CW00448381

# THE STOLEN CHILD

## ALEX COOMBS

Boldwood

First published in Great Britain in 2021 by Boldwood Books Ltd.

A CIP catalogue record for this book is available from the British Library.

Paperback ISBN 978-1-80048-808-3

Large Print ISBN 978-1-80048-804-5

Ebook ISBN 978-1-80048-802-1

Kindle ISBN 978-1-80048-803-8

Audio CD ISBN 978-1-80048-809-0

MP3 CD ISBN 978-1-80048-806-9

Digital audio download ISBN 978-1-80048-801-4

Boldwood Books Ltd
23 Bowerdean Street
London SW6 3TN
www.boldwoodbooks.com

# 1

The compact, concrete shape of the World War Two gun emplacement crouched, hunkered down into the shallow, gravelly soil above the beach on the Essex side of the Thames Estuary near Southend. It overlooked the wide, grey shallow waters on whose far side lay the Isle of Grain and Sheerness. Hanlon guessed it was somewhere out there in those cold, steely waters that the proposed island airport for London might one day take shape. She thought, fleetingly, it would be a pity in a way if it happened. The North Sea waters had a chilly quality that she found rather beautiful. She looked around her slowly, the sky above enormous after London's claustrophobic horizons. A heron stood on a boulder near the beach, shrugging its wings like an old lady arranging a shawl around her shoulders. Cormorants bobbed along on top of the water and she could see guillemots, their wings folded back like dive-bombers, thundering into the water. The calls of the birds floated towards her on the stiff sea breeze.

The tarmac track that led down from the main road above them was old, cracked and weed-grown. The ex-army building's pitted, grey, artificial stone surface was now camouflaged with yellow, cream and blue-grey lichens and grey-green moss, so that it seemed almost organic, a part of the landscape like a strangely symmetric rock formation. There was a fissured, concrete apron next to the bunker and Hanlon pulled up adjacent to the large, white Mercedes van that she guessed belonged to the forensics team, then got out of her car. She stood for a moment by her Audi and closed her eyes. She felt the cold, fresh sea air against her skin and the breeze tugged at her shoulder-length dark hair. She could smell the metallic warmth of her car engine and the salt tang of the sea. The sound of the small waves breaking on the stony beach a hundred metres or so away were nearly drowned out by the throbbing of the generator next to the Mercedes. She could hear the keening of seagulls, much louder now, wheeling above in the sky. Hanlon stretched the powerful, sinewy muscles in her shoulders and arms and opened her eyes, which were as expressionless as the North Sea in front of her. She looked out over the water, feeling its call. Hanlon loved swimming in the open sea. Earlier that morning, at 6 a.m., she had swum for a steady hour in her local swimming pool, but pool swimming was nothing compared to real salt water. She guessed at this time of year the temperature would be only two or three degrees, colder than a fridge. That wouldn't deter her.

She could taste its saltiness, carried to her lips by the wind.

A red power cable looped its way from the generator through the heavy, open metal door of the bunker. The door was rusted and pitted by time and the elements, but still substantial. Hanlon stepped over the line of police crime-scene tape that secured the area, blowing like bunting in the sea breeze, and approached the building. Earlier that day, the place would have been bustling with her colleagues from Essex. Now the uniforms had gone and the outside of the bunker, included in the search area, reopened. She didn't go inside through the forbidding-looking portal designed, she guessed, to be blast-proof, but walked instead along the side wall until she came to one of its long, slit windows that overlooked the beach and the far horizon.

Hanlon had already spoken to the crime scene manager in charge to clear her access to the site and she remembered her conversation on the phone with the CSM. It had been straightforward enough. 'We've done what we can with the access route to the crime, DI Hanlon. It was vehicular, we've searched the surrounding radius of the bunker to within half a kilometre, foreshore, beach, in case the body was brought in by sea or inland, on the off chance it was carried here, but nada. We assume it was driven here.' The CSM had carried on. 'Basically, you're fine by us as far as access is concerned. Why the interest anyway?'

The intonation of Hanlon's voice conveyed a shrug. 'AC Corrigan wants me to have a look. Ask him.' And that's how the call had ended.

The World War Two building still had a certain forlorn power about it even though its original purpose – observation? Defence, maybe? – was long forgotten or possibly preserved somewhere, buried deep in a government archive. Now it was being noted by officialdom again.

Hanlon peered in through the glassless window. Inside the hexagonal interior of the building she could see the two CSI men in their white disposable overalls, gloved and booted, masked, and in plastic caps, working in the blaze of two powerful arc lights powered by the generator outside. She watched as they carried on with their high-intensity light source photography. The inside of the bunker was comparatively clean. The chained door had kept people out and there was none of the usual smell of urine or detritus like old beer cans, food wrappers, odds and sods of soiled clothing, cigarette ends or the drug paraphernalia of roaches from joints and needles that you'd normally find in abandoned, solitary buildings – the spoor of kids, tramps and junkies, the natural denizens of places like this. When she'd first joined the force, places like this were always littered with scraps of photographs torn from pages of porn magazines. She'd often wondered why. If you wanted to look at porn, why do it in a dank, derelict building? Maybe you had to. That sort of litter had become a rarity these days. She guessed it was the digital revolution. Times moved on.

The bunker certainly wasn't odour-free, though. Hanlon had a keen sense of smell and her nose could detect the lingering aftermath of charred flesh and petrol that still coated its concrete shell. It smelt like burnt cooking, a barbecue gone horribly wrong. She looked upwards at the ceiling and there, as she thought she might, she could see small patches of black, greasy soot where bits of burnt remains had drifted in the updraft from the flames and come to rest.

Hanlon was invisible to the men inside working behind the glare of the lights and she watched unseen as the taller of the two figures started to put photographic equipment away into a dimpled, metallic, silver-coloured carrying case. Despite the noise of the breeze, she could hear their conversation clearly.

'So, are we done now, Jim?' one of them asked.

The smaller of the two men removed hat and mask, revealing a bald head and a thin, good-humoured face. She recognized him. Hanlon was glad it was James Forrest. He was old school, thorough and experienced, not the kind of man who'd make foolish mistakes. In the last year Hanlon had seen two perfectly good verdicts overturned by defence lawyers because of stupid, procedural blunders. Forrest wouldn't do that.

'Pretty much,' Forrest said. 'I'd like you to start packing all this stuff away. I'm going outside now, Hanlon'll be here soon.' 'What about the PolSA?' asked the other man. Only after the scene had been signed off by that officer, the police search adviser, could the scene actually be cleaned and returned to

normality. Hanlon guessed that in this case there'd be no big rush. It was hardly in anyone's way, like a stabbing on Oxford Street would be. The only people inconvenienced out here would be dog walkers and beachcombers.

'We'll secure the premises and speak to the SIO later,' said Forrest.

The younger man carried on disassembling the cameras and putting the parts away in their respective compartments. It had been an unpleasant day. The girl's naked body had been so charred they'd had to wrap her limbs carefully in oiled clingfilm so that when they moved her, she didn't break up. One of the officers present had made a joke about liking his meat well done. No one had laughed. 'So what's she like, boss, this Hanlon? They say she's a bit of a ball-breaker,' said the young CSI.

'Is that what they say, Thomas?' said Forrest courteously but firmly. His tone made it clear he had no interest in this line of conversation. He was annoyed with his assistant now. He disliked gossip. 'You shouldn't listen to tittle-tattle.'

Ball-breaker, Hanlon thought. Is that what I am? Well, she thought dispassionately, I've kicked a fair few in my time. She had the rare quality of not caring what others thought of her. She had long ago reached the conclusion that she had risen as far as she was likely to get in the police force. Hanlon didn't particularly mind.

She'd forgotten Forrest's old-fashioned turns of phrase. Tittle-tattle. Stuff and nonsense. Argy-bargy. Golly. Those kinds of expressions. He'd never been known to swear. Forrest was a kind of living legend for that alone.

She'd once been with him at the scene of a triple homicide. A drug deal gone wrong. Shotguns had been used. Two of them. Great chunks had been blown out of the victims' bodies. A shotgun is a very messy weapon; it does an all too predictable amount of damage to a human body. It looked like the room had been painted and decorated in blood and tissue, arterial spray and brains, far worse than an abattoir. Even Hanlon had been impressed by the carnage. Two or three police had to go outside and be sick. It was memorably horrible. Forrest had slowly surveyed the scene, eyebrows raised, cocked his head to one side and said simply, 'Good Heavens.' Hanlon had savoured that moment. She appreciated understatement.

'She's always been perfectly pleasant to me,' said Forrest. 'Now, get this lot cleaned down and I'll see you outside.' He was very fond of Hanlon. His voice was suddenly acerbic. The way he emphasized 'Now' was like the crack of a whip. His young assistant jumped and set to with alacrity.

She turned and retraced her steps and waited for Forrest to emerge from the bunker. He did so, looking tired and preoccupied, then, as soon as he saw Hanlon, a delighted smile transformed his thin, mobile, slightly ugly face.

'Hanlon!'

'James,' she said. They shook hands, both pleased to see each other.

'So what brings you down here?' asked Forrest. The sea breeze whipped again at Hanlon's hair and she pushed it away from her eyes as she looked out over the water at the mouth of the estuary. She could see in the far distance the low bulk of two tankers heading for the port facilities on the unseen opposite shore.

By way of explanation she said, 'You heard about my new job?'

'Vaguely,' said Forrest. 'Congratulations on the medal, by the way.' Hanlon smiled thinly. Her mouth wasn't designed for humour. In December she had been given the Queen's

Award for Gallantry, a decoration for bravery usually awarded posthumously to dead police. It was almost the equivalent of a Victoria Cross. It was this that Forrest was referring to.

She shrugged, dismissing all talk of the medal. 'Corrigan gave me this post on the back of it.' Her hard eyes looked out to sea. 'He wants the Commissioner's job, it's no secret, and he's worried that there'll be some internal cock-up that'll get in the way and screw his chances up.' Forrest nodded and Hanlon continued. 'You can imagine, another Stockwell, another police killing, some stupid balls-up that we've made.' She looked out to sea, the wind still whipping her long, dark hair.

'Like Tottenham,' said Forrest pleasantly. Hanlon narrowed her eyes; it was the riots that had nearly finished her own career. 'Exactly. No more own goals, well, not in our bit of the Met anyway. If anyone else cocks up, preferably one of his rivals, so much the better for us. We don't care if heads roll so long as it's not ours. If Corrigan's a bit paranoid, I can't say I blame him. How many police have we got in the Met anyway?'

'Thirty-one thousand officers the last time I counted. Bound to be a few bad apples.'

'Well,' said Forrest diplomatically, 'Public Relations is part of his job after all. I suppose this one,' he jerked his head in the direction of the bunker, 'is going to generate a bit of press interest. It's not on your patch, though.'

'May as well be. You're only down the road,' she said. 'So, what have we got here then?' she asked the forensics man. 'Witchcraft killing, is it? At least, that's what I was told.'

Corrigan had heard this might be the case and had sent her down to check up on the facts rather than wait for an official report to be delivered. The AC shared Forrest's view. A witchcraft killing in his opinion was newsworthy. If reporters were going to ask questions he didn't want to look uninformed.

It was off his patch as Forrest had said, but it was so close to London it might as well be there.

Forrest started removing his protective suit. 'What we've got, Hanlon,' he said in his gentle, measured way, 'is the charred body of a pubescent African girl who was killed elsewhere, brought here, and set alight. I'm guessing diesel was the accelerant but we'll have to wait for the GC results on that. Her teeth and hands are intact so I'm guessing she won't feature on any UK or Interpol DNA database, she won't have any dental records and there'll be no record of her fingerprints on NAFIS or HOLMES.' Hanlon nodded. Anyone who had the kind of personality needed to do this to a child would not hesitate to remove such

obvious clues to identity.

'That's only a guess, mind you,' said Forrest. 'We'll obviously know soon enough.'

'OK,' said Hanlon. 'What else, James?'

'There are also some crude designs scratched on the floor and the remains of a chicken and a couple of candles. And a crucifix. That would seem to indicate some kind of occult mumbo-jumbo, some sort of ceremony, but...' Forrest looked at her keenly.

'But?' asked Hanlon. They were both thinking of two similar cases. The 'Adam' killing in 2001 when the torso of an African boy was found in the Thames – just the torso, no limbs or head. That had been a witchcraft killing, most probably Nigerian. Then, more recently, there had been the murder of Kristy Bamu in London by his sister and her boyfriend. They had accused the boy of Kindoki or witchcraft. Attempts to exorcize him had led to horrific injuries and the boy's death. Hanlon thought that had been Congolese. African Christianity seemed keen on this sort of thing. While driving through London recently she'd been listening absently-mindedly to

Radio Four and heard two African Anglican ministers

discussing the existence of witches as a verifiable fact. She'd turned angrily to another station.

Forrest smiled at her. 'But a cursory examination showed extensive vaginal trauma.' He sighed. 'The poor girl was naked, legs splayed so it's just visual evidence. We'll know more after we've examined her properly but she had been circumcised, the clitoris excised, the labia sewn up. It's partly why it was so easy to see she'd been assaulted.' Hanlon frowned. FGM, or female genital mutilation, in her view was not taken nearly as seriously over here as it should be. The French, she knew, adopted a much harder line. There were virtually no prosecutions over it in this country. 'I'd guess, personally, she was Somali. They've got a 98 per cent female circumcision rate. Well, she looks Somali anyway. As I said, it's early days yet. We'll know more after we've run tests. So I think we've got a murdered rape victim, not a witchcraft victim. I think I'm correct in saying that witchcraft victims are usually the by-products of African Christianity, often Congolese or Nigerian, not Islam. Do they have witches in the Qur'an?'

'I don't know,' said Hanlon. 'I don't think so. I seem to remember that there's something about women blowing on knots as a form of sorcery, but I don't really have a clue. Mind you, I don't think there's much about them in the Bible, come to that. Witches, I mean. That hasn't stopped anyone before, has it.' Certainly not you two idiots, she thought back to the two men of God she'd heard on the radio. The unspoken implication had been that killing a witch was quite reasonable.

'I guess not. Well, anyway,' said Forrest, 'I think it was just staged. The body made to look like a witchcraft killing. I think it's old-fashioned rape, murder. But, of course, that's your job, not mine. I just do forensics.'

Hanlon nodded. She could see that if the motive was sexual rather than occult it would widen the search parameters hugely.

There were only a certain number of Kindoki practitioners in London, but a vast pool of potential rapists. Several million.

'Then,' said Forrest, 'and this is purely a personal observation by someone who's from this area, you don't get many Congolese or West Africans around here, not near Southend. Whoever dumped the poor child here knew this part of the Essex coast very well. You wouldn't find this place by accident. I think, for what it's worth, when you find him, he'll be white and local. And as for that poor girl, well, I'll email you the post-mortem results together with any relevant forensic information. I'm assuming you'll just want the highlights of any report?'

Hanlon nodded; she just needed the gist of things. It wasn't her case.

'When's the management team meeting on this, James?' she asked.

'There'll be one tomorrow morning. I'll send you any relevant info. Martin Horrocks is the SIO for this one, do you know him?'

Hanlon shook her head.

'He's good,' said Forrest. He looked out over the estuary and watched as another gannet exploded into the sea, putting an Olympic diver to shame with its easy grace. 'There's quite a lot that needs follow-up, obviously, but whoever did this was careful. There's no trace evidence. No useable tyre prints or footprints; nothing left by whoever deposited her here. I've got prints to run through the PNC but I doubt if they'll have any relevance. This looks like a relatively professional job, but you never know. That'll be in the next couple of days, we haven't got a great deal on.'

'Who found her?' asked Hanlon.

'A woman walking her dog,' said Forrest. 'Thank God for dog walkers. Dog walkers and joggers. If it wasn't for them, God knows how many bodies would go undetected.' Hanlon nodded in agreement. 'The door there,' he indicated it with a nod of his head, 'is usually chained and padlocked but today her dog ran inside. It was open, so she went looking for it. That's when she called us.'

'It was open?' said Hanlon in surprise. She'd have expected it to be at least pushed to, more of an attempt at concealment made. It was as if someone had intended the body to be discovered. Forrest nodded. 'Open. The chain was cut with bolt cutters.

It was lying on the ground. It's bagged and back at the lab.' 'How long's she been in there?' asked Hanlon.

'Not long,' said Forrest. 'One of your lot told me the dog walker comes by every day and yesterday the door was chained and padlocked. I'll know more when I've got back to the lab.' Hanlon nodded and Forrest's assistant appeared through the doorway of the bunker, carrying lights and cabling. Thomas stood blinking in the afternoon light, staring at the slim, con

troversial figure that was Hanlon.

During the London riots a police community support officer had found himself, through a mixture of bad luck and unfortunate timing, caught up on the fringes of the Tottenham riots. When he'd started his beat patrol, alone, as his partner had called in sick, everything was more or less normal. Elsewhere in the borough, sporadic acts of vandalism, like Brownian motion in a lab, were coalescing into what eventually turned into the most alarming street violence in living memory. To James Brudenell, the hapless PCSO, it was like being trapped on a mudflat by a tide racing in, as the flood of lawlessness bore down on him from all sides, leaving him bobbing around like a piece of helpless driftwood. It was the speed of it all that was

maybe the most frightening thing. One minute the shopping parade had been a picture of normality. Five minutes later the street was full of noise, rampaging masked youths shouting, normal people caught up in it running for cover or in flight, the strident, deafening wails of alarms from businesses and cars, shopkeepers frantically pulling down security screens if they had any, sirens in the distance, news and police helicopters overhead, shouting and screaming, breaking glass.

The PCSO had stood bewildered, paralysed with indecision, feeling ridiculously conspicuous in his uniform, very much alone. He had never imagined anything like this happening. He felt he couldn't have been much more of a target if he'd tried. It was then that he felt a blow strike him from behind. He wheeled round to confront his assailant and found himself looking at a group of about ten youths. One of them had thrown a half-empty can of Red Stripe at him, which had splashed him with beer as it hit him and now lay at his feet. He could smell it. The faces of the kids suddenly seemed very adult, very hostile as they stared at him. Brudenell thought with a sudden, terrible clarity: they want to kill me. They threw more things at him. Various missiles struck the PCSO: stones, a half-brick, a bottle and a full can of Coke which hit him on the forehead, breaking the skin. Blood coursed down his face and the sight of it was like a signal to the group, who

surged forward towards him.

There were police officers in an adjacent street who had been ordered not to engage with the crowd, even though there were reports that an officer was under attack nearby. They stood around helplessly, trying to look purposeful. The truth was that nobody really knew what to do. The helicopter overhead had called the situation in but they were impotent. They were not to 'inflame' the situation or 'escalate' tension. They were

to contain it. No one was quite sure exactly what that meant. Hanlon had been with them.

Ignoring orders, she had taken a baton from one of the PCs, walked away from the police line and strode through the rioters, round the corner, just in time to see the fallen PCSO surrounded by half a dozen figures, all kicking and stamping. Hanlon didn't weigh up the risks of what she was doing. She didn't calculate the odds. She just acted.

Accounts didn't differ as to what happened next. What caused the argument was the legality of Hanlon's actions. The police federation lawyers argued that Hanlon had identified herself as a police officer and that it was all by the book. Civil rights lawyers claimed that Hanlon, not in uniform and not readily recognizable as a police officer, had attacked innocent members of the public. It was unprovoked assault by a dangerous thug hiding behind a police badge. The PCSO's blood on their clothing and shoes was proof of proximity, but not of guilt. The CCTV cameras that could have caught the action had been damaged by this time and no one came forward as an eyewitness on either side. What was uncontestable was that, on the one hand, Hanlon had hospitalized three men aged between seventeen and thirty-two and, on the other, had saved the life of a fellow officer. Several doctors had testified to the fact the PCSO would have probably died had the attack continued for very much longer. The list of his injuries was extensive, from skull fractures to broken wrists to smashed cheekbones to ruptured kidneys. One of the rioters had stamped on his face so hard you could see the imprint of the sports shoe manufacturer embedded on his skin from the sole of the trainer.

Throughout the following investigations and enquiry by

the IPCC, apart from when directly questioned Hanlon had preserved an enigmatic silence.

It was a tricky problem for the Met. She was certainly guilty of disobeying orders, flagrantly so, but then again, to discipline her or sack her would make them look ridiculous. Not only ridiculous, but unpopular and out of touch with public opinion, which was in a vengeful mood. People wanted the rioters punished. Society wanted an eye for an eye. Prosecuting Hanlon would have been a PR disaster. They'd compromised on a medal and a decision to sideline her from front-line duties. In an ideal world, and heavy hints were dropped, Hanlon would resign through some unspecified stress- or health-related problem and would be handsomely paid off, pension intact. Irritatingly, she showed no signs of wanting to do this. She'd spent about three months in limbo in the system and no one really knew what to do with her, no one wanted her, until Corrigan had taken her under his wing. Thomas thought she looked disappointingly ordinary. She was tall and slim with a long, unsmiling face and bleak, grey eyes. She didn't fit his warrior princess preconceptions. There was no glamour. She was wearing dark clothes and they made her face even more pallid. There were smudges under her eyes as if she habitually slept badly and her shoulder-length black

hair was slightly greasy and ragged-looking.

As if suddenly aware of Thomas's scrutiny, she turned her eyes on him again and he blushed and started busying himself securing the halogen lights away in the van. She had hard eyes, cold, unfriendly.

Forrest bent down to help Thomas stow the lights in the back of the van, then he turned back to Hanlon. 'There is one thing. It might be important.' He took an iPad out of the van and scrolled through images until he found one he was looking for.

'Here,' he said and passed the tablet to Hanlon.

She took it and found herself looking at an image of a section of rough concrete wall next to a ruled mark that showed the

distance in centimetres from the floor. There was a downward slash and next to it an inverted V. She looked at Forrest and shrugged.

Forrest said, 'I went to Morocco on holiday last year and I learnt some Arabic, including the way they write numerals. That,' he indicated the twin marks, 'says "eighteen". This mark means "one".' His finger pointed to the downward stroke. 'And this one "eight", here.'

This time he pointed to the inverted V. 'Written in pencil. Whoever left the body, left that. The pencil mark runs through some of the carbon deposit on the wall from the girl's body, so it's post-mortem, post-burning. I just thought you'd better know.'

Hanlon handed the tablet back. Eighteen. The unspoken thought, just in case someone's keeping count, hung in the salty estuary air.

# 2

He had just finished unloading the contents of the shopping trolley on to the conveyor belt at the checkout when Reyhan, his four-year-old daughter, looked up at him suddenly and said, 'Papa, I need to go to the toilet.'

Mehmet sighed out loud and scratched his beard in irritation. He looked down in exasperation at the little girl. She tugged at one of her pigtails and the morning sun, flooding through the huge, long, low front window of the supermarket, shone brightly on the small, gold earrings she wore. Three times earlier in maybe the past hour, he had checked, at the restaurant where he worked, at the library where they had gone to change books and get a DVD, and, as they'd walked in to the supermarket at the entrance, now thirty checkouts away, 'Do you want the toilet?' The answer to which, each time, had been a definitive, 'No, Papa.'

'I need to go to the toilet.' It was a form of shorthand. Mehmet knew from past experience that what it really meant was, 'I'm going to the toilet any second now.' He looked around him for inspiration.

The supermarket in Wood Green in North London offered him little obvious help. It was huge. Mehmet was from Nevs̡ehir in the centre of Turkey, which is a fairly large city, but it had nowhere that was anything like the size of this monolithic

shop. Mehmet had been initially daunted by the supermarket's vastness, but not any more. He'd become a regular. Familiarity had tamed the enormous retail space. He came here, without fail, with his two children every Thursday at 11.30 a.m. Nur, Mehmet's wife, found the place intimidating. Nevs, ehir is not a multicultural city, and the black and Asian faces surrounding her when she went shopping were unfamiliar, frightening and unsettling, even though she'd been in London for over a year. So it was that the weekly bulk shop passed to Mehmet.

Mehmet, like more or less everyone in the supermarket, staff and customers alike, had a strict routine. He himself used the place largely for non-food items. He was here mainly for Baby Ali, his eighteen-month-old son, to buy Pampers, wet wipes, nappy sacks, the kind of things that toddlers need. He hardly ever bought food there. Vegetables, Nur bought at the local market where many of the stallholders were Turkish and she felt more at home, for her English was practically non-existent, and meat came from the Halal butchers near their small flat. Again, she could speak Turkish to them. The stallholders were mainly Northern Cypriots, who make up most of the four hundred thousand Turks in London, and their Turkish sounded strange to her ears, but it was Turkish nevertheless.

Ali was sitting in the baby seat at the front of the trolley,

his legs in their romper suit poking out in front of him, little blue boots laced on his feet. His small face was solemn. He was a very self-possessed child, one hand holding on to the front of the trolley for balance, the other holding Grey Rabbit, his favourite toy. Grey Rabbit went everywhere that Ali went. They were inseparable.

'Papa, please!' said Reyhan desperately.

Mehmet had pushed the trolley to the farthest end of the supermarket where the queues were the shortest. The toilets were

at the entrance to the shop, now maybe a hundred metres away.
Today there was no one else at checkout thirty and checkouts
twenty-nine to twenty-seven were closed. Checkout thirty was self-
service. Its fellow self-service checkouts stood clustered together
near the entrance to the shop, in a semicircular huddle, but this one
stood alone as though it had been exiled to the end for some
unknown reason. Maybe it had been a prototype, but it worked well
enough. It also meant he wouldn't have to talk to anyone. Mehmet
didn't like speaking to people, even at checkout. Mehmet rarely
spoke to anyone, even in his own language. He was a very shy
person. His own English was extremely limited. He hardly ever had
a chance to practise, though it was unlikely he'd have taken it if the
opportunity arose. He spoke Turkish at work and at home. He lived
in a self-created Turkish bubble. When he had the chance to go to a
mosque he went to the Turkish Suleymaniye Mosque in Hackney.

He was in the UK illegally and he half expected, even though

he knew it unlikely, the police to descend on him at any time.
He was a worrier by nature and if he didn't have anything concrete
to fret about his mind would invent lurid, frightening scenarios.
Right now, his mind was fully occupied with the fear that Reyhan
was going to relieve herself on the shop floor. He could imagine the
puddle spreading outwards beneath her on the non-absorbent tiles
of the floor, wider and wider. People would stare and point. Maybe
he'd be banned from the supermarket. Management would shout at
him in English and he wouldn't understand. He felt himself beginning to panic. Then there was the problem of his shopping. Half of
his goods were in the trolley, the rest still on the black rubber of the
conveyor belt. Mehmet's desperate gaze was met by a woman – he
guessed she was a manageress – who he took to be Muslim, wearing
a headscarf. She was standing near the checkout. Her staff

name tag pinned to her top said Aisha. It was a comforting name. It was nice and traditional. There were several Aisha's, or Ayse in Turkish spelling, in his own family. This one was in her late twenties, Mehmet guessed. He noticed she had a small horseshoe-shaped scar between her eyebrows. This slight blemish made her pleasant face seem even more trustworthy. Mehmet was very tired. He worked a six-day week, fourteen hours a day, split shifts, in his cousin's restaurant, and when the girl smiled at him and said, 'I'll look after him and the trolley for you,' he barely hesitated. In Mehmet's world, women looked after children, men worked; it was the natural order of things. Maybe if he hadn't been so exhausted, if he hadn't been so convinced that Reyhan was about to go all over the supermarket floor, if the woman hadn't been so transparently trustworthy,

he wouldn't have done what he did.

He smiled his thanks, picked up Reyhan and strode quickly back down the long line of checkouts to the toilets. Ali watched them go, his head cocked to one side, a quizzical expression on his small face. His small fingers curled around Grey Rabbit.

About five minutes later, not much more, Mehmet and Reyhan were returning to checkout thirty. At checkout twenty-five Mehmet felt a terrible constriction start in his stomach as if a giant invisible hand had begun to squeeze the life out of the core of his being. He picked his daughter up in his arms. She could feel the sudden tension in her father's body and his grip tighten round her and she put her arms around his neck for comfort. His stride lengthened and then became a run. He stopped short by the self-service checkout.

Checkout thirty was now deserted. There was no sign of his shopping. The manageress was gone. His trolley was gone. His son was gone. He gently put Reyhan down and stared around him in bewildered disbelief. His heart was racing and his mouth very dry. This can't be happening. This can't be happening. Momentarily he thought he was going to faint. Sweat broke out on his forehead and his heart started racing.

He looked around him, at the orderly shelves, the other customers. Surely, he thought, there has been some kind of mistake, some kind of mix-up. They must be round here somewhere. He gently put Reyhan down on the floor.

He thought: Where is he?

He thought: This can't be happening.

He thought: I don't believe this.

He stood there, stupidly, his head swivelling left and right. Outside the huge, glass window of the supermarket, cars and people came and went, life continued, while Mehmet stood as if frozen in some kind of aquarium.

Reyhan stared at her father and then bent down and picked something up that had fallen out of Mehmet's line of sight under the lip of the checkout. She could sense the tension in her father but wasn't sure why. Perhaps this would help.

'Look, Papa,' she said brightly. 'It's Grey Rabbit.'

It was then Mehmet felt despair and fear hit him harder than he could ever have imagined. His son would never have been separated from his toy. He knew then with a terrible clarity that Ali was gone.

# 3

If you looked out of the window of Assistant Commissioner Corrigan's office you could see the iconic sight of the Thames on one side and the green of St James's Park stretching away to Buckingham Palace on the other. It was typical of Corrigan, thought Hanlon, that he had managed, while professing no interest at all in the matter, to install himself in a room with one of the most spectacular views that the twenty-storey glass, concrete and granite building that was New Scotland Yard could provide.

People often underestimated Corrigan, usually to their cost. His enormous size (he was six foot five), shovel-like hands and builder's-slab face made people think he was a street copper promoted way above his ability, maybe to fulfil some kind of quota. He looked that way. He looked anachronistic. People seemed to expect senior police these days to behave and sound like management consultants. Corrigan didn't. He had the face of the old-fashioned Irish navvy that his grandfather had been. He also shared his grandfather's strength. The old man had reputedly been able to straighten a horseshoe with his bare hands. Corrigan couldn't do this, but he looked as if he could give it a bloody good go.

In fact the AC had a highly attuned grasp of politics allied
with an almost feminine sensitivity to mood and thought and
nuance. It suited him down to the ground to be thought thick.
You usually only got one chance to underestimate Corrigan; he was
adept at slipping the knife in. He'd ended several rivals' careers,
fellow officers who'd underestimated him, who now sat shuffling
paper or reading their emails in disappointing dead-end jobs in
Hendon or Basingstoke.

Another of the AC's survival skills was the ability to smell the
way the wind was blowing. It had brought him promotion in the
past and he was hoping it would do so again. Currently he was
steering a delicate path between multi-ethnic policing and a rising
backlash against it from critics citing police unwillingness to tackle
difficult issues in case they were branded as racist. It was a difficult
juggling act.

Framed citations, decorations and awards were hung over the
walls of the office. Most of these had been assiduously and
discreetly lobbied for by the assistant commissioner. While on the
surface he claimed that such things were meaningless to him, that
what counted was getting the job done, he enjoyed the celebrity
part of his job. He liked being recognized, enjoyed being feted. He
was a great one for backing into the limelight. There were photos
too. Corrigan sharing a joke with the home secretary, Corrigan
waggling a pair of handcuffs at the prime minister. Corrigan with
the mayor. There was a gap in the wall where Corrigan had taken
down Ken Livingstone. As soon as the results were in and Ken was
yesterday's man, down he had come. Hanlon noted as she sat down
opposite him that the home secretary's photo too had gone now, to
be replaced by a smiling Arab in white robes and a headdress.
Corrigan obviously had little faith in her future. That boded ill for
the politician. Corrigan had a finely tuned nose for that kind of
thing.

The Arab, Hanlon guessed, would turn out to be the interior minister of some oil-rich state where Corrigan would wind up doing very well-paid consultancy work should his bid to become Metropolitan Police commissioner fail. She could see Corrigan in somewhere like Doha, advising the Qataris. Corrigan would have several insurance policies on the go; he was that kind of man.

Right now, Corrigan was in a bad mood and it showed. He had supported Hanlon when no other senior figure would dare. Politics and police work inevitably go together and Hanlon was politically troublesome. The Metropolitan Police is a huge organization, employing some fifty thousand people with a budget of over four billion pounds. In common with all large organizations it does not encourage maverick individuals. It can't afford to and it doesn't want to. When a precedent is set, others will follow. If more police followed Hanlon's lead and disobeyed orders, recklessly endangering themselves and potentially inflaming an already explosive situation, it would be disastrous. But she had saved a fellow officer's life and she had shown exceptional bravery. And Corrigan liked her a lot. So he had thrown his considerable weight behind Hanlon and was beginning to suspect he might regret it.

'So this witchcraft killing?' he began. As soon as he'd heard about it he had sent Hanlon down to check on it. It was the kind of story the press would get excited about.

'Is probably not a witchcraft killing at all, sir,' said Hanlon. 'Really?' said the AC sceptically. 'I thought all these feathers and stuff, the crucifix... what about all of that then?'

Hanlon shrugged. She was wearing a V-necked black cashmere sweater and the AC could see the delicate but powerful muscle that ran from her neck to her shoulder, her trapezius, move under the skin like an elegant cable as she did so. Having Hanlon in his office always had the effect of making him feel overweight and out of condition. Last week he'd had a

mandatory work medical and had been warned about his BMI. He wondered what Hanlon's BMI would be. Crazily low, he suspected. Maybe that was why she seemed to live in a state of constant irritation. Maybe that's why she also looked so tired all the time.

'Sources say that she had been extensively sexually assaulted and is probably of non-Christian origin, sir.'

'So it's assault and murder; it's straightforward then,' said Corrigan.

'So it would seem, sir,' she agreed. Straightforward was Essex police's view. The SIO on the case had been unmoved by the 'eighteen' on the wall of the bunker. 'If that's what it is, so what? Have we got seventeen other missing black girls? No, we haven't. Have we got seventeen other burnt bodies? I haven't seen any. Life's complicated enough without looking for problems,' he'd said in a dismissive tone. Hanlon wasn't so sure. Corrigan looked at Hanlon with his shrewd eyes. 'So it would seem' was very much an evasive answer. Hanlon was careful with words. She weighed them carefully before she used them, like a miser with money. She was returning his gaze coldly. He thought to himself, you're not telling me everything. There was little he could do about it. You couldn't push Hanlon or intimidate her. He decided to bring this conversation to an end.

'Well, Detective Inspector, if I'm asked I'll say that police experts have cast doubts on the witchcraft theory and if anyone

perseveres, I'll refer them to you.'

Hanlon nodded. 'Fine by me, sir. The SIO is copying me in on their findings and I'll summarize it for you. It'll be on your desk the day after tomorrow.' She stood up. 'If that's everything, sir? I've got an appointment, if you don't mind.'

Corrigan waved her away absent-mindedly. He had a briefing to give to the London Assembly and was behind his

own self-imposed schedule. More issues with trigger-happy policemen. Sometimes his own force seemed more trouble than the criminals. Hanlon left his office.

She signed herself out of the building and crossed the road to the art-deco St James's Park Underground where she walked down to the Circle and District line. Victoria Street was a mass of snarled traffic. As she waited for a westbound train, she checked the time again on her BlackBerry: 8.30 a.m. She had emailed DS Whiteside, her former colleague from the Serious and Organized Crime Group, just before she entered the station.

After the riot incident, SCD 7 had washed their hands of Hanlon, but although they were finished with her she still had unfinished business with a case she'd been involved with at the time. Hanlon didn't like unresolved business. Whiteside's reply confirmed they were still on. Their target was alone, and at home.

Hanlon rode the tube train two stops down to Sloane Square and exited there. She walked up into the wide-open plaza that reminded her of a European city in its spaciousness, not London with its typically narrow streets like a turned-up collar against the rain, and looked at the Peter Jones store opposite. Hanlon was no great fan of shopping, nor of Sloane Rangers, the ostentatiously wealthy women who frequented the area, but she did like buildings and the sinuous late-1920s art-deco lines of the large shop gave her a great deal of pleasure.

She walked through the expensive streets, moving quickly out of the borders of the exclusive areas of Chelsea and into the marginally less price-tag-heavy Fulham. A one-bedroom flat here would still be about a dozen times her annual salary, if not more. You didn't have to deal drugs to live in Fulham, but it helped.

Although her legs still ached from the hour she'd put in at the gym between six and seven, before her 8 a.m. meeting with Corrigan, she was enjoying the walk. She loved the streets of London with a visceral passion. Today she'd been working on her thighs, calves and shoulders, high-weight, low-repetition work, and she could still feel the muscles protesting. She ignored them. She was old school: no pain, no gain. Hanlon's gym was defiantly old-fashioned, full of free weights, barbells and dumbbells, its soundtrack being grunts of effort and clanking metal.

Her eyes softened slightly as she saw the well-dressed figure of DS Whiteside sitting on a low wall at a corner of the street where their target lived. Today the sergeant looked like an Indie rocker in tight skinny jeans and a fashionably distressed leather jacket. The clothes emphasized the powerful body beneath rather than concealing it. As she waited to cross the road to join him, a couple of Sloaney girls walked past her, frankly ogling him as they did so. She heard one say to the other, 'He's a bit of all right.' The other replied, lasciviously, flicking back her glossy long hair with an expensively manicured hand, 'Yah! I most certainly wouldn't say no!' Hanlon shook her head sadly. You really are barking up the wrong tree, she said mentally to the young girls as they disappeared along the pavement.

She crossed over to where Whiteside was sitting. He smiled up at her, supremely confident as ever. He had, she reflected, an insanely optimistic attitude on life.

'Did you know you're a babe magnet, Sergeant?' she asked. 'Morning, ma'am. Some of us have got it, and some of us haven't,' he said, with a grin.

He's ridiculously attractive, thought Hanlon. 'Shall we go and wake young Toby up?'

She nodded. 'Let's go then.'

They crossed the road together. Whiteside's eyes were gleaming with pleasure at working with Hanlon again. Life had been so boring without her.

Toby Manning had a basement flat and the two of them walked down the steep stairs that led off the pavement, in single file. They stood in the stairwell next to some dead potted plants while Whiteside rang the bell. He looked at the plants. Toby's gardening skills were not the best. He had to ring three times before they heard a muffled 'All right, OK, I'm coming' from within. There was the sound of a bolt being drawn back and then the door opened a crack and a bleary, unshaven face appeared.

With one practised, synchronized movement, Whiteside shouldered both Toby and the door back, Hanlon stepped regally inside and Whiteside wheeled round, closed the door and leant against it, while Toby stood with his back to a wall, wearing nothing but a dressing gown and a puzzled, frightened look.

'Who—' he began to say. The sergeant had no intention of letting Toby speak. He wanted to establish in Toby's slow mind who was in control. Whiteside grabbed Toby by the lapels of the ragged dressing gown and roughly pushed him into the centre of his own living room where Hanlon was now standing, looking around her with an air of distaste.

'Sit down, Toby,' she ordered, pointing to a scruffy-looking armchair. The flat was probably worth between half to three-quarters of a million in its SW6 location, but inside it was a dump. Toby did as he was told. The living room hadn't been cleaned in a while and smelt of stale cigarette smoke, grass and old booze. There was still a half-smoked joint in an ashtray on a coffee table. Next to it a folded wrap of paper and a mirror.

There was an underlying sweet/sour smell of rotting food from the kitchen.

Hanlon produced a warrant card and held it in front of Toby's face. She leant forward, invading his personal space, literally in his face.

'We're police.'

Toby had shoulder-length permed hair and lined, unhealthily pale features. He looked as if he'd wandered in from another era. Hanlon guessed he didn't really keep up with current trends except narcotics. His lifestyle was catching up with him quickly. His arms and legs beneath the short, silk dressing gown were pallid and thin. Hanlon knew he was only twenty-nine, but he could have passed for forty in the struggling sunlight from the uncleaned windows that dimly transformed the native gloom of the basement into a murky greyness.

'You look like shit, Toby,' said Hanlon conversationally. 'Like you've crawled out from under a rock.'

There was a sideboard in the living room and Whiteside had pulled a drawer open. He slipped a pair of latex gloves over his fingers.

Toby looked alarmed. 'What are you doing?' he said in a dry, frightened tone. 'Have you got a search warrant?' His voice was expensively educated. It went with the flat in a way that the rest of Toby didn't. Hanlon knew that Toby was a Trustafarian whose private income and accommodation provided by his tax-exile parents did not cover his drug expenditure, so he had turned to coke dealing to his friends and acquaintances to make ends meet. He was an amateur dealer, now hopelessly out of his depth, and beginning to realize it.

'Ma'am?' said Whiteside. He was looking into the open drawer. You beauty, he was thinking to himself. There, in the drawer, were electronic scales, a zip-loc bag of white powder, a

plastic screw-top container of dextrose that he assumed was for cutting the coke and another transparent plastic bag containing small, wrapped packages, like miniature origami envelopes, that Whiteside guessed would contain one gram deals of coke. He lifted this out of the drawer and held it up. Toby looked at it with fear.

'Well, well, well, Toby Manning. What's this then?' said Whiteside. 'Hardly for personal consumption, eh, Tobes?'

Toby had risen to his feet. 'That's not mine. I'm looking after it for a friend,' he said. 'I want a lawyer. I don't think you're allowed—'

Hanlon guessed the rest of the sentence would have been 'to do this' but she'd had enough of Toby. With a scythe-like move of her foot, she kicked his legs from underneath him at ankle level so he fell back into his chair. She leant over as he collapsed, startled, into the welcoming fabric of the armchair, seized a handful of his hair and yanked it hard. His head snapped back on its neck and he was staring upwards at the ceiling. Hanlon's face, her grey eyes boring into his, appeared menacingly in his line of vision.

'You listen to me, you cretin,' she said. 'You have two options. Cooperate and we won't prosecute. Don't cooperate and you go down for dealing coke. Do you understand?'

Toby wanted to say 'You can't do this'. But the policewoman was doing this, his hair felt like it might be ripped out at any second, it was very painful and he was very frightened. He badly needed the toilet, he felt his bladder might burst. The coke had been bringing on panic attacks for a while and he was in the middle of one now. Her eyes looked totally insane. He thought his heart might explode, it was galloping so.

He heard the other policeman say, 'We don't need a warrant, Toby, because you invited us in and the drugs were in plain

sight. I think you've got about a hundred grams here, Toby, old chum. Plus your paraphernalia, the scales, the bagged-up gear.'

'That's called dealing, Toby,' said Hanlon. She gave his hair an extra hard tug for emphasis.

'Help us and you walk, we'll be out of here,' said the other one.

'We'll even let you keep all your gear. Don't help and you're going down. Seven years, Toby. That's what you'll probably get.' 'That would be the going rate,' agreed Hanlon. The dealer digested this unhappily. Then the policeman went on. 'Oh,

and Toby...'

The policewoman let go of his hair and he sat up straight in the chair and looked nervously at the bearded policeman. 'All those stories, Toby, you may have heard about prison showers and what happens to innocent young men in them.' Toby nodded. He swallowed painfully, wary of the mad bitch policewoman who was staring at him with those unnerving eyes. The policeman went on. 'Well, the thing is, Tobes, they're all true.' He smiled as Toby's mind flooded with horror stories he'd heard about prison or seen in films.

'I wouldn't like to be an ex-public schoolboy inside, Tobes.

They'll eat you alive. As the actress said to the bishop.'

'What do you want me to do?' he asked in a small voice. 'Go and get your phone, Toby,' said the policewoman calmly.

'I want you to text one of your clients. That will be more or less it.' She picked up a DVD case from his coffee table and looked at it with distaste. 'Then you can return to watching *Bangkok Thai Anal Babe Whores Three* at your leisure.'

Toby stood up and fetched his phone. 'What do you want me to do?' he said.


Bingo, thought Whiteside triumphantly.

# 4

In Finchley, in North London, Kathy Reynolds poured another cup of tea for the woman from the property-letting company. Clarissa Morgan, she thought, was exceptionally helpful. Albion Services had been a real find. Other estate agents, other letting agencies, had proved utterly useless, in some cases worse than useless, when it came to finding a property. The level of incompetence she had encountered was shocking. Kathy was extremely efficient herself at her job and it caused her bewilderment when she came across people manifestly not up to doing theirs. She really didn't see how hard it could be. They were estate agents, for heaven's sake, not astrophysicists or surgeons. It was surprising really when they had all the relevant information, knew her price range and her requirements – single mother, one twelve-year-old child – the number of unsuitable properties she'd been offered, everything from penthouses suitable for single, wealthy bachelors to eight-bedroom houses or downright slums. Not so with Clarissa Morgan. Clarissa Morgan was a beacon of ability. Kathy had known Clarissa would be good, ever since she first saw her bright, intelligent face under her short square-cut fringe of dark hair, and they'd become friends.

An observer might have thought that Clarissa and Kathy could be used in some advertising campaign that required two Caucasian women

who were physically virtual polar opposites.

Kathy was tall, blonde and slim. She looked, and was, reserved by nature. Time had etched fine lines on her face but she still had an exceptionally good figure, and she was aware that she was still extremely attractive. Peter, her son, had inherited her good looks. He was too young to think about girls but Kathy knew that before he was much older, he'd be in great demand. That wasn't just a mother's biased judgement; there was independent verification. Her friends frequently remarked upon it. He was exceptionally handsome.

If Kathy was ethereal, then Clarissa was earthy. She was stocky in build, dark-haired, swarthy. Kathy guessed, correctly, that she had to work hard to keep her weight down and her hair under control. She could, and did, wear bold colours, vivid nail varnish, scarlet lipstick. She wasn't conventionally pretty, her figure was indifferent, but she'd played the hand she'd been dealt extremely well. Kathy knew that when Clarissa walked into a room or down a street, male heads would turn. She was sexy and she knew it. It was the aura she obviously liked to project. At first sight she wasn't the kind of person Kathy naturally warmed to. Clarissa looked like the sort of woman who didn't like women, but now Kathy felt she had misjudged her. Clarissa's competence and friendliness had thawed her.

Albion, unlike the other agencies, had taken the time to draw up a detailed profile of her and her needs so they could find her the property she wanted, and Clarissa had even taken a keen interest in her twelve-year-old son, Peter, helpfully restricting the search to areas accessible from his school and to properties that fitted her price range. Kathy was immensely proud of Peter and, although she suspected that a healthy interest in your client's children always made sense from a business point of view, Clarissa's questions about Peter seemed inspired by genuine affection and concern. She'd even, with Kathy's permission,

put a picture of Kathy and Peter on her phone, in fact several pictures. 'I like to show potential clients the kind of customers we have on our books,' she explained. 'Particularly women on their own. I'm a single woman myself and you can't be too careful these days who you trust, especially when it comes down to really important things like where you live. Also who you meet. I'm very wary about male clients on their own until I've got to know them.'

Clarissa now leant back in her chair and sipped her tea. She'd called round to tell Kathy they were thinking about putting cable into the property and wanted to check that was OK with her. Kathy had hired the flat on a one-year lease while she considered her options. After her husband's death and the sale of her South London house, she didn't feel up to the strains of buying a property. It would have taken an energy she didn't have. She didn't want to think about anything important for the time being. This particularly went for house-hunting. The endless visiting, the wasted time, the depressing traipsing around other people's houses, the brief, unwanted snapshots of their lives. Above all, she didn't want to make any decisions. She looked at Clarissa and thought, when I decide to get a place, I'll get her to find it for me. She's someone I can trust.

Today Clarissa was looking Tatler-esque. She was wearing

a well-cut jacket and skirt that looked expensive but not off-puttingly so. She had a silver ring with a large red rectangular-cut ruby on the ring finger of her right hand. It matched her lipstick. She asked, 'So, how is Peter?' She always asked after his welfare. She was very solicitous. She leant forward as she spoke. She had a husky, slightly emphatic, voice.

Kathy, who frequently had to make presentations to large groups of people and speak at conferences, had once paid for a couple of sessions of professional training from a voice coach

who worked in the theatre. He had shown her how to project her voice, using her breath and the muscles at the base of her diaphragm to reach the back of a room. Clarissa did this, she had noticed. Vaguely, she wondered if Clarissa had received theatrical training too. She did look slightly stagey and had those mannerisms that Kathy associated with Peter's drama teacher at school, deliberately overemphasized movements, particularly hand and arm gestures. She put the thought from her head, it was hardly relevant.

Kathy smiled and automatically looked at the school photo of Peter in his chorister's robes. The school prided itself on its choir. She wondered, as she sometimes did, if he would keep his voice when it broke. His father had had a beautiful voice. 'Getting over things,' she said, in answer to Clarissa. 'It's like his dad said before he died, "I'm too old now for it to be a tragedy, just think of it as a bit of a shame".' She missed Dan, but above all she worried about how his death might affect her son. Would it make her too much of a clingy mother? Would it matter if her son didn't have some sort of male role model?

Luckily, she thought wryly to herself, I'm usually too busy to think about things like that, too busy to brood.

'It must be difficult,' said Clarissa in her caring voice, and looked at the family photos framed on the windowsill. Kathy's son was very good-looking, she had decided. Very good-looking indeed. She gently touched the small, horseshoe-shaped scar between her eyes. It was a habit she had when she was thinking.

# 5

Patrick Cunningham was starting to go crazy. He knew this, but it was so much part of the craziness that had taken over his life that he had come to accept it as normal.

He impatiently parked his red Porsche in a residents-only parking bay. He wasn't a Notting Hill resident himself, but he'd represented a fair few of them in court and felt more than entitled. He hurriedly walked across the road into the upmarket pub. All the bars in Notting Hill seemed to have been gentrified since the film with Hugh Grant. He ran his eye along the bottles in the refrigerated cabinet behind the barman and ordered a Kirin. He stood by the bar, pretending to read a *Metro*, the free London newspaper, one eye firmly, and, if he were honest, slightly desperately, fixed on the clock above the optic rack.

The doors had just opened and there were only another two customers, their rosy faces witnesses to their owners' early starts and late finishes in the pub. It was 12.15 p.m. Cunningham had a hell of a coke habit. That was his problem, the root source of the craziness. The motherlode.

Today he'd rescheduled face-time with a client to see Toby

Manning, his dealer. It was extremely unprofessional. This was far from the first time he'd done this. He was beginning to run out of plausible excuses for cancelled meetings and, maybe more worryingly, he was beginning not to care. Work was becoming

almost an irrelevance.

Cunningham's own chambers were becoming both perplexed and alarmed at his behaviour. Eyebrows were beginning to be raised by his erratic work habits. He didn't care. Real life was cocaine-centred; it was dominating his life. He was either doing coke, getting coke or thinking about coke. Then Toby had texted him to say he couldn't come and he was sending an associate, but not to worry, the guy was reliable.

Come on, come on, come on, thought Cunningham to himself impatiently. He didn't drum his fingers on the polished wooden bar counter but he felt like doing so.

He drank some lager. He didn't want lager, what good was that to him. He wanted Charlie.

Then, at twelve thirty, as promised, the dealer appeared. Cunningham knew it was him as soon as he walked through the door. The lawyer breathed a huge sigh of relief. It wasn't as if the man was dressed in a hip-hop, pimped-up style, like some of Cunningham's wealthier, cash-rich, clients. He was dressed inconspicuously, if expensively, but he stood out from the other customers in the pub. The other people in the bar looked normal. They had educated, relaxed, comfortable faces. This man didn't belong in their cosy Notting Hill world. It was the aura of matter-of-fact menace, the look in the eyes and the face that bore the traces of past violence – a broken nose, a hairline scar, a misaligned jaw disguised by the current trend for beards that was sweeping the media and hipster world. The man reminded him of Anderson. Cunningham had met a lot of criminals. It was his job after all. The innocent didn't hire him. He knew what he was looking at now. It was the unmistakable face of crime.

Toby's stand-in too immediately recognized the tall, thin, angular frame of Patrick Cunningham, leaning against the bar, as soon as he walked into the pub. He had seen him in action in court a couple of times. There, he had been effortlessly in charge of the situation. Most people are used to seeing lawyers in TV dramas where they're well rehearsed, eloquent and effective. The reality is often the reverse. Cunningham, however, looked like a famous actor being a lawyer. He gave a polished performance. He gave good court. The dealer thought the lawyer was one of those people who believed so strongly in themselves that others were drawn into it, judges included. He had made the other legal team appear amateurish, stupid.

Patrick Cunningham, his languid frame physically dominating the court, had looked slightly bored as he effortlessly demolished arguments and evidence given by the prosecution and the police, or introduced reasonable doubt in the minds of the jury. They'd been almost cheering him on. It was like watching a Grand Slam tennis player turning up at a club-level tournament.

He went up to Cunningham. 'I'm George,' he said quietly. 'Toby can't make it. He said he'd called you.' Cunningham looked at him closely and nodded. He asked George what he wanted to drink, bought the dealer a beer, and they both sat down at a quiet corner table. The pub was popular and was beginning to fill up. George looked around him. He recognized it from a decade ago when it had been a defiantly drinkers' pub that no one but the desperate would have used, with a sticky carpet, a jukebox and a fruit machine. The fibre of the carpet had been so soaked in spilt beer over the years it was like walking on Velcro. Now its walls were Farrow & Ball grey, not nicotine yellow, the ageing alcoholics who'd been its loyal patrons either dead of alcohol-related disease or dispersed. Miles

Davis was playing in the background. Tonight it was full of professional people like Cunningham. I'm getting old, thought George.

Notting Hill had changed too. George could remember when
it was rundown, the Portobello Road a haven for ageing hippies,
when bands used to play under the Westway, the motorway
bridge vaulting upwards high above the roof of the open-air concert
area. It had smelt of exhaust fumes, cement dust and hash. He'd
known it when it was a dump of a place and every other person
seemed to be a dealer. Now it was the haunt of millionaires and
models. George preferred the old days.

Still, he thought, some things never change. Drugs then, drugs
now, and there would be drugs tomorrow. He said, 'I've got something for you from Toby,' and discreetly took an envelope from his
jacket and slid it to the lawyer under the table. It contained ten one-
gram wraps of cocaine, and Cunningham in turn pressed a wad of
folded twenties silently into George's hand. George put it in the
pocket of his jacket. He knew it would be correct.

A hint of a smile now played around Cunningham's tight,
bloodless lips. George noted, slightly to his surprise, that
Cunningham was almost shaking with suppressed eagerness.
George knew a lot of people with big drug problems; he hadn't
expected Cunningham to be one of them. You've got it bad, mate,
he thought to himself.

'Thank you very much, George,' said Cunningham. Like Toby,
his accent was privately educated, expensively vowelled. George
noted with amusement that he was trying to look nonchalant while
trembling, practically shaking, with coke desire. 'Toby did say it was
going to be exceptional. I hope he's right.' His voice tailed off. He
was salivating. 'If you'll excuse me.'

Cunningham disappeared, practically ran, into the toilets with
his coke. George raised his eyebrows; drugs were a great social
leveller. It really doesn't matter where you're from, an addiction is

an addiction, an addict, an addict. George recognized that semi-insane look of overexcited eagerness in Cunningham's eyes, and it wasn't the look of a casual user. The lawyer was a man

with a monkey on his back. He took a slow mouthful of beer and thoughtfully picked up Cunningham's paper.

A while later Cunningham came back into the bar. George was still at the table, reading the lawyer's paper.

'Everything OK?' asked the dealer without looking up from the paper.

'Fine. Exceptional even,' said Cunningham, his eyes glittering. George raised his eyes, then his eyebrows. Cunningham was wired, coked out of his mind. How much did he just do? wondered George. The lawyer's jaw was rotating like he was chewing invisible gum. His eyes were starting out of his head as if they'd grown and the sockets had shrunk. Sweat beaded his forehead. Coke sweat. George knew that if he put his head close to Cunningham he'd be able to smell the metallic tang in his perspiration from the drug.

Cunningham stood smiling down at him, shifting his weight from foot to foot. He was so out of it he really didn't know what to do. God alone knew what was happening to his brain; synapses were exploding like fireworks. 'Tell Toby, next week, same time, same place,' said Cunningham, self-importantly. He grinned wildly again. His nose ran and he sniffed loudly.

Jesus Christ, thought George. And this is supposedly one of Britain's finest legal minds. 'OK,' he said mildly. 'Take care.' As he watched Cunningham's back disappear through the frosted glass of the pub's Victorian doors – a suitable image, thought George, for the man's brain – he wondered if the lawyer were due in court that day. He guessed the judge might not notice, but Cunningham's low-life clients certainly would. Oh well, he thought. That's his problem, not mine. He went back to the paper. The headline read:

*Burnt girl not 'witchcraft' killing, say police.*

**6**
_____

Cunningham left the pub, stepped off the pavement and was very nearly hit by a four-by-four he hadn't seen, as he euphorically strode into the road without looking. He was finding it very hard to focus. The driver angrily sounded the horn. Cunningham gave him the finger. He crossed over to his Carrera and climbed inside. He closed his eyes momentarily and told himself to concentrate. As he sat on the leather-upholstered seat, sweating in his expensive suit, the temptation to do another quick line before driving back to his office was overwhelming. No one will notice, he thought, and even if they do, fuck 'em. His hand made contact with the envelope in his pocket.

A tap on the driver's window made him jump. For a second he wondered what the noise was. He also wondered how long he'd been sitting there staring into space. He'd lost track of time. Momentarily he was disorientated, wondered where he was. He looked up and around, half expecting to see George, and instead saw the dark blue uniform of a policeman. His heart started pounding and he felt an unpleasant lurch in his bowels. He didn't want to be dealing with the police. Whenever he usually saw them, they were safely in a witness box or deferentially escorting him to a witness room in a police station. Not like this. He opened the window.

'Would you mind getting out of the car, sir,' said the officer politely.

He did so, now extremely conscious of the curious glances of passers-by on the pavement. Man in a Porsche being pulled over. Good, they probably thought. He was also extremely conscious of the presence of enough quantities of a Class A drug on his person to be facing jail time. Oh shit, thought Cunningham.

Half an hour before, Hanlon had looked approvingly at Detective Sergeant Whiteside as he shrugged himself into the brown suede jacket that felt as soft as warm butter and slipped a pair of Armani glasses on where they rested comfortably on the slight ridge in his nose from one of the three occasions it had been broken, twice in the line of duty and once in his own time. Hanlon had borrowed the clothes from the property store of goods confiscated from convicted criminals that were awaiting auction. The sergeant was dressed in the seized goods of a busted drug dealer the same build as Whiteside. It seemed appropriate to Hanlon that if Whiteside were impersonating a drug dealer he might as well dress the part. She felt it was a kind of poetic justice. The dealer's wardrobe collection seized by the police, not including shoes, was probably worth a conservative fifty thousand, or would have been, when new. Whiteside loved clothes. Having the opportunity to wear an entire new outfit without worrying about the cost was a welcome novelty.

'Do I get to keep these?' asked Whiteside.

'Why not?' said Hanlon. The evidence storage manager

shrugged. 'Fine by me. Just submit a report later saying they've been damaged in police use and are no longer suitable for resale, so it's all kosher. If DI Hanlon signs it, that'll be good enough.'

'There's your answer then,' said Hanlon.

Whiteside grinned happily. The civilian in charge of the confiscated goods in the property room, Dan Brudenell, was the brother of the PCSO whose life Hanlon had saved. It was Dan who had come to her after the event to say if ever she needed a favour, no matter what, just to ask. He'd been delighted to help when asked to kit Whiteside out. Whiteside's own wardrobe was carefully selected and good quality, but Hanlon wanted him in the trappings of the genuine dealer. Whiteside wouldn't spend three grand on a jacket even if he could afford to. 'George', his new alter ego, would.

Hanlon now watched with amusement as Whiteside rubbed his short, clipped beard while he studied his appearance in the mirror of the sun visor of the unmarked police car. 'I should have requested a Rolex,' he said. Sergeant Thompson and Constable Childs, sitting in the back, studied the rear of his head.

'You look so gay, sir!' said Childs. Thompson put his hand over his mouth to mask a smile. Whiteside was actually gay, a fact known to just about everyone he worked with, but obviously not Constable Childs.

Hanlon's expressionless eyes met Whiteside's. The sergeant decided to spare Childs' blushes. His hard brown eyes rested on the reflection of the two policemen in the rear of the car. Childs was kind of cute, thought Whiteside speculatively. The prospect of action always made him horny. 'Well,' said Hanlon, as if divining his thoughts, which wouldn't have surprised Whiteside. It was as if the woman was psychic sometimes. 'Off you go, George. Time to make your dope deal.'

Whiteside got out of the Ford and closed the door gently behind him. Hanlon watched his muscular back stretching the fabric of the

jacket as he walked to the upmarket Notting Hill pub where he was
about to sell ten grams of coke to one of London's top criminal
defendants. It was coming up to half past

twelve and already the lunchtime customers were beginning to
stream into the gastropub. In half an hour it would be packed.
Hanlon was about to risk what was left of her career purely to
settle an old score. It was revenge, nothing more, nothing less. If it
went wrong she faced all sorts of trouble: dismissal from the police
and the loss of all pension rights, charges – valid ones – of entrapment, perjury, false witness, false imprisonment, plus possibly
several other lesser crimes. Thompson, the uniformed sergeant in
the car with her, knew what was going on. He had met Hanlon
when she'd been in Specialist Crime and they'd got on well. He
too was delighted to have the opportunity to bring down Anderson, which is what all this was about. Cunningham, 'Jesus' Anderson's tame lawyer, was also, in Hanlon's judgement, his Achilles
heel. She was going to bring Anderson down by using the man
who'd so far been spectacularly successful at keeping him out of
prison.

Childs hadn't got a clue what was happening. He was just
excited to be there.

If it went according to plan, she would be able to arrest one of
North London's most notorious drug dealers. David Anderson, to
anyone who lived in his manor, was a household name. Hanlon and
Whiteside had nearly had him two years ago when they were both
working for the Serious and Organized Crime unit of Specialist
Crimes and Operations and liaising with the drug squads in various
boroughs. The case had collapsed because of witness intimidation.
It was par for the course with anything involving Anderson. Hanlon
wanted him badly. She'd taken his acquittal as a personal affront.
As Whiteside knew, there was an obsessive streak to her and there
was no such thing in her world that equated to drawing a line

under something. She was out to get the man and she would, even if it meant the destruction of her career.

Hanlon was sure that Cunningham knew a great deal about Anderson's business. Cunningham had boasted as much to one of Hanlon's informants while the two of them had been involved in a marathon coke session round at the informant's house. Cunningham had bragged about how much he'd learnt about Anderson, about how much information he had on deliveries and prices. If what the man said was true, and if Cunningham decided to share the information, they could arrest Anderson with a sizeable drug delivery on his property. This time there would be no witnesses to retract stories, no coercion, just simple, undeniable possession.

'I couldn't help but notice you leaving that pub over there, sir,' said the sergeant, who was accompanied by a young PC who looked about twelve to Cunningham. 'You were nearly struck by a car as you crossed the road. Have you been drinking, sir?' Cunningham took a deep breath. Although they had no reason to search him, the five hundred pounds' worth of coke in his inside pocket felt the size and weight of a breeze block. The police hate lawyers. If they nicked him, he would be disbarred from the legal profession and they'd be turning cartwheels of joy at whichever station these two operated out of. Cunningham

was widely known and disliked by the police.

'I've had a drink, yes, but only a half of lager.' The lawyer's nose ran a little and he gave a loud involuntary sniff. He noticed the sergeant's eyes narrow suspiciously.

'Well, I'll have to ask you to take a breathalyser test, sir,' he said, producing the small, transparent plastic bag and fitting it with a tube. Cunningham followed his instructions and blew into it. The sergeant studied it carefully and said, to his huge relief, 'Well, sir. The test indicates the presence of alcohol but within the permitted limits.'

Yes! thought Cunningham. Thank God for that.

Then, 'However, sir, your general behaviour and inability to focus would indicate to me that you may be under the influence of drugs, which is an offence under the 1988 Road Traffic Act. I am afraid this means I must ask you to accompany me to the local police station where we can establish whether or not you have been driving under the influence of a controlled substance.' A few times in his career, Cunningham had seen clients found guilty who had been expecting an acquittal and now he knew very much how they felt, running confidently forward off a cliff, legs pumping furiously on thin air, like a cartoon character, like Wile E. Coyote or Road Runner, only to look down and realize that the ground beneath their feet no longer existed, before plummeting to the earth. It was more or less

how he felt now.

'Could I have your car keys, sir?' Cunningham opened the door and got out. He locked the car behind him. When he returned to it, he knew it would be clamped or towed. He might as well sell it anyway. He wouldn't be able to afford it in the future. He wouldn't have a future. He wouldn't have a job. He knew what would happen at the police station. 'Would you mind emptying your pockets, sir.' If they believed they had reasonable suspicion that he possessed drugs, which they did, he couldn't refuse. The discovery of the coke would follow, as would a mandatory mouth swab or blood test to see if he'd been under the influence of drugs while intending to drive. The crazy thing was, what he cared about even more than losing his driving licence, or losing his job, his career, was losing the coke in his pocket. He even found himself mentally working out how long they'd hold him for, so he could give Toby a call and get some more. It was the end of the road for his legal career,

that much was for sure.

He followed the sergeant, the constable at his side. At least they hadn't cuffed him. They'd spared him that embarrassment. Their police car was parked round the corner. The sergeant opened the door and put Cunningham in the back, then sat in the passenger seat. The younger policeman got in behind the wheel. He started the engine and then Cunningham, staring at his knees to avoid eye contact with curious pedestrians, hoping to God no one he knew would walk past and recognize him, and wondering which nick they'd take him to, was aware of the window being wound down and a woman's voice.

The engine stopped. The other rear door opened and a dark-haired, unsmiling woman stepped in and sat next to him. The uniforms got out and walked away from the car. Cunningham looked at her in surprise. He didn't recognize her. She had a hard, pale face and there were dark patches under her eyes as if she had trouble sleeping. She looked like trouble on legs.

He wondered who she was and what she wanted. It couldn't be anything good. Not with a face like that.

The coke euphoria was beginning to wear off and he was feeling a growing sense of agonized doom. He just wanted the day to end.

She looked at him and said, 'My name's DI Hanlon. I'm liaising with the sergeant from Serious Crimes and I think you're Patrick Cunningham, the lawyer, and you are in very serious trouble.' She paused to let the concept of serious trouble sink into the lawyer's mind. He stared at her blankly. She repeated the phrase. 'Very serious trouble.'

Hanlon wondered if maybe he'd gone into shock at the prospect of being arrested. She'd seen it happen before with people who had never been in trouble before with the police, had never dreamed it would be possible, and found themselves way out of their depth. Or maybe he was about to spring some

devastating legal objection she hadn't foreseen. Some procedural lapse that they'd committed. He was a lawyer after all. His mind had to be working like crazy to find a way out of the mess he was in. They'd nicked a judge for speeding a while back and he'd turned up for his court appearance with eight ring binders full of paperwork to try to get the charge quashed on a technicality. God knows what Cunningham might try. He was facing a lot more than three points on his licence.

She shrugged mentally and carried on. 'Now, if you give me the information I want, you can go free; if not, well, it's up to you. So far, nothing is yet official. You haven't actually been charged. You can walk away from all this mess. It's up to you whether it stays that way, but if you'd rather, you can accompany us to the police station and we'll allow the due process of the law to take over, with all that implies.' Hanlon waited for the man's reply. It was more or less the line she had used with Toby, but Toby was a sad failure of a man, in way above his head, and Cunningham was a top-flight lawyer.

Momentarily she wondered if he really was all there mentally. He did look remarkably stoned. She never tried to predict reactions or outcomes but she had been expecting some form of protest, not this silence.

'What do you want?' said Cunningham. Eventually. It was not the voice of despair. She had arrested professionals before, white-collar workers with no criminal history who had burst into tears at the thought of their careers being destroyed, the shame they'd brought on their families, feelings not shared by the majority of her clients to whom arrest was either a nuisance or an occupational hazard. Cunningham seemed more resigned than anything else.

'Information leading to the arrest of David Anderson.' Hanlon looked at the lawyer speculatively. It was like a raise in poker; the question was whether or not Cunningham would call her bluff or fold. She was asking a lot. Would the dangers posed by betraying a man they both knew to be a killer outweigh the end of Cunningham's life as a lawyer? Hanlon had told herself that Cunningham's ego would not allow him to consider the possibility of failure. He would rather take the risk of Anderson than the certainty of the loss of his livelihood. The latter was of course her gigantic bluff. His arrest was based on a lie; she could not carry the charade further than the confines of the car. For Cunningham, an entrapment defence would be tricky since he'd have to prove or show that he wouldn't have acted illegally unless the police had talked him into doing it. It would be hard to make a jury credibly believe that you'd been sweet-talked or bullied into buying five hundred pounds' worth of coke by an undercover officer and then stuck a load of it up your nose. However, her sting operation was not officially sanctioned. The drugs that he'd been busted with had been supplied illegally. She could imagine, if she chose to, the scene in court. 'And where, Sergeant Whiteside, did you obtain these drugs?' Kicking Toby's door in and threatening him was certainly beyond the remit of the police. Theoretically, Whiteside wasn't simply posing as a dealer: he had been dealing. She had no case, but Cunningham didn't know that. The end of her career or Anderson behind bars instead of swaggering around his North London estate like some lord of the manor: the outcome lay in Cunningham's

frazzled mind.

For Hanlon, it was a perfectly acceptable gamble. She felt completely calm. If she'd been hooked up to a monitor her heart rate would have shown fifty beats per minute. Cunningham stared at her for what felt like a very long time.

He must know, she thought. He must realize that he's been set up rather than nicked randomly.

What Hanlon didn't know, couldn't know, was that because Cunningham had, for a while now, been behaving so outrageously professionally, been involved in so many lies through his habit, he had come to expect this moment in some form or another. To him it had an air of terrible inevitability. He knew all the things he'd been up to and he suspected that others must know too. His view of the world was skewed through the drug bombardment he was subjecting himself to. Paranoia is a common side-effect of prolonged cocaine abuse and Cunningham had been very edgy for a while now. Reality was a hazy concept for him these days. That he should be arrested came as no real surprise. For Cunningham, sitting in the police car, it had not been a question of 'if' but 'when'. He was prepared to bow to the inevitable. He felt he might as well get it over and done with.

'OK,' he said simply. 'What do you want to know?'

Hanlon blinked in surprise. She had won. She was startled by how easy it was all proving to be, but it didn't show. Her face was impassive. The heart monitor would have remained unchanged. She took a notebook out of a pocket and explained. Cunningham listened carefully.

'I won't have to testify, of course, or appear as a witness,' he said.

'No,' replied Hanlon. 'It'll all be off the record, I'll make sure your name doesn't appear anywhere.' Cunningham nodded. He started talking.

He talked quickly and fluently: names, dates, times and methods of delivery. He wanted to get back to his flat and do some more coke. He certainly wasn't going back to work. Not after all this. The quicker this was over, the better. Hanlon's pen moved over the paper, Anderson's fate sealed in biro with his lawyer's complicity.

## 7

Detective Sergeant Enver Demirel was not a happy man. If he had read his horoscope in the newspaper he'd found on his desk, it would have promised him a challenging twelve hours ahead and that was certainly the kind of day he was having. Challenging. Today's challenge was not to feel too despondent. When police work went well, Enver thoroughly enjoyed his job. When he had days like today, it felt like trying to empty the sea with a bucket: utterly futile. A five-week, painstaking investigation into a prolific local burglar was now, to all intents and purposes, dead in the water. All that time, all the hopes they had raised of burglary victims who felt that for once the police were doing something more constructive than issuing them with a case number to facilitate insurance claims, wasted.

It had really irritated him because it was the kind of policing

he felt they should be doing. Proper policing, not faffing around with celebrities or distractions like bloody Plebgate. Haringey, the London borough that his patch Wood Green lay in, had about a quarter of a million people living in it. It was probably the population of Iceland, thought Enver. It was certainly big enough. Last year there had been about three thousand reported burglaries. Percentage-wise it was over double the national average. The burglar they'd been after had caused misery throughout Wood Green. Many of these people would have been uninsured. There

were big pockets of poverty in the borough and premiums were high. It was the kind of crime that most people worried about, that and being mugged or attacked. The kind of crime that directly affected them. It wasn't just the nicked electrical goods or jewellery. It was the door kicked in, the smashed window, the ransacked flat, the feeling of invasion.

Phil Johnson, their target, was a prolific criminal and his arrest would have shown the local community that the police were working for them, not against them. It would have won hearts and minds. It would have been a high-profile statement that the police were doing something useful, catching criminals, not just issuing crime case numbers for insurance claim purposes. Yesterday the case against him was rock solid. But now, all this had changed. As of this morning, he had a key eyewitness who was refusing to coop-erate and a suspect who'd left the country for the Caribbean, indefi-nitely. Despite the other evidence they still had on him, Enver knew that once the momentum was lost Johnson would slip down to a fairly low position on the 'to do' list when he returned. And now, courtesy of his own extended relatives, he had this new problem to deal with.

Today, in his lunch hour, he was in the back room of a mosque

in Wood Green while family pressure was gently but ruthlessly applied by the imam of the mosque, his Uncle Osman. The small room with its wooden floor smelt of furniture polish overlaid with acrimony.

The conversation was taking place in heavily accented Turkish, which Enver, who was born in London, didn't really speak too well, and English. He had to keep interrupting, to ask for clarification.

'So, let me get this straight. He,' Enver pointed an accusing finger at Mehmet who sat unhappily and powerlessly in his chair while these two men, the policeman and the imam, decided his

future, 'didn't come forward on Thursday to report his child missing because he's here, in the UK, illegally and didn't know what to do?' Enver's tone of voice was incredulous. 'It's a missing child investigation, not visa fraud! What was he thinking?'

Osman nodded wearily. He looked hard at his nephew, Enver Demirel. He knew he was emotionally blackmailing him, but it was in a good cause. Mehmet Yilmaz was in the most terrible trouble a parent could be in and it was their duty to help. Whether or not mistakes had been made was neither here nor there. What's done was done. He could appreciate Enver's rage. But that would pass. Enver was a good person and Osman was sure he'd deliver. It was just that Enver was judging Mehmet using British frames of reference. If you were in trouble in Turkey, the police were not automatically your first choice for help. Family and community were. Turkey, as Turkey, had only really been around for a century or so. It was a strange mix of the new and the old. Corruption ran deep at most official levels and the police were no exception. He looked into Enver's angry brown eyes.

It was a while since he'd seen his nephew and he was surprised and a little concerned by the weight that Enver had put on. His nephew seemed to have morphed from whippet thin to gently fat in the blink of an eye. Majid, his brother, Enver's father, had died of a massive heart attack in his fifties and looking at the suddenly corpulent son, who had also grown a thick, drooping moustache since he'd seen him last, Osman realized he looked uncannily like Majid. He looked so like him it was disturbing. Osman was worried history would repeat itself.

The old imam spoke. 'He was frightened and confused. He doesn't speak much English. Hardly any in fact. He got friends in the community to speak to the supermarket management. They knew nothing. They don't employ anyone who has the name Ayse or who matches her description. We told people in

the local Turkish mosques at Friday prayers. That's probably a good two thousand people. Would the police have that kind of coverage? Would they treat a missing illegal immigrant seriously?' He looked gently at Enver. They both knew the answer. 'Now we're coming to you for help and advice. That's all.'

Osman had also approached the local Turkish London radio station and newspapers. They had all said they'd be delighted to do everything they could to help, but the police would have to be informed. Mehmet had been adamant. No police. Approaching Enver had been Osman's idea of a compromise.

The old imam, immaculate in an antique three-piece suit, winced gently from the pain of the arthritis in his left hand and then smiled at himself. 'Why me?' he had been on the point of thinking. Why did God see fit to inflict arthritis on me. Then he thought, Majid got the heart, I got arthritis. I shouldn't complain. I mustn't be impatient. It is not my will, Osman thought, that is important. What I will does not matter.

Enver sipped his Fanta and glared at the hunched, bearded figure of Mehmet. The Sergeant was normally a very patient man but Mehmet's slowness in coming forward had made any investigation hugely difficult. Mehmet sat on his chair, shoulders rounded, twisting his fingers uncomfortably. He was hollow-faced, dark rings around his eyes. He hadn't slept properly since Thursday. Life, for Mehmet, had taken on an unreal, nightmarish quality, as if he was living in some kind of cave and events were flickering away on the wall, like a terrible hallucination. It's Monday today, Enver was thinking, and this abduction had happened on Thursday. Four days, gone. His frustration at this time lag was clearly visible on his face. Osman gently recapitulated for Enver's benefit the problems that Mehmet faced and why he had done, or more to the point, hadn't done, what he did.

The biggest problem was of course that he was here illegally

and there was currently a crackdown on Turkish illegal workers. If Mehmet had been Kurdish, he could maybe have claimed some form of asylum, citing Turkish persecution, but coming from a country that had wanted to join the EU, and indeed had been backed in that by the British government, it was hard to see an asylum request being granted.

The next problem was one of debt. Mehmet owed a great deal of money to his family in Turkey for getting him over here. It was money that had to be repaid. It was a debt of honour as well as of hard cash. Currently half of everything he earned went straight back to Cappadocia, remitted to pay back what he owed. Mehmet paid no tax or National Insurance and both he and Mehmet's employers were keen to keep it that way. They did not want the local Inland Revenue on their backs. Tax avoidance and the employment of illegal immigrants were very hot topics at the moment; trouble was to be avoided at all costs. Osman explained to Enver that Mehmet was working off a debt of about twenty thousand pounds for the fraudulent paperwork and the various bribes that had got him and Nur, his wife, over here. If he were deported, he could never pay it back.

And now Reyhan, his daughter, was at school and Nur

pregnant again. Mehmet had been hoping – though maybe hope was the wrong word – that Ali had been kidnapped for money. In Cappadocia such things were not too unusual. If that had been the case, somehow he'd have found the cash. But as the days had gone past and no demands had come, it had become obvious to him this wasn't so.

Enver looked again at Mehmet, at the short, stocky muscular peasant who in turn looked at the police sergeant with anguish, as if it lay within Enver's grasp to somehow make everything OK again. It was infuriating to be made the repository of such blind, unrealistic hopes. They wanted him to launch an unofficial

investigation into a child's disappearance, somehow using as much of the Metropolitan Police's official time and resources as possible. He made up his mind to say 'no'. If we do this at all, he thought to himself, you can go through official channels. I'm not an unofficial cheerleader for London's Turkish community. If he said yes, he suspected – no, he knew, he didn't suspect –

it would be the thin end of the wedge. He could easily visualize endless petitions from London Turks. 'Go to Enver, he'll sort you out. He did it for Mehmet Yilmaz, he can't refuse you.'

He cleared his throat to say, I can't help you. It was an official-sounding noise, the prelude to a statement. He put his official face on, straightening his posture to add authority. As he did so, Mehmet produced a small, grey, woollen rabbit from his jacket pocket. Mehmet cradled it gently in his hands. He looked at it and Enver heard his breathing change to a deep, agonized rasp, as if putting as much air as possible inside his lungs would somehow compensate for the pain.

The stitching along the knitted toy's spine had long ago come adrift and the toy rabbit had been neatly, lovingly, sewn back together with black thread. Enver could guess what it was and who it had belonged to.

'Please,' said Mehmet, holding out Ali's toy rabbit like a talisman to Enver. His eyes filled with tears. It was the only English word he'd spoken so far. Maybe the only one he knew. It was enough. Enver knew then he was going to help.

Enver cursed himself mentally for a fool and took his notebook out. He knew too he was going to regret this. Well, he could always put in for a transfer to Norfolk. He'd heard it had the lowest number of immigrants in the UK. King's Lynn, he guessed, would be Turkish free. He would be safe from his family out there. He turned to his uncle. 'Tell him to go through the events of last Thursday.' Mehmet started speaking; Enver started writing.

## 8

There are some two thousand miles of canals in Britain, about two hundred miles or so of which – such as the Grand Union Canal, the Hertford Union Canal and the River Lea Navigation

– loop and meander, or strike purposefully, through London. One of the oldest of the capital's waterways is the Regent's Canal, which runs through the heart of London like a secret artery from Islington to Little Venice, built about two centuries ago. The uses of the canals have changed from transport to leisure but they've survived more or less intact.

It was a man called Ron James who found the body. There was an inset day for teacher training at his grandson's school, and his daughter and her husband were both at work. He had taken the seven-year-old to fish on the Regent's Canal down near Maida Vale. The towpath gets quite busy and Ron and the boy had arrived early to stake out a place. There were some nice roach and perch in the water down there, maybe a carp if they were really lucky. His grandson enjoyed fishing and Ron was pleased to have this bond with him. He particularly liked showing him how to tie the knots and bait the hooks. The boy was good at knots and was always fascinated by the maggots writhing in their small, polythene tub.

Most of the people on the canal bank at that hour of the day were runners and joggers, with the occasional dog walker, paying no attention to the canal's waters. There were few fishermen around.

'Can I put the maggot on, Granddad?' asked the boy.

''Course you can, son. I'll just get this on for you.' Ron slid the fine nylon line through the eye of the float and let Jared, his grandson, carefully bait the small hook with one of the maggots. He cast the line into the water for the boy and then he noticed the small bundle floating down by some rushes that grew near the lock gates and had escaped the last canal clean-up in the previous year.

'Jared,' he said quietly. 'Yes, Granddad?'

'Do you see that man sitting back there, the one with the really long rod?'

'Yes.'

'Could you go and ask him if he's had any luck so far today? See if the fish are biting.'

'Sure, Granddad.' The small, self-confident boy walked happily back the way they'd come.

Ron had never seen a dead body before outside of a hospital, but he realized immediately what he was looking at. It was far too realistic to be a toy. He had hoped it might be a large doll but he knew, almost instinctively, it wasn't the case. This year there had been a lot of algal bloom on the canal, but here by the lock it was comparatively clear. The child's hair floated gently around the back of his head in the dark, still waters. He wouldn't have noticed it if he hadn't been scanning the surface of the water for possible obstructions to his line.

He waited for Jared to move a little distance down the towpath to ask the fisherman how he was doing so the child wouldn't overhear his conversation, then he took his phone out. Ten minutes later the first couple of police arrived.

Baby Ali had been found.

The lock gate, a few metres away from where the body was snagged on the reeds, had been recently repainted black. White numerals denoting its number on the canal were stencilled on to the top lintel of one of the two powerfully thick mitre gates that controlled the flow of water in the lock. Ron noticed – the numbers didn't signify anything to him – that it was Gate 18.

# 9

Enver watched the two police divers from the marine policing unit as they gently and carefully moved the body of the child into the webbing of the cradle, so it could be pulled free of the water and up on to the bank of the canal. The water of the Regent's Canal was mournful, dark and still. It was now II a.m. on Tuesday morning and the towpath and canal banks had been cordoned off on both sides. On the other divide of the police tape, a group of TV reporters had assembled. They eyed each other disdainfully. By contrast, most of the technical crew with them – cameramen, sound engineers and other outside broadcast personnel – knew each other from similar, past occasions and there was a sense of, if not quite a party atmosphere, then a definite feeling of good cheer, of camaraderie, as they caught up with news and gossip. This was not shared on the other side of the police line. Grim efficiency was the pervasive atmosphere. There was very little talking beyond what was necessary.

Enver had worked on two previous child deaths, liaising with CEOP, the child protection people. He knew the statistics, themselves a subject of controversy. NSPCC figures put the number of deaths of under-sixteens at one child killed on average every week and one baby killed every twenty days in England and Wales. However, alternative sources put the

figures much higher, at one to two hundred per year. The figures weren't huge but they all knew that the investigation would be depressing enough. Whichever way you looked at it, it would be depressing. It could hardly be anything but. The chances were statistically high that the parents were involved and there would be a tearful litany of denial and attempt to shift the blame elsewhere if they were the killers. The alternative, that there was a child killer on the loose, an Ian Huntley or an Ian Brady or maybe even children involved in killing children, like the Bulger case, was perhaps even worse. Social services would be involved, newspapers, external agencies; it would be a messy and unpleasant investigation. And to make the investigation even more problematic, it would be conducted under an intense media scrutiny and an atmosphere of public semi-hysteria.

He watched as the small corpse, now on the bank, was

carefully and gently zipped into a child's body bag. Enver found the sight of the small container with its pathetic contents deeply distressing. He thought of Mehmet, his anguished, tear-stained face. He thought of Ali's toy, Grey Rabbit. He couldn't tell if he felt angry or depressed. Above all, he felt numb and slightly sick. The MPU men climbed out of the water, this part of their job done. Soon they would be joined by the Underwater and Confined Spaces Search Team to check that there were no more bodies down there. Enver guessed visibility would be dreadful in the canal. He'd often wondered why anyone would want to work for UCSST. He could understand people liking diving, not a passion he himself shared, but moving around, groping about in zero visibility in polluted canals, rivers and flooded buildings in search of bodies or evidence was hideous. Even when the search area wasn't aquatic, UCSST would be crawling around unpleasant places. He'd seen them once having to extract a body from a ventilation flue in a pub in White City.

A burglar over Christmas had tried to break into the premises like a criminally minded Santa, by crawling into the hood of the extractor fans from the kitchen, which rose funnel-like from the roof behind the building. He'd become trapped inside and because the pub kitchens were closed for three days, no one had heard his cries for help. He'd been in there for ten days while the kitchen staff had tried to work out where the terrible smell was coming from.

Enver knew the body they'd found had to be Mehmet's son, Ali. Today was the day after he had spoken to Mehmet and his uncle. So far, all he had been able to do was confirm that the supermarket had no CCTV record of the incident. The shop system was an old XDH one, connected to twenty-eight cameras internally and half a dozen externally. It was a good system: colour and high-resolution. There were so few external cameras because the shop car park was relatively small. The security manager, an ex-soldier, had been very helpful, but they only stored images for three days, seventy-two hours.

And, of course, they had no member of staff either called Aisha or answering to Mehmet's sketchy description. And that was as far as he'd got in his unofficial capacity. At least now they'd be able to do things properly, although Enver suspected it would all be too late. If only Mehmet had come forward earlier. He knew too that he would be in for an uncomfortable time explaining to his boss, Detective Chief Superintendent Ludgate, why he was able to identify the body. It wasn't that he had done anything particularly wrong, he hadn't had time, but he knew Ludgate would be in a bad mood and he'd be in the firing line.

He could see Jim Ludgate now, stocky and balding, wearing a suit that looked slept in, talking to a slim, dark-haired woman he didn't recognize. Ludgate looked irritated; the woman, expressionless. Enver was a believer in doing unpalatable things quickly. Oh well, he thought, may as well get things over with. Hopefully, Ludgate won't be too interested to know how one of his officers had managed to become personally involved with the illegal immigrant parents of a murdered child.

He walked over to the DCS. Movement made him aware of the weight he was carrying. He was suddenly and ridiculously conscious of the tightness of his shirt against his growing belly. Enver was an ex-athlete. He'd been a boxer before becoming a policeman and now, freed from the constraints of having to train and diet to make a weight, his stomach had relished its freedom with predictable results. A section of unwearable shirts in his wardrobe was steadily growing. They were simply too small. Some he could no longer even button around his stomach. It wasn't just his belly. He felt he could live with that. Even worse were the rolls of surplus flesh on his sides, above his hips. I've got love handles, he'd think to himself gloomily. Quite often he would grasp the fatty flesh in each hand and jiggle it up and down angrily in a fit of self-loathing. It really wasn't the time to be thinking about dieting, he thought, as he approached Ludgate.

'Morning, sir,' he said.

Ludgate looked up, away from the woman. Enver saw her face properly for the first time. He noticed that her long dark hair could do with cutting and she had a pale, intense face, bare of make-up. He had no idea who she was. He guessed she was one of the scene of crimes people. There were dark circles around her eyes as if she habitually slept badly. She looked like the kind of person you might see in a line-up as a fanatic for some militant cause.

'Morning, Sergeant,' said Ludgate. There was an unmistakably sour note to Ludgate's voice. He knew Enver by sight and, although Enver had a good, some would say very good,

record, the DCS had never really acknowledged him. It was a slight that had not gone unnoticed at the Wood Green station, particularly by Enver. Enver put it down to racism. Most people liked him. He was an easy-going man by nature and not used to hostility, except as a result of his job.

It was unusual to see the DCS at a crime scene. Ludgate had very nearly put in his thirty years and was well known for studiously avoiding anything that might be regarded as hard work. He was a popular enough figure, though, loyal to his men and trustworthy. Or that was the myth anyway. Ludgate waved a vague, dismissive hand at the canal scene behind them. 'Bad business, Sergeant.'

'Yes, sir.' Enver was aware that the woman was studying him with cold, intelligent eyes, as if trying to work out something about him, maybe to place him. He was still vain enough to wonder what she made of him, a powerfully built thirty-year-old with thick, black hair, a drooping black moustache and sad, sleepy brown eyes. And, of course, a fat stomach. Despite himself not finding her remotely attractive, he tried to suck it in. All that happened was the band of iron-hard muscle he still had around his middle contracted, but the flab stayed where it was. And the love handles. You couldn't suck those in. He must do something about it. It wasn't like he didn't know what. He didn't even have the excuse of ignorance. I need more will power, he thought. More exercise, less carbs. He wished she'd go away. He didn't want SOCO there witnessing what could well be an unpleasant conversation. One that could lead to a very public bollocking.

'Was there anything in particular, Sergeant?' Ludgate was beginning to look impatient, evidently willing him to get to the point. Enver didn't want to speak in front of her but he was left with no choice.

'I think I might have information about the child's identity, sir,' he said.

Ludgate raised an eyebrow. 'That's quick work, Sergeant. Oh, this is DI Hanlon, by the way, I'm sure you've heard of her. Our Tottenham Riots Pin-up Girl.'

Enver kept his face expressionless. Ludgate's old-school policing habits, he knew from rumour and anecdotes, extended into casual racism according to some, hardcore racism according to others, or harmless 'banter' if you believed his supporters. That made Enver dislike him on a secondary level. Personal rudeness to himself; racial rudeness to others. Maybe the two were interlinked. Now it seemed Ludgate didn't like women either. There was no mistaking the venom in Ludgate's voice behind the Pin-up Girl jibe. It was also hard to imagine anyone less like a vapid lingerie model than Hanlon.

Hanlon remained silent, impassive. Enver was impressed. It wasn't that she was blanking Ludgate out; it was if he didn't even exist. Her face was like a mask. There was no narrowing of eyes, raising of eyebrows. No reaction at all. So, he thought, this is the famous Hanlon. Everyone knew the riot story. There were other rumours too about Hanlon and violence. Rumour had it she'd hospitalized a fellow officer for calling her a 'fag hag', some rumour about her and her sergeant. He had also been told by someone that she was a triathlete and competed in several Iron Man competitions. Reputedly, she was one of the top amateurs in the country. Enver knew that an Iron Man event meant a 2.4 mile swim, a 100 plus mile cycle race and then running a full marathon. He doubted he could waddle

2.4 miles, let alone run a marathon. He doubted he'd be able to swim a length; he certainly hadn't tried since school. He did have a cycling proficiency certificate, though, from primary school. The thought of getting on a bicycle made him shudder.

'Ma'am,' he said respectfully.

Enver realized too, at that point, how still she was physically. Ludgate scratched his head, moved his weight around, coughed, fidgeted. DI Hanlon looked as if she were playing a game of statues like children do.

Years spent in the boxing ring had taught Enver to weigh up opponents very quickly. A fight is sometimes over before you've even got in the ring. You know that standing before you is someone who is going to spend the next maybe thirty-six minutes trying their best to beat the living shit out of you, and you're going to be doing the same to them. You get good at assessing threat levels. You have to. He suddenly thought to himself that if you had Hanlon advancing towards you, you'd better know what you're doing, or give up. She was formidable. She looked at him speculatively. 'Who is the child, Sergeant?

I'm sorry, I didn't catch your name.'

'Demirel, ma'am. Sergeant Enver Demirel.' Against a background of car doors slamming, bursts of radio noise and raised voices as the body was put into a waiting vehicle, he quickly ran through what he knew of the history of the boy. 'If indeed it's him, sir,' he added for the benefit of the DCS. Enver was relieved. Ludgate hadn't exploded. He'd simply told him to report all that to the senior investigating officer once he'd decided who that was going to be.

Ludgate now looked out at the scene by the canal and at the TV people. He'd already spoken to them briefly. Ludgate was good on the TV. He came across well. He always looked and sounded like he knew what they were doing. His easy confidence went down well at all levels. 'Well, the kid looks pretty Turkish from here. There can't be that many of them bobbing about in the Regent's Canal, Sergeant. Go and bring the parents in for identification and questioning. And we'll

need an interpreter – two interpreters, I suppose, male and female, and a social worker for the daughter. Jesus Christ, the cost of all this is getting bloody ridiculous.' His voice was full of irritation. 'As for Jacques Cousteau and his chum over there,' he pointed at the divers, 'I've got to pay for them too. We're supposed to be making cuts.' He glared at Enver as if he were part of the conspiracy to sabotage his budget, then he turned away and headed up the towpath back to where his car was parked.

Enver felt a hard knot of rage tie itself in his stomach. He could still see the dead child's favourite toy in his memory. He could still see the father's gentle way of holding it, the only link to his missing son. Nobody would play with Grey Rabbit now or ever again.

'I saw you fight, Sergeant.' It was Hanlon. She ran her eyes over him speculatively like a butcher eyeing a piece of meat of dubious quality, and Enver straightened his back into a more erect posture. He was jerked back to reality, back to the present. 'About five years ago. You beat someone called Tyler Mirchison on points. It was a good fight.' She paused, remembering details, as did Enver. You never forget your fights. He was amazed, though, that she'd seen it. It hadn't been televised; she must have actually been there, in Finsbury Park, on a freezing February night. And to remember his opponent's name was an uncanny feat of recall. Mirchison had long since disappeared into obscurity. Then she said, 'Enver, "the Iron Hand" Demirel. That's what they billed you as, wasn't it?'

He blinked in surprise. He hadn't heard anyone call him

that for ages, for years. He used to love the way the MC would introduce him, with the swooping emphasis and stress on the words that was unique to boxing. 'Aaand in the Blue Corner,' Blue stretched to two syllables, 'Berrloo'. 'All the way from

Tottenham (Tot – Ten – Haaam!), North London, Enver, the Iron Hand Demirel.' For an instant he could hear the roar of the crowd, invisible to him and his opponent in the bright, white light of the ring, the universe shrunk into a tiny square. 'Are you ready to rumble!' The smell of sweat and blood would still be there from the previous fight, hanging in the air like perfume, the canvas floor of the ring speckled rusty red here and there. And then he blinked again and he was back on the canal towpath, the glory days gone, the future contracting. 'Demirel means "Iron Hand" in Turkish, ma'am,' said Enver, by way of explanation.

'I know that, Sergeant,' said Hanlon.

Mirchison, a tough, angular Scot, may have lost the fight, but not as comprehensively as Enver, who had won the fight but lost the war. Mirchison had a powerful right hand and in the course of the eight rounds Enver suffered a detached retina in his left eye, which led to him losing his fight licence from the British Boxing Board of Control. He could never box again, not legally. It was the end of his career. It was then that he'd joined the Met.

'Well, Sergeant. Boxing's loss is our gain.' She turned and looked at the top of the lock gates for a while, lost in thought. The gates seemed to fascinate her. Her eyes kept drifting to them. 'I'll be seeing you again, Sergeant,' she said in a tone of finality. 'There are things I'll have to talk to you about regarding

this murder.'

'Yes, ma'am,' said Enver dutifully as he watched her walk away. She was joined by a tall, bearded, burly plainclothes officer who had been waiting for her at a respectful distance. Enver watched as she acknowledged him and he inclined his head down closer to her level so they could talk discreetly as they walked. You could tell by their body language that they were very much at ease with each other's company. He wondered if they were seeing each other, they seemed so intimate. For some reason he felt a sudden stab of jealousy.

He tried to shake free the image of Hanlon as he too turned and made his way back to his car. He had a lot to do.

## 10

Kathy cleared up the remains of the breakfast from the table in the living room. Peter had left for school some twenty minutes before. The ground-floor flat that Clarissa had found them was perfectly located for Peter's secondary school, which was about a quarter of an hour's walk away down (relatively, she thought ruefully) safe streets.

This part of North London, Finchley, was actually where Kathy was from. She'd been born at the Whittington Hospital down the road in Archway, some forty years earlier. She'd always lived in London and couldn't imagine living anywhere else. There is a saying in German: the air of a city makes you free – 'Die Luft einer Stadt macht frei'. That more or less summed up her attitude about the capital. London always seemed to her a city of infinite possibilities. After her husband's death, she had sold the house in Barnes, needing to downsize. It was bought, to her amusement, by some French people. She wondered if maybe there was a Gallic equivalent of *A Year in Provence* – *Une Année en SW13* – a nostalgic French look at the charming, rustic English Barnes, peopled by amusingly stereotypical English people, and it was almost with a sense of relief, of coming home, that she had decided virtually immediately to return to Finchley. There was no question in Kathy's mind of leaving London.

The narrow streets of Finchley, with their small, pale-grey

houses, seemed to welcome her back. And look, Peter, she had said, there's the archer outside East Finchley tube station. The archer waited, as he had always waited, his bow perpetually readied as he knelt to defend East Finchley from its foes. It was where she belonged. Barnes was where Dan belonged. Dan had been quite posh. He'd been taken to the theatre a lot by his parents as a treat, he had gone to a private school, and his mother had a tagine and an Aga before anyone had heard of things like that.

Without Dan, life in Barnes was pointless. Not so Finchley. She remembered how she had always felt as if she were on an island in the borough. It was an island bordered by Mill Hill on the periphery of London, Muswell Hill, isolated without an underground, gateway to Ally Pally and poor relation of now cool, hip, Crouch End. Then to the south, Highgate with its cemetery and vampire and Karl Marx, and Jewish Golders Green. To the north, the countrified Totteridge and Whetstone. Coming back was coming home. She knew she'd made the right decision when she saw the statue of the archer again, her old friend, frozen in time and space, kneeling as he endlessly fired his arrow from his bent bow.

There had been the odd occasion walking the streets that she

had grown up in, when the sense of the past had almost overwhelmed her, when she was momentarily not Kathy Reynolds, aged forty, mother of Peter and Overseas Business Development Manager for PFK Plastics, but Kathy Markham, aged fifteen, in her tartan school uniform skirt, hair in pigtails, school shirt a dazzling white and with creases ironed into it that could almost cut you they were so sharp, living where Margaret Thatcher, the milk snatcher, was the local MP. Who could have ever imagined her first senile, now dead, or that Meryl Streep would play her in a film? Her mother, now in a home, senile too, had been a

champion ironer. Anything that could be ironed was ironed – socks, pants, you name it, everything.

Now she had a laptop; then she would have had pictures of Adam and the Ants and Duran Duran, cut from *Smash Hits*, painstakingly glued on to her schoolwork folder.

Sometimes her current self seemed insubstantial and ghostlike, as if she were haunting East Finchley like a time-travelling spirit, as if her younger avatar was more real. Some afternoons it wouldn't have surprised her to see her younger self coming home from school, laughing, with a satchel on her back, while she stood, a wraith, looking wistfully on from the other side of the road.

Life was so much more fun then. It certainly wasn't fun at the moment; it was bloody hard work, coloured with problems and bordered with tragedy. Fun had upped sticks and left a long time ago. The death of her husband had coincided with her mother losing her mind to dementia. She gritted her teeth and got on with things. What else can you do? Whatever her younger self had imagined, it wasn't this. This life wasn't in the script. What, she often wondered, would have been the reaction of her younger self to the older woman she had become, had she been able to see her? Bemused, thought Kathy. I always wanted to be self-confident when I was young, she thought. I am now. I always wanted to be a success. I am now. And I used to fret about my looks. I'm the wrong side of forty and I can still turn heads. I should be grateful really, but I'm tired. I wish I could go back to when *Dallas* was on the telly and me and Karen Jenkins would go to the wine bar. Wine bars were new then. She fancied Bobby Ewing but I kind of liked Ray, in his tight jeans and checked shirt, even though he walked in a funny way, almost bent double – perhaps it was the cowboy boots.

Her friend Karen would take the piss out of him sometimes

and say, 'Hey, Kat, who's this?' and do a Ray walk and imitate his accent, which used to have her in fits. Well, *Dallas* is back, she thought, but I'm not going to watch it now. I don't want to see them all old, or dead. I'd rather remember them as they were. And sometimes we'd go to Cinderella Rockefeller's in North Finchley and lie about our age, and dance to Donna Summer and Kajagoogoo and Gloria Gaynor and Sylvester. Later, of course, it would have been Wham!

I wish I could practise our dances like we used to in her living room. Her parents had a Bang & Olufsen stereo which Dad said cost as much as his car. Everyone had rubbish cars then and we didn't care. We didn't care about brands. It was a lot more egalitarian. She lived in Canada now, Karen did, in Vancouver. She'd married a doctor. Far away. They still exchanged Christmas cards but that was as far as it went. You can never go back, can you. She returned her thoughts to the present.

She looked at the diary in front of her where she'd written down the day's to-do list. She'd got the morning off work because Peter's diabetic nurse was due round and they were to review his blood-sugar levels, carb-counting, diet and exercise. She knew the nurse would be pleased with his performance. Her son was very diligent. The diabetes was not a problem but it was a persistent and ever-present issue that had to be dealt with. She sometimes had nightmares that Peter would be away somewhere inaccessible without his insulin. She was determined she would never become overprotective.

She looked at the photo of Peter on the mantelpiece, absurdly handsome in his school uniform. He was taller than she was now, and he had the same loose-limbed, muscular grace that he had inherited from his father. Peter's restricted diet because of his type-one diabetes had also trimmed any puppy fat away from his frame, so that his long muscles stood out like anatomical drawings. Even his stomach was ridged with muscle. He's got a six-pack, she had thought wonderingly.

She was glad that Peter was going to be so powerfully built for reasons other than a parent's simple delight at their child's attainments. Peter was a frighteningly pleasant boy, considerate, kind. Sometimes she worried that he was too nice for his own good. It wasn't just her who felt that way. Several of her friends had made the same comment. He would be a sucker for a girl with some hard-luck story.

On Saturdays he worked as a volunteer for the local branch of the North London Canine Defence League, helping to exercise and care for maltreated dogs. He desperately wanted a dog of his own but Kathy had been adamant. She travelled too much for it to be really practical. It was often hard enough to find a friend who could look after Peter let alone Peter plus dog. That was one of the benefits of living in rented accommodation. The no-animal policy meant the question would not even get raised. His school reports were straight A's for effort, because, as he explained, 'I want Daddy to be proud of me and I want to make you happy now he's gone.' She was frightened that because of Dan's death, she might be overly protective, let alone because of the diabetes issue. She felt her eyes fill with tears and blew her nose loudly on a tissue. Oh, for heaven's sake, she thought, pull yourself together, and straightened some papers on her work table. She picked the phone up and tapped out the number for the Siemens office in Stuttgart, where she was bidding for a seven million euro contract for her company. The negotiations were going smoothly. PFK's product had been approved on a technical level and now it was simply a question of persuading the industrial giant of their own commitment, their own ability.

She knew that it was going well and she also knew that it was mainly down to her.

'*Ja, guten Morgen. Ich heisse Frau Reynolds, ja, stimt, mitt ein "R",
nein jetzt.*' She paused, listening to the woman on the other end of
the line. '*Ja, Max Brucker bitte.*' She waited to be put through, then
she was speaking to the Siemens procurement manager, '*Max! Wie
geht's? Wie ist das Wetter in Stuttgart?*' The conversation continued
for a few minutes and she pictured Max's calm, intelligent face, his
short-cut, thinning, dark hair, his elegant, muscular body, as they
discussed the technical questions that she could have answered in
her sleep. She was always formidably well prepared. Then, '*Also, am
Freitag um zwölf Uhr. Auf wiederhören, Max.*'

'*Auf wiederhören, Kathy.*'

She put the phone down with quiet satisfaction. Max wanted
her out in Stuttgart in three days' time for a Friday twelve o'clock
meeting, to make a last, formal, presentation. It would be the
clincher. She smiled at Max's pronunciation of *Freitag*. *Freidag*. It
was so *stereotypically Schwäbische Deutsche*. Kathy really fancied
Max, even down to his Swabian Stuttgart accent. She'd have to
arrange some kind of childcare for Peter. He was used to her travel-
ling around the world at short notice. She'd ask Annette. She was
irritatingly scatty but Peter liked both her and her son Sam, and of
course he adored her dog.

Just then her front doorbell rang and she raised her head in
surprise. She looked through the front-room window and there,
outside the front door, with her habitual, charming smile, was
Clarissa from the agency.

Kathy got up and let her in. It was always good to see Clarissa.
Presumably she was here to finalize the arrangements for the cable
installation. Maybe today, once they'd finished discussing that,
she'd tell her to start looking for a permanent house in the area for
her and Peter. But first they could have a good old talk about what
they were both up to.

# 11

Hanlon was back in Corrigan's office for the first time since the Essex murder. The public had forgotten about it. Deprived of the oxygen of interest supplied by the words 'witchcraft killing', the story had died its own death.

Hanlon was now working on a draft document for Corrigan with a provisional title, 'Seizing the Initiative: Building on the Legacy'. The legacy was the post-Olympic Games spirit; 'seizing the initiative' was Corriganspeak for increasing the size of his department. Hanlon didn't like doing paperwork, but she could apply herself diligently to most things if she chose and the right sentiments flowed from her fingertips on to the screen. Corrigan himself was quite inarticulate in written form. Verbally he was great, but he needed people to interact with. Hanlon was famously unable or unwilling to engage with people, so in some respects they made a not unreasonable team.

He was pleased with Hanlon's work, pleased until rumblings from the arrest of David Anderson reached his ears. The rumour
– there was no actual proof – was that Hanlon was behind it. Hanlon was not supposed to handle anything operational; she was

toxic as far as most of the Met were concerned. But now, if the story was to be believed, and it sounded horribly plausible to Corrigan, she'd gone and done it again, launched her own initiative to arrest someone she didn't like. It had the Hanlon

hallmark of a praiseworthy thing done, the arrest and certain conviction of a dangerous criminal, with a cavalier disregard for legal process. It differed from Tottenham in that she'd roped some accomplices in to help. He'd had a couple of acrimonious unofficial meetings about the Anderson bust. Hanlon's name had been mentioned in connection with that sergeant she was still close with. Corrigan didn't know for sure, but he'd bet a lot of money that if he chose to ask he'd find Hanlon and Anderson had crossed paths before. Corrigan had gritted his teeth and stood by her. He felt like strangling her, and here she was, in his office, unrepentant as usual.

'So, let's go over this Anderson arrest again. Why's he called "Jesus", did you say?' he asked. Hanlon was sitting opposite him on the other side of his desk, tired-looking, but holding herself very straight in her chair. He'd never seen her slouch.

'Because he crucified someone to a door once,' said Hanlon, 'with a nail gun.'

'Was that proven or is it just a rumour?' asked Corrigan, curious despite himself. Hanlon shrugged. She was irritatingly self-composed. Then again, thought Corrigan, she always was. Although he was much bigger physically, it was the still, motionless body of Hanlon that somehow dominated the room.

'Well, he was never charged with it,' she said.

Corrigan shook his head in irritation. 'Typical,' he said. 'They all do that kind of thing. Nail guns,' he added to himself in an angry tone.

Hanlon couldn't work out if the assistant commissioner was annoyed by the crime itself or the laziness of using a nail gun. She half expected him to say something along the lines of, in my day, when I was young, criminals used hammers for this kind of thing. Not any more, couldn't be bothered to get off

their fat arses. 'The point is, what were you doing nicking him?' My job, I suppose, thought Hanlon. She decided not to say it and further annoy Corrigan. She knew he had, after all, saved her career when there was a call for her to be got rid of. Nobody else had wanted her. For that she was genuinely grateful and, deep down, quite touched. Corrigan was usually so politically and career motivated. Helping Hanlon, she knew, could not be considered a wise move. She knew she was very good at certain aspects of police work, but she was perfectly aware she was trouble. Her performance appraisals made that abundantly clear. She didn't care. It was quite touching to discover that the AC was actually a fundamentally decent man, although the fact that it should surprise was an alarming indictment of

the society they were in.

'I didn't make the arrest, sir. The officer in charge was DS Whiteside.'

Corrigan grunted contemptuously. 'Pull the other one, Hanlon. Whiteside wouldn't wipe his arse unless he'd cleared it with you.'

'If you say so, sir.'

Corrigan was fishing, thought Hanlon. There was no definite proof she was involved in the arrest. Whiteside had given his DI the information that had led to the bust as coming from an informant, which it had. Neither Toby Manning nor Cunningham had complained. Thompson, the uniformed sergeant, was notoriously silent and Whiteside said he had it on good authority Childs wouldn't talk. They'd all closed ranks and mouths. So, no loose ends.

The AC leant back in his chair. He was in his shirtsleeves and the sun through the windows sparkled on the crowns on the shoulders of the epaulettes on his shirt. 'Do you know who Kevin Briggs is?' asked Corrigan tetchily.

'Yes, sir. He's assistant commissioner, territorial operations.'
'That's correct. It was a rhetorical question,' said Corrigan. 'And you'll doubtless know the name of the assistant com

missioner for specialist operations.'

'Yes, sir,' replied Hanlon. She could guess where this was leading. She didn't bother answering, he used to be my boss. They both knew that. They also both knew he had tried to have her dismissed from the police force.

'Well, I've had both of them on my back about Anderson's arrest. Compromising investigations, treading on people's toes, up to your old tricks, I'm sure you can imagine the row you've provoked. Can you?'

'It was nothing to do with me, sir,' she said levelly. 'I think you'll find it was Haringey drug squad that made the arrest. I don't know what they're on about.' They looked at each other, Hanlon's gaze steady. 'Quite frankly, sir, I'd have thought they had other things to occupy their minds with.'

Corrigan stared back at her. 'Just, just, don't, OK.' He motioned with his hands to try to indicate the areas she should keep clear of. It was an expansive gesture. 'You've got enough enemies as it is, I'm sure you can appreciate that.'

'I'm sorry to hear that, sir.' His eyes narrowed. Not I'm sorry, but I'm sorry to hear that. In no way, shape or form was that an apology. She was no longer part of Special Crimes and Operations but Whiteside was, and she knew that she hadn't compromised anything by what she'd done. Credit for the Anderson bust had, like she'd said, gone to the Haringey drug squad. She was mildly surprised to find herself having this conversation. Someone must have talked.

'I've had to spend a lot of time explaining to ACSO and ACTO that you probably had nothing to do with it. I said it was all hearsay.'

'Yes, sir. But—'

'No buts.' Corrigan held up an enormous, admonitory hand, palm outwards. 'Please try to remember that you work for me, not in some unspecified vigilante capacity. Is that clear?' Hanlon didn't look contrite as she nodded.

'Yes, sir.'

Corrigan absent-mindedly rubbed his expanding paunch. He'd always been fond of food and, courtesy of Fleet Street, had eaten his way through the menus of most of London's top restaurants. PR after all was one of his duties. He had to keep the media informed and if the media chose to be informed over agreeable lunches, so be it. Now the mood had changed. Corrigan was aware of the zeitgeist and adopted the new hair-shirt strategy. The Leveson Inquiry into the press and their lavish wining and dining of Scotland Yard was going to hit the assistant commissioner's stomach hard. Today he'd eaten at the canteen. It hadn't been very nice. He tried again to lay down parameters.

'Let's get this straight, Hanlon. I got you out from that

disciplinary enquiry you were facing and, until the dust settles, you're supposed to keep your head down and ideally help me, not chase high-profile criminals that you have a personal grudge against. Is that clear?'

'Crystal clear, sir.'

'Don't take the piss, Hanlon.'

'No, sir.' She didn't add, I wouldn't dream of it, for fear of sounding sarcastic.

He looked hard at the woman sitting opposite him. Hanlon returned his gaze equably. Oh well, thought Corrigan, it's not as if I didn't know what she was like when I gave her the job. I brought this on myself. I might as well be talking to the wall. He was genuinely fond of Hanlon but he found

her impossible to understand at times. Most people fitted in to the police force – it was a broad church – whether they were crusaders or career officers or simply the kind of people who temperamentally like large organizations. But she was none of those things. She was an enigma. She was... then the expression came to him from yesterday's phrase of the day... *sui generis*. He was pleased with it. *Sui generis*. One of a kind, or, more literally, 'of its own kind'. Well, that was something to be grateful for. David Anderson wasn't *sui generis*; he was generic, he was a violent nutter of which London was not in short supply. Join the queue, Anderson, he thought. Violent crime in the capital was getting like football. The local talent was being overshadowed by players brought in from abroad. The Russians and the Albanians. Globalization was making his job increasingly hard. At the lower end, criminals were being undercut by the Poles and Romanians. You could get someone killed for a couple of grand these days, maybe not very professionally, but it was remarkably cheap. London was awash with Eastern European ex-Warsaw Pact firearms and Eastern European criminals who'd all done military service and were very much at home with guns.

What annoyed him about this situation, the reason he was

giving what he recognized as an ineffectual bollocking, were the signs of Hanlon's meticulous planning and executing, right down to the phrasing in Whiteside's reports. He knew her handiwork when he saw it. Worthy as it was, she had engineered this arrest when she knew she should have been doing no such thing. She would go too far one of these days and then she'd give the Met the excuse it needed to sack her. She'd got away with it this time by the skin of her teeth.

Hanlon sat in front of him, irritatingly self-composed. I'm getting nowhere here, he thought. I might as well cut my losses.

'OK, Hanlon, let's move on. These child murders, the Essex one and the baby in the canal, anything I need to know? We are doing everything sensibly, I take it. We haven't cut corners? We haven't fucked up?' His eyes were resting on the report she'd sent him about the Somali girl.

'No, sir.'

Corrigan raised his gaze from the paperwork. 'And they're not related at all?'

Hanlon met his eyes. God, that man is shrewd, she thought. Now isn't the time, she decided. Not yet. Her suspicions, her certainty, that the two deaths were linked would for now remain unvoiced. Both were sexual in nature, both involved children, both were connected by the use of the number eighteen which had been added like a signature. She had worked once in paedophile crime and she knew how overstretched the team was. And that was before Operation Yewtree. You were dealing with an unusual group of criminals, usually highly organized, highly secretive and generally extremely intelligent. They also covered all sections of society. File-sharing on the Internet and people-trafficking with cheap travel to Far Eastern countries where policing was lax and more corrupt than Europe only added to the problems.

No, thought Hanlon. I think I'll look into it myself before

I bring anything to Corrigan. He's cross enough over this Anderson business, he'll go crazy if I tell him about this.

'They would appear to be very different crimes, sir,' she said diplomatically. Corrigan noted the delay in reply, the careful wording of the answer, but let it pass for now.

'Who's in charge of our one? The Maida Vale one,' he asked.

'DCS Ludgate's in charge of the canal one, sir.' She paused. 'If

I were you I'd have a word with him about his racial attitudes.'

She knew that would grab Corrigan's attention. Ludgate had a track record of offensive remarks both on and off the record.

Hanlon figured that one sure way to get close to Ludgate, who was leading the Baby Ali investigation, would be to do it under the guise of ensuring he did nothing to further discredit the Met in terms of racism. Corrigan had made a big display of his determination to tackle the issue. She should know, she'd incorporated it into his strategic plan for him. She felt sure he'd want her breathing down Ludgate's neck, forcing him to keep to the straight and narrow. It would give her the perfect excuse to monitor the investigation.

Corrigan rolled his eyes in exasperation. 'I'm sure Ludgate won't say anything too stupid,' he said.

Hanlon shrugged. The gesture spoke volumes. 'There are four hundred thousand Turks in London, sir. In one form or another. I'm including North Cypriot immigrants in those figures. They're a sizeable constituency, sir. They have their own newspapers and radio station.'

'You've clearly done your research, Detective Inspector.' 'I've clearly done my job, sir.' Rhetorically speaking, she

thought.

'OK,' said Corrigan with irritation. 'Point made, Hanlon.'

He knew Ludgate well enough from a couple of meetings to realize that any faith in Ludgate mollifying a sizeable ethnic community would be based more on hope than experience. He knew she was right, as she usually was. 'I'll officially appoint you my liaison officer on this. You can keep an eye on him. Tell him if he steps out of line I'll be down on him like a ton of bricks. Try and do that tactfully. If you can.'

Hanlon nodded. I do wish she'd wear something other than black, white or grey, thought Corrigan, looking at her. It's like she was perpetually dressed for a funeral.

'You do realize, sir, that the DCS doesn't like me very much.
I can't see him being cooperative.'

Corrigan rolled his eyes again, 'And when,' he said acidly, 'were you ever concerned with your personal popularity, Detective Inspector. Ludgate is part of a fairly sizeable queue of people who don't like you very much. Your leaving party would be packed, DI Hanlon, with people eager to wave goodbye.'

He picked up the landline phone on his desk. Hanlon listened as he told the unseen person to get hold of DCS Ludgate as a matter of urgency. Corrigan drummed his fingers for a while and then Hanlon listened to a one-sided conversation designed to save Ludgate's face. Mayoral initiative, placating feminist lobbies, no reflection on Ludgate's abilities, the *Guardian*, yes, they would get together, yes, it was political correctness run mad, yes, we all knew what those sorts of people were like, fine, bye.

Corrigan shook his head wearily. 'Well, Hanlon, there you go. You can shadow him. He doesn't sound terribly happy about it but he'll cooperate. In fact he'll be taking you out to dinner tomorrow.' He noted with amusement the look of surprise and distaste that flickered across Hanlon's normally expressionless face. 'It's the North London Traders' Association Executive Committee. Someone called Harry Conquest is hosting it. It's a party, you'll love it.'

He smiled at Hanlon. He knew she hated parties. She had told him once she hadn't been to one willingly since she was nine years old. He also knew how much she and Ludgate hated each other too. 'It's quite formal seemingly. Wear something nice. Phone Ludgate's nick later, his secretary will give you the address and details.'

She nodded and stood up. As she reached the door he said, 'Oh, Hanlon. Please be diplomatic. Try and win friends and influence people.' Fat chance, he thought. 'That includes Ludgate and Harry Conquest. He's got a lot of clout politically.

That means he's rich, Hanlon, and gives generously to political parties. So be nice. Be loquacious. Not your usual silent self.' Corrigan had a new app on his phone called 'Word Power'. It aimed to build your vocabulary. It was where he had found *sui generis*. He was pleased to have found an excuse to use today's word, 'loquacious'. It was hard to work into a conversation. Hanlon stared at him as if he'd gone mad. 'It means talkative,' he said plaintively. Hanlon didn't reply but let herself out of

his office, silently.

Corrigan looked pensively at the closing door. He thought, she knew that. It was as if she had decided to bring the interview to a close, as if she had been in charge all along. It was a sensation he often had whenever he met her. The door clicked gently but firmly behind her. He felt somehow deflated.

## 12

The Bishops Avenue was only about a mile and a half geographically from Kathy Reynolds's two-bedroomed ground-floor flat in East Finchley, but it was a world removed both socially and economically. The Avenue itself was unremarkable. It was a long, wide, charmless road, a stone's throw from Hampstead Heath, flanked by about sixty very large, charmless houses. Only the very rich lived on the Avenue, Saudi and Qatari Royal families. Lakshmi Mittal, the steel magnate, had a house here. There were Russian oligarchs, media moguls and several property developers, Harry Conquest among them. This made Conquest a very rich property developer. A house on the Bishops Avenue was a warning from God that you have too much money.

There was no unifying architectural theme to the road.

The houses on the Avenue were built in various styles. Faux-Palladian, Barratt home on steroids, Asda-style supermarket and mock-Spanish hacienda. None were architecturally distinguished; all were ostentatious. They could hardly be otherwise, not in the Avenue. It wasn't a modest place.

Hanlon rolled her eyes in distaste as she drove in through the enormous, scrolled-iron gates that guarded Harry Conquest's short, wide drive and expertly parked her Audi with mathematical precision between a Bentley and a Maserati. The luxury cars were too in your face for Hanlon's taste, vulgar, as were the

houses. Vulgar described Bishops Avenue very well. Whatever money could buy, good taste wasn't necessarily part of it.

Hanlon was fascinated by architecture. She wondered sometimes if it was a reaction to having to deal with people all the time. A lot of police have hobbies where they can avoid people and escape into a world of their own. Fishing, for example, cycling, or birdwatching. Forrest, the forensic guru, had a passion for lawns. You could crawl across his grass and not find a single weed or hint of moss. You weren't allowed to walk on it in shoes, bare feet only.

'There are seven different varieties of grass in my lawn,' he'd told her. 'The secret really is feeding and drainage.' It had been a long lecture.

Hanlon liked buildings. They spoke to her in a vernacular that excluded lies, unlike people.

By Bishops Avenue standards, Conquest's house was a fairly modest affair. It could have strayed in from nearby Hampstead Garden Suburb, it had that kind of arts and crafts look about it, and then grown unfeasibly large in its new environment, like a foreign species introduced to a native environment, like Japanese knotweed, giant hogweed or rhododendrons. Hanlon guessed it would probably have about seven or eight bedrooms upstairs. It was that kind of size. She walked towards the front door, which had a colonnaded porch and, flanking the entrance, a statue of a seated lion on one side and a unicorn on the other. She thought they were incredibly tasteless, Essex garden-centre chic. It looked like the entrance to an expensive but tacky nightclub, the security on the door adding to this impression. They were three large men, two black, one white, dressed in dinner jackets. They turned to face her.

Up close, the dinner jackets had seen better days; they
were stained and shiny, and the fabric strained on the men's
freakishly pumped-up arms. Their shaved heads gleamed
under the porch lights. They didn't really match the Bishops
Avenue; they looked like they belonged in a rougher part of town,
Bethnal Green or Camden. They straightened themselves up as
Hanlon approached.

Hanlon was wearing a simple black cocktail dress, Thirties-
style, that she knew flattered her toned body. She rarely went out,
she disliked socializing, but when she did she took care with her
appearance. She had a black-lace, antique shawl that had belonged
to her grandmother, and her colleagues would have been interested
to see her wearing heels. She had tied her unruly hair back, which
emphasized her long, slim, muscular neck. Modigliani would have
loved Hanlon. Without breaking her stride, Hanlon had perfect
balance despite the stiletto-like heels on her shoes. She removed
her invitation from her clutch bag and held it as she would a
warrant card, thrusting it into the face of the head bouncer.

'Hanlon,' she said, her voice sharp with the peremptory
tone of those used to being obeyed.

She stared into the hard, aggressive, brown eyes of the man. The
top of his shaved head was tattooed geometrically, like a sergeant's
stripes, as were his knuckles, but with writing in a Gothic script.
She didn't know him personally but she had arrested enough of his
kind to feel a contemptuous familiarity. Like many experienced
police, she had a finely tuned nose for criminals. Like calls to like.
He, in his turn, recognized her for what she was. She hadn't said DI
Hanlon but his brain automatically allocated her a police rank.
They understood each other. They had faced each other's kind
many times over scratched and chipped tables in endless interview
rooms where it always seemed to be one in the morning and the air
was perpetually stale. She knew he had form. She

could smell it on him as strongly as his Lynx aftershave. He had a clipboard but obviously felt no need to consult it. He didn't need to know who she was; he knew what she was. He nodded at one of his two companions and the door was opened to Hanlon. She stepped inside, the door closed behind

her and her eyes widened with surprise.

The outside of Conquest's house was a form of Lutyens design, whether fake or real Hanlon didn't know. It was made of unadorned brick, that alone distinguishing it from its stuccoed neighbours. The adjoining houses were all brilliantly lit by spotlights and shone a uniform gleaming white. His didn't. It had an arch over the front door and long, narrow, leaded windows – suitable for archers, she thought, but not for much else, and not for admitting light. The inside, however, by total contrast, was pure art-deco. It was a disturbing clash of styles. She looked down at her clothes. By coincidence she was perfectly dressed for Conquest's peculiarly retro interior design.

She was now standing just inside the door that had closed behind her, on a wide, shallow balcony overlooking a huge room below. It was like stepping into the lounge of a 1930s Cunard liner. The huge floor was sprung plywood, the sweep of the lines of the room sinuous, with Thirties-style decorative tiling in friezes running across the walls. The railings and bannisters were nautical in style, made of chrome and steel; they gleamed in the lights above. Furniture was again full of period detail. Her eyes made out chrome-framed chairs, Bakelite-topped tables, sharkskin and zebra coverings on seats. Futurist and vorticist art was displayed on the wall. Hanlon recognized a Marinetti here and a Wyndham Lewis there. Good-quality reproductions, not prints. You could have filmed a Thirties costume drama in here without changing a thing.

A string quartet of girls wearing Thirties-style flapper clothes played their way gently and undemandingly through a classical-

style medley, while a hundred or so guests in black tie helped themselves to food from an enormous, expensive-looking buffet. Adjacent to the long tables under their white linen coverings, silver
serving trays and ice sculptures, slowly melting in the heat of the
room, was a champagne and wine bar that was doing brisk business. The recession was certainly not affecting Conquest.

Hanlon raised an eyebrow in quizzical surprise. The North
London Traders' Association must be doing well for themselves,
she thought, if this was a typical evening out. She could begin to
understand Corrigan's insistence she did nothing to offend the man
and why Ludgate had wanted her here. Look at my connections was
the none too subtle message.

The noise was cacophonous. It was swimming-pool acoustics
with little or nothing to baffle or absorb the sound. She looked
below her in the crowd for Ludgate and saw him chatting to a
couple of paunchy men in a corner. All three of them had over-
loaded their plates with food, in the way that the greedy do, just in
case something coveted disappears before they can refill – not that
there was any sign of it running out. Ludgate's chin was jutting out
aggressively, his scalp shone through his comb-over, and she could
see him emphatically using his fingers to count off points in whatever argument or discussion they were having. Hanlon made up her
mind to avoid him if at all possible. She saw him look up and
register her presence before resuming his conversation. He hadn't
acknowledged her. Evidently Ludgate felt the same about her.
Good, she thought. The partygoers were conspicuously wealthy;
they certainly gave off that rarefied perfume of money that the rich
have, even from a distance. Money has a smell, and here it reached
to the
heavens. Excess was anathema to Hanlon. She looked down at
the crowd with an expression like that of Oliver Cromwell and the
Puritans looking at a group of Cavaliers or a wolf eyeing cavorting

sheep. She was a barbarian at the gates of Rome. Momentarily she wondered what she would have done if she'd been in charge of a riot team and seen the angry hooded and masked mob frenziedly swarming down Bishops Avenue. She had a sneaking suspicion she'd have pulled back and let them do their worst. They'd be welcome to the place.

The women were heavily turned out and Hanlon recognized iconic handbags – Birkin, Hermes, Vuitton and Chanel – carried like heraldic, totemic badges. Dresses were designer, haircuts expensive. She saw a couple of politicians she knew and several journalists, as well as two judges and some lawyers whom she recognized from court appearances. She also caught sight of Cunningham who had his back towards her but whose face she could see reflected in a large mirror with a decorative stylized silver frame bordered with bas-relief sphinxes. She thought she'd try and avoid him too. She felt a twinge of guilt momentarily. If Anderson ever found out it was his lawyer who had supplied the information on the coke shipment they'd busted him for, Cunningham's fate would be truly terrible. He wouldn't just be killed, he'd be made an example of. Anderson had crucified a man for less; God alone knows what he'd do to his trusted lawyer if he discovered it was he who had grassed him up. Then she thought, well, that's Cunningham's choice. You make your bed, you lie down in it.

That Hanlon was not a party person was obvious from the somewhat sour look on her face as she gazed down at the crowd below. She despised occasions like this. Before coming, she had managed to fit in an hour at the gym where she'd worked on her legs, shoulders and abs. Her muscles still ached from the relentless pressure she'd subjected them to. She liked that feeling. She liked working her way through pain, it was cleansing. Hanlon tortured her muscles until they cried out and could barely function. She'd held a mental picture of Ludgate as she upped the weight on the smith bar, using her intense dislike of the man as an energy to transform the screaming torment in her upper thigh muscles into a healing agony, as she squatted up and down.

She decided to ignore Ludgate and go down to the buffet. She could feel her body craving protein. Let the property developer pay for it, she thought. Unlike other athletes she knew, she didn't consult a dietician in her training for the Iron Man competition in California in the autumn. She didn't particularly care where she placed; the challenge was her versus the event. The challenge was overcoming the pain. The reward was victory over self. The reward was paradoxically that there was no reward.

Hanlon was contemptuous of honours. Her medal for bravery was stuffed at the back of a drawer in her bedroom, various athletic awards in a cardboard box, and her degree still in the envelope it had come in when the university sent it to her. She hadn't gone to the ceremony either. 'They can post it to me,' she'd snapped. She was famous for biting the hand that fed her. She knew that. She didn't care. Whiteside had collected the medal for her and lied, saying she was ill as a result of injuries sustained in the riots. He implied it was post-traumatic stress. No one there who knew Hanlon had believed him.

She shook herself out of her reverie. She'd better be careful with these disapproving thoughts or she'd end up arresting someone for doing drugs in one of Conquest's doubtless lavish washrooms. Just for the hell of it. Or maybe picking a fight with someone. It wouldn't be hard. It wouldn't be the first time. She thought to herself, remember why you're here. Don't

lose your temper. You're supposed to get close to Ludgate, to the murder investigation you're not allowed to be part of. Concentrate.

Then she saw Conquest.

From her perspective, literally looking down on the crowd below, Conquest – flanked by two minders or members of staff,

Hanlon couldn't really tell – cut a swathe through his guests like a boat through water. Up here, she could see the wake he left as he passed. Several of the women were looking at him with naked lust. Amazing what a house on Bishops Avenue can do, she thought to herself. From this distance she could tell he was grey-haired, distinguished-looking, with a tough, humorous face. She guessed he was about fifty. She'd certainly learnt tonight that Conquest had a way with the ladies.

He stopped at the foot of the stairs, then looked up to where she was standing and their eyes met.

'DI Hanlon,' he called up to her. 'Do come and join me.'

It was more of a command than a request. Hanlon was suddenly conscious of his very blue eyes locked on hers and she was aware of the aggressively persuasive strength of his personality. She revised her opinion of the man. It wasn't just the aphrodisiac quality of owning a very expensive property. Conquest had charisma. She wondered how on earth he knew who she was. Still, she was hardly in a position to say no. It was his party. She smiled, rather coldly, and walked down the steps to join him. Several of the women standing behind Conquest narrowed their eyes at her jealously, probably willing her to stumble on her heels and crash down the stairs in an ungainly, embarrassing fashion. She allowed her smile to broaden slightly. I don't do requests, she thought.

Conquest met her at the bottom of the stairs and shook her hand warmly and firmly, his eyes locked on hers. His hand was large and powerful and he was a head taller than she was. He was very good-looking, almost theatrically so, a silver fox.

'A pleasure to meet you, DI Hanlon,' he said. He had the successful salesman's knack of making you feel that you were the most important person in the room. 'I'm Harry Conquest.' He smiled and pulled a face as he looked around in mock despair at the opulence that surrounded them. It was a look that said, isn't all this ridiculous, we both know that.

'Good evening, Mr Conquest,' Hanlon said. Around them the party whirled and eddied. Its noise level made conversation hard. Conquest showed no sign of wanting to leave her. He was looking at her with an almost pleading intensity.

'Harry. Please,' he said.

She nodded. He smiled charmingly at her in a practised way. Hanlon wondered if he was trying to flirt with her or if he was just one of those men who found the police fascinating. Neither was an appealing prospect but she was determined to be on her best behaviour. Any complaints about her and Ludgate would be able to get rid of her all the more easily.

She wasn't surprised when he suggested they go somewhere quieter to talk. 'I'm an independent councillor in Finchley as well as a developer and I've got some questions I'd love to ask you about police policy, off the record.' He practically had to shout to make himself heard over the noise. His voice was pure London, educated barrow boy. She found herself agreeing, not just because of Corrigan's order to be nice to him, to win friends and influence people, but also out of genuine curiosity.

Hanlon followed him across the crowded room. She noted his suit was well cut and she also noticed his muscular build. Conquest obviously liked to keep in shape. He led her through a door on the other side. They walked down a short passageway

to another light-panelled door. It led into a small, comfortable living room. Here the remorseless Thirties art-deco theme ended. The room was large and simply furnished. As he opened the door, two dogs, German shepherds, ran excitedly over to Conquest. They ignored Hanlon and stared at their master lovingly. Conquest beamed with genuine pleasure and stroked their heads. The dogs panted happily. They continued to ignore Hanlon, which suited her. She wasn't really a dog person.

There were a couple of sofas and a low coffee table between them. The furniture was well designed, stylish. It whispered, I cost a lot of money. Conquest indicated one of the settees to Hanlon. She sat down and he sat opposite, the dogs lying at his feet. She noted that the sofa was incredibly comfortable. Conquest looked at her with frank interest.

The situation felt oddly like a job interview. The door must have been quite heavy because the noise of the party was scarcely audible through its panelling. He breathed a sigh of relief.

'Thanks for that,' he said. 'For what?' asked Hanlon.

Conquest smiled. 'For giving me an excuse to escape. I can't stand parties,' he said, pulling a mock-rueful face. 'But in my line of work I need to put myself about. It's part of the image. I'm a successful property developer.' He made little inverted commas round the phrase to show he was being ironic. It was a gesture Hanlon particularly disliked. 'I'm supposed to have a lavish life-style. It reassures my investors.' He shrugged. 'Do you want a drink?'

Hanlon said, 'I'm driving.'

'And?' said Conquest. He stood up and made his way to what she'd thought was a sideboard but turned out to be a kind of lavish minibar. The side flapped down to reveal bottles and glasses. 'I've got a wide variety of soft drinks, including eight

varieties of water.' She accepted a glass of mineral water and Conquest followed suit.

'Tell me about the house,' said Hanlon. She was genuinely interested.

'It is an odd building,' he said thoughtfully. 'I bought this place in the Eighties, when I was a yuppy, remember them? I had a Porsche, a

Filofax and a Barbour jacket, even one of those huge old mobile phones – it ran off a car battery. Happy days. The enterprise economy they called it back then.' He laughed at the memory. He drank some Perrier; that had been popular too in the Eighties. 'It had belonged to an Israeli in the film business and this Thirties stuff, that's all his. He had the place gutted downstairs, knocked through, so he could hold big parties, like tonight's. It's great for that, but it's practically unliv-able. He went bust and I got it at a really good price.' He drank some water. 'I mean a seriously good price. The locals were terrified Boy George would buy it, but in the end he found somewhere down the road, on the Heath, and I bought it instead. To be honest, I hardly use it. Do I, Prince, do I, Blondi.' The dogs looked at him adoringly at the sound of their names and Prince's tail swished on the carpet. Conquest leant forward and scratched them gently behind the ears.

'This place is my pension fund.' The dogs panted happily.

'I can't say I'll miss it when I sell it.'

She nodded. Then she asked, 'Conquest is an unusual name.

Are you related to the historian?'

Another charming smile from the man opposite her. He really was quite attractive, thought Hanlon. His face was hard, but humor-ous, his eyes intelligent. A shame I find it hard to believe in you, she thought. Hanlon was used to people lying to her, or at best being evasive. She'd had two decades of it. In her view, Conquest was telling the truth, but it was a partial

truth, an edited truth. I'm sure you are a property developer, but that's not everything, is it. There's more to you than that. I can smell it on you, just like I could on your security at the front door. He shook his head. I bet you know Jesus Anderson, she thought, or more likely his father.

'I wish I was. I'm not that bright, I'm afraid. I left school at fifteen.'

Oh Christ, thought Hanlon, don't give me the 'I'm an educated peasant' routine.

'I do like history, though. I researched it. No, the surname means from Le Conquet in France. It's in Brittany, so I guess it makes sense. It's not too far to come.'

'I suppose not,' said Hanlon. And, she added mentally, there can't be too many of you to go through when I do some of my own research. 'Now,' her voice became businesslike, 'you had some questions to ask me about policing.'

If Conquest was disappointed at her brusque tone he hid it well. 'Yes, I do. As a councillor I'm involved in the Safer Neighbourhoods scheme, so I'm more than aware of the valuable input of our local PCSOs. It's how I met your DCS Ludgate,' he said with a smile. He opened the folder that was on the coffee table and looked at a list of questions. 'He tells me that you have the ear of one of the assistant commissioners, is that so?'

'Yes,' said Hanlon. She felt no urge to elaborate.

'So, may I ask, what brings you up here to Hampstead?' asked Conquest.

'Crime,' said Hanlon. Once again she made no attempt to explain. Conquest raised his eyebrows. If he felt aggrieved at the closing down of this line of questioning he took it in good grace. 'Well, I do have a few general questions about the police and the future of community policing. Quite a few, really, you don't mind, do you?'

Now it was Hanlon's turn to smile. She had to admire the way that Conquest had prepared a fallback position just in case his attempts to find out exactly what had brought AC Corrigan's attack dog, as she was known in certain circles, up to Hampstead were rebuffed. It was very slickly done.

'Not at all,' Hanlon said. I'd best be loquacious, she thought to herself.

## 13

The following night Hanlon parked her Audi outside Whiteside's small, one-bedroomed apartment in Holloway, in North London. She stood outside the large house he lived in that had long ago been divided into flats and looked up at the soft light coming from his living room. The long, broad, quiet street was empty of people but most of the windows were lit, like so many TV screens, each featuring dozens of different individuals or families, all from different backgrounds, all with different stories to tell. Hanlon loved the diversity of London, its cool anonymity. Despite the large number of families, of people in the street, there was a sense of isolation in a London scene that echoed an Edward Hopper painting. You could be very alone in London, a feeling that she found deeply attractive. She yawned and rubbed her eyes; she felt very tired.

Whiteside buzzed her in when she rang the bell and she

went upstairs to the first-floor flat. Whiteside was framed in the doorway at the top of the stairs, his muscular bulk filling the space of the open door, backlit in the darkness. There was a coat-rack on the left-hand side of the wall as you walked in and Hanlon's sharp eyes noticed a police uniform jacket that obviously wasn't White-side's hanging there. Beneath the coats was a shoe-rack and Hanlon's eyes registered a pair of boots that weren't Whiteside's size. Whoever the jacket belonged to

had quite small feet. As they walked past the bedroom she heard the light, slithery rustle of someone turning over under a duvet. The sergeant was obviously not alone.

Whiteside led her into his small, immaculate lounge and disap-peared to the kitchen for something to drink. There wasn't much furniture in the living room: a sofa, a chair and a glass coffee table. There was no clutter. His tidiness bordered on the obsessive, as indeed did Hanlon's. There were three pens on the table, a copy of *GQ*, a Scissor Sisters CD and an iPod. All of them were aligned at precisely the same angle. The books on the shelf were arranged in alphabetical order; everything was precision placed. Everything that could gleam, did gleam. It was freer of dirt and dust than an operating theatre. Hanlon thoroughly approved.

She sat down on his sofa and tucked her legs under her. Her shoes she'd left at the door. Whiteside was very protective of his carpet; he hated dirt, marks or any form of stain on its fabric. Whiteside reappeared with a bottle of wine and a Perrier for Hanlon. He put three coasters carefully on the table and poured himself a large glass of Pinot Noir. Hanlon sipped her mineral water. He was dressed for bed in a T-shirt and shorts. Whiteside had a great body, thought Hanlon approvingly. He was muscular, but not overly so. Hanlon couldn't stand the bodybuilder look, the Gym Martha. It had everything to do with vanity and little to do with utility. I'm such a muscle snob, she thought. Whiteside would warrant an eight out of ten from Hanlon. Whoever was in the bed was a very lucky man in her opinion. Running your hands over Whiteside would be a

thoroughly exhilarating experience, she imagined.

Briefly, she filled him in on the previous evening. Whiteside listened with amusement, scratching his neatly trimmed beard occasionally.

'And then he invited you to his study for a chat, did he?' smiled Whiteside.

He wondered if maybe Conquest had made a pass at Hanlon. He suspected most men would be too scared of her to do so, even if they fancied her. Hanlon was certainly intimidating. Conquest must have great self-confidence. Or, he thought, even if the DI didn't scare you, would you necessarily want to spend the evening with her? These things cut both ways. She didn't have much small talk and so much of intimacy is bound up with just that, whispered sweet nothings. The idea of Hanlon chatting amicably was simply unreal. What would she find to talk about? Crime? Triathlons? How much Hanlon could any man take? He realized that despite the years he'd known her they rarely talked about things other than work-related issues. He knew very little about her. She liked architecture and history. She liked boxing, a taste they both shared. She would come over and they'd watch it on Sky Sports. That was more or less it. Sometimes she'd stayed over and slept on his sofa but she was still an enigma. They themselves didn't talk much, content with each other's company like a long-time amicably married couple. He smiled again in amusement.

'He did indeed, Sergeant,' said Hanlon. 'And why are you grinning like that?' She sounded irritated.

'I was just wondering what you two young kids found to talk about,' said Whiteside teasingly. 'Was it everything and nothing? This and that? Setting the world to rights? The whole crazy, mixed-up world of policing the UK's capital city.'

'No, it wasn't,' said Hanlon, annoyed. 'It wasn't so much of a chat as a Q-and-A session about community policing. He said it was because of his position as head of that traders' group.' There we go, thought Whiteside. I knew she wouldn't follow Corrigan's advice to be loquacious.

She'd told Whiteside about the meeting with the assistant commissioner. She hadn't told him, though, her reason for getting involved as the AC's information officer on the Ali Yilmaz murder. Hanlon always played her cards close to her chest. When she had proof that Baby Ali's death was not a one-off but connected to the Essex killing, she'd tell him, but not until then. Meanwhile, let him think it was because the AC thought Ludgate might screw it all up.

'Oh, and he told me how much he admired me,' said Hanlon. 'And that went for everyone he'd met and everyone at the party. How at least I'd had the guts to tackle the rioters and how the country needed more police like me.'

'That's nice of him. I bet he fancies you too,' said Whiteside. 'Get him to put it in writing. You can give it to that disciplinary board. You don't have many prominent fans, ma'am. They'll be impressed. Start a campaign. They might give you your old job back.'

Hanlon smiled, or rather her lips twitched momentarily, despite herself. She continued, 'Conquest's an independent councillor in Finchley, with access, according to him, to the mayor's office, so maybe I should.'

'Well then.' Whiteside shrugged. 'That's good, isn't it. He's not a criminal after all.'

'Well,' Hanlon said, 'I didn't buy any of it.'

'How do you mean?' asked Whiteside, sipping his wine. Hanlon noted that, as usual when he drank, he held his little finger up. It was an odd quirk he had, like refined old ladies are supposed to do when they sip their tea.

'I'm not the local police community liaison officer. I'm also not a household name. And how did he know I'd be around here to attend this party?' said Hanlon. Whiteside thought she had a point, but equally he couldn't see where she was going

with this. 'It had to be Ludgate's doing. He got me the invite and I want to know why.'

'Maybe he wants to make friends?' said Whiteside with a humourless smile. He knew how much they detested each other. 'Yeah, right,' replied Hanlon sarcastically. 'I think Conquest wanted me to reveal what I'm doing on Ludgate's patch, what I'm spying on for the AC. Ludgate must have put him up to it. What I want to know is what Ludgate is doing cosying up with some multimillionaire property developer. It doesn't smell right.'

Whiteside scratched his beard. 'You think DCS Ludgate's bent?'

'Yes,' said Hanlon simply. 'Besides, I'm sure Conquest is.

You lie down with a dog, you get up with fleas.'

Whiteside looked at her dubiously. 'You're sure that's not just because you don't like him?' That's putting it charitably, he thought. 'There could be any number of reasons why Ludgate wanted him to ask why you're here. I'd be curious too, in his position. And annoyed. It is you, after all. And why shouldn't he be mates with a property developer? The DCS is up for retirement soon; he might be after wangling a nice little job as a security consultant. I wouldn't mind that myself. Couple of hundred quid a day for advising on anything from how to secure against squatters, to scams, to the best person to approach in the council. Ludgate knows everyone round here. He's been here since the ark.'

'I ran Conquest through the PNC,' said Hanlon. Her face

was stony. She was not amused. Whiteside recognized the look. He supposed there was some point to all of this but he couldn't see what.

'And?' he asked.

'Nothing, he's clean. Not even a driving endorsement or an unpaid parking ticket.'

'Well then.' Whiteside shrugged. 'That's good, isn't it. He's not a criminal after all. Hoorah. We can all sleep easy in our beds.'

Hanlon said, 'I know shit when I smell it, Sergeant. And when I've got Conquest under my nose, I don't smell roses. I've spent twenty years in the police and I know that man's got a record, I don't care what the police national computer thinks.' Whiteside guessed she'd say something along those lines.

One of Hanlon's greatest strengths was her terrier-like tenacity. She never gave up. The Anderson arrest was typical Hanlon. She'd been out to get him ever since the first attempt had ended in failure. Now Conquest was in her sights. Maybe Ludgate too. If she was convinced of their guilt she'd move heaven and earth to prove it. Hanlon handed him a piece of paper with a name and address.

'Here,' she said, 'look at this.' Whiteside took it and read it. 'Who's Dr S. Cohen and what's the Shapiro Institute?' he
asked.

By way of answer she said, 'I met Conquest's dogs, Prince and Blondi. German shepherds. Nice animals.' She looked at Whiteside. 'Do those names mean anything to you?'

Whiteside thought momentarily. 'No. No, they don't. Eighties pop stars?' What on earth is she on about now?

'They're the names of Hitler's dogs,' said Hanlon.

Whiteside laughed. 'Oh, come on,' he protested. 'They're really common names – well, Prince is for a dog. Even if he is a Nazi sympathizer and the dogs are named in honour of the Fuhrer, I don't think that's a crime in this country anyway, not unless he's, say, inciting racial hatred. Is he?'

Hanlon twisted a lock of her dark hair. She chose to answer Whiteside's question obliquely. 'Prominent fascist supporters are very often engaged in criminal activity, Mark. And like I
said, Conquest smells funny to me. I told you I don't believe any of this hoohah of wanting to speak to me about community

policing and telling me how much he admires me. I think he, like Ludgate, wanted to know what a senior officer associated with Corrigan – whose main issue is anti-racism, let's not forget

– is doing in his neck of the woods.'

Whiteside nodded. 'Let me get this straight.' He used the kind of voice you might use to patronize a small, annoying child. 'So he's worried that you might discover, what? That he doesn't like Jews?'

'If I'm wrong, I'm wrong,' said Hanlon. 'In the meantime you can humour me. We're not the only people with criminal databases. The Shapiro Institute has a very good one. You can ask them if they know Mr Conquest.'

'Who are they?' asked Whiteside, curious despite himself. 'They're a think tank that monitors far-right and neo-Nazi activity in this country and Europe. If Conquest or Ludgate is involved in illegal right-wing activity, they'll know. Conquest is a prominent citizen; he's anti-Semitic. I bet they've got something on him, even if it's just rumours. I want to know. Sol Cohen is the director. He's a busy man but he'll give you half an hour on Saturday at eleven.' It's my day off, damn it, thought Whiteside.

Then, she knows that of course.

'Surely they don't work on Saturdays?' he asked.

'Sol Cohen does. He's not orthodox, in fact he's an atheist,' said Hanlon. 'So you don't need to worry about that side of things.' 'I'll do my best,' he said sarcastically. 'And what do I tell him? That we, you, think a property developer might be anti-Semitic? It's hardly the crime of the century, is it? Even to a

Jewish think tank.'

'No,' said Hanlon with laboured patience, 'you tell him you're a journalist investigating anti-Semitism in the property

industry with links to organized crime.' Whiteside shook his head in mystification. 'Organized crime?'

'Organized crime,' repeated Hanlon firmly. 'I think Conquest's a criminal and he most certainly is organized. I checked out his business at Companies House. They made a small profit last financial year, nothing like enough to fund his lifestyle. You should have seen that party, that house. He's got an underground garage with a Maserati, a Mercedes and a top-of-the-line Range Rover as well. His clothes, shoes and watch come to your annual salary alone. Something doesn't add up. He's spent a lot more money than he's earned legitimately.' Hanlon paused. 'You'll need these.' She handed him an envelope which he opened.

Whiteside found himself looking at a photo driving licence and NUJ card that identified him as Michael Dunlop. There was also a covering letter written in Hebrew on Israeli Embassy notepaper. He looked inquiringly at Hanlon.

'That asks that the Shapiro Institute grant you every assistance. I phoned someone I know. Saul Gertler is the Chief of Security at the Israeli Embassy here in London; he provided this. They take millionaire neo-Nazis with police connections quite seriously even if you don't.'

'Why can't I just be me?' he asked. 'What's wrong with being Sergeant Whiteside? I can play that role. I've studied it for years. I was born to play it. Why undercover?'

Hanlon snorted. 'The institute doesn't trust the police. Shin Bet, yes; Scotland Yard, no. The police have connived too often in the past at shafting Jews. Who do you think rounded them up and sent them to camps, the Salvation Army? They wouldn't let you through the door, Sergeant. The institute is very security conscious. Not only that. They're always worried about information leaking. I can't say I blame them. I don't fully trust the police and I work for them. If I'm right, and

he is dirty, someone deleted Conquest from the PNC. That's probably one of our colleagues. I think we'll just keep this to ourselves for now.'

'If Corrigan finds out he'll have a blue fit,' said Whiteside warningly. You'll be sacked, he thought, and I'll be demoted. 'Corrigan won't find out,' said Hanlon. Whiteside recognized the tone in her voice. It meant, don't argue. 'That letter in Hebrew identifies you as a freelance journalist who is accredited in Israel. Your address I've given as this one. Is that OK with you?' Whiteside nodded. He doubted they'd be adding him to their mailing list. 'If anyone gets inquisitive tell them to ring Gertler at the embassy. No one will dare. He's not the kind of

man you'd want to bother.'

'You just did,' said Whiteside.

She looked at him imperiously, her grey eyes dark in the soft light of Whiteside's living room. Her chin lifted slightly in a combative way. 'That's true,' said Hanlon equably, as if it were nothing out of the ordinary. 'But I'm me.'

What can you do, he thought admiringly, faced with someone who shortly after leaving a dinner party has contacted the head of Israeli Intelligence in London, whose number she has on her mobile phone, and got him to do this. The range of people that Hanlon knew was extraordinary. What was even more extraordinary was the way they all tended to do her bidding. Himself included. Hanlon was looking at him expectantly. 'OK. OK,' he said. 'I'll go. What exactly do you want?'

'Like I told you. I want whatever they've got on Conquest. There'll be something. He's dirty, I can smell it. The fact that the PNC has got nothing on him doesn't impress me.'

Whiteside, who knew Hanlon much better than most, was surprised at the level of venom in her voice. He thought it boded ill for Conquest, guilty or innocent. Nothing would

get in her way. Whiteside had worked with her for five years. She was unstoppable.

'That's straightforward enough,' he said.

Hanlon took another sip of water. 'I also want to know if the number eighteen has any significance.'

'Eighteen?'

'Yes,' she said. Whiteside paused expectantly. Hanlon looked at him as if to say what more do you want.

'Are you going to tell me why this number's significant?' he asked.

She shook her head. 'I'd rather not,' she said.

'OK, fine. Be like that.' His mock irritation was not entirely mock. 'And how about you, what'll you be doing tomorrow?' he asked.

Hanlon stood up to leave. 'I'm seeing Sergeant Demirel about the murdered child. That, Sergeant, is what this is all about. Catching criminals, not feeding my ego.' She looked at him commandingly. 'Is that clear?'

'Yes, ma'am,' he said.

## 14

Clarissa sat in the front of the small, white Ford Transit van parked just down the road from Kathy and Peter's flat and felt the excitement rise in her body and mind as the adrenaline started to flow. She was growing to love this sensation. It was like that feeling she had before she used to go onstage, would she remember her lines? Would the audience love her? It was like being at the top of a roller-coaster ride, waiting for the moment when the car would plunge forward into the abyss, or standing on a bungee platform, but far, far better. This was life and death. This must be how God felt. What she was about to do was apocalyptic. She would utterly shatter Kathy and Peter's lives. She thought:

I am Destiny. I am Vishnu.

I am the Destroyer of Worlds.

Today would be the third time. First the Somali girl, then the Turkish boy, now this. One of their best clients had requested a young, white child and Clarissa had the perfect candidate. Clarissa was looking forward to taking Peter. He would fit the customer's specifications in every respect but, first and foremost, it would break Kathy's heart, it would destroy her, and Clarissa hated Kathy.

She quickly ran through her list of resentments against Kathy again, just to inspire herself. How Kathy reminded her of the

oh so superior girls at school who had looked down on her, who had sneered at her, who had belittled her, the girls who had ruined her childhood. She represented all the girls who had never liked her, never let her join their gangs. Well, suck on this, Kathy!

Then there was her career. Clarissa was a failed actress; Kathy an in-your-face successful businesswoman. Who did Kathy think she was with her high-power job, swanking around all over the world (in Clarissa's mind Kathy didn't travel, she swanked, every step of her elegant, high-heeled shoes leaving footprints of smugness), attending meetings, speaking her foreign languages. Oooh, look at me, I'm speaking German. Oooh, look at me, I'm speaking Italian. Oooh, look at me, now I'm talking French. Are you trilingual? I bet you're not.

Then there was her beauty. Clarissa knew she herself was reasonably good-looking, and quite sexy, but she had to work on that, and there was no way on earth, no matter how many diets, how much aerobics, how much Zumba, that she would ever have Kathy's long legs, Kathy's neck, Kathy's classic, fine-chiselled features. Women like Kathy were in the Style section of the *Sunday Times*. They modelled clothes for Boden. Clarissa despised them. She was everything that Clarissa wasn't, but had longed to be, in one package. Slim, sophisticated, successful, almost certainly popular. She'd have been one of those girls who had taunted Clarissa (then called Clare) at primary school. The girls who used to sing:

'Clare Yate, Clare Yate
    Don't kiss her at the garden gate! Don't touch her, isn't she big!
    Look at her, she's a big fat pig.'
    Well, she wasn't at school any more, she wasn't called Clare Yate

any more, and thanks to remorseless self-discipline, she wasn't fat any more, and people didn't chant hurtful things about her in playgrounds. Today she was Clarissa Yeats. And today she wasn't going to eat any more shit in her life. She'd had a bellyful of it growing up. She didn't take pain any more; she dished it out.

It's not as if the woman needed her looks anyway, not with her 'career'. To make matters even more galling, Kathy always seemed to be doing something worthy, baking, yoga, exercise, ironing, reading foreign journals. In the toilet there were *The Economist*, *Der Spiegel*, *Paris Match* and the *FT*.

Clarissa felt she was a living reproach. Kathy even had tragic glamour as a result of being a widow. Her husband would never grow bald, fat and old, never have hair sprout from his ears, never break her heart by having sex with a girl in his office or her best friend. He would remain an iconic, shining memory.

And then, of course, there was her beautiful son.

When the judge has finished with him, when Robbo has finished with him, he won't look so beautiful then, Kathy.

I can never have what you've got, Kathy, but I can, and I will, take it away from you, she thought. And it starts today. The Somali girl she had lured into a car where Robbo had dealt with her. The Turkish toddler she'd taken while following Mehmet. She knew the family routine and the gods had smiled on her when the man had left the boy of his own volition in

her care.

She shook her head with irritation when she thought of Robbo, huge, packed with weightlifter's muscle, his shaved head decorated with those three inverted V's like sergeant's stripes. He'd really started to go off the rails of late. Clarissa blamed the drugs he took for his bodybuilding. Human growth

hormone, extracted from some dead guy's pituitary gland, as if that would do you good.

The Somali girl he'd left in that bunker where the police had found her. They'd accepted his explanation that he'd thought it would be blamed on kindoku (Just don't think, OK, said Conquest). Then the boy dumped, highly visibly, in the canal. I panicked, Robbo had said, I thought the Old Bill were going to pull my car. Well, Robbo didn't know, but his future was under review and it would be a severance package, quite literally. They couldn't put up with his erratic behaviour any more.

Neither of them even began to suspect that Robbo, in his own way, had been paying tribute to the historic figure he truly venerated.

Today was her third, then, and she knew it would go well. Peter was more of a challenge. Much more. He was tall and strong and, above all, she guessed he would be a fighter by nature. Not like the others. Destiny had already dealt Mariam, the Somali, a series of dreadful blows so it was almost as if she accepted her fate, she hadn't fought back. Baby Ali couldn't.

The boy wouldn't either. Not through choice. The boy wouldn't know what had hit him.

Earlier that day she had watched from the van as Kathy had left for the airport. Kathy had told her about the trip and her movements. London was such a perfect environment to work in. No one noticed vehicles. She left the van where she'd parked it so she wouldn't lose its place. She had a council parking permit displayed on the dashboard. The plates on the van were fake. She knew from talking to Kathy – 'It must be so hard for you when you travel to make arrangements for Peter! How do you manage?' – the boy would be home about four thirty and was due to shower, change and then go to a friend's party from seven until ten, then go to a sleepover and stay at

another friend's until Sunday evening when Kathy would pick him up. It would all work perfectly.

She rehearsed it again in her mind. It was foolproof.

Clarissa came back to the vehicle at four in the afternoon, accompanied by the dog. She had thought about leaving it in the van but was worried in case it started barking. You could commit virtually any crime in Britain and no one would do a thing, but leave a dog unattended in a vehicle and they'd lynch you.

She had thought about taking the boy in the flat where there would be privacy, but he was tall and strong, and in the inevitable struggle she was worried about leaving DNA evidence. Of course, she had been in the flat for professional reasons, as an employee of Albion, so there was no reason why there shouldn't be traces of her around, but she was thinking about blood or hair, things that shouldn't be there, things that might look suspicious. There was going to be one hell of an investigation over Peter's disappearance, that was for sure. A Somali and a Turk both with questionable pasts, both here illegally, were not so newsworthy. There was a public feeling it was almost their fault for being here in the first place. Nobody had asked them to come to Britain. Mariam hadn't made any of the national papers. Baby Ali had warranted a paragraph. Even the TV footage from the canal hadn't been used. A photogenic white boy with a beautiful, tragic mother, that would be a gift from the gods to journalists. That would go national.

No, she thought, the street would be best, if all went accord

ing to plan, and she could see no reason why it shouldn't, the whole thing would be over in seconds. She had rehearsed over and over; she had used props. She knew her lines, the direction was thorough and clear, now she was impatient to get on stage.

She looked at the clock in the car. Four fifteen. It was time to get ready.

Showtime.

* * *

Peter walked slowly home from school and turned into his road. The street was always quiet at this time. He had a lot to carry on a Friday. There was his PE kit, his heavy schoolbag with his textbooks and exercise books, and today he was further burdened with a papier mâché model of a cat that he'd made in art and had decided to give to his mum as a birthday present. He hadn't painted it yet; he would do that at home. He was still undecided as to the colour scheme. Black and white would be easiest but tabby more of a challenge. His mum liked cats. She liked dogs too but when he asked, as he often did, about getting one, she'd always say that it would be too much of a responsibility. One day, thought Peter. One day, I'll have a dog. It was, he decided, an achievable dream. He was a very practical boy.

Not like Kemal in his class. Kemal wanted a horse. Like
that was going to happen in Finchley.

As he rounded the corner he saw the woman and the spaniel. It was a cocker spaniel, or similar, with a brown and white coat and one of its front legs was heavily bandaged. He guessed it had to be a stray. The woman, one leg kneeling on the pavement, was wearing a blue uniform and the van had the Haringey Council logo, a kind of asymmetric star, that to Peter's eyes was strangely similar to the NATO emblem he'd seen on the military channel that he liked watching on TV.

The dog-warden lady had managed to get the animal into a small, portable cage but she had some kind of cast on her hand, maybe it was broken, and would obviously struggle to lift the steel container, now heavy with dog, into the back of the van.

Peter stopped and said politely, 'Hello. Do you need some help?' He was a very helpful boy. His school reports usually mentioned this. 'Peter is very popular with the other boys and always ready to help out.'

The woman looked up at him from where she was crouching

beside the dog on the pavement. 'If you don't mind,' she said, and smiled at him warmly.

Peter noticed she was very pretty. He was just beginning to notice girls. There was a U-shaped scar between her eyebrows, which strangely made her look even more attractive. It was a paradox. He thought, maybe when I'm older I'll understand things like that.

'He's got a collar but no tag,' she said, pointing at the spaniel. The dog looked at them mournfully through the wire mesh of the cage as if it knew it was being talked about. 'I need to take him back to the office so I can see if he's been chipped.' She looked ruefully at her bandaged wrist. 'If you could get him into the back of the van for me? We can't let him wander around the streets.'

'Sure,' said Peter, glad to be of help. The woman opened the back door of the van and Peter picked the cage up and placed it carefully on the floor.

'Could you move it right to the front?' she asked. 'I can secure it better then. I don't want it sliding around.' Of course not, he thought, it'd scare the dog. Peter slowly and gently pushed the cage in, murmuring to the dog to relax it, and climbed in himself so he was squatting with his back to the woman.

When undergoing an operation or a surgical procedure and injected with an intravenous anaesthetic and asked to count back from ten, it is round about five before darkness washes over the patient. It is often a derivative of sodium thiopental that has been administered. That is what was in the body of the

syringe that Clarissa plunged into him as his back was turned, together with benzodiazepine to keep him under.

Peter had to inject himself four times a day with insulin because of his non-functioning pancreas. That's the price paid to live as a type-one diabetic, and he was more aware than most people of the sensation of a needle going into his flesh. He realized immediately what was happening. Two thoughts flashed through his mind: I've been injected, and, why? He felt the sting in his right buttock, but both of his hands were still wrapped round the cage with the dog and he was bent uncomfortably, confined in the narrow space of the small van. He tried to turn round but the woman's hand was suddenly on his neck, jamming his head uncomfortably against the cage. He tried to kick, but the weight of her body was pressed against his heels.

For a second he was more confused than alarmed. Is this some kind of joke? was his last, coherent thought, then he felt a roaring in his ears and a blackness darker than night enveloped him like a cloak.

## 15

Several hundred miles and an hour's time difference away from London, Kathy flew into Flughafen Stuttgart, the city's airport, home of Mercedes and Porsche. She had only hand luggage with her and there was no queue at passport control. She walked into the main concourse and looked around the clean, modern building with genuine pleasure. The Germanic lettering, the umlauts, the capital letters of the nouns, and the signature letter of the 'esset' that represented double 's' in German script and looked like the Greek letter for Beta, greeted her like old friends.

Kathy loved Germany. It was a love affair that had started as an exchange student in grimy, flat-as-a-pancake Berlin, been nurtured in a six-month ERASMUS university stint in Hamburg, and had been topped up ever since. She even quite liked the food. She spoke excellent German and the signs around her and the conversations she heard were as easy to understand as if they'd been in English, but they were, to her eyes and ears, pleasingly exotic. She heard a man's voice call her name; it was her Siemens contact Max Brucker.

'Max, good to see you. *Wie geht's*? What are you doing here?' she asked.

Max smiled. Kathy was tall, about five ten, one metre seventy, but she only just reached Max's shoulder. She was

surprised by the rediscovery of just how big he was. '*Bestens, Kathy, und wie geht's du?*'

He took her solitary piece of hand luggage. 'I thought I'd come and meet you,' he said in English. Now it was Kathy's turn to smile. She had forgotten, or maybe hadn't acknowledged to herself, just how attractive she found Max. She thought to herself, just for a few hours I'm going to behave normally. Just for a few hours I'm not going to brood on the past or worry about the future. Maybe I'll even flirt with him. Peter'll be fine round at Sam's. I worry too much about that boy, it can't be healthy. Max smiled back. He thought Kathy was very attractive.

Five streets away from where Peter lived, Annette Fielding took a migraine tablet out of its disproportionately sized piece of packaging, the same as a book of stamps, containing just the one blister-packed tiny tablet, and washed it down with some water. She didn't like taking them. She thought she'd start building up an immunity to them and they were incredibly expensive, but she had no choice. Her head was killing her. The events of the next few hours certainly wouldn't help.

Sam, her son, had three friends over for the sleepover that was happening later, making four twelve-year-old boys who had to be fed and entertained. Tonight, with the agonizing pain in her head, she was dreading the noise levels. Frederica, her daughter, was out with some girls from her school but had promised to be back at a reasonable time. Like that's going to happen! she thought. Freddie was sixteen and always vague about time. Declan, her husband, was stuck in Newcastle because of some systems glitch at work and wouldn't be home until about 2 a.m. Well, she'd cope, she always did, but by God, she thought, I feel awful. If only she could crawl into

bed, close the door and spend the next couple of days there. But that wasn't going to happen.

She made a cup of tea and looked despairingly round the small kitchen that still had a pile of washing up left from breakfast waiting patiently by the sink. The plates with their congealed food were stacked on top of each other; the cutlery sat there accusingly. The dirty tines of the forks pointed at her, why haven't you cleaned us yet? She opened the dishwasher. That was full – at least it was full of clean plates rather than dirty ones, let's be thankful for small mercies – and she started to unload it.

To put them on to a work surface she had to move a basket of laundry whites in a crumpled, sulky heap waiting to be ironed – school shirts and Declan's shirts mainly (why was she the only one in the house who seemed able to iron, for Christ's sake? Why couldn't Declan do some, it's not that hard, is it?), and another basket of coloured laundry waiting to be washed. The dog nudged her hopefully with its damp nose; he needed feeding. And they were running short of milk. There was a bowl of fruit going off on the kitchen table and a big stack of the children's schoolbooks that needed sorting out. There were unopened letters on top of the fridge, some of them bills and credit card statements, and she had seven messages on her phone, she could see the red digits glowing at her. Even inanimate things were nagging her now, and the whiteboard in the kitchen for messages seemed to be covered in reminders of other things that needed doing.

Sometimes, and tonight was one of those nights, Annette felt completely overwhelmed by life, outraced by the tide of things that needed to be done.

The migraine headache was really kicking in now. Christ, I feel awful, she thought. Annette sat down on the tiled floor

of the kitchen and buried her head in Dizzy, their retriever's, fur for comfort. She felt nauseous and hoped the pill would take effect before she was actually sick. The dog smelt warm and comforting and licked her hand consolingly. Down at this level she could see that the kitchen floor needed cleaning and so did the skirting boards. Why did skirting boards have a groove in them that served no function but to get clogged with dirt? Whose bright idea was that? Why have I even got skirting boards in the sodding kitchen? She felt like crying. No, she thought, I feel like howling and then crying.

There was something she felt she hadn't done, something important, but couldn't bring it to mind. She was feeling too ill to concentrate on the thought. Then her stomach spasmed and she thought, 'Oh God, here we go,' and quickly made her way to the toilet. She ran the taps in the basin in case any of the boys over-heard her, and was sick into the bowl as quietly as she could be, holding her hair up with one hand so it didn't get dirty.

Jesus, now she really did feel terrible. All she wanted to do was curl up on the loo floor but that simply wasn't an option. Dimly, she heard the phone start to ring in the kitchen.

'Oh, go away!' she groaned.

In Stuttgart, in her comfortable room at the five-star, quietly luxurious Althoff Hotel, Kathy let the phone ring five times and then hung up. She enjoyed staying in hotels. She liked the solitude and anonymity. Annette must be busy, she thought. She had promised Peter she wouldn't phone him anyway – 'It's like you're checking up on me, Mum.' He'd be fine. She undressed and got into the shower.

It was roomy, spacious and had a large, powerful jet, much better than the one at home. She turned the heat up to the maximum her body could bear, revelling in the

sensation. A shower after a journey, she thought, what could be more fun than that. The bathroom gleamed and shone through the transparent shower screen. She felt intensely happy.

The only thing she didn't like about business travel was eating alone. It was particularly unenjoyable in hotel dining rooms where many of her fellow diners tended to be single businessmen who would surreptitiously stare at her speculatively as she ate, a book or a Kindle propped up on a cruet set in front of her.

Tonight would be different, though. Max was taking her out to dinner and she was determined to enjoy herself.

Peter Reynolds had regained consciousness and was lying on his back, taking stock of his surroundings. He felt remarkably calm, considering. He was feeling very weak and he could feel the hypo coming. This meant his blood sugar was very low and he knew he was not far off fainting. Despite the panic and fear he was feeling at his abduction, he knew he had to get some sugars into his body before he collapsed. He felt in his pockets for his blood-testing kit to check how low he was, then remembered it was in his schoolbag. His blood sugar had to be below four, he thought, the danger level. Four's the floor. He patted his pockets again, hoping to find a sweet, but it was no good. There was nothing there.

He had no way of knowing what time it was but he guessed,

judging by the way he was feeling, it was probably late on Friday night. He breathed deeply and looked around him again.

It did not take long to complete an inventory. He was in a small, bare windowless room. The walls were smooth brick, painted a battleship grey. It was lit dimly by a recessed light covered with a grille. The metal door of the room was painted a dull green, with two square hatches, one at shoulder level, the other at floor level, and an eyehole. The room was about

the size of his bedroom at home, he guessed. It wasn't very big but the lack of furnishings made it seem larger than it was. A metal toilet was bolted to the wall, no seat, with some toilet paper next to it. There was a small washbasin, also metal, with a mixer tap, some soap and a plastic cup. In one corner of the room was a fixed shower head and mixer tap, with a drain below it set into the floor. He was lying by the far wall opposite the door on a thick, blue padded plastic mat, rather like they had at school in the gym, with a thin pillow that his head was resting on and a neatly folded blanket by his feet. In the ceiling corner above the door was a CCTV camera so he could be observed. That completed the inspection of the room, apart from one thing that made his misery more bearable. By the door was the dog in its cage.

Peter carefully got to his feet, rubbing his head, and opened

the cage door. The dog flinched in fear. Its brown eyes were troubled and it trembled slightly. The boy put his arm slowly into the cage, allowing the dog to smell his hand to reassure it, and spoke soothingly to it. The animal let him stroke its head and when Peter withdrew his hand the dog crept nervously out of its cage and came to him. It lay down in front of Peter as he stroked its warm fur. It was still trembling. Peter could sympathize. The dog licked his hand and Peter kissed its head. As he did so, he heard footsteps that stopped outside his cell and felt he was being observed through the spyhole. He lifted his head.

'I'm diabetic and I'm about to go into a coma unless you give me the emergency glucose that you'll find in my schoolbag. And get me some orange juice.' He spoke loudly at the blank, metal door. He paused, his head ached so. The coma was no idle threat. 'I'll need my blood-testing kit too. I'd hurry if I were you.'

The footsteps on the other side of the door started to move away, much more quickly than they'd arrived. A couple of minutes later he stood up as he heard the bottom hatch in his cell door being opened, and he moved forward to take the two cases that contained what he needed. Then the hands of the unseen person – a man's hands, he noticed, so not the woman who had kidnapped him – passed him four individual cartons of orange juice. He noticed that the hands of the unseen man were furred with coarse, dark hair and heavily and intricately tattooed with Gothic lettering; the words weren't English.

Quickly he sat down and tested his blood. He raised his eyebrows. God, he was low. He drank the juice and crunched three of the dextrose tablets between his teeth. He could almost feel the palpable relief in his body as his sugar levels rose. He felt a bit happier now. 'At least I'm not dead,' he whispered to the dog.

He sat back on his mat and the dog climbed into his arms, and Peter buried his nose in the animal's fur for reassurance. Above him the light shone remorselessly and the camera watched over him like a malignant, vigilant eye.

## 16

The Shapiro Institute was discreetly housed in a small side road off Marylebone High Street. The area was extremely fashionable and, for the residents, reassuringly expensive. As well as its ten-minute proximity to the good end of Oxford Street and Bond Street, it was very close to Harley Street, destination of the wealthy ill or those in need of cosmetic body upkeep. Although he lived in London, Whiteside hadn't been to this part of the city for years and had forgotten how attractive it was, with its red-brick facades, the windows neatly edged in white stuccoed stone, and village-like feel. He thought, it probably doesn't have much crime, except tax evasion. It was homely, with everything on a reassuring scale, unlike parts of London built to impress, like, say, Regent Street, or built to overawe, like the City.

He walked up the small flight of steps to the entrance of what had been a narrow, three-storey town house, looked up at the camera over the door that mutely returned his stare and pushed the buzzer. The intercom crackled into life and he gave his new name to an unseen woman. The door swung open. So far, so good, he thought.

As he walked through into the building, he gave a professional glance at the door, which was unusually – several centimetres

– thick. He noticed it was a kind of sandwich. It was made of

sheet steel between laminated wood with no obvious hinges. They must have been recessed into the wall. You'd need a bazooka to break it down.

Inside the doorway to the street was an entrance room with an airport-style security gate and an X-ray machine for any hand luggage. This was manned by two hard-faced men, one of them wearing a yarmulke, who Whiteside guessed would probably be Israeli ex-forces. Then again, he thought, almost everyone in Israel is in the military in one form or another.

Ex-military usually have a certain air about them. They had it. They eyed him professionally in an unfriendly way. The guards examined Whiteside's credentials and ID with a far from impressed air. Perhaps Gertler had fired them from embassy security, he thought. As one of them patted him down, a dowdy woman in her late thirties, wearing a tweed skirt, cardigan, thick brown tights and sensible shoes, came down the staircase. 'Michael Dunlop? I'm Celia Westermann, Dr Cohen's assis

tant. Would you come with me, please,' she said.

Whiteside followed her up the stairs while Westermann apologized for the security. 'Not too intrusive, I hope. Obviously, we have to be a bit cautious, being who we are.' Whiteside, who noticed such things, thought to himself that Westermann was dressed as though frumpy was obligatory at the Shapiro Institute. Her clothes were like something her mother should be wearing. It was as if she were making some kind of subtle point. He was innately suspicious of people who dressed like their parents or went the other way and aped their children. Both were wrong, in his opinion. He shrugged mentally. Westermann's attitude, whatever it may be, could hardly affect him, he thought.

As they walked up the broad stairs, they passed a large, gilt mirror and Whiteside caught a glimpse of his own reflection: burly, tough, reddish-sandy hair and close-cropped beard, punctuated by a broad diagonal scar on the right side of his jaw. He looked like a streetwise thug, exactly how you might imagine a right-wing terrorist to look. No wonder the guards had been dubious.

They stopped on the first floor. The institute smelt like a college, of carpet and books. 'Now,' Westermann said brightly, 'this is Dr Cohen's office.' She knocked and opened the door. 'If you'd like to go in.'

Whiteside did so. The door closed behind him and a small, white-haired man stood up from behind his desk. He looked professorial. He was wearing an antique-looking three-piece suit with a fob watch in his waistcoat. His hand was outstretched and Whiteside shook it. He smelt of books and eau de cologne, the scent of academia.

'Ah, Mr Dunlop. Do come in and sit down, I'm Dr Sol Cohen.' Whiteside did so. Cohen opened his laptop. That wasn't old-fashioned: it was a new Apple Mac.

\* \* \*

While Whiteside was in the expensive, sought-after suburb of Marylebone, DI Hanlon was in the rather less desirable Wood Green in North London. There is nothing particularly treelined and leafy about Wood Green. It's the kind of area you might think of if you were going to film a low-budget drama on drug dealing.

'Do come in and sit down, Sergeant Demirel,' said DI Hanlon. 'I take it you remember me.'

'Yes, ma'am,' said Enver.

They were meeting in a room at Wood Green police station that was used as a kind of storage area. Storage area was a euphemism: it was a junk room. The office lay at the end of a short corridor that led nowhere. The window looked out on to

a brick wall a few feet away giving it no natural light, just what the brick wall chose to reflect, which wasn't much. Inside the room there were several desks, chairs and two tables, as well as half a dozen filing cabinets pushed close together. Some old computer monitors were stacked up on top of the tables, there were eleven (Hanlon had counted them) old cardboard boxes containing out-of-date stationery, paper of the sort that used to be used by old-fashioned ink-jet computer printers, the kind that had perforations in strips along its edges and used to fit through a sprocket. Several lever-arch files gathered dust on a table in the corner and there was a National Trust calendar from two years ago on the wall. September 2010 featured Waddesdon Manor in Buckinghamshire in its autumnal glory. Ludgate had made this room available to Hanlon by way of an insult, a calculated snub. You can go in there with all the other unwanted junk was the message.

Ludgate was sure Corrigan had sent Hanlon down to spy

on him and he was not happy. This was one way of showing it. Another was to not copy her in on emails, to not inform her of meetings, in general to ignore her, to pretend she wasn't there. Hanlon had complained about this and received a grudging apology, Ludgate blaming it on insufficient technical support. The intention behind the room had misfired, though. Hanlon rather liked this secretive, out-of-the-way lair. It suited her nature. She could come and go as she pleased without anyone noticing. And she liked the fact that nobody could suddenly barge in. It was physically impossible. To reach the corner where she sat, you had to thread your way slowly through the labyrinth

of disused office furniture. Enver was doing this right now.

There was no question of a surprise appearance, a casual

craning over to see what you were up to. It took time and effort to reach her desk and it helped to be slim.

'Didn't you used to be a middleweight, Sergeant?' said Hanlon, rather pointedly, as Enver squeezed his way through the obstacle course of the room to the spare seat opposite her. He was carrying a good few extra pounds around his middle, she noticed. His paunch had brushed against the disused screens of the old computer monitors and left a wide streak of grey dust across his white shirt.

'It's been five years, ma'am,' he protested. 'Even then it was a struggle to make the weight.'

She nodded. Enver looked at her. He doubted she carried any surplus flesh. When she moved her head to one side, he could see the long, elegant muscles in her neck stretch. Under her white cotton blouse, where the top buttons were undone, he could see the strong trapezius muscles across her shoulders highly defined under her skin. It was a while since he'd weighed one hundred and sixty pounds, which had been his fighting weight. Strangely, despite the evidence of mirror and scales, he was still in the habit of thinking of himself as slim. It was becoming an expensive habit. He'd bought two new shirts recently in his last size. He'd put one of them on this morning and had to suck his breath in to button it up. When he'd relaxed and breathed out, his stomach pushed tightly against the fabric and he felt his flab redistribute itself around his middle. It's all going pear-shaped, he thought, quite literally. I look like a pear. He felt a stab of self-loathing, revulsion at what his once beautiful body was becoming. He had looked in the mirror in his bedroom and decided he looked grotesque. His fat was visibly rippling over the waistband of his trousers and was outlined by the shirt's material. It didn't disguise it; it emphasized it. I'll need a bloody kaftan soon, he thought.

Enver had shaken his head mournfully. His dad, dead of a heart attack, had been fat too. He took the shirt off, his flab hanging over the waistband of his trousers, hung it up and put on one two sizes bigger. He'd put the shirt in the side of his wardrobe reserved for shirts and suits that no longer fitted. It was a growing collection. The replacement shirt was too long in the arms for him and the cuffs poked out of the end of his jacket sleeves in an odd way. Still, better that than the tight shirt. He didn't want to look like a beached whale in front of the DI.

Enver was becoming increasingly drawn to Hanlon. Ever since their first meeting by the canal he had found himself thinking about her at odd times. He told himself he didn't find her attractive but he realized now that he was starting to obsess about her. He thought, I'm doing it again, staring at her thick, black, unruly hair, her dark, graceful eyebrows, her long, strong fingers. He was acutely aware of her clothes and her body and he thought, slightly desperately, I must stop this. Hanlon was looking at him impatiently. Whatever inner turmoil Enver was going through never showed on his face.

He raised his sleepy brown eyes to her grey ones and shrugged apologetically.

'Who was champion then?' she asked. 'Ma'am?' He was confused.

'When you were fighting, Sergeant. Who was UK champion? At your weight.'

'Howard Eastman, ma'am,' he said.

'The Battersea Bomber,' said Hanlon thoughtfully.

She'd seen Eastman fight. All she could remember was his dyed beard, that and his speed. The beard had looked strange. He'd coloured it yellow, she seemed to remember, and he was black. From a distance he'd looked really old, the beard appearing snowy white under the harsh ring lights, whereas he'd only been about thirty something. Hanlon liked boxing very

much. The discipline, the aggression, the artistry, the nobility, the pain and the purity of the sport, all of these were things she admired most in life. Also, its solitary nature appealed to her. 'You're not a team player, Hanlon' – an accusation, and a true one, that she'd lived with most of her life.

'Did you ever fight him, Sergeant?' she asked.

'No, ma'am. I would have done but, well, the business with my eye put paid to that,' explained Enver.

Hanlon nodded sympathetically. She placed her hands flat on the table and looked at her fingernails, then she raised her eyes to Enver. Eastman would have slaughtered him, she guessed. 'So what's happening with your investigation, Sergeant?

Any further forward?' Hanlon had read most of the reports and spoken to the personnel concerned, but the collective feeling was this was a case that would go nowhere.

Enver shook his head. 'Because Mr Yilmaz left it three days to report the child missing, we don't have any CCTV footage from the supermarket. They wipe it after three days. It occupies too much computer storage space. So no footage of the woman and no footage of whatever vehicle was used to move the child. Nothing useful either from any of the staff. He's also very vague on what the woman he left looking after the boy looked like. "Very brown eyes" and "young".' The sergeant rolled his eyes. 'Mr Yilmaz is not the sharpest knife in the box.' Hanlon nodded. In one of the case notes, someone had made the comment that Mehmet Yilmaz had learning difficulties. It didn't make their lives any easier.

'Ethnicity?' asked Hanlon.

'He's got no idea.' Enver shrugged. 'She was wearing a headscarf so he couldn't see her hair. Not Turkish, Caucasian, that's as good as it gets.'

'So you've got nothing?' asked Hanlon.

Enver nodded unhappily. 'No. Nothing from the supermarket, no witnesses have come forward, no forensic evidence, nothing.

We're going to stage a reconstruction, a walk through, next week, but I'm not optimistic.' This is London, he thought to himself, not a village. Not only did people not notice things, they didn't want to notice things. It's hardwired into the DNA of a city-dweller. If you see trouble, you avert your gaze. We're in the kingdom of the three monkeys. See no evil. Hear no evil. Speak no evil. This was particularly true in Wood Green, as he knew to his cost. He'd long ago given up saying 'Somebody must have seen something'. These days he hardly even thought it.

'Well, at least it'll refresh people's memories,' said Hanlon. 'Maybe it'll get it back into the papers.'

Public response to the case had been disappointing. London could be a callous city and it was as if the population had collectively shrugged its shoulders over Ali's death.

Enver nodded. 'The e-fit image the father managed to produce is so generic it's practically useless. She's got a nose, two eyes and a mouth, that's about as far as it goes.'

'So no question of parental involvement in your judgement, Sergeant?'

'No, ma'am. Of course, it's complicated by the fact that the child was never officially here, so we have no health visitor records or GP surgery attendance, but the post-mortem exam showed a perfectly healthy child apart from the injuries, sexual in nature, that were inflicted on him prior to his death.' She looked at him enquiringly and he shook his head. 'No semen traces, ma'am. No foreign DNA. Anyway, nothing to link the parents. Nothing indicating long-term abuse.'

'I read the report,' said Hanlon.

It was sickening, but how could it be otherwise. Aside from the assault itself, what particularly got to her was the way the

body had just been tossed in the canal near that number eighteen. It was a kind of boast. It was saying, Look at me. I've done it again and I'm going to do it again. And what significance did that number have? Once more she briefly considered going to Corrigan with her feeling that this was linked to the Essex case. Once again she dismissed the idea. When she had more evidence, maybe. Right now, both cases were getting nowhere. What good would her contribution be even if believed? She knew there was a strong lobby that would dismiss anything she suggested simply because it came from her. What could you do? Warn everyone there was a child killer on the loose while the police were powerless to act?

'I gather it's unusual, ma'am, for a woman to be involved

in what looks like false imprisonment for sexual purposes,' said Enver.

'Maybe, but not unknown,' said Hanlon. 'Look at the Moors murders for a start. Or Rosemary West.' She looked again at Enver. 'What do you think happened, Sergeant?'

'The child was taken by a woman either dressed in supermarket uniform, or near as damn it, with a reasonably convincing ID hanging round her neck. Either she'd gone there to abduct any old child or she had possibly followed Mehmet Yilmaz there for that purpose. She almost certainly had an accomplice outside with transport. The child was taken to order, ma'am, that's what I think, and frighteningly efficiently too.'

'And the disposal of the body? So obviously?'

Enver shrugged. 'The most popular theory is the rape and murder took place locally. That stretch of canal is a CCTV blackspot; the killer may have known that or may have just got lucky.' He stroked his moustache. 'I'd hate to speculate, ma'am. To be honest I can think of three or four reasons to leave it

there, including simply it's as good a place as any. Maybe even just to taunt us.'

Enver's phone indicated he had a message. He muttered an apology to the DI. He read it and raised his eyebrows. 'Well, well,' he said with something approaching excitement in his voice. 'That was the incident room. Mehmet Yilmaz has finally been in touch to say he's remembered something about the woman. He wants me there because he wants to make sure he's understood; his English is not that brilliant, to put it mildly. Ludgate wants me to go and see him at home this afternoon. One o'clock.'

'That's encouraging,' said Hanlon.

'Yes,' said Enver. 'I'm not counting chickens, but at least it's something. It all sounds very vague.' Enver nodded. In spite of his reservations, he was pleased. About bloody time too, he thought.

'I'll come with you,' said Hanlon. 'I'll see you in the car park at half twelve. I'll take you.'

Enver nodded and stood up. 'Thank you, ma'am,' he said. Hanlon watched him thoughtfully as he retraced his steps through the obstacle course that was her office. She was beginning to warm to the gloomily efficient, Eeyore-like Sergeant Demirel.

She turned to her laptop and wrote an email to Corrigan, detailing what had been happening on the Yilmaz case. Her unofficial view rather than Ludgate's version, although, to give the devil his due, Ludgate had handled everything with consummate ability. He'd even reined in his usual, casual racism. His organization had been exemplary, probably better than she could have done. She'd always been poor at administration, and management in general. It's what she had used Whiteside for.

She added a note praising Enver. Corrigan was always on the lookout for talented, ethnically diverse police. An endorsement from me would probably torpedo Enver's career chances, she thought, but one from Corrigan could send you on your way up the ladder. She finished her email and pressed send. As she did so, she wondered how Whiteside was getting on.

## 17

Whiteside took a seat opposite Sol Cohen. He tried to look journalistic. Although he'd been interviewed innumerable times by journalists, print and TV for various cases, he couldn't remember what equipment they carried. He'd settled for a notebook. He placed it in front of him, together with his phone. He had a police issue MP3 recorder but thought Cohen might recognize it as such. Through the window came the noise of the London traffic. Once again, he had the feeling, looking at Cohen in this pleasant, airy, book-lined room, of being in an academic's study, pleasingly isolated from the outside world. Between them lay the desk: modern, sleek, Scandanavian-looking.

On the wall was a large computer photo-frame and a variety

of faces, predominately white, jowly, middle-aged, came and went on the screen, one after another, a succession of images. He recognized none of them in the endless video picture parade. He wondered if it might be some art installation, a counter to the framed photos of David Ben-Gurion and Jacob Bronowski on the opposite wall. Cohen noted Whiteside's interest.

'My rogues' gallery, my "lest we forget",' Cohen said. '"Those who forget the lessons of history are doomed to repeat it." I'm sure you know the quote?' Whiteside nodded wisely. 'We're now looking at Gergely Pongrátz,' noted Cohen, pointing at the screen.

He suited his name, thought the sergeant. An elderly man with archaic moustaches, silver hair and old-fashioned braiding on his jacket, filled the screen. Whiteside looked at him; the folkloric clothing gave him a deeply sinister air, a character out of Grimm. Whiteside would have picked him out of a line-up as almost certainly the nutter who'd done the axe murder, he had that air of rustic insanity.

Cohen said, 'The founder of Jobbik, The Movement for a Better Hungary. Mr Pongrátz isn't keen on Jews. The party line is we shouldn't be complaining about this but instead be, and I quote, "playing with our tiny, circumcised dicks".' Cohen laughed. 'Mr Pongrátz has a way with words. Quite popular they are, too, in his country. In fact, according to the Hungarian police trade union, no less, Hungary should be preparing for armed battle with the Jews.' Cohen's tone was very much that of a teacher giving a lecture to a slightly dim pupil. Whiteside could begin to see why maybe Cohen didn't have a particularly rosy view of the police.

'You can't always trust the law,' Whiteside said, helpfully, enthusiastically. Cohen shrugged eloquently as Pongrátz faded away to be replaced by another face. 'Nikolaos Michaloliakos, from the Golden Dawn of Greece, with their trademark, 'I can't believe it's not a swastika' symbol. You'll know them from the recent news, they did rather well in the Greek elections.' Michaloliakos shrank to a corner of the screen. 'In Athens police are recommending victims of crime go to them for assistance.' 'Oh,' said Whiteside. Now a fat-faced, tough-looking man filled the screen.

'Holger Apfel. National Democratic Party of Germany. Bit of a synonym for National Socialism, no?' Cohen sighed. 'We monitor anti-Semitism, Mr Dunlop. It's as old as the Jews themselves and I would say it's making a comeback;

these are all current figures, not bogeymen from the past. The truth is, anti-Semitism never went away. In Britain alone we logged six hundred anti-Semitic incidents last year. So, as you can see, the reason for our funding is as important as ever. Plus of course we have Iran that wants to destroy us completely – well, and all the Arab countries. Unfortunately, our future here at the institute looks extremely secure. If only we weren't needed I'd be a happy man.' Cohen picked up a small remote. 'There's a lot more stored on the files for that photo-frame,' he said. 'I just wanted to give you a flavour of what we do, put a face to our persecutors.' He pressed a button and changed the right-wing portraiture for a blue-green picture of an attenuated violinist, floating dreamlike in a night sky over a village.

'Marc Chagall,' said Cohen. 'Let's cheer ourselves up a bit.

Some positive Jewish artistic achievement, eh.'

He looked at Whiteside with disconcertingly intelligent eyes. 'So, how can we be of assistance?'

'Harry Conquest,' said Whiteside. He spelt the surname for Cohen.

'OK then, Mr Dunlop.' Cohen smiled as he said the name.

It sounded ridiculous to Whiteside himself. Who thought of that name? Perhaps they were working their way through tyre brands. He could have been Bridgestone, Pirelli, Marangoni, Goodyear or Michelin. Presumably not Continental. Mr Continental.

Cohen opened a laptop and typed away. 'Ah ha,' he said. 'Well, we do have Mr Conquest on our files.'

Despite himself, Whiteside nearly jumped with surprise. He hadn't been expecting that.

Cohen swivelled the screen round for Whiteside to see. 'Do you read Hebrew?'

'Unfortunately not.'

'Never mind. I'm sure you can use shorthand,' said Cohen, nodding at Whiteside's notebook.

At that moment there was a knock on the door and Celia Westermann came in with coffee. Whiteside glanced at her. She looked so self-effacing he had the strange sensation again that, like the clothes, it was some kind of act. She behaved as if she was playing a secretary from the past. Cohen ignored her. Perhaps this was normal for the institute. As she busied herself pouring the coffee, Whiteside wondered if journalists these days did know shorthand. It sounded archaic. He wondered if it was some kind of joke by Cohen, like an apprentice being sent to buy tartan paint or a sky-hook.

'I'll just record what you say on my phone, Dr Cohen. Dyslexia,' he said ruefully by way of explanation. 'Dyslexia, a journalist's nightmare, Doctor.'

Cohen nodded. It was now obvious to Whiteside he didn't believe a word of anything he said.

'Well, well, here he is.' Cohen pointed to the sturdy Hebrew characters filling the screen with the end of a biro. Whiteside looked suitably blank. 'Better switch your phone on then, Mr Dunlop,' said Cohen. There was now surely no mistaking the ironic inflection in the elderly Jew's voice. He looked at Celia. 'Do you want to stay, Celia?'

'No, Dr Cohen,' she said. 'I've got things to do.' She smiled benignly at Whiteside and left the room.

The gist of Cohen's file entry was short and to the point. Conquest had been born in Lewisham in South London in the early Sixties. He had left school at fifteen. In the late Seventies, aged seventeen, he'd joined the Hell's Angels, what later became the infamous Windsor Chapter, and also become a member of Combat 18.

'What's that?' Whiteside had asked sharply. He'd never heard of them, but the number caught his ear. It was part of what Hanlon had wanted him to ask about. Cohen's reply was, '18 is 1 + 8. What's the first letter of the alphabet? Mr Dunlop?'

'A,' said Whiteside.

'That's right, and now the eighth?' 'H.'

'Mm hm,' said Cohen. 'Put them together and you have A.

H. Now, who do you think that might possibly refer to?' 'Adolf Hitler,' said Whiteside. Cohen nodded happily. Well,

he thought. Hanlon was right. He also thought, so what? Conquest liked Nazis.

Cohen explained that Combat 18 was a small and disorganized racist group. The members were more of a threat to themselves than anyone else. Very much so. In fact, their founder was inside for murder, having killed a fellow member in some internal dispute. At the time, the major right-wing party, the then BNP equivalent, was the National Front, but Combat 18 believed in direct action. Luckily, the only people they had killed were each other.

In 1980 Conquest served a year at Feltham for petrol-bombing a synagogue in Stamford Hill. It was this that had brought him to the attention of the Shapiro Institute. All UK anti-Semitic attacks were logged by them and this one had their highest rating in terms of threat level. In 1982 he was acquitted of dealing Class A substances (amphetamines) and in 1985 he was acquitted of armed robbery of a Hatton Garden jewellers. 'A Jewish business,' said Cohen. In both the last two cases, witness intimidation and tampering with evidence had been cited as the reasons for the trials' collapse.

This was more like it, thought Whiteside. Ludgate could hang out with former Nazis till the cows came home; for all

anyone knew Conquest had long changed his political or racist views, or become a Buddhist, an advocate of rational peace and harmony, but consorting with a drug-dealing armed robber would take some explaining.

In 1985 he started Albion Property, funded, according to the file, by the robbery proceeds. And that, said Cohen, is more or less that. He disappeared off our radar. He looked at Whiteside's impassive face.

Whiteside considered the implications of what he'd just learnt. For Whiteside, the absence of Conquest's record from the PNC was the most important thing. It was a very serious matter indeed. He remembered the year before a court official had been sent down for three years for taking bribes to delete motoring offences from the police national database. He knew too, historically, that a great deal of police information had been transferred from paper records to fledgling computer systems in the early Eighties and a lot of low-grade crime records had simply been destroyed or junked. They'd been deemed not worthy of keeping. Conquest's records were too important for that. Someone in the criminal records system had deliberately removed them. Conquest had to have had some serious influence.

Well, Hanlon had been proved right. Conquest did have a

record. He was, or had been, dirty. He wondered, though, if what he'd learnt was remotely important. It could be argued that Conquest was a triumph of the system. He had done time for his crimes, well, one of them anyway, and had built himself a success-ful, legitimate, life. But he knew Hanlon too well for her to be satis-fied with that. Hanlon believed that, on the whole, leopards don't change their spots. Something else was going on other than redemption for Conquest to have paid a great deal of money to have his records expunged. Property was a good way

to launder money. He thought of Conquest's lavish lifestyle, the former connections with drug dealing. He remembered what

Hanlon had said about the money he was spending outstripping the reported income. He guessed that's what Hanlon was assuming, money laundering, but he didn't know.

If Hanlon had any faults in Whiteside's opinion, it was that she played her cards too close to her chest. But then again, Whiteside wasn't overly concerned with larger pictures. One thought occurred to him as he switched his phone off.

'Dr Cohen, does that file mention any known associates?'

Cohen glanced at the screen. 'He set up Albion, the name of his business – the poet Blake would be turning in his grave

– with a partner, a Paul Bingham, in the Eighties, but there's no more mention of him.'

Whiteside felt a surge of elation and excitement inside. Bingham. Paul Bingham, could it be? He struggled to keep the tension out of his expression. 'This Bingham, does he have a nickname?'

Cohen raised his eyebrows and peered at the screen. 'Yes, he does,' he said. Please God, please let it be Rabbit, prayed Whiteside. 'Rabbit. Does that help?'

'Yes, yes, it does,' said Whiteside. Oh my God, yes, it does. 'Will there be anything else?' Cohen asked.

Whiteside shook his head. Rabbit Bingham. No wonder Conquest wanted any criminal details keeping off his record. If Conquest was involved with crime it was something far more disturbing than drugs. Far worse. He could see now why Conquest would do anything to keep off the police radar. No wonder he was trying to find out what the DI wanted the other night. He must have been shitting himself when Hanlon, a woman with a fearsome reputation for direct action, had turned up on his doorstep.

'Thank you very much for your time, Dr Cohen. I'll see myself out.' Whiteside could have punched the air with elation. Bingham!

As he walked down the stairs Whiteside thought, now I know what you're thinking, Hanlon. Child sex abuse and murder. You lift a stone and what do you find under it. Rabbit Bingham. And now Conquest. He couldn't wait to see Hanlon's face.

When she was delighted, she would raise her left eyebrow. Grim satisfaction, Hanlon's version of happiness, was a wintery smile. What he now had was maybe enough for the two together. As soon as he was outside in the street he phoned the DI. Her phone was switched off so he left a message. 'Ma'am, you were right. Most importantly, Rabbit Bingham, yes, that Rabbit Bingham, was one of Conquest's associates. Oh, last thing, that number question: 18 is A. H.' He wouldn't need to explain what that meant. Hanlon would know. Those bloody dogs of Conquest's. If he'd called them Rover and Spike, Whiteside

wouldn't even be at the institute.

Whiteside wasn't Hanlon. He didn't hide emotions. He grinned as he flagged down a taxi. Time to go home and celebrate.

Celia Westermann sat upstairs in what had been an attic room at the top of the building and watched Whiteside on one of the twelve CCTV monitors she had on her desk. Her face was no longer that of the amenable, put-upon drudge. It was implacable and cruel. There was no trace now of the downtrodden secretary. Invisible, a malignant ghost sitting at her desk, she had tracked Whiteside's progress on camera down the stairs, back through security, past Zev and Reuben, the guards on the door, and into the street. She clicked on the icon on her screen where she had herself accessed Conquest's file and picked up her

own phone while she looked at the image of Whiteside as he talked on his mobile.

People say that there are two requisites for betrayal: love and hate. Eta Westermann, Celia's mother, had dementia. Physically, she was fit for her age, she could live for years, but mentally was another story. She was a seventy-eight-year-old baby. She had a baby's needs: nappies, washing, feeding, attention. The home that she was in was wonderful. The staff were highly trained and motivated, the building light, airy, clean. It was also extremely expensive. Celia could not afford it on her salary. That was where the love came in. Then there was the flip side of love.

Celia felt she practically ran the institute. She had been here for twenty-six years now, running virtually all of the administration, from IT to wages, and got as much thanks as the expensive computer equipment that surrounded her. Less maybe. She was regarded by the predominantly male workforce as an old maid, practically pitiable despite the fact she probably did three people's jobs. Indeed, to replace her, they would need three people. Zev and Reuben earned more than she did – she authorized their pay checks for God's sake, and what did their jobs entail, looking menacing and checking bags. A dog could do that job. A chimpanzee could do it. A retard could do it. And they had the gall to look down their noses at her.

Almost a year ago a bill from the home had arrived that she simply couldn't pay. The next day she took out a bridging loan from her bank and the same evening, accessing the institute's encrypted files, worked out who was selected for 'action' by the London branch of Shin Bet, Israeli intelligence. She chose one of three names. With the recent assassinations of scientists in Tehran still fresh in Muslim minds, the person concerned was more than grateful for the tip-off.

Payment from the Arab had been swift and generous. Since then, each transaction becoming morally and practically easier, she had done it three times more. Today would be her fifth. From another database, she accessed Conquest's mobile number and called it. He answered immediately. Celia liked that in a man. He was curious to know who the unknown caller was. She told him why she was calling, using a voice changer to disguise herself. It was a man's robotic voice that read out over the phone to an increasingly disturbed Conquest the contents of his file. For a price she would give him the name and address of the journalist who'd accessed it. Payment would also ensure she kept an eye on any further access of his details, which she would pass on.

Conquest agreed, as she'd known he would. How could he refuse? Her screen showed the bank balance of the account she had set up to handle these transactions. Within a couple of minutes the balance increased dramatically and she gave him Dunlop's name and his address from his business card. She hung up. What Conquest did with the information was up to him. Mother had another six months of care.

Well, *lekh tizdayen*, Zev and Reuben. *Lekh tizdayen*, Dr Cohen, and *lekh tizdayen*, Shapiro Institute, and *lekh tizdayen*, Mr Dunlop. She almost giggled at herself. She never swore usually.

Celia Westermann checked she had left no trace of her recent activities on the computer system. She was as thorough as she was unappreciated. Then she went downstairs to fetch the coffee cups from Cohen's office. She was a tidy woman.

The address that Enver had for Mehmet and his family was in a depressed-looking street just off White Hart Lane, where a rough area of Wood Green shades into a slightly rougher area of Tottenham. It was the kind of place he had grown up in. The kind of place where you joined a gang to get girls, money, respect, to avoid getting targeted and, perhaps most importantly, to fit in with the others. Peer pressure is huge when you're young. It's also one of the peculiarities of life in a city, particularly when you live on or near an estate, that there's an almost village-like sense of agoraphobia. Enver still knew grown men he'd been at school with who had hardly ever ventured out of Tottenham, more specifically their area of Tottenham. Turkish kids don't stray into Greek Tottenham and vice versa. They'd re-created the kind of no-go areas their Cypriot parents had moved to Britain to avoid.

The afternoon was sunny for once; it had been a grey, cold, wet spring and the May sunshine transformed even this North London road into somewhere almost pleasant.

Hanlon parked her Audi A3 with practised skill and the two of them got out of the car. A group of youths eyed them curiously. In this kind of neighbourhood strangers were few and far between. You didn't visit unless you had to. Hanlon's car itself stood out from the others parked by the kerb. We might

as well have come in a marked police car, thought Enver. That's the only time anyone round here sees a roadworthy vehicle, if it's the Old Bill, a drug dealer or social workers. He wondered if the car would be intact when they returned, or if it would be keyed or otherwise damaged. They should have brought a uniform to look after it.

It was these kinds of streets that had made Enver a boxer. He had been a quiet, pudgy child and he had never really fitted in with the other Turkish kids. He used to think it was because, like Mehmet, his parents were Turkish, although from Rize province, not Cappadocia, and the other kids were from North Cypriot backgrounds. Now he was older, much older, he thought it was probably nothing to do with that, he just didn't join gangs. He wasn't that kind of person. Because he lacked the protection, the security, of being in a gang, he signed up for boxing classes that were held by the ABA in the local church hall. It was there he discovered he had a talent for it.

How far he would have got he would never know. He'd had a good amateur record and when injury stopped him, he'd had eight pro fights, winning all of them. It was a promising start. He had been known more as a puncher than a boxer, that's to say he was ponderous in the ring but one good blow from Enver could, and did, end fights. 'Iron Hand' was the right fighting name for him.

He looked at Hanlon and thought that in her dark jeans, training shoes and black bomber jacket, she maybe looked more like a female bouncer from one of Tottenham's tougher clubs than a police officer. To his annoyance, he was still acutely aware of her body under her tight-fitting, expensive-looking shirt. Less controversially, he was also acutely aware of his own body. He could feel his stomach pressing against his belt. He was wearing a cheap, dark blue suit, made of a slightly

shiny, cheap fabric, and a garish patterned tie. And I suppose I could be the fat, Turkish club owner, not a very successful one at that. Some dive in King's Cross. All I lack is the cheap aftershave and the two-tone shoes and maybe a gold tooth and some Samsun cigarettes.

There was a parade of three shops in the street between the houses. The kind of shops you find in a place like this – a Bargain Booze, a Pakistani grocer and a newsagent. There was a tough-looking, battered pub at the end of the road. Mehmet's address was above the newsagent. They went round the back, into the service lane behind the shops, with overflowing green plastic wheelie bins and piles of stacked-up empty boxes and plastic crates. There was a strong smell of rotting food and urine. Between a couple of the shuttered and graffitied back doors to the retail premises there was a flight of metal stairs that gave access to the roof above the shops where the flats were. Hanlon led the way, almost floating up the stairs, while Enver, his knees protesting, panted up after her. The stairs seemed interminable. Over a low parapet the roof spread out in front of them, left and right like a terrace. Facing them were the backs of the flats, each with its own door. Outside the middle flat, sitting leaning forward on an old plastic chair, was a scrawny white-haired pensioner in a string vest, once white, now a piss-coloured yellow, and stained, grey baggy trousers, smoking a cigarette. Faded blue and green marks, old tattoos long since blurred, discoloured the slack skin on his thin arms. A smell of cabbage and old, rancid fat was exhaled by the open doorway. He screwed his face up inquisitively as Enver and Hanlon appeared over the parapet and stood framed

against the skyline.

'You're with the Environmental Health as well? Cos your mates left half an hour ago.' The old man hawked phlegm and

spat a large green gob of mucus offensively close to Enver's shoe. His tone was aggressive and unpleasant.

He and Hanlon exchanged a quick, worried glance. Hanlon wordlessly strode to the far left door.

'We're police,' said Enver, producing his warrant card. The old man spat again. He was unimpressed.

'Screaming and shaartin', jabbering away in their facking lingo. Paki Turk bastards, coming over here. They should be arrested. Forrin bastards.' The pensioner's red-rimmed, rheumy eyes were full of hate. 'Taking our jobs!'

Enver shook his head and went to join Hanlon. Her face was devoid of expression, stonier than ever. Hanlon tried the door, locked, on its latch. She shrugged and rang the bell. They listened to its buzz. It had that mournful sound that a bell makes in an empty house. A bell that there is no one to hear. They looked at each other. They both knew nobody would answer.

The pensioner filled them in on events, like a solo, senile, Greek chorus. 'Three big bin bags they took away, the caarncil done. Oh, they can find the money for the effnics.' He repeated the word for emphasis. 'The effnics, for the gippos, what abart the whites, that's what I say. Bet it was food what they was hoarding. Attracts the rats, hoarding does.' The old man smacked his lips on the word 'hoarding' as if it gave him pleasure. He overemphasized the 'h', Hoarding, for emphasis. 'Facking forrin hoarders. Oi, you, I'm talking to you.' He pointed a shaking finger at them. 'No bleeding respect. Not these days.'

With no warning, in one fluid motion that Enver guessed took under a second, Hanlon drew her right knee up to her chest, pivoted on her left leg and lashed out with her right foot. There was a very loud crash and the door flew open.

Hanlon, followed by Enver, strode in. Enver remained by the door as Hanlon moved carefully through the flat, touching nothing, anxious not to contaminate what they both felt would be a crime scene. It took less than a minute to ascertain the flat

– one bedroom, lounge, kitchen, bathroom – was empty. It was as they had suspected, as they feared. The small galley kitchen was a wreck. There was smashed crockery and cutlery on the floor to the right of the sink. On the work surface a jar of instant coffee had smashed, milk and soft drink bottles lay on their sides. There were other food items on the floor too, stepped on and squashed on to the cheap linoleum. The kitchen was directly in line to the door. Hanlon guessed that Mehmet had answered the door and then been slammed backwards into the kitchen where the struggle had taken place. She could imagine it happening, the door opening and the attacker's shoulder thudding into the body of the unsuspecting man. It's how she would have done it. There was a sizeable pool of blood on the countertop. Hanlon examined it, careful not to touch anything. The epicentre of the blood was on the edge of the work surface. The cheap wooden laminate had splintered under a terrific impact and Hanlon could see shreds of skin and some coarse black hairs adhering to the surface of the counter. She guessed that it was Mehmet's forehead that had been slammed down into the wood at hairline level. The force of such a blow, hard enough to break chipboard, would probably have killed him, certainly he'd have lost consciousness. She crouched down to look further. The other two, Nur and the little girl would be easier to subdue, particularly once they'd seen Mehmet's skull cracked open, his

body slumping to the floor.

'Ma'am,' called Enver.

She left the kitchen and joined him in the doorway of the neighbouring room. They didn't go in. Inside the small living

room were more signs of a struggle, less dramatic, equally

depressing to the two police. The old sofa was beige. On the floor was a bloodstained cushion. A coffee table had been upset. Broken glass from little dainty cups shone in the sun coming through the windows. On a battered old sideboard was an embroidered lace cloth and a plastic model of the Sultan Ahmed mosque in Istanbul. There was an electrical cable coming out. It would light up. A souvenir of life in Turkey. Hanlon looked at the cushion. She guessed that the blood probably belonged to the wife, Nur. She shook her head sadly. The other room was the bedroom. She could see a cot from where she was standing that would have belonged to Baby Ali. There was a small mattress on the floor where Reyhan would have slept.

She went back into the kitchen.

On the floor, puddled with blood which had dripped off the counter, underneath the jutting ledge of the work surface, by the skirting board, was a small scrap of paper, torn, she guessed from a Turkish newspaper. Two words. Crouching down, she read them. Enver was putting his phone back in his pocket.

'Everyone's on their way, ma'am,' he said.

She nodded and they both went outside into the fresh air. Three bags. Three bodies. Hanlon's eyes narrowed. Someone knew they were coming and at what time. Someone had tipped them off. It had to come from their end, from the team investigating the Baby Ali murder. There really was no other possibility. She was glad now that she had told no one about her thoughts that the Baby Ali murder was connected to the Essex killing. They knew now they were not looking for a single perpetrator. Two men had done this. Paedophiles were normally organized, usually highly so, and they did operate in groups, but violence like this – direct, professional – from a paedophile was unheard of. This had more the hallmarks

of organized crime. It was no sex attack. It was an efficient, organized hit. It was the sort of thing the Andersons of this world did.

'Sergeant, what does "*on sekiz*" mean in Turkish?' she asked, referring to the words on the paper.

'Eighteen, ma'am.'

Hanlon nodded. She thought so. The images of memory obligingly lined up in her head. The pencilled eighteen on the bunker wall. The lock gate. Now this. The same number. The same killer. Different victims. There could be no shred of doubt now that they were the same perpetrator. Better make that plural. Well, she'd have to report this to Corrigan. He wouldn't be best pleased. Serial killings and a police informer. Not good. The unusually blue skies and hot sun overhead gave an almost Mediterranean feel to the roof in contrast to the darkness of the scene within the flat.

'Tell SOCO when they get here and start work there's a piece of paper under that counter I want bagged as evidence. I don't want it overlooked.' That would annoy them, she thought, being told how to do their job.

'Why take the bodies away, ma'am?' asked Enver in a puzzled voice.

Hanlon had worked paedophile and rape cases before in Special Crimes. Enver hadn't. Because the woman and daughter probably weren't dead yet, thought Hanlon. That would come later. That was the reason. Baby Ali had been assaulted numerous times but there was no DNA trace. Hanlon guessed that mother and daughter wouldn't be found. There would be no need for caution on their abductors' part. She didn't feel like going into it now.

'I'm not sure, Sergeant.' she said. 'What I am sure of is that we're looking for two powerfully built men. Three bodies carried down in a single trip. One presumably carried the man; the other, mother and daughter. That's a lot of kilos. I don't think it was the woman who abducted Ali that was involved. She wouldn't be physically capable.' Her voice was distracted. 'Anyway, Sergeant, I'll leave you to it. Right now, I've got things I need to do. I don't have to tell you your job. Do what needs doing. Tell whoever arrives to call me on my mobile or text me. I'll be back in the office later anyway. I can't see that I've got anything to add that you can't help them with.'

Enver registered the fact she was leaving without surprise. Like she said, it didn't need two of them to stay, but he was interested to notice his regret. There was something very reassuring about Hanlon's presence. More than that, he relished her presence.

'Do you know who did this, ma'am?' asked Enver. He looked hard into Hanlon's long face. It was as expressionless as ever, her eyes flinty-grey, impenetrable. He realized that was as much of an answer as he was likely to get.

'Oi, you two!' shouted the old man. They had forgotten about him. 'What was it then, rats?'

Hanlon, suddenly letting her anger off its leash, strode over to him. She'd had enough. 'Hello, darlin', come to make an old man happy,' he leered at Hanlon. She leant forward until her face was over his and he was suddenly aware of the sun being blocked out by her long, tangled, black hair that haloed her face. It was like a terrible eclipse. He looked up and saw her features transfixed by rage. It totally unnerved him. He had never seen anything like it. She looked inhuman, devoid of any feelings other than fury, her face a mask of pure anger, and then to his mental fear was added physical and he gasped in agony as Hanlon's long, shapely, immensely strong fingers crushed the ulnar nerve near his elbow, the so-called funny bone. It's painful enough when you bang it

on something; this was drawn-out pressure that hurt him like nothing he'd experienced in seventy-five years. He thought he was going to throw up with the pain. He cowered backwards in his seat as the pain mounted.

'I know where you live,' she hissed. 'Do you want me to come back and visit you? When there'll be just you and me? Do you?' He shook his head emphatically, pleadingly. Her face, a gorgon's mask, the features of Medusa, was almost touching his. He looked into her pitiless eyes as tears trickled down his face. 'My colleague will ask you some questions, I suggest you be helpful.' She released her grip.

Enver had seen her stoop momentarily over the old man and then, a couple of seconds later, stand up. He had absolutely no idea what had happened. He could see even at this distance the terror on the man's face. It was almost pantomime-like in its characterization of fear. He wondered what on earth she'd said to him.

Hanlon walked past him, radiating aggression and rage. 'Get a witness statement off him now he's in a cooperative mood. Remember to secure the crime scene. Nobody up here but police,' she snapped. 'I'm off to see Whiteside.'

Enver watched as she climbed gracefully down the steel staircase. Again, for the second time since he had met Hanlon, he felt a stab of jealousy directed at the other sergeant. He walked over to the old man who gave him a frightened, placatory smile. He cowered away from Enver, trying to make himself small in his chair.

'No 'ard feelings, eh, son,' he said, in a wheedling voice. 'No 'ard feelings.'

\* \* \*

Peter had tested his blood again in his cell earlier that morning. Five point eight, which was good. His initial panic at his

predicament had died down to a general unease coupled, strangely, with boredom. Peter felt he was a survivor. He had survived the illness and death of his father. He had survived type-one diabetes; every day was, in a sense, a triumph. Sixty odd years ago, before synthesized insulin, he'd have been dead too. He would survive this.

He had nothing to do in the cell other than stroke the brown and white spaniel and eat the food that was provided. So far it was supermarket packed sandwiches together with bottled water. Breakfast had been sausage sandwiches. He didn't like cold sausage but as a type-one diabetic he had to eat. He had given the dog its food that came in a bowl at the same time as his evening meal. There was a small, circular drain in the corner of the cell under the shower and the dog had, rather cleverly in Peter's eyes, decided to use that as its toilet. Cleaning up after the animal was simply a question of sluicing it away.

Beneath the unremitting light from the bulb that never went out, he was measuring time by the amount of insulin injections he was giving himself. It was four a day. He had kept aside an old hypodermic needle and he made a scratch on the wall every time he injected himself. His body had developed a rhythm over the past couple of years and he knew that his timings were pretty accurate. Besides, the blood-sugar levels themselves would let him know if he was miscalculating time. Without this diabetic clock he would have no idea of how long he'd been there. By counting the scratches, he did. There was no clock in the cell, he didn't have a watch, there was no natural light, and there was no background noise, nothing at all to provide a clue. All he had to measure the passing of time were the scratches on the wall. So far he had three of them, which meant he'd been there under twenty-four hours. Friday evening, Friday night, Saturday morning. By his reckoning, this made today Saturday

afternoon. He wondered what would happen when his insulin ran out. He had seven days' worth of NovoRapid insulin, more or less, the dose varied according to the amount of carbohydrate in his meal and what his blood-sugar levels were before he ate. He used the NovoRapid three times daily after meals. Usually at home and at school, he would calculate the dose of insulin by weighing his food. Here in the cell he didn't have any scales but fortunately, either by accident or design of his captors, he had the carb levels printed on the packaging of the sandwiches. He also had a week's supply of Glargine, the slow-release insulin he took at night. If he was in the cell longer than a week, he'd be in trouble. Well, he thought, perhaps I'll be free

by then. I certainly hope so.

What he couldn't understand was why he was there, why he was being held captive. Peter had tried various scenarios: kidnap, mistaken identity, terrorism; none of them made any sense. Why would anyone want him? The main thing, he decided, was to be brave, not to cry.

Having the dog helped enormously. He whispered his thoughts in its ear and shared his food with it. Perhaps when all this was over, his mum would let him keep the dog. Assuming they let the dog go with him. He was trying to think of a good name for him. It had to be worthy of the animal, something with a ring to it, something defiant.

And all the while the CCTV camera watched him. And fifty miles away in London, Lord Justice Reece periodically logged on to see how he was doing. He was looking forward to giving the boy what he needed, but anticipation was a huge part of the pleasure. He had rehearsed various scenarios in his head many times. Soon, he'd be able to put them into practice. It was what set us apart from the savages, in the judge's opinion. Deferred gratification.

He had to fly to Brussels that evening, but he'd be able to view the boy whenever he wanted on his laptop until they were finally together in the coming week. An Internet feed was such a boon. The wait would only increase the pleasure, particularly now he could see what Conquest had arranged for him. Conquest had surpassed himself. The child was perfect, perfect in every way.

The judge thought back to when he was a child the same age, a very different child. He hadn't been good-looking. 'Blubber lips', that's what the other boys had called him at his boarding school, as had most of the teachers. His parents had been equally dismissive. At home, the judge had felt like an unwelcome guest who'd overstayed his welcome. But the judge had survived the bullying and the beatings. He'd survived through hard work, intelligence and the fierce will that they would not crush him. Every exam passed with an A grade, the scholarship to Pembroke, the first-class degree, all were battles he had won to get back at them. And now his time had come. They would dance to his tune. Those prefects who had beaten him, who had devised excruciating torments for him, and were now the Establishment, let them dance and grovel. Those good-looking boys who would never have reciprocated the judge's schoolboy passions, let them dance the way he wanted them to dance.

He stared hungrily, lasciviously, at the boy's straw-blond
hair and licked his thin, juridical lips, lips that were so used to pronouncing judgements with pedantic, legal precision. Watching as the boy stroked the dog, the judge felt himself stiffen. Come Unto Me, that was how the school song had gone. And now he was calling the tune. It would be very soon now. Soon you will Come Unto Me, he thought. Very soon indeed.

## 19

In Germany, in Stuttgart, Kathy had finished her meeting with the line manager and the procurement director from the Siemens subsidiary, and she knew the contract was hers. The trip had gone far better than she could have anticipated. What was particularly pleasing was that the Germans had extended the contract period from three to five years. That was a huge, unexpected benefit to PFK. She was now looking forward to Monday to report to her company how things were going. Pleasant visions of the future danced across her imagination. She'd finish early and meet Peter from school and take him to the cinema for that new action film he wanted to see, the one she'd told him she wouldn't have time to take him to. She was sorely tempted to call her MD, Tim Morgan, at home to tell him the good news, but decided to leave it until she went in to work. She had a reputation for coolness that she was proud of and she didn't want to compromise it.

She was due back on the four o'clock flight to London and had accepted a lunch date from Max Brucker, the Siemens man. She had found herself the night before hoping that he would make a pass at her; she found him extremely attractive. She had spent a year mourning Dan; now she felt it was time to come out of her shell of bereavement. Nothing had happened last night but she knew that if he had tried anything, she'd

have flung herself on him. She wanted him very badly. She looked at her left hand. She was looking at her marriage band. Gently, she worked it off her finger. She held it in the palm of her hand, the golden symbol of her past life, and stroked the circular indentation it had left in the skin of the third finger. She said, 'I'm sorry, darling' to Dan's memory and undid the simple gold chain around her neck, then slid the wedding ring through and replaced the necklace. There, she had done it. It was a simple gesture, but a powerfully symbolic one. She was no longer married. She wondered if Max would notice. No, that wasn't true. She knew Max would notice. How could he not? It was why she'd done it. It was a signal as clear and unequivocal as the 'Please Make Up The Room' sign she would hang on her door handle when she vacated the room.

She was wearing her hair back in a ponytail today. It had

been her lucky hairstyle before she'd been married. Maybe it would work again. She knew she'd be back and forth to Germany with increasing regularity so there was no need to rush things. Then she thought, no, sod it, I've had enough of this. If he doesn't make a pass at me today, I'm going to make one at him. We're both adults after all, and I'm bloody attractive. She looked at herself in the mirror and pouted, then grinned at her reflection. She tossed her head and watched the ponytail bounce with the motion. I feel frisky, she thought. Who could ever have imagined. She felt happier than she'd done in ages.

She tried Annette's house again but got the answerphone and left a brief message about Peter, asking her to tell him she'd be picking him up from her house about seven. Annette's mobile number was on a business card that she'd left in her other purse so all she had programmed on her phone was the landline number.

Annette put down the two heavy bags of shopping with a thud on the kitchen table and filled the kettle to make tea. They were plastic bags and they eyed her reproachfully. The cupboard under the stairs contained the reusable hessian and jute organic shopping bags and a quantity of heavy-duty plastic Bags for Life that she'd bought over the years. These she inevitably forgot when she went to the supermarket. Her husband had taken Sam and his friends to the local swimming pool and the house would be mercifully quiet for the next couple of hours. Thank God, she thought. The house was wonderfully peaceful. She thought, I'll have a cup of tea and then I'll lie on the sofa and relax. God, that'll be wonderful. She yawned and checked her BlackBerry for messages. Nothing.

As she drank her tea she felt the soft, warm weight of Dizzy rolling on to her feet under the kitchen table. Stroking the dog's warm body with her toes, she thought suddenly of Peter Reynolds who adored the animal. She froze with the teacup in her hand as abruptly as if she were a TV image that had been paused on a remote. No, no, it couldn't be. She thought, I'm imagining things. Her heart started to pound like a trip hammer. Calm down, she thought, calm down.

She found she was holding her breath tightly. I'm having a panic attack, she thought. She forced herself to breathe deeply and evenly. She had suddenly remembered that Peter should have been at their place the night before. Or should he? Or was this a false memory? Did she think that, or did she think she thought she remembered he should have been there? Had it been discussed with Kathy and then dropped? Now she was confused between what had, and hadn't, been agreed. If she was supposed to have him, wouldn't Kathy have phoned by now? She felt very worried indeed. If she had agreed to take Peter and forgotten about it, where could he be? Perhaps he'd gone to

another friend's house. He had lots of friends, he was a popular boy. She looked again at the BlackBerry. Oh God, please let it not be the diabetes. Had he had an attack? Do you get attacks if you have diabetes? Surely Kathy would have phoned up about Peter if he was supposed to have been staying? Or emailed her? She always did that when she went away. She'd already thought that. She was going round in bloody circles. Run over, what if he'd been run over? Someone would have phoned, wouldn't they? James Ramsden's mother, she'd have phoned. She'd phone everyone about every-thing, like when Mrs Taylor the physics teacher left her husband for another woman. I just thought you ought to know. That was her catchphrase. Or it would have been on the news. She hadn't seen the news. Oh God, this was getting nightmarish. There had to be a perfectly normal explanation. The alternative was too dreadful to think about. It couldn't happen. They lived in Finchley, for God's sake.

This wasn't South London.

She had to grasp the nettle. She picked up the BlackBerry, looked at it, counted one, two, three, go! and called Kathy. She hadn't any idea what she would say to her. The best-case scenario would be Kathy saying something like 'hang on a minute, I'll just get Peter to turn the TV down.' Or maybe 'Annette, you dimwit, how could you have forgotten. Thank God Peter had the presence of mind to go to so-and-so's house.' That would be acceptable. Other-wise how do you say to another mother, 'Should I be looking after your child at this precise moment in time? I don't know where he is.'

She listened with a mixture of relief and worry to the ringtone giving way to voicemail. Hello, you have reached... Why do people say that? It's not a stop on the way to a destination, the way you might reach Coventry before you get to Birmingham. It was now a problem postponed, not a problem solved. She

emailed Kathy and started to agonize over the message. How do you word something like that? She settled on, 'Please phone me asap. Urgent.' That set the right tone at least, she thought. Her husband would be in the pool now with Sam. Sam might know, but he hadn't said anything last night. Did that mean anything? Should she go to the pool anyway and ask him? Annette felt paralysed with indecision. She sat at the table, her tea forgotten and growing cold, staring at the BlackBerry.

Kathy had turned her mobile and her BlackBerry off. She found it passionately annoying when people she was with in restaurants left theirs on. It was so rude. Particularly when they lined them up in front of them like an uninvited guest. She was early for her lunch date with Max and was enjoying sitting by herself at a table, looking out of the window at Schillerplatz and the busy shopping streets of central Stuttgart. She liked people-watching. There was a heavy gilt mirror on the wall opposite and she could see her reflection, a tall, slim woman with an enviable figure and her lucky ponytail. She thought about the contract she'd won, she thought about Max. I'll have a glass of champagne, she thought. Why not? It's not every day you have something to celebrate. She looked at her naked left ring finger; she felt incredibly daring. Her heartbeat increased with pleasurable excitement.

'*Entschuldigung,*' she said, stopping a waiter.

The hatch in the bottom of Peter's door opened and a tray was pushed in. It must be lunchtime, thought Peter. The hatch closed and he took the tray over to the ledge where the blue mat was. The dog watched with interest. He knew it was food. Peter sat down and picked up the small device that tested the sugar level in his blood. He pricked his finger to get a drop of

blood, touched it with a testing strip and fed it into the small Accu-Chek machine. The digital readout was a five point one. Peter shook his head ruefully. Imprisonment seemed to be very good for him somehow. He looked at the sandwiches: chicken salad. The spaniel looked at him expectantly and licked his lips. Tito, thought Peter suddenly with delight, that's what I'll call you, like the Yugoslav partisan leader we did in history, the one who later became president.

'Hello, Tito,' he said and ruffled the dog's fur. Tito looked at him adoringly and wagged his tail. The two of them shared the sandwiches in companionable silence.

Above him the camera watched silently and in his bedroom, his packing complete, the judge watched the boy eat his sandwiches. He stared in rapturous fascination at the boy's full lips and beautiful mouth. His breathing quickened. Soon, you little bitch, soon, he thought.

## 20

Whiteside had paid off the taxi and let himself into his flat. He now looked out of the large sash window of his first-floor living room on to the generously proportioned grey Victorian town houses opposite. He was still euphoric at the way his morning at the Shapiro Institute had gone. Whiteside, loyal as he was, had been doubtful about Hanlon's theory that Conquest would be criminally dirty. Dirty, yes, but it was a question of degree. Everyone was, to a greater or lesser extent. Hanlon herself flagrantly flouted the rules as if they didn't apply to her. True, she wasn't motivated by money, but money, thought Whiteside, is just a means to happiness and fulfilment and so is altruism. She'd framed, well, entrapped Cunningham to get to Anderson. That was a criminal act in itself. He still had the ex-drug dealer's clothes that he'd liberated from the property store. That was theft. Where do you draw the line? He expected a certain amount of venality from any property speculator. Tax evasion, bribery disguised as 'presentations' in expensive hotels in exotic or luxurious locations. It wasn't as if it was just the property sector. Everyone was at it. The Met weren't immune either. Amazing the interest an inter-police liaison forum could create when it was held in the Caribbean in the winter. These were the kinds of things he expected Conquest to be mixed up in. Possibly even direct bribery of local housing authority officials.

What he hadn't expected were arson attacks on synagogues, more because of the unusual commitment to violence than anything, drug dealing and other armed robbery. That was one of the virtues of a Bishops Avenue address, he guessed. You wouldn't be thought of as a gangland criminal. Arms dealer, maybe; armed robber, no way. In many ways, thought Whiteside, I'm being a bit naive. Now I come to think of it I can recall at least one other multi-millionaire tycoon with an equally chequered past. Well, I'll talk about it with Hanlon later. It'll be the Rabbit Bingham connection that will interest her. Now that is something unusual.

Whiteside went into his small kitchen, opened the fridge and poured himself a glass of Sauvignon Blanc, returned to the lounge and stared out of the window again at the houses opposite. There was hardly any movement in the street. When it was hot, which it was at the moment, London was torpid. Like a reptile, the city dozed in the heat. Upper Holloway was quiet today. Down at the other end of the Holloway Road at Highbury and Islington, where Upper Street began, it would be a different story. There, the affluent young middle-aged would be out feeding their addiction to contemporary or retro furniture and *objets trouvés*. They'd be sitting outside the bars and cafes or pubs with their Farrow & Ball paint jobs, discussing the new developments at the Tate, the Tanks, the Turner or politics. Islington was getting staid now; it was old hat. The hipsters and medianistas had moved to Old Street or were reclaiming King's Cross. The more adventurous were going south of the river. The iconic Hoxton White Cube was closing.

Whiteside loved London. North London anyway; he felt out of touch in East, West or South London. If he could have afforded it, Hampstead would be his ideal location, but it was way, way out of his price range, which is how he'd ended up

here. Holloway is probably best known for its women's prison but it had come into being as a Victorian middle-class suburb, large town houses in a then far-flung area of London.

In later years most of these houses had been divided into flats. Irish immigrants had moved in; Johnny Rotten, he seemed to remember, was from here. One of these days he'd get a blue plaque. Now there were more diverse incomers but the area still retained its architectural beauty despite the house conversions. The streets, by London standards, were wide. It had a spacious, airy feel. He'd come to like it very much. It was relaxing.

His phone beeped to say he had mail. He checked it. It was from the Shapiro Institute to say Dr Cohen had some documents for him that he was sending over. The text explained they couldn't email them because they had to be signed for.

He replied to confirm he'd be in.

He drank another mouthful of wine to toast the success of the day. He wondered what they could be about. Conquest, maybe. The Sauvignon was clean and robust against his palate. He thought of 'Rabbit' Bingham. He wasn't clean and robust. He conjured up Bingham's face, his scant fair hair brushed over his balding head. His pale, pudgy body. What was startling about Bingham was his charm. The word 'monster' normally follows 'paedophile' but Bingham wasn't monstrous, he was utterly charming. That was the problem, really. Self-deprecating, witty, humorous; if Whiteside had children he'd probably have entrusted them to Bingham without a second's thought.

He'd met Hanlon on that case, when he was working briefly

for the Met's child abuse unit. Hanlon had been investigating a child prostitution murder. Like many paedophiles, Bingham had been uncomfortably bright, and, now he remembered, quite wealthy. He thought of Conquest immediately. Money for services rendered? Was it possible that Conquest was a fellow

paedophile? Bingham had worked in IT, he remembered that much. He remembered too that Hanlon had looked into the source of Bingham's money and drawn a blank. There was a conspicuous gap between Bingham's earned income and his lifestyle. Hanlon had been sure he was dealing in child porn via secure subscriber websites. The CPS hadn't been interested in that. Everyone just wanted Bingham sent down with the maximum speed and the minimum fuss. Bingham, like many paedophiles, was very good at hiding things. They'd only arrested him because of a tip-off. Bingham would still be free if it hadn't been for that.

Bingham had been jailed in the end for possessing several thousand graphic, sexual images of children and babies. Some of these were now irrevocably lodged in Whitehead's own memory. Before he'd joined the unit he didn't know how you had sex with a baby, now he did, and he would have to live with that knowledge for the rest of his life. He'd never really understood the true meaning of depravity until he had seen those images. Unfortunately, they had proved unforgettable. It was the only time in his life he had ever experienced such levels of rage and disgust at others that he'd felt truly murderous. He had looked into the face of true evil. The charming face of 'Rabbit' Bingham. For weeks, months even, after he left the unit he'd felt defiled.

Whiteside, however, was not telepathic. He had no way of

reading minds. Other people too had been irrevocably affected by Bingham's trial. Lord Justice Reece had been the trial judge. He too had seen the images but he'd drawn very different conclusions from Whiteside, very different indeed.

The judge had pored over them in the rooms reserved for him in the court building. For years he had fought against this side of his nature and refused to acknowledge it to himself. Only when he'd been drunk had he allowed himself to think about children. But now the forces inside him were too powerful to control and he felt as if this trial had been sent to free him, to liberate him. The serpent had proffered the apple: take, eat of this fruit of knowledge. And the judge did. And it was good. He could hear the old school song 'Come Unto Me' as they'd sung it in chapel all those years ago, ringing in his ears.

He'd stared at the pictures. The delicate, innocent flesh excited him tremendously. At first he'd resisted, but Bingham's photo collections were the sexiest, most erotic things he had ever imagined in his life. The pictures gave him a window on a world he had never seen before. He'd intuited its existence but he had never dreamed that such nirvana was attainable, and Bingham had been there. They were the most arousing pictures he had ever seen. Bingham was like an explorer who had returned from an unknown continent that the judge longed to visit.

He was extremely grateful for the prosecuting QC who had insisted on the most extreme descriptions and illustrations of the degrading sexual acts that had been forced on the children. Bingham's defence lawyer had kept up a barrage of 'objection', Reece a counter-offensive of 'overruled'. The QC's intention had been to ensure, without any shred of doubt, the hideous guilt of the defendant in the minds of the jury. The judge had found these commentaries and pictures incredibly erotic. He'd wanted more. He'd been profoundly grateful for the fact he wore long robes during the trial.

At one point his eyes had met Bingham's. In the course of his legal career the judge had done this countless times. This was different. Bingham had recognized a true soulmate. He made no sign to the judge. There was no smile or nod of the head, it was just a look, but it had been enough. They both knew

what it meant. The jury, the audience in the gallery, the lawyers and court officials all had seemed suddenly insubstantial. He knows, he'd thought with a shock, he knows. Like calls to like. After the trial Reece had discreetly used his lobbying power and got himself appointed as the legal expert on a parliamentary committee to look into paedophilia. The authorities were delighted that such a senior figure had been so public spirited to volunteer for such a depressing job. He'd used it to engineer

a meeting with Bingham.

'Hello, Judge,' Bingham had said with a knowing smirk when they finally met.

* * *

There was a ring at the doorbell in Whiteside's flat. That must be Cohen's messenger, he thought, and pressed the button to let them in.

## 21

The first time Clarissa had seen, felt and handled the Makarov handgun (Eastern European, as predicted by Corrigan) had been a moment of true love. She had never seen a handgun in real life before. She was so used to the visual reality from TV and film that she expected it to have no real resonance, for it to be just a tool, like a cooker or an iPod. Far from it.

First of all was the physical beauty of the weapon, which she hadn't been expecting. Form follows function and good design has a timeless, classic grace. The gun had grace. It was a fairly standard-looking automatic and quite small, an ideal size for Clarissa. Its black metal body was sleek and functional. It smelt of oil, a scent she was unused to, slick and heavy. It gleamed dully when she held it to the light. She had balanced it in her palm and felt its weight with fascination: 700 grams, she learnt later. That 700 grams was nearly the weight of a large bag of sugar, but concentrated in the small frame of the gun it felt supernaturally heavy.

Conquest had shown her how to load the magazine, sliding the 9 mm bullets into its spring-activated mechanism. He knew the

Makarov well. It had been a standard-issue firearm in Eastern Europe in the old communist days, and a large number of the guns were still in circulation. They were cheap and reliable. This one had cost Conquest 300 pounds, coincidentally

the same sum he'd spent on the same night entertaining a client at the Ritz.

In Clarissa's eyes, each glowing copper-jacketed bullet with its lead tip looked like a miniature, deadly, metal lipstick. Loaded, it felt physically not that much heavier, but emotionally, well, that was a different story. Holding the handgun, she was now more than the equal of any unarmed man. She could walk up to someone like Mike Tyson, pull the trigger nine times – the gun was semi-automatic – and there would be no need of a referee's count to decide the outcome. Holding the gun was power. Holding the gun was freedom. Holding the gun was heaven.

Firing it for the first time was a sexual thrill. She felt it in the same visceral, physical way. In some ways it was more exciting than that physical act. Even the actions were arousing. Pulling the trigger was like a metaphor for sex. Even the wording, 'pulling the trigger', sounded like a sexual reference.

He showed her on the range he had on the island how to shoot. The stance, 'You can always tell a good shooter, he stands like a gay man,' he had told her. The grip, how to pull the trigger; most importantly, how to breathe when she aimed. Hold your breath when you align the sight, he'd said. She'd taken it all in and then almost cried out in frustration as the empty glass bottle and cans he had put out at a ten metre distance stood unscathed as every shot she fired missed.

Conquest had smiled at her incompetence. Don't snatch the trigger, he had said, be gentle. Squeeze it gently. The gun will do the work.

She had improved since then, and today she would be firing into a man's body from a distance of probably under a metre. She couldn't miss.

Bald Paul, another of Conquest's employees, a mate from the old days, who lived at the lodge house opposite the island,

had dropped her off a mile away from Whiteside's in Upper Holloway. She checked her reflection out as she walked past a shop window: shoulder-length, blonde hair, large red-framed sunglasses, short denim skirt, ankle boots. Anyone looking closely at her face would not have seen the scar between her eyes, she'd foundationed over that, she would never make that mistake again. She knew that soon all the CCTV around here would be searched again and again. She was carrying a canvas tote bag with her, the gun inside. She walked round the corner into Whiteside's street.

It was now lunchtime and the pavements were eerily deserted. The day was unusually hot and hardly a breath of air moved in the streets of Holloway. The lime trees stood like silent silver pillars, their bark bleached and peeling in the bright sunlight. It was fairy-tale-like, as if North London were holding its breath, as if some enchantment had sent everyone to sleep.

She walked up the steps to the heavy front door of the house that Whiteside lived in and rang the bell that had his name beside it and the words 'Flat One'. There was a noise from the buzzer and a click from the lock as it sprang open. She was obviously expected. Conquest's text had done the work. She walked into the spacious hall, through the door with his flat number beside it, which stood ajar, and then gently closed it behind her with her foot. She was careful not to touch anything. After she'd finished, the place would be forensically examined in minute detail. She walked up the narrow flight of stairs to the first-floor flat, heart thudding, hardly able to breathe.

Lights. Camera. Action. She thought: take one. The victim's
flat.

'Hi!' she said brightly to the figure framed in the doorway above,
filling the space, who stood looking down at her. In

the flesh the journalist looked frighteningly unstoppable, the
kind of man who could absorb bullets. She hadn't expected him to
be so big; he looked huge. The Makarov had been highly effective
against tin cans and empty wine bottles. It had punched holes in
paper targets. Would it be any good against him? Her heart was
racing now and her mouth was very dry. She badly needed some
water. She wondered if she would be able to speak.

'Come in,' he said and she suddenly thought, what if he's not
alone? What am I going to do then? She started sweating and she
felt faint. Clarissa's training as an actress meant she was unusually
good at detecting what was real from what was false in the image
that people projected. She was really good at detecting bullshit.
There was none here. He wasn't playing a role. He wasn't just
tough-looking; he was tough. She had a mad desire to just give up,
run out of the door or, even more crazily, give him the gun and
surrender herself to him. I must do this quickly before I lose it, she
thought to herself.

She slid her right hand inside the canvas bag she was carrying
and tightened it around the butt and the trigger. The feel of the gun
lifted her spirits. She remembered Conquest getting her to shoot a
watermelon, the massive damage the small bullet had inflicted.
There was a tiny hole on the outside but when they'd looked inside,
there you could see what it had done. Whiteside's formidable
muscles would no more deflect the bullet than the skin of the fruit.
He led the way along a short narrow corridor, past a bedroom and a
bathroom. Both had their doors ajar; both, she noted, were empty.
Then a narrow galley kitchen to the right, again, unoccupied.
Ahead, at the end of the corridor was what looked like a study. This

had no door, it had obviously been removed to create an illusion of more space, and that too was empty. She felt her spirits rise.

They moved into the living room, its huge windows flooding the room with light. They were alone. Relief flooded through her. Clarissa felt calm and in control. She knew now everything would be all right. She smiled at the man standing before her. 'So,' said Whiteside. It was the last word, the last syllable he would say to Clarissa. He had turned away, maybe to open a window, and his back was to her. She took the gun in a calm, easy motion from the bag, slid the safety off, and – remembering to squeeze, not snatch, the trigger, be gentle and let the gun do the work – shot him in the back at a distance of a metre

and a half.

The gun kicked in her hand and the shot made a noise like a loud, dry crack. The bullet caught him, not in the spine which was what she had aimed for, but in the side. The shiny, bright copper-coloured shell casing was spat out by the gun and she caught an intoxicating smell of the smoke from the gunpowder as it rose out of the pistol. Whiteside felt as if he'd been hit with a sledgehammer. He staggered forward as if pushed by an invisible hand and turned. Clarissa took a step forward, and this time shot him in the stomach. Whiteside's legs gave way and he crashed backwards on to the floor as if he'd sat on an invisible, non-existent chair. She was smiling now. Everything was working brilliantly. He made no sound. Automatically, he put a hand over the entry wound and dark-red blood seeped through his fingers. He watched as it soaked into the carpet. He felt no pain. Stupidly, he found himself thinking, that stain's going to be hard to shift. There was a roaring in his ears and he felt as though he was falling. He had an overwhelming sense of unreality crashing over him like a wave in slow motion. This can't be happening, he thought.

He turned his head to look at Clarissa. She looked down

at him triumphantly, sprawled on the carpet of his flat, which was gently absorbing his life blood. She had won, he had lost. All that muscle, all that experience, all that character, all that crime-fighting expertise reduced to, what? A human rag doll. Her lips were parted and her eyes glinted with excitement as she carefully sighted the gun, and that was the last thing Whiteside saw as he lay there helplessly, the black hole at the end of the handgun's barrel, the eye of the Makarov. Then her third 9 mm bullet hit him in the face and he knew no more.

She shook her head to clear it. Time had ceased to mean anything. Clarissa felt as if the last couple of minutes had extended for hours, but a glance at her watch confirmed that it really was only a hundred or so seconds. She glanced briefly at the man lying on the floor, dead or dying. Blood was still oozing out of him and she avoided looking at what was left of his face, which was now a bloody mask. She slid the safety catch on to the pistol, put it in her bag and pulled on a pair of latex gloves that she had in her pocket.

First of all she quickly retrieved the three casings from the shots she'd fired and put them in her bag. His mobile was ridiculously easy to find, lying on the coffee table. She had his number programmed into hers and she quickly called it, just in case he had more than one phone, but it rang immediately. That was the phone she was after. She switched it off and put it into her bag. Next to where the mobile had been was his wallet. She added that to the bag. Then she pulled off her blonde wig and dropped it into her bag too, followed by the sunglasses, and slipped a pair of small, heavy-framed glasses on to her face. Transformed from blonde siren to dark-haired intellectual, she let herself out of the flat, peeling off and pocketing the gloves at the last minute as the front door closed behind her.

As she walked down the street, she passed Constable Childs on his way to Whiteside's flat. Childs didn't notice her. He was a man very much in love, with sex on his mind. His libido was rampant, he was as hot as the surrounding streets. He put it down to the sunny weather.

## 22

Hanlon turned her car into Whiteside's road and immediately stamped on the brake. The street was like a disturbed anthill. She saw an ambulance, five police cars, two police vans and about twenty police in uniform milling frantically around outside Whiteside's house. There was a loud roar and clatter as the police helicopter flew overhead. With a terrible, swift certainty, Hanlon knew immediately what had happened. This level of manpower on a Saturday afternoon had to be for a fellow officer.

She parked the car and walked up to the sergeant's house, stony-faced. The engine of the ambulance started, its lights and siren came on and it pulled away. Behind it, she could see two officers sealing the entrance to the building with incident tape. She heard a senior officer that she didn't know shouting, 'Block off that road. Jesus Christ. Will you hurry up. And cordon off those pavements, will you.' His voice was sharp with tension, his face thunderous, tense and angry.

'Hurry up. I don't want any traffic moving up or down this street.'

A uniformed officer blocked Hanlon on the pavement. 'I'm

sorry, madam.' She opened her bag for her warrant card but a voice called, 'Ma'am, ma'am.' Hanlon looked past the PC and there was Childs. He was wearing a white disposable

boiler suit and overshoes on his bare feet. Hanlon thought, they must have removed and bagged his clothing. Childs' forearms and wrists were rusty with dried blood and there were more streaks of blood on his face.

'It's Mark, ma'am. DS Whiteside. He's been shot,' said Childs. He stood there awkwardly on the pavement, a beseeching look on his face. He looked even younger than usual. The uniform was still standing between them. It's as if Childs believes I can wave a wand and everything will be somehow all right again, thought Hanlon. Behind Childs was the usual activity of crime scenes, but carried out with far more grim urgency than normal. In the background she could see DCS Ludgate directing the action. Hanlon felt a surge of anger towards him. He must have been inside the house when she arrived. Of all the people that this investigation could have fallen to, he was the one that she'd least like to have in charge. It was almost an insult to Whiteside to have Ludgate here as the senior investigating officer.

'How badly?' Hanlon said. By that she really meant, was he still alive?

Childs shrugged helplessly. 'I don't know,' he said. 'He'd been hit in the head and the body. I know that.'

Oh God, thought Hanlon, a head shot. Childs had obviously done his best. The blood that soaked him was testimony to that. Behind Childs three SOCO officers had arrived and were busy suiting up. In a minute they'd be starting on the house and Whiteside's flat. Now that the crime scene had been preserved, other officers were gathering at both ends of the now sealed-off road to search that perimeter. She could see Ludgate pointing at houses in the street and sending officers off for house-to-house enquiries. She couldn't fault Ludgate for efficiency, that was for sure.

She turned her attention back to Childs. The uniform had stood aside to let them be together. Childs looked immensely vulnerable. Tears rolled down his face. 'I did my best, ma'am.' He started to shake and sat down heavily on the pavement, as if he was going to faint.

Hanlon sat next to him. She wanted to put her arm round him. She wanted to squeeze him tightly to her, heedless of the sticky blood that adhered to the youngster's body. But she couldn't. Not yet. She made gentle, soothing noises like you do to calm a child. In the distance she could hear the bad-tempered officer shouting, 'Where the hell are those temporary barriers, I want this road properly sealed off, and tell those idiots over there to get back inside. The whole road's a crime scene until I say otherwise.' Windows down the length of the street were open and faces were looking out, intrigued by the commotion. 'It's not your fault. You did everything you could have done,'

she said.

Childs' head was bowed and she could smell the heavy, ferrous tang of Whiteside's blood. She saw his shoulders heave as he sobbed and she thought, he's only nineteen. Her grim-faced colleagues were taping off Whiteside's door at what was now the centre of a crime scene.

A sergeant approached Hanlon hesitantly. 'Ma'am,' he said, 'I'll take Tom back to the station now, if that's OK.'

She nodded. She herself would have had Childs down there practically immediately. Theoretically, Childs, the discoverer of the body, was a suspect. It would be time for him to make a formal statement and doubtless for his hands to be tested in a kind of embarrassed way, for GSR. Hanlon spoke softly to the boy and Childs nodded and stood up. The tracks of his tears had put streaks in the dried blood that smeared his cheeks. He looked at his blood-covered hands and arms almost in surprise.

'Go with the sergeant, Constable,' she said gently. 'I'll be round to see you later, but just now I've got work to do.'

Childs nodded and the sergeant led him away to an unmarked car. Hanlon straightened up and looked for someone she knew. A senior officer who she recognized, DI Clarke, waved her over to him. As she walked towards him she was stopped by Sergeant Thompson, who'd been there with her for the Cunningham bust. 'Sorry, ma'am, I know you're busy, I just want to say how gutted we are.' Thompson was shaking with suppressed emotion.

'Do you know how he is, Sergeant?' asked Hanlon. She knew that Thompson was a friend of Whiteside's. They were sports fans and drinking buddies. They'd go and watch cricket together in the summer, rugby in the winter. Thompson shook his head. 'No, ma'am, not yet. I know one of the paramedics who attended but there was no time to talk. At least he's still alive. The one good thing is that young Childs over there found him shortly after and called it in. Otherwise Mark'd be gone by now. But gunshot trauma is really a hospital job, they got him there as soon as possible. When I know more I'll text you. I've got your number.'

'You do that, Sergeant,' she said. 'You do that.'

Thompson said, 'I don't know who'll lead the investigation but I hope it's you, ma'am. I hope you get the bastard who did this.'

Hanlon had been looking at the activity around them while he was speaking. Now she looked directly at him and the sergeant saw into her eyes for the first time. He knew her well enough and obviously their gazes had met in the past, but this time it was as though a darkened window had been opened and he could see the real Hanlon. The rage that burnt there was frightening. Later, when trying to describe it to a colleague,

all he – a Catholic – could come up with was, 'like the fires of hell'. Now she didn't need to reply. She blinked and it was as if the shutters had come down again, and Thompson was looking into her habitually expressionless eyes.

He knew then with a quiet certainty that Hanlon would make someone pay. He was grateful for that. Whiteside was his friend.

Hanlon moved towards DI Clarke and Thompson breathed again. He noted, almost without surprise, that he was standing as rigidly as if he'd been on ceremonial parade.

## 23

Annette's husband came home with her son, Sam, about one o'clock. They were both gleaming with that healthy, overwashed glow that swimming gives you and smelt strongly of chlorine. Sleek from the pool, they were like upholstery that had been steam-cleaned, or a valeted car. By contrast, there was a tangible air of gloom in the untidy sitting room.

'You OK?' he said to his wife, who looked unusually preoccu-pied. Declan wondered if something bad had happened to her mother, who wasn't in the best of health.

'In a minute,' she said, holding her hand, palm up to him to forestall any conversation, then, 'Sammy, darling, did you see Peter at school yesterday?'

Sam looked puzzled. 'Yes, Mum, but I didn't get to speak to him. We had that football match in Southgate, and he's not in the team, and then when we got back, like after lunch, he was in the field for biology looking at their insect traps, Bradley McDonald got a stag-beetle! Everyone was like, a stagbeetle, and we're in different sets for maths. Why?'

'Oh, no reason,' said Annette. So far, so good, she thought. Peter obviously wasn't due to come here or Sam would have known.

Her son went upstairs to play Black Ops or some such game on his Xbox. Declan had dropped the sports bag containing

their towels, costumes and dirty clothes on the floor by the sofa. Bet he leaves it there, she thought, he'll be off down the pub in a minute. He picked up the phone, the landline, and punched in the number to check any missed calls. She watched as his face grew puzzled. He put the phone back on its holder.

'That was Kathy Reynolds. She was calling to tell Peter she'd pick him up from here later today. She's abroad again. Is he staying somewhere else? He usually comes here, doesn't he?' Annette suddenly felt very sick indeed. Her head swam and she felt faint as the terrible implications sank in, her worst fears coming true. 'Oh God, Declan,' she said to her husband. 'Oh

my God.'

Declan stared at her, uncomprehending, and Annette told him what she thought that meant. Jesus Christ, said Declan. Annette started crying while he tried to comfort her.

For a couple of minutes they sat together on the sofa as they tried to think of something other than the obvious to do. Declan broke the silence. 'We'll have to call the police,' he said. 'And Kathy. Do you want me to do it?' Annette sniffed and shook her head.

'I'll do it, darling. But I'm going round to her flat first, I want to check he's not there. He might be there right now, you know, like *Home Alone*. He's got a key, after all. Please, it's only five minutes away.'

Declan nodded and acquiesced. Why not? he thought. He had a terrible desire to shout at Annette, to attack her verbally. How could you be so forgetful? he wanted to shout. How could you have been so criminally stupid! He managed to control himself. He stood up and kissed her hair and squeezed her hand. She automatically squeezed his hand back.

'Oh, Declan,' she said. 'What have I done. It's all my fault.' Yes, he thought. It is.

'It's not your fault,' he said. 'Go round there, take your phone. If he's not there call the police, Kathy, and then me, OK. I'll be waiting here for your call. I'll keep an eye on Sam.' She nodded and stood up. She left the room and returned a second later. 'Have you seen my car keys?' she asked. 'I don't

know where I've put them.' She started to cry again.

Annette sat outside Kathy's flat in her old, scuffed Ford Mondeo. The pockets in the door of both the driver and passenger side were full to overflowing with old parking tickets from machines and empty sweet and crisp packets. There was a child's woolly hat on the floor in the passenger well, left over from March's cold weather, and a stack of magazines that she'd meant to get rid of in the recycling but hadn't.

Her friend's small, ground-floor flat looked immaculate. There was a tiny piece of front garden, the lawn a manicured strip of green between the flat and the road, and the path was swept, with a little tub of flowers. It was all so neat. Just like Kathy's life.

She thought of her own house. Its small, rusted, metal gate falling off its hinges, the path choked with weeds, and what was left of the lawn dotted with old plastic toys of Sam's that she'd never got round to clearing away. The paint around her windows was flaking badly; she couldn't afford to pay anyone and she didn't have the time to do it herself. Annette felt as though she was slowly drowning in a sea of inescapable tasks while every day the tide rose higher.

The hope that maybe Peter would be there after all had proved illusory. She had thought it would. No one had answered the door. Peter had gone.

She took a deep breath and looked at her mobile. Its screen full of harmless apps seemed to mock her. They promised so much: cookery apps so you'd never run out of ideas or

knowledge, restaurant apps so you'd always know where to go, games so you'd never be bored, search engines so you'd always know everything, Google Earth, so you'd always know where you were.

But, she thought bitterly, it was all lies, wasn't it. The cookery apps were pointless. Her food was 90 per cent convenience: pizzas, sausages, fish fingers, burgers, baked beans, the usual things that people actually ate and 10 per cent what the family as a unit would agree to eat together. Planning meals was like a Venn diagram, one would eat one thing, the others wouldn't, and she didn't have the time, patience or money to cook three different variations on a theme every night. The only unanimity lay in dishes like spaghetti Bolognese, chilli con carne and cottage pie. We're a family bound together with mince, she thought. She couldn't afford to go to restaurants, TripAdvisor, don't make me laugh, so much for those apps, and she didn't have time for games.

And what use Google Earth with its pinpoint accuracy?

Would it find Peter? No, it wouldn't. Would playing Candy Crush distract her from guilt? No.

Briefly, she wondered what the number was for non-emergency police calls, then she thought, if a twelve-year-old missing since end of school yesterday doesn't qualify as an emergency, what does?

Heart thudding, head throbbing, stomach knotting, she dialled nine, nine, nine and asked for the police, took a deep breath. 'Hello, yes, my name's Annette Fielding and I'd like to report a child missing.' Tears started to run down her cheeks and she rested her forehead on the steering wheel.

* * *

And in Stuttgart Max had ordered coffee and left the table when Kathy checked her voicemail and called Annette. Her

conversation was short and to the point. Kathy didn't cry, she didn't scream, although she felt like doing both. She clicked her phone off. She looked around the restaurant in disbelief, as though she was amazed that life could carry on so normally. All thought was virtually suspended. Every beat of her heart said, this cannot be. She felt as if the roof had fallen in on top of her. There must be some mistake.

The fat man on his own carried on eating his spatzeli. The two young lovers were still holding hands and looking at each other over the tablecloth. A tired-looking, quite drunk, English businessman in a crumpled suit was reading a book propped up on the salt and pepper in front of him. All was as before, except in her head, where everything had exploded into Edvard Munch-like despair. I must get home, she thought.

Images of Peter flashed through her head in bewildering succession. Terrible thoughts of what might be happening to him, mixed with random memories of his face. The police would meet her flight, Annette had said. She had felt Annette's guilt and pain through the iPhone in her hand, but she had no desire to say anything comforting. She felt like throwing up. She was stunned. I must go, she thought, and stood up, then immediately sat down. She was too unsteady on her feet. Her legs were like jelly. I must tell Max I'm going, she thought. But I can't say why, I can't face talking.

When Max rejoined her at the table, he thought to himself as he saw her across the restaurant that she looked ethereally beautiful. Before, she'd been funny, sexy, warm. Now, she was like a woman transformed. She was staring expressionlessly into space. Momentarily he wondered if he had done something, or said something, terrible to offend her. They had been speaking German, Kathy's was so good Max had to keep reminding himself how unusual this was from a British person. Now she

switched to English. Her beautiful eyes held his and she spoke as if she were reading a script, her voice flat and uninflected. 'Max. I need to leave now. Something's happened. No, I'm not going to talk about it now, I'm sorry. There's a taxi rank on the corner.' He opened his mouth to speak and she touched him gently as a feather on the lips. 'Please don't say anything.

I can't talk right now.'

She stood up and left. He watched her back retreat through the restaurant. Kathy always had excellent posture, she didn't stoop like some tall people, but now she was walking drawn up to her full height in an almost exaggerated way. She didn't look back or left or right. 'Entschuldigung. Zahlen, bitte,' he said to a waiter, asking for the bill.

He realized she had left without taking her small suitcase. He would look after it for her until he saw her again. He guessed it had to be serious. Most of us can recognize when someone has just had bad news, but Max couldn't even begin to guess how bad it could be.

# 24

Enver watched from his position outside the flat as the SOCO officers came and started their work, while various other uniforms sealed off the premises and started searching the roof and alley. These were the parameters that he had defined as the primary and secondary search sites. He had already started a crime-scene log, which he'd handed over to the SIO. He had also taken a witness statement from Mr Colin Hargreaves, the formerly abusive, but now extremely cooperative, pensioner. Hargreaves seemed pathetically eager to help. He kept smiling nervously at Enver, his false teeth slipping around wetly in his slack mouth. He reminded Enver of a chastised dog, keen to make amends.

What he told Enver was this: two men in council workclothes had arrived, had been admitted to the Yilmaz flat, there'd been some shouting, a general commotion which the old man had put down to objections to doing what they were told, then silence. The men had emerged carrying the large refuse sacks of the kind that were reinforced and strong enough to contain builders' waste and rubble. Hargreaves said he assumed the bags contained rubbish. No description of the men beyond the fact that they were white and burly, both with hats, one a baseball cap, one a blue beanie. Hargreaves had no idea of the vehicle the men had arrived in. He said he'd heard doors

slam after they disappeared down the staircase, so he assumed it was a van.

The officer who had been put in charge, the SIO, was DCI Murray, someone Enver knew fairly well. Murray was regarded as reliable and thorough, but Enver thought he was actually a lazy sod who liked to spin things out for overtime purposes. He was known as 'Never Hurry' Murray. As if to confirm this nickname, as soon as he'd cordoned off the service road and checked the initial plan of action with Enver, Murray had put Enver in charge of the crime scene and disappeared to 'sort things out, logistics wise. We need an incident room.' In Murray speak, that meant finding an office and drinking a lot of tea. Enver resigned himself mentally to a very late finish. He sent officers to check the shops below for CCTV footage and to get witness statements. He arranged to have door-to-door enquiries down the street and he also sent an officer to try to track down the gang of youths who'd been hanging around when he and Hanlon had first arrived. If anyone had seen anything, they would have, although the chances of them helping the police with their enquiries would be

practically nil.

He had been so preoccupied with the various tasks in hand, determined not to let Hanlon down, that strangely, the first he heard of the Whiteside shooting was when the outsize bulk of Corrigan, all six foot five of the assistant commissioner, loomed up the metal steps that led to the roof where the flat was. Like Enver, he was finding the metal stairs hard going and he appeared in Enver's sight inch by impressive inch as he grimly hauled his way up, knees protesting. The top of his head came first, followed by the rest of him in slow motion. It was like the visitation of a deity. Everyone stopped what they were doing and stared. He climbed on to the flat roof, followed by

two of his own men, hard-faced police that Enver had never seen before, one in uniform, one not. They fell in behind Corrigan, one on either side, like attendant priests.

In the absence of Murray, Enver had been busy contacting the council for traffic and other CCTV sources to see if anything could be made of the van. If they had the number plate they could use the ANPR system. He wasn't optimistic. They'd probably have fake plates, but it was worth a try. He told the council employee he'd be back in touch later and, like everyone else, he stopped what he was doing and stared at the assistant commissioner. Although Corrigan was wearing civilian clothes, chinos, a baggy shirt and deck shoes, Enver recognized him immediately and saluted. Like everyone else, he wondered, what had brought the assistant commissioner up here. To his horror, Corrigan bore down on him.

'Are you Sergeant Demirel?' Corrigan asked.

'Yes, sir,' said Enver uncomfortably. He wondered feverishly what all this could possibly be about. The AC's acolytes stared at him silently. It was very unnerving.

'Come with me, Sergeant.' The assistant commissioner indicated the hatchet-faced plainclothes policeman to his left. 'DI Ralphs will take over from you.'

'Yes, sir. Do you want me to fill the DI in on what I've done already?' asked Enver.

Corrigan looked at him as if he were insane. 'No. No, I don't,' he said, as if speaking to a child. 'I want you to stop what you're doing and come with me. Ralphs is perfectly capable of following procedure, which I take it you have been doing?'

'Yes, sir,' said Enver.

'Good,' said Corrigan. 'Where's the SIO here?' 'Back at the station, sir.'

'Is that so?' said Corrigan.

'Yes, sir. I'm acting SIO, in his absence.'

'Well, Ralphs is now,' said Corrigan. He looked unimpressed by Murray's absence. Someone's in for a bollocking, thought Enver. The AC ordered, 'You, Sergeant, come with me.'

'Yes, sir,' said Enver and fell in beside the AC. Corrigan swung his bulk over the roof's edge and descended the stairs. Enver followed him. The sergeant came up to the other man's shoulders; he hadn't felt this small in years. He wondered what on earth Corrigan might want.

In the comfort of the black leather back seat of Corrigan's air-conditioned Mercedes, parked in the street below, the driver standing discreetly outside, the big man looked at Enver.

'I need to talk to you and not down the nick. Where can we go that's private and convenient?' Enver's mind went blank. He looked around the car for inspiration.

'I'm not sitting in here talking,' said Corrigan, 'that's for sure.'

'Errm,' said Enver. Corrigan sighed in exasperation.

'You do know this area, Sergeant, don't you? Somewhere we can go? Somewhere quiet?'

Enver thought furiously, North London addresses and venues whirring crazily in his brain, before he said, 'My uncle's house, sir. That's near.'

'Fine, Sergeant. Let's go there then,' said Corrigan.

'Do you mind if I phone my aunt, sir?' asked Enver. It sounded ridiculous.

'Please go ahead, Sergeant.'

* * *

In Uncle Osman's front room, in the house off the immensely long Seven Sisters Road – the room that Enver thought of as his uncle's study with its shelves full of gloomy-looking theological works in Turkish, Ottoman Turkish and Arabic, souvenirs of

Istanbul on the wall, the floor covered with Turkish rugs – they were drinking sweet tea from glasses. Corrigan, helping himself to some immensely sticky baklava, proudly brought in by Aunt Fatima, said, 'You know DS Whiteside, I believe?'

'Vaguely, sir. We've met anyway.'

'I take it you haven't heard the news then?' asked Corrigan. 'No, sir,' said Enver, puzzled. 'I've been busy with the Yilmaz

murder.'

'It's not a murder case yet, Sergeant,' said the AC. 'They've technically gone missing. At this stage anyway.'

'Yes, sir,' said Enver. 'But surely the shouting, the blood, the disappearance of the three of them?' It could only be murder, he thought.

'It could be abduction, false imprisonment, it could be staged,' said Corrigan. 'It's not the only thing that's been happening.'

'I'm sorry, sir?' said Enver, bewildered.

'Sergeant Whiteside has been shot, at his flat.' Corrigan sipped his tea thoughtfully.

He looked around the imam's study with a policeman's eye for detail. It was the room of an elderly scholar, no more, no less. The glasses from which they were drinking their tea were small, about the size of sherry glasses, and held in a filigreed silver holder. They were absurdly dainty for Corrigan's huge fingers.

Enver took in the news of Whiteside's shooting. Various thoughts crowded his mind – amazement that such a thing could happen, a terrible sympathy for Whiteside that a man so full of vitality – he'd only seen him that one time – had been struck down, professional responses, why hadn't he known before, how many would be on the investigation, shamefully (to his mind) a selfish relief that it wasn't him.

'Is he...?' Enver hesitated.

Corrigan supplied the answer to the unasked question. 'Not yet. Two body shots, but they missed vital organs – well, that's not strictly true, his bladder's been, well, I'll spare you the details, extensive trauma, massive blood loss – only the third shot, he was shot in the face.' Corrigan grimaced. He had seen gunshot head injuries before; he hoped to God he'd never need to see another one again. 'The bullet shattered his jaw, then the cheekbone and lodged in the front of his head. They're operating now to remove it.'

Enver shuddered inwardly. He didn't mind bodily injuries. He had boxed for ten years, including three as a semi-professional, from the age of fifteen to twenty-five, and his own body had, literally, taken a pounding. But to live the rest of your life brain-damaged, to be there but not there, to be no longer you since you are defined by your personality rather than your physical abilities, struck him as awful. Of course, brain damage was a perpetual risk in boxing, but things had been tightened up a lot since the Michael Watson fight. A Whiteside with a permanent catheter was still undeniably Whiteside. So would be a Whiteside in a wheelchair. A Whiteside with permanent mental impairment, well, was that still Whiteside? If he survived physically, how mentally affected would he be? It was a terrible thought. Enver could face life physically disabled, or felt he could, but not as a vegetable.

He thought too of Hanlon. 'Who's heading the investigation, sir? DI Hanlon?'

Corrigan's eyes bulged in disbelief, emphasized by his eyebrows arcing upwards. 'How much punishment did you take in that boxing ring, Sergeant?' he asked. 'Are you crazy? Hanlon in charge? Think about it for a minute.'

Enver did so. He didn't know the DI that well. She had a reputation for toughness, a superlative arrest record, that much was canteen knowledge, and, of course, there was the

famous riot incident. And the rumoured propensity to violence. None of these, though, was particularly remarkable. He could think of half a dozen police that these qualities fitted, himself included, to a certain extent. There was the fact that she was remarkably physically fit, he'd heard about the triathlons, but again, there were probably quite a few athletes in the Met. He stroked his moustache pensively. Corrigan lost patience with him. He was beginning to wonder if Hanlon had been right in her glowing references.

'DI Hanlon has a history of bending or breaking rules, Sergeant, as well you know,' he said irritably, 'and she has got away with it so far because she's been very clever and very lucky. And also because she has a number of people, myself included, who have gone out on a limb for her. Quite frankly, she is the last person anyone would want in charge of this investigation. One of Hanlon's biggest problems is she does take things personally and this Whiteside business...' Corrigan shook his head; he didn't bother finishing the sentence. 'Hanlon is quite capable, Sergeant, of taking matters into her own hands. God alone knows what she might get up to, or God forbid, do to a suspect.'

He looked shrewdly at Enver. Corrigan had undertaken

a bit of digging into the Anderson arrest. There were several niggling details that had caught his eye, particularly with regards to the information leading to the drugs bust. He didn't think Hanlon had fitted Anderson up or entrapped him, but something felt fishy. Now he would have to let the thing go. Whiteside was in no position, maybe never would be, even if he survived, to help him. The point was, he, Corrigan had helped Hanlon and she'd repaid him by stabbing him in the back. Don't ruffle feathers, he'd told her; what had she done, assaulted a chicken. And that was down to her wanting to get even with someone who'd merely outwitted her legally. God knows what she was capable of doing to avenge Whiteside. Hanlon needed to be reined in. Simply making sure she wasn't part of the investigation wouldn't be nearly enough. She'd be forever checking up on its progress, interfering, driving the SIO mad. And Hanlon had enough devoted fans in strategic positions to keep her well informed of everything she'd want to know. Reading her the riot act would just be a waste of breath.

In an ideal world, Corrigan would have seconded her to somewhere far away, Wales or Yorkshire, anywhere out of London. But failing that, he would find her a babysitter. He wasn't going to share any of this with Enver, but his reputation as a grim, methodical copper might slow Hanlon down. He knew from Hanlon's memo that she considered Demirel a good policeman and the checks Corrigan had made on his record backed that up. If he teamed him up with her, she'd accept it.

Corrigan had wondered momentarily if Anderson were behind the shooting of Whiteside by way of revenge. It seemed unlikely. Although the man was certainly capable of murder, had indeed committed it if the stories were to be believed, he was a professional criminal and would accept police activity as an occupational hazard. But you could never be sure. Anderson was capable of crucifying someone he didn't like; he was capable of anything.

Enver began to see what Corrigan was getting at. Hanlon would be on the warpath. Corrigan continued, 'For one thing, she has licences for two hunting rifles, a .22 and a .243, and three shotguns, one double barrel, one up and over and a pump action, and that's just what she officially owns.' He had stressed the word 'officially'. Enver nodded. Hanlon could probably get

anything she wanted in London, come to that. Enver could himself if he wanted to. He knew an underworld armourer, two in fact. You could even hire guns on a deposit basis for a couple of hundred quid plus deposit, non-returnable if the firearms were used.

Enver suddenly thought to himself, Corrigan thinks she might kill whoever did this. This is what it's all about. 'Why are you telling me this, sir?' he asked. He wanted his suspicions confirmed.

Corrigan poured himself some more tea. The glass looked ridiculously fragile in his massive fingers. 'Hanlon's unstoppable, Sergeant, once she's made up her mind. Why am I telling you this?' He hesitated and rubbed the bald patch on his crown thoughtfully, 'Because I like Hanlon a lot and I think you do too.' He paused. 'She can be her own worst enemy.'

'What do you want me to do, sir?' Enver was confused by Corrigan now. He had always thought that Corrigan would hang anyone out to dry who might get in his way. He hadn't realized the extent to which the assistant commissioner was prepared to shield Hanlon.

'I suppose I would like you to save her from herself, Sergeant. DI Hanlon has enemies in high places who would very much like to sack her. I want you to find out what she intends to do and stop her. That is what I want you to do, Sergeant. Needless to say, this conversation never took place.'

Sure, thought Enver. And stopping Hanlon doing anything is going to be really easy. 'Thank you, sir,' he said, purely to annoy Corrigan. 'Then what are you doing here, sir? Officially, I mean. For when people ask me what the assistant commissioner wanted to talk to me about.'

The assistant commissioner didn't miss a beat. 'Building bridges, Sergeant, with the London Anglo-Turkish community. My secretary has arranged an interview with *Olay Gazetesi* and *Londra Gazete* for later.'

Enver nodded admiringly. You're slick, he thought. They were the two Turkish-language newspapers in London. The AC had been in touch with them both. Corrigan had a rare talent for PR. Nothing was wasted.

'I'm looking forward to meeting your uncle, the imam. We're going to have our photos taken. I gather he's highly respected,' he said. 'Meanwhile, here is what you'll do about Hanlon

'
.

## 25

At 7 p.m. that evening, Enver was standing under the large Victorian railway viaduct in Bermondsey, a stone's throw from the Shard. It was still light, but the sky was darkening and the narrow streets around here never really seemed to get much sun. He looked around. It was a strange juxtaposition, the gleaming, futurist construction rising skywards like something out of a sci-fi film, like *Metropolis*, and the gloomy, red-brick Victorian train viaduct. The enormously tall building looked deceptively short to Enver. This was, he thought, the tallest building in Europe but it certainly didn't seem that way. It was hard to impress Enver.

Enver was a North Londoner. South London, the other side of the river, was alien territory. To want to live in South London seemed almost perverse. The very thought almost made him feel ill. To cross the Thames was to cross into another country. London was two distinct nations, but Schengen-like; you didn't need a passport to travel between them.

Bermondsey, Enver decided from a short walk around it, was a schizophrenic part of London. It didn't know what it wanted to be. It was like Barbara Windsor married to Damien Hirst. Bermondsey has a private art gallery, the White Cube, which is huge, both in reputation and size. Internationally famous artists like Gilbert and George, Anselm Kiefer, Tracey Emin

and Antony Gormley show there. Following the art gallery, he guessed, like the Cantona seagulls around a trawler, or asteroids pulled in by the gravitational tug of a giant-like Saturn, came the hipsters, the fashionistas and the art-school students and the media types, and what was once a solid working-class environment had now become an odd mix of contemporary chic flats and Boho apartments in converted warehouses. Enver grimly noted sand-blasted walls, lots of glass, nautical-style architectural flourishes, tiny balconies that mirrored ships' decks, with hawsers as guard rails and panoramas of shiny stainless steel, at exorbitant prices. There were mini-piazzas with fake cobbles. He loathed these chichi details with a passion that surprised him. These bijou flatlets stood cheek by jowl with traditional council estates which Enver person-ally wouldn't risk walking around without a local in tow. It's Hoxton all over again, he thought.

Enver had been out in his youth with several girls from art-school-style backgrounds. He'd been a big hit with the students of Goldsmiths and St Martins. He was local colour. He was exotic. Art school was a country he'd visited often. He wouldn't like to live there but he enjoyed staring at the colourful natives. A bit like Turkey. He'd lost count of parties where he'd been paraded as a kind of odd freak for the intellectuals to look at. 'You must meet my boyfriend, Enver. He's...' here the categories had changed over the years but the point, he's not one of us, had been the same... 'half-Turkish/a boxer/a policeman/his uncle's an imam, how weird/his dad's got a kebab house in Southgate, but not in an ironic way, it actually is a kebab house!' Perhaps that's what I share with Hanlon, he thought, stroking his drooping moustache, we don't fit in, and we don't really want to.

Even the defiantly grim railway arches had been colonized
by the arty interlopers. Underneath the red-brick, shallow
arches of the railway bridge were small businesses and pop-up
restaurants, the odd night club and, more prosaically, the occasional road that ran underneath from one side of the construction
to the other. Enver was on the pavement of one of these thorough-
fares, the vaulted roof of the bridge overhead, the noise of the traffic
compressed to a loud, echoing roar by the constrained acoustics of
the confined space. Despite the recent dry weather and the unusual
heat, it was cold and damp in this shadowy place that never saw the
light of day. It smelt of damp and piss and poverty. It was resisting
gentrification. Enver patted the clammy, sweating brickwork. Good
luck, he thought. Enjoy it before you get claimed as a 'found'
artwork, dismantled and put in a gallery.

Some elements of the old Bermondsey remained, however.

Halfway along the tunnel was a doorway with a fading sign for
'Bob's Gym, Boxer's Welcome'. Enver knew there was something
wrong with the punctuation, with the apostrophe, but wasn't quite
sure what it was. Punctuation wasn't his strong point. What it did
send out was the message that Bob was untroubled by such things.
The sign didn't mention popular quasi-boxing sports such as boxer-
cise or, Enver's personal bête noir, white-collar boxing, where office
workers pretend they're boxers. You're such a snob, he told himself.
You're not a boxer any more. Look at you. A city accountant could
probably take you, you fat lump. His obese stomach mocked his
former slimline self. You wouldn't need to hit me in a ring these
days, just run around, I'd collapse trying to catch you.

He opened the door and it was like going back in time. His
own boxing gym, the one that he'd fought out of in North
London, was relatively smart. 'Gentleman Dave' Jones, who ran it, a
sixty-year-old former middleweight like Enver, but, unlike Enver,
annoyingly trim, embraced modernity and was

also a cleanliness fanatic. He was an ex-army champion and the army had left its mark not just on his face, his posture and his language, but on his attitude. Everything that could gleam, did gleam. There was usually a smell of paint overlying the scent of sweat and effort that comes with a gym. And if it didn't smell of paint, it smelt of polish. Not here. Not at Bob's. Mildew, body odour, grim effort and violence, that's what was in the air. Enver snuffled it with greedy pleasure. He realized with a pang how he had missed that smell.

He walked up some steep, shabby wooden stairs. The walls were a dark green and every so often, every few steps, there were old, framed posters for fights featuring long-forgotten names of boxers from the past. The smell of the gym – old sweat, damp, disinfectant – grew stronger; he would be able to guess where he was blindfolded. Enver opened a door at the top to a rudimentary reception area. No Nespresso machine here. Just a kettle. A lime-scaled kettle.

There was a man of about fifty behind the desk, short and wiry, with a nose that had seen better days. The computer monitor in front of him was old-fashioned and massive and beige. He looked up, his eyes hard and suspicious. 'We're closed. Opening hours are listed on the door.' His tone was unfriendly. 'I'm not here to join,' said Enver. His own tone was flat and matter-of-fact. His eyes wore their usual sleepy look but the other man recognized a kindred spirit in them. He sat up in his chair to better pay attention. He saw a thirty-year-old man with a gut but he also took in Enver's powerful musculature, the slightly marked face and the attitude. Enver was impressively

menacing.

'How can I help you then?' the manager asked. Momentarily he wondered if he was going to be made an offer he'd be foolish to refuse. Enver did have more than a hint of gangland enforcer about him. He could be quietly threatening when he wanted to be. Boxers intimidate.

Enver produced his warrant card and showed it to him. The man behind the desk looked at the ID, singularly unimpressed, and asked, 'What do you want then, Sergeant?'

'DI Hanlon.'

The man looked up at him, this time actively hostile, eyes narrowed. He leant forward slightly in an aggressive way.

Enver returned his stare with his own heavy-lidded, sleepy look. Come on then, come on! was the message his own look sent out. Enver felt his pulse rate increase and he welcomed it. The brutal truth was that Enver would have been delighted if the manager started a fight. It had been a long, frustrating, highly depressing day, if not week. Not only that, it was complicated. The whole situation was complicated. A simple, satisfyingly violent fistfight would suit him nicely. It wouldn't be the manager he was hitting, it would be everything that was getting him down. The case, Ludgate, the Whiteside shooting, maybe life in general. Enver would feel a lot better if he beat someone up.

'What if I told you she wasn't here?' said the manager. He relaxed back in his chair. It was a submissive gesture; he was backing down.

Enver sighed. Corrigan had said that every Saturday from six to eight she was here, provided she wasn't working. And Enver knew that after a piece of really grim news, the Whiteside incident, she'd want to be here, working out her anger, working out her pain. Where else would she go? A support group? Friends? Of course she'd be here.

Then the man looked again at the warrant card that Enver was still holding and said, with dawning recognition, 'Demirel, eh? Did you used to box?' Enver nodded. 'Were you Iron Hand Demirel?'

'Yes,' he said.

The gym manager grinned, stood up and proffered his hand. 'Freddie Laidlaw.' Enver took his hand and shook it. 'I saw you fight at the Vauxhall Recreation Club in Luton. I won a monkey betting on you.' His attitude had changed completely. 'You were a big hitter, bit slow on your feet, if I recall right.'

Enver remembered the fight. It was a northern boxer from Blackpool, Jason Clitheroe, that he'd fought then. He'd stopped him in the fourth. He shook Laidlaw's hand. Laidlaw had become a lot friendlier now he knew that Enver was an ex-boxer. Or maybe it was because he'd won five hundred pounds on him. 'Sorry I was a bit unfriendly,' he apologized. 'The DI likes

to come here when we're closed. Some of the members have got form, are a bit tasty, if you see what I mean. I used to think she'd seen enough criminals at work and that's why she wanted to avoid them, but to be honest, I think she just prefers being alone. I can't imagine any of them would worry her. They'd leave well alone. Do you want to speak to her?'

Enver shook his head. He decided to tell Laidlaw the truth, or at least a version of it. He seemed a decent man. 'I'm supposed to babysit her,' he said. 'Follow her around, protect her back.'

Laidlaw was looking at him doubtfully. 'You're supposed to protect her? Are you sure?' He placed a very heavy emphasis on the last two words.

Enver was stung by the obvious implication he wasn't up to it. 'Yes. Yes, I am sure,' he said. 'DI Hanlon has quite a few enemies at the moment.' He didn't bother adding that they were mainly to be found within the police.

'Oh well, follow me, I'll take you to her.' Laidlaw didn't sound as though he believed Enver was up to it.

'It's not that simple,' said Enver. 'It's supposed to be without her knowledge.' Laidlaw frowned. He was obviously puzzled.

'I guess it's because she'd refuse protection if she was offered it,'

Enver explained. He didn't like lying but this contained more than a grain of truth. Anyway, thought Enver, it was probably true. Hanlon, from what he knew of her, would not accept protection even if she needed it.

Corrigan had told him to make sure she didn't do anything stupid, by which Enver assumed he meant maim or kill someone in retaliation for Whiteside. He'd told him to stick close to Hanlon, intervene if necessary.

'OK,' said Laidlaw decisively. 'Come with me and we'll see how she's doing. I know her routine.' He motioned Enver round to a door behind the desk that he opened. More stairs led upwards into darkness. 'The gym's got a gallery above it. The lights are out and she won't see us. Just be quiet and I can work out how much longer she'll be.'

The two men walked quietly up the wooden stairs, which groaned slightly under their weight. The stairway was unlit save by the light from the reception area filtering upwards. Laidlaw opened a door at the top and, as they went through, gently closed it behind them. They moved silently on to a wooden spectators' gallery with half a dozen rows of seats. As the manager had said, the gallery was unlit and ran round three sides of the gym hall so they were shrouded in blackness. Below, Enver could make out two boxing rings in darkness. Spotlights on gantries hung above them. Between the two boxing rings a heavy bag was hanging from a chain attached to the ceiling. This was lit by two of the spotlights, a circle of brilliant white light. In front of the heavy bag was Hanlon, wearing dark blue tracksuit trousers, a baggy grey top and heavy gloves.

She was throwing combination punches at the bag, jab, jab, cross, then jab, jab, right hook. Her punching was fluid, graceful and very fast, particularly her left jab. Enver thought if he were fighting her, he'd be very wary about being caught with that. As she punched, her head swayed, almost mongoose-like, so as not to present a static target. The two former professionals watched admiringly, Laidlaw with more than a hint of proprietorial pride. Hanlon moved beautifully. Enver guessed he'd coached her. Moving like that she'd be very hard to hit. He noted too the way Hanlon's chin, the most vulnerable point on a fighter's face, was kept tucked in, just like it should be. The bag below thudded with the impact of her punches and he could hear her forceful breathing and the occasional squeak of her trainers on the polished wooden floor. The blows, the bag, her breaths were the only real sounds.

'She's bloody good,' whispered Enver.

Hanlon's punches were hard, vicious and fast. Even from up here, at this distance, you could sense their power, not only by the movement of the heavy bag, but the percussive noise her gloves made on its surface. Laidlaw nodded, then put a finger to his lips.

Hanlon's top was soaked in sweat in an inverted triangle on her back and as she punched more sweat ran down her face, as wet as tears. He could see it shining like jewels on her skin in the harsh white light from above. Her hair was slick and matted with perspiration. She hadn't tied it back and it flew around her head as she moved so she looked like Medusa.

She stopped throwing combinations and steadied the heavy bag with her arms, putting them round it as if she was embracing it. He could see the powerful muscles snake-like under her smooth skin. The bag, which was swinging on its chain like an erratic pendulum from the force of her punches, came to a stop. Hanlon switched to practising body shots on the bag. Enver watched in amazement at the power behind the gloves. Her face, when he glimpsed it through the curtain of her hair, was set in tranquil

viciousness. She punched again and again at the same spot, creating, driving a football-sized dent, into the canvas of the bag. Enver knew how hard those things were, the canvas stiff and unyielding. You'd almost need a sledgehammer to do what she was doing to the bag. Faster and faster she hit the bag, each blow accompanied by a loud grunt of effort as she expelled air from her lungs, until with a final shout she landed a last punch that sent the bag arcing away from her. As it returned, swinging back towards her, she drop-kicked it with tremendous force. The bottom of the bag was what would have been, on a tall man, crotch level. The heavy bag jerked visibly up in the air on its chain, the metal links rattling, then stopped dead in its tracks, with a percussive thud. Enver shook his head disbelievingly.

'Christ almighty,' he heard Laidlaw whisper. The force Hanlon exerted on the base of the bag with her leg was unbelievable. He guessed she had just kicked forty-odd kilos of mass visibly upwards.

Hanlon stood for a moment, her gloved arms by her side, motionless, and then with a dancer's grace sat down cross-legged on the floor and bowed her head. Her gloved hands rested on the ground and Enver could see the rise and fall of her shoulders heaving as her body tried to re-oxygenate her blood. He stared at her in respectful fascination.

He felt a gentle tug on his jacket as Laidlaw motioned him away, back through the door, down the stairs and into his reception area. Laidlaw sat down behind his desk.

'She's fucking wonderful,' said Laidlaw in loving reverence. 'Isn't she.' It wasn't a question. He didn't wait for Enver's reply. The sergeant knew he was with another of the DI's fan club. Corrigan, Laidlaw, himself and barely alive Whiteside.

'Like I said to you before,' said Laidlaw, eyes on Enver, 'You're supposed to protect her? I really don't think she needs it. I wouldn't like to try and attack her, would you?'

Enver looked steadily at him. 'I think I'm supposed to protect her from herself, Freddie.'

Laidlaw nodded thoughtfully. 'I heard about her colleague,' he said.

'There you go then, Freddie,' Enver replied.

'I take your point,' said Laidlaw. 'That was for him, wasn't it?'

Enver nodded.

'Someone's going to pay, aren't they?' It wasn't really a question.

Enver looked at Laidlaw noncommittally. 'Don't tell her I've been here, please.'

The manager nodded again. 'No, I won't. So what's your plan now?' he asked.

Enver shrugged. 'I think I'm supposed to follow her, discreetly.'

Laidlaw snorted in derision. 'Yeah, like that's going to work. That's a plan, is it? Good luck with that one. Follow Hanlon,' he said sarcastically. 'Or are you going to tell me you're really good at covert surveillance?'

'No,' said Enver simply. 'No, I'm not. Did she drive here?' Laidlaw shook his head. 'No. Tube. There's no parking round here. I think the tube's your best bet. Go and wait for her at London Bridge Station, that's closest. I think that's the one she uses. I'll speak to her before she leaves, I'll offer her a lift there. If she shows any sign of not using the Underground

I'll phone you. Give me your number.'

Enver did so. Freddie Laidlaw keyed it into his phone. 'You'd better go now,' said Laidlaw. 'She'll be out in a minute.' They shook hands. 'Come and see me again,' said the manager. 'You look like you could do with some exercise.'

Enver rolled his eyes.

'I bet you a pony she susses you before you even get on a train.'

'Deal,' said Enver and grinned.

As he opened the door, he heard Laidlaw say, 'Oi, Ironhand.' He looked back 'Don't let her catch you with a body shot, mate. You're a big man, but you're out of shape.'

Enver flicked two fingers at him and grinned. As he walked down the crepuscular, gloomy stairs to the dark Bermondsey street he thought, at least I can afford to lose twenty-five quid. I don't think Laidlaw will have to pay up.

Enver walked along Tooley Street, past the expensive dockside developments like Hays Galleria, to London Bridge Station. Inside the station, echoey and windswept, its lights bright and harsh after the dimness of the gym, there were two possibilities, if she used it, Jubilee or Northern Line. If Enver had known where Hanlon lived he'd have been able to make a more informed guess, but he didn't. He assumed she'd head home. She was a solitary person, he couldn't see her wanting to be with anyone or to go to a bar or restaurant, and for the same reason he knew she wouldn't want a taxi. She'd be asked to talk. The driver might say, 'Penny for your thoughts,' or 'Cheer up, love, it might never happen.' He knew she'd hate that. Even the proximity of a potentially talkative stranger would be unwelcome to Hanlon, so the anonymity of the tube would be what she wanted. He knew that. He walked into the station. He now had a one in four chance of guessing correctly. Two lines, two directions on each line, north to south, south to north, for the Northern Line, east to west, west to east for the Jubilee.

Where would Hanlon live? Enver wondered. He guessed either East or North London. East because it was, inasmuch as London is, more affordable on a police salary and slightly more real than West London, which like many North Londoners he thought of as poncey. South London he disregarded, purely on prejudice; Wandsworth, the brighter borough, yeah right! Pull the other one. Battersea, to Enver, meant not the dog's home but Sloane

Rangers, driven out by Russian money, forever exiled by the river from Chelsea, their spiritual home. He was after all from Haringey, home of Spurs and Alexandra Palace, home of Muswell Hill where the Kinks came from and of Highgate Cemetery where Karl Marx is buried. Haringey, whose council was rated by the Audit Commission as the worst in London and the fourth worst in Britain.

North London, though, made him think. She was, or had

been, based in Islington, that much he knew of her police history. He'd be willing to bet, though, she wouldn't live there. He associated it with people who ate polenta and read the *Guardian* and liked performance art. He couldn't see Hanlon in that kind of milieu. It would make her cross. She wouldn't be going to see experimental theatre at the Almeida. She'd been caught up in the riots in Tottenham, so maybe she lived somewhere around there, Hackney maybe, Stoke Newington possibly. Also, there is something slightly gloomy about North London that he felt might have influenced her as a choice of district. She wouldn't live somewhere frivolous, somewhere like Kensington or Notting Hill.

He chose north.

## 26

Enver swiped his Oyster card over the electronic sensor on the gates leading to the Underground platforms, the electric barrier parted and let him through and he went down to the northbound platform of the deep, twisting complexities of the Northern Line. On the diagrammatic map of the tube, Harry Beck's legacy to the world, like an exploded wiring plan, the Northern Line is coloured black, a sombre warning to passengers of what lies ahead. Its regulars know it as the Misery Line. It's notorious for delays, overcrowding and whimsical rerouting. He stood at the far end where the train would come in so he had an uninterrupted view of the platform. The platform itself wasn't busy; there were only a dozen or so people on it. He picked up a discarded *Metro* newspaper and used it to partially shield his face while he pretended to read. He felt extremely conspicuous, also slightly ridiculous, and was half sure that Hanlon would notice him immediately, assuming she came. The air from the tunnels smelt metallic, sooty, industrial and gritty.

Five minutes and one train later Hanlon walked out on to

the platform, gym bag in hand. Enver felt a surge of delight at having guessed correctly. He saw the whiteness of her face, emphasized by her sombre clothes, as she glanced up at the electronic arrivals board with its orange lights spelling out destinations and times. She looked neither left nor right, just

waited with her back to the wall of the platform, seemingly lost in thought. He felt the rolling warmth of the stale air from the tunnel gather speed around him, the breeze from the tunnel growing stronger as the train came closer, and the sudden rumbling noise getting louder and louder until the tube train burst out of the tunnel with a rattling crescendo of sound to pull into the station, and they both boarded. She was half the length of the train away from him.

The Underground train was old and it rattled its way up the Northern Line, its worn-out brakes squealing as they rounded corners or stopped with a screech at stations: Bank and Moorgate in the City and Old Street. Then came Angel, one of the stops for Islington. Enver was right in his assumption she wouldn't be getting off there. Enver got out at each stop and moved compartments until he was in the adjacent one to Hanlon. He was beginning to feel the thrill of the hunt. Through the interconnecting door between the carriages he could see her dark hair obscuring her face as she sat hunched in her seat. The question now occupying him was where would she get off?

He had a gut feeling she would make her move at King's

Cross or Camden. Both were large and busy, both would offer the anonymity that he suspected Hanlon needed. He felt that Hanlon had to live in the city. He couldn't imagine her getting on an overground train and commuting to the countryside in Herts or Essex. Neither could he visualize her in some outlying suburb like, say, Pinner or Ongar. It would be absurd to think of her getting on the Metropolitan line to Metroland, as Sir John Betjeman had called it, places like Harrow on the Hill, Northwick Park, Little Chalfont or Chesham. Hanlon would not want to live somewhere friendly where she would have to talk to people. Her natural haunt would be large and impersonal

but probably expensive. She would not be able to put up with noisy neighbours, and money, if nothing else, buys thicker walls. It insulates you.

There was a certain amount of wishful thinking too in his choice of possible exits for Hanlon. He didn't want to get out with her at some desolate station where just the two of them would be left together staring at each other on an otherwise deserted platform, High Barnet, for example, this train's terminus. If that happens, thought Enver, I'm not getting off. I'll stay on the train. Corrigan could hardly be surprised if this harebrained idea of his failed.

He still hadn't realized that Corrigan wanted Hanlon to see him, wanted her to know that his eyes were on her. Enver wasn't the medium; he was the message.

King's Cross came and went, as did Camden, then Kentish Town. She stayed seated. Enver studied the advertising posters on the wall as the train pulled away. So she's not going to see the Alabama Three at the Forum tonight, he thought. There's a surprise. Please God, not Tufnell Park, thought Enver. Hardly anyone ever got off there at night in his experience. As the train pulled out of Tufnell Park he saw Hanlon stand up. Archway, then, Enver was sure must be the one. It was the next stop. He stood up too and moved as far down his carriage away from Hanlon as he possibly could. To his relief, a group of about ten large drunken Australians stood up too, shielding him from view.

The train stopped, the doors slid open and they left the train,

the noisy Australians a good-natured, shouting, human shield. Through their bodies he could see Hanlon heading for the exit. Archway has a single very steep escalator and Hanlon was standing on the right as it moved up, about fifteen people away f rom Enver. Even if she turned round she wouldn't see him.

He followed her out into the street. Archway commands a good view of London and he could see the city spreading out beneath him. There, marooned like an island in a river, by the main arterial road down into London, the bottom of the A1, was the large bulk of what used to be a huge pub that he remembered being used by Irish builders that now seemed to have become a café. Just up the way was the semi-industrial conurbation of the Whittington Hospital, its name a reminder of where Dick and his cat had turned again, a jumble of ugly disparate buildings. Northwards, uphill, against the darkening sky, you could see the Gothic, Victorian bridge that spanned the deep cut of the road at the base of Highgate. The locals called it the suicide bridge for obvious reasons. It was a popular way to go. Handier than Dignitas, thought Enver, a lot closer than Switzerland.

Hanlon was making her way to the underpass and Enver took the surface route, running across the busy main road, climbing the railings in the central reservation, and hurrying over to the other side. From there he could see her slim, dark-clad figure emerge from the pedestrian tunnel and walk eastwards towards North Holloway. Enver was really beginning to notice how unfit he had become. Tonight was the first time he'd walked any distance in a while and he was feeling it acutely. He still had an out-of-date mental image of himself as being in terrific shape, if a little overweight. But just like a once handsome man who's lost his looks yet stubbornly clings on to the dream that women still find him attractive despite the evidence in the mirror, so Enver – now an enthusiastic user of escalators, lifts, cars and sofas, a man whose idea of heaven was the travelator at an airport, that wonderful moving pavement, so soft and springy underfoot – had refused to come to terms with the fact that times had moved on. He himself hadn't moved faster than a walk for years. Running across the Archway Road had been a nightmare, almost in the true sense of the word. Like in a dream he'd run as fast as he could, yet seemed to be going nowhere. He'd misjudged totally how quickly he could move; he'd only just managed to break into a speedy waddle. Cars had been forced to brake to avoid hitting him. Horns had sounded angrily. The waist-high railings had proved embarrassingly hard to get over.

Hanlon on foot moved speedily and lightly. Enver trudged after her through what had become the endless streets of Holloway, like an Escher drawing. His legs ached, his lungs laboured. She turned a corner, the sergeant following, grimly determined, in her footsteps. The sky was a rich purple-blue, it was now almost night, and he turned into the new street that the corner revealed and Hanlon was gone.

He stood, hands on his hips, gazing hopelessly down the empty road, waiting for his heart to slow down. Where the hell was she? An unfriendly voice behind him asked, 'Looking for someone, Sergeant?'

At five to six Kathy's Lufthansa flight had landed at Heathrow's Terminal Three and she'd been fast-tracked by a customs officer and a waiting police officer and taken through a maze of back, employees only, corridors until she cleared airside. There, at Arrivals, she was met by a tearful Annette and a sympathetic WPC. The woman was a family liaison officer who explained as they moved quickly through the airport what they were doing to find Peter. From there she was driven in an unmarked police car to Highgate police station in North London, close to where she lived. Here she was escorted through the tall security gates at the back of the building to an office, where a team of three police officers were waiting. She was briefed

on what they knew about his disappearance and what steps they were taking.

Annette had already provided them with information on Peter's diabetes and they asked about his insulin, how much he would have had on him when he was taken. She didn't know, probably about a week's worth. The police exchanged significant glances. If he hadn't been found within a week, he almost certainly wouldn't be found alive anyway, insulin or no insulin.

They moved on to issues like friction at home, could he have run away following a row or maybe just in search of excitement? Had there been trouble at home or school? Had he got any trouble with friends? Did he belong to a gang? She understood that these questions had to be asked but she felt like screaming at them, you morons, he's been taken. No one made the suggestion, nobody implied it, but she was beginning to feel, rightly or wrongly, that they viewed her as partly responsible. Absent mother stays in lap of luxury in posh Stuttgart (home of German luxury cars, Mercedes and Porsche) five-star hotel while child vanishes. She gave them a list of friends and relations, anyone that he could have gone to. 'My son wouldn't do this!' she said.

The worst of it all was returning with the FLO to her flat to

check that Peter hadn't left a note, or packed a suitcase of his own volition. Of course he hadn't. In his bedroom, neat and tidy, he was unusual in that respect, she'd asked the FLO for a moment, closed the door and sunk down to her knees and wept into his duvet, head buried in the material that still smelt slightly of him. There by his bed was the Artemis Fowl book he'd been reading, there folded by his pillow were his pyjamas.

She stood up and dried her eyes. I won't cry again, not until he's found, she told herself. She rejoined the FLO.

'His overnight bag's still here,' she said. 'The one he'd packed to take to Sam's. I doubt he ever came back here.'

The FLO nodded, then asked hesitantly, 'Could you let me have his toothbrush and maybe his comb or hairbrush?'

'Of course,' Kathy said, then in puzzlement, 'Why?'

'For the DNA,' the FLO said simply. She saw Kathy's face crumple. 'I'm so sorry,' she said. It was all she could think of. Then it was back to the police station. It was painfully obvious to Kathy that they had very little information, and any steps were essentially constrained by this lack of knowledge. One part of her brain was still working analytically, although the rest of it was frozen with disbelief and misery. She was assured that an expert profiler was being brought in to help the investigation, that Peter's description and photo (taken from a file on Annette's laptop, recent and a good likeness of him) had been circulated nationwide to press and media. She said she was happy for it to be used from now on; she didn't have a better one. They told her all ports and airports had been informed, he had been entered on to the PNC, that it was only a matter of time before he was found. She wished she had more faith in

any of these measures.

Kathy had impressed everyone with her dry-eyed stoicism, her bravery in the face of every parent's worst nightmare. The reality behind the facade of calm was one of nearly utter hopelessness. In her heart, she did not believe that, barring a miracle, she would ever see her son alive again. And she was not the kind of person who believed in miracles. She felt totally vacant, a shell of a person. The mantra, this can't be happening, was running over and over in her head. Without much hope she prayed to God, as a policewoman brought her tea and the others tried to look busy and purposeful. It was a simple prayer, a plea bargain. In return for going to church

every day for the rest of her life, let him be found now. Alive. Or even better, if You exist and You're omnipotent, make it so none of this ever happened. You could do it with a blink of Your eye. It would be as simple as pressing 'return to last scene' on a DVD remote control.

Her tea grew cold. The clock ticked. Nothing changed. The asked for miracle didn't happen.

First Dan had died, now Peter had been taken from her. It was that simple. Well, Fate was in the running for a hat trick. If Peter didn't come back alive, she had no intention of carrying on without him, that was for sure. And she knew exactly how she would do it. No suicide bridge for Kathy. No need for that. She had enough insulin at home to kill an ox. She would leave a note on the bedroom door, swallow a handful of Valium, get into bed and inject herself with twenty-five units of NovoRapid. Within a few minutes her body would be rapidly exhausting all the sugars in her blood, she would black out and enter a coma from which she wouldn't wake up. If Peter died, she would too. She had no doubt in her mind whatsoever. What would be the point in carrying on? She nodded her head to herself in confirmation of her plan. It seemed quite foolproof.

The police in the room watched her solicitously but almost

nervously, as if she were suffering from something that might be contagious. No one could think of anything particularly helpful to say.

Kathy's mobile phone and her BlackBerry sat side by side in front of her in case the kidnapper called. Both had rung several times but she had recognized the caller in each instance and let it go through to voicemail. An officer was at her flat for now, another family liaison officer (what family? she thought bitterly) and she would monitor the landline. None of the police really expected the perpetrator to call. One of the police was saying something about a press conference that had been convened, was she up to doing it? It was always good to get the media involved.

'Yes,' she said in a clear voice immediately. She'd always been good at making decisions; it was one of the reasons she was so valued at work.

\* \* \*

On the street in North Holloway, Enver stroked his heavy, drooping moustache. 'Yes, ma'am,' he said. He turned round to face her.

Hanlon's face was inscrutable, her grey eyes cold, devoid of expression. Her hair was still damp from the shower at the gym. It was very thick, he thought, it would take a long time to dry. He suddenly wished he could touch it. The street around them was quiet. A few people passed by on the broad North London pavement; one glanced at the two of them curiously. Enver thought, we probably look like a married couple about to have a huge fight. She's furious and I'm standing here looking guilty.

'I take it this wasn't your idea?' she said with an air of menace.

Now there was a distinctly ugly look in her eyes and she moved closer to Enver. He was beginning to understand why people who knew Hanlon were wary, to say the least, of upsetting her. The ex-fighter in him understood why, either consciously or subconsciously, Hanlon was moving herself into his range. She was six inches shorter than him at least, so she was positioning herself for where her reach could make contact. Enver hoped it wouldn't come to that. If it did he'd most certainly fight back. There'd be no mercy from Hanlon and he didn't want her doing to him what she'd done to the heavy bag at the gym. He decided he would flatten her with

no compunction if he had to. He was a slow mover but he had fast hands and there was no way she would be able to block a punch from his sledgehammer fists. She was too light. He thought,

and because it's her, I probably wouldn't even get into trouble officially. I'd be offered counselling. Maybe a promotion. 'No, ma'am.'
He moved back a step. He felt slightly more

comfortable now he was out of her reach.

'Did Ludgate send you?' The two syllables of the DCS's name
were virtually spat out. Enver could almost see them lying on the
pavement.

'Ludgate?' he said, amazed at the thought. Hanlon stared up at
him impatiently. Enver realized she'd had enough of asking questions. It was time to come clean. 'Corrigan, ma'am, the assistant
commissioner, he told me to follow you.'

Hanlon snorted derisively through her nose. Enver wondered if
this were a Hanlon version of laughter.

'Corrigan,' she said, shaking her head. She stood before him,
irresolutely. Enver could almost see the tension, the adrenaline,
drain from her arms as she relaxed. She breathed deeply. 'Come
with me, Sergeant,' she commanded. 'You've got some explaining
to do.'

He followed her a hundred metres or so down the street until
they stopped outside one of the large terraced houses, and
suddenly Enver understood where they must be and whose flat
they were going to. Hanlon let herself in with a key. Enver realized,
with a pang of jealousy, how close the two of them must have been
and he followed her inside.

The house had been divided into flats and in the entrance hall
was an internal door that obviously led upstairs. You could see the
panelling in the hallway where a narrow staircase had been boxed
in. Police crime-scene tape sealed the door. Hanlon reached into
the pocket of her jacket and took something out

that fitted snugly in her hand. There was an audible click as the
blade sprang out of the flick knife. She severed the tape and opened
Whiteside's door. She looked at Enver.

'I cleared this with forensics, they're done here,' she said. They walked up the stairs into the flat. More stairs, thought

Enver, breathing heavily. He followed her inside the flat and into the lounge. Beneath the large window, overlooking the street, was the stain on Whiteside's carpet where he had lost so much blood. Hanlon stood with her arms folded, looking at it. Her face was drawn and thoughtful. She had a strong urge to touch it, to smear some on herself, if it was still wet enough, as a kind of tribute or talisman to her injured colleague. She turned away from Enver and he could see her raise her arm and, he guessed, wipe her eyes. She thought, he would have hated that stain on his beloved carpet. I remember when he bought it. He was so pleased with it.

'Sit,' she said to Enver, indicating the sofa where Whiteside had been facing her only the other night.

How can things happen so quickly? Hanlon was thinking to herself. Investigations seem to take forever; most of the people I've known personally who've died all had time to adjust or at least had an inkling something was coming, if only through age. It should only be strangers who die violently. Last night Mark was here where Demirel's sitting, and now... She couldn't, wouldn't, finish the thought. She looked at Enver. His sad, brown eyes reminded her of a dog, maybe a Basset hound. Looking at his well-upholstered form, shining with sweat, shirt bulging over his waistband, it was strange to think he'd once, not that long ago, been a boxer. Maybe when his dream died so had his athleticism. He'd sounded terribly out of breath walking up Whiteside's stairs. She thought of how amused Whiteside would have been by that, of his wolfish grin. Now he

was lying in a drug-induced coma with various drips attached to him, while they hoped for the bruised swelling in his brain to subside. Oh God, what did they do to you, Mark?

Hanlon's face showed nothing of her inner thoughts. 'So, what did Corrigan say to you about me?'

He replied to the question. He left nothing out. When Enver had finished talking, she hadn't moved. She was still standing, looking at the patch of bloodstained carpet. Hanlon hadn't put any lights on in the flat and the only illumination came from the street-lights in the road whose yellow gleam cast a soft glow into the room. Her face was mask-like.

'So Corrigan thinks if I found out who did this I might take the law into my own hands,' she said softly.

'Yes,' said Enver simply. He was beginning to find it increasingly easy to speak to Hanlon. You didn't need to qualify things.

'And he actually thinks I have a supply of illegal weapons?' she said contemptuously.

Enver said in an official tone, 'Well, according to the Restriction of Offensive Weapons Act 1959, ma'am, switchblades, such as you possess, are deemed illegal, not to mention the 1988 Criminal Justice Act, which makes the carrying of knives longer than three inches also illegal. So, in a sense, ma'am, he's already been proved right.'

Hanlon's head moved slightly once, as if she had nodded. In Turkey, this is a sign for 'no' but he interpreted it as Hanlon's way of conveying amusement. He knew Corrigan was right. Hanlon would almost certainly possess illegal firearms, he'd cheerfully bet money on it. It wouldn't be a gamble; it would be a certainty.

'Do you know who shot Whiteside, ma'am?' he suddenly asked.

'Yes,' she said. 'Well, I know who was responsible for ordering it.'

Enver breathed deeply. 'And are you going to take the law into your own hands, ma'am, like the AC fears?'

Hanlon looked at him. 'Oh, yes,' she said, in an almost surprised tone of voice. 'Very much so, Sergeant. That is exactly what I intend to do.' Enver looked lonely and bulky on his sofa, like a seal, she thought, his eyes sleepy as ever. 'Are you going to tell Corrigan?' she asked him.

It was Enver's turn to look surprised. 'No,' he said. 'No, I'm not.' I can't believe what I'm doing, he thought. 'Tell me, are they responsible for the Yilmaz killings too?'

Hanlon nodded. He thought of Mehmet, twisting his fingers nervously as he'd watched him and his uncle discussing his future. He thought of his little daughter, Reyhan, and their hopes for her future. He thought of the tiny body bag that had awaited Ali by the side of the canal and he thought too of Grey Rabbit. It was the toy that was maybe the clinching factor. He felt his eyes moisten and he was glad of the protective darkness of the room. He wouldn't have wanted Hanlon to see. This is for you, Grey Rabbit. Enver took a deep breath. 'Well, I'm going to help you then.'

## 27

HMP Wendover, thirty miles west of London, is a Category A prison. There are four bandings in the penal custodial system, which refer to the danger posed to the general public by the prisoner. Category A is for the most dangerous inmates. Dave 'Jesus' Anderson was now a high-risk prisoner in a high-risk jail.

He was currently on remand after his arrest for possession with intent to supply five kilograms of uncut cocaine with a conservative value of a quarter of a million pounds. He had been taking delivery of it with two of his men when Whiteside and the drug squad had busted him. It was a textbook scenario, a large lock-up garage, car, sports bag, bench, scales, drugs. It had looked to the police like a film set for a drugs bust. The photos that SOCO had taken alone would probably ensure a conviction.

Anderson knew immediately that someone had grassed him up, the moment the police had burst through the door. He had been over and over candidates for the informer's identity in his head more or less continually from the second the handcuffs went on him up to now, but with no credible suspect. He could not understand how anyone who knew would dare to do it. Who would have the balls to do this? Somewhere out there was a dead man walking.

He had been in Wendover for some time now. He had been arrested, appeared in court the following day; bail was denied, even with Cunningham passionately arguing his case. He hadn't been surprised by the decision and he was now here waiting on a court date for his trial. There had been a work-to-rule by the PCS Union and this had delayed legal proceedings. Meanwhile, he had tried to make the best of things. He was no stranger to prison.

Anderson's family were drug dealers. They were career criminals; Anderson was born into it. All ancillary crime, the beatings, the money laundering, intimidation, the occasional killing, were professionally driven. It was a family business, started by Malcolm, his father, thirty years ago and run now by Dave and his two brothers, Terry and Jordan. Dave, the middle brother, was the head of the operation. Terry would have been capable but was fundamentally lazy and Jordan had neither the brains nor the temperament. All three brothers were violent, both by nature and nurture, but the temper that burnt inside Dave Anderson was controlled. It was like a blowtorch: it was always there, usually on a pilot light, but when he wanted he could turn up the gas to a white-hot, incendiary degree. Jordan couldn't restrain himself when it came to violence. He would explode unpredictably. He was currently doing ten years in Armley Prison in Leeds for attempted murder and GBH over a pointless road rage incident. His absence made Dave's incarceration all the more troublesome. It had taken him two days and ten grand to get a mobile phone inside Wendover. He guessed he would have to run things from in here for a while. Malcolm, his father, was being treated for lung cancer, in fact had recently had a lung removed, and was in no frame of mind to work. They all knew, Malcolm included, the future was not rosy. Life had given him a sentence and the sentence wasn't life.

Anderson's cell was in B Wing. There were five wings at Wendover, A to E. They were ageing, red-brick structures, following the usual prison pattern of cells built on several floors, three high at Wendover, around a central, netted well. The net would catch anyone who jumped, fell or was pushed from one of the galleries, before they hit the ground.

Anderson hadn't been inside for a while, but it all came flooding back quickly enough. Nothing had changed. The echoing acoustics of prison were what he noticed first. Everything was metal, stone or brick, with the qualities of a claustrophobic swimming pool. Any sound was instantly magnified, from the slam of a door to a barked command. From a whisper to a shout. Then there was the smell of prison. Canteen cooking and men's bodies, and air that was never quite fresh enough, overlaid with pungent disinfectant. The noise was constant. It was multilayered. The jangle of the screws' keys on their belt and the squeak of their shoes on the flooring, the shouting, even the quietest of conversations, added to the hubbub. Just about all sound was amplified in here. And he'd forgotten too, the colours of prison, the yellow paint. Prisons always seemed to favour yellow. Anderson guessed some study must have claimed it soothed people – either that, or it was cheap – and then there were the blue denim uniforms of the prisoners and the dark ones of the warders, the grey of the ubiquitous metalwork. Finally, there was the durability of everything: iron staircases, iron bars, iron doors, stone walls, reinforced glass. Everything was designed, unlike normal places with comfort or style in mind, so it couldn't break or be broken, or smashed or used as a weapon. There was nothing soft in prison, nothing soft except flesh.

B Wing was controlled by a mass murderer. To be classified as such, you had to have killed at least four people and he just qualified for this. He had killed them without any 'cooling down' time and so was not deemed a serial killer. He was an old-timer called Andy Howe, who had butchered his father, his step-mother and two other people in one blood-drenched, murderous evening. He had used a machete. Andy was never going to be released. He'd been sentenced to a whole life tariff which meant he would never be freed unless by order of the Home Secretary. Nobody, Andy included, believed this would ever happen. This gave him a certain cachet in the small world in which he lived. He had quasi-celebrity status. Both guards and inmates were wary of Andy. In the fifteen years he had been inside, he had occasionally been challenged by other prisoners. It had been a mistake on their part.

He knew of Anderson by reputation and had gone out of

his way to be helpful. Anderson was offered cigarettes, grass, home-made booze, porn, various drugs. His father's illness had put Anderson off smoking anything, but he accepted alcohol and some Temazepam to help him sleep. Prison at night could be annoyingly noisy; sounds carried. Someone coughing could keep half the wing awake. He also accepted a very desirable job, cleaning the educational block. This job cost him another five thousand pounds to arrange. He could use his phone in there without being disturbed.

The educational facility was a brick-built building which stood alone in the prison grounds, unlike the other wings which were interconnected. It reminded Anderson of a village hall, if you pretended not to notice the bars on the windows or the metal door and the building's unusually stout construction. It consisted of two rooms joined together by an arch, with a small kitchen and toilet and storage facilities in the mid-section. The walls of the educational block were decorated with prisoners' art and motivational quotations from things they'd written.

'Reform starts from within' read one. 'Rage = Despair!' read another.

That kind of thing.

Anderson was able to use his time in the block to keep in touch with Terry, his brother, via his illegal mobile and generally relax, although he did do a certain amount of cleaning, just for form's sake. He could, after all, be in for a very long time, but like all experienced prisoners Anderson lived in the moment. You never serve a ten-year stretch, it's just one day. That's all you need to get through. One day at a time. And if you can't, do one day, do half a day, or do five minutes. That's the length of your sentence. It's a permanent 'now'. If you started thinking of the future, it would be intolerable. It's how you do a prison sentence. Anderson lived one day at a time. It was OK.

* * *

Peter Reynolds was not an experienced prisoner and he was being kept in conditions that would not be allowed in a UK prison. True, his cell was clean and he was reasonably fed and he had the dog, Tito, for company, but he was in total isolation. That would be regarded in the prison system as wrong, both from a practical point of view, because it tended to reinforce antisocial behaviour, and from an ethical point of view. His mood had changed from terror and incomprehension, to fear, to worry, but what he was feeling now, on this Sunday, was mainly excruciating boredom. The fear and the worry were still there, but they were like an ocean current below the surface.

He had scratched another two marks on his wall, which by his reckoning made today a Sunday and the current time, the afternoon. Incomprehension was another major part of what he was feeling. Peter was unable to think of a good reason for any of this. He had decided someone must be keeping him here for some sort of ransom, but probably not money. He knew they weren't poor but he knew his mum didn't have enough wealth to warrant this kind of attention. It had to be for some kind of unspecified favour or service. It must be something to do with her work. He only had a hazy idea what she did, other than travel a lot, but PFK Plastics made plastic things that went into machines. Maybe 'they', his kidnappers, wanted her to sabotage something or maybe 'they' wanted her to steal some plans. Maybe she didn't really work for PFK but was a spy? It had to be something like that. It seemed implausible, but what other answer made any kind of sense? Nobody would kidnap him for himself.

Salvation for Peter came later that day when two books that had been in his schoolbag were put through the hatch, together with a snack. He now had *Animal Farm* to read and a book on European history. He never thought the time would come when he would want to read George Orwell, he preferred Artemis Fowl or the Cherub books, but now he opened the dystopian novel with real joy. Anything to take his mind off the situation he was in. He worried about Tito too; the dog must be going mad with the confinement. He certainly was. He hoped his mum would do whatever they wanted her to do quickly. He had a physics textbook too in his bag. He knew that if the day came when he was looking forward to reading that, then he was definitely in trouble.

He stroked Tito's thick fur gently and the dog rolled on his

back and stretched. 'Poor love,' said Peter. He scratched its stomach with his fingertips and the dog groaned in ecstasy. Tito must be craving exercise, he thought. Oh, Mum, please come. Please God, let her come soon.

\* \* \*

It was the worst and longest Sunday of Kathy's life. At least when Dan was dying she had Peter, she had friends, she even had Dan, although he was slipping away from her. She could at least touch him as he lay in a morphine haze, to try and keep the pain at bay. This day she was in limbo. She couldn't think, she didn't want to do anything. There was nothing to do. She sat on the sofa in jeans and a sweatshirt, trainers on her feet, just in case they found Peter, so she'd be ready. A WPC, she'd forgotten her name, another support officer, fielded any telephone calls on her landline. She monitored her mobile and her email. This wasn't living. It was a living death.

\* \* \*

Hanlon had run ten miles that morning, really pushing her body to extremes, relishing the pain and the tiredness, feeling it cleanse her spiritually. As she ran through the London streets and parks, she thought about the events of the day before. In Hanlon's mind it was a question of personalities as much as of events and as her legs rhythmically moved and her feet bounded along the streets of London, traffic very quiet on the Sunday morning, she thought of them like a deck of cards, fanned out in her mind's eye. Hanlon had a very visual memory. Whiteside, the handsome, bearded Jack of Clubs. The Knave of Hearts, Rabbit Bingham; Corrigan, the King of Diamonds; Ludgate, the Jack of Diamonds; the shadowy Queen of Spades, the woman responsible for abducting Baby Ali, her face veiled from sight, obscured by shadow. I'll get you, you bitch, thought Hanlon. She was sure it was the same woman who had shot Whiteside. She did not believe he would have invited a man he didn't know into his flat. There was another card too, the Joker, face down so she couldn't see his face, Conquest's man, or possibly woman, hiding their true colours behind a Met uniform, one of her colleagues. And behind them all, the Dealer, Conquest himself, with his deck of souls, supplier of children. Every step she took hardened her resolve; every beat of her heart

strengthened her will. I will triumph, Conquest, and you will lose. It was as simple as that.

After Whiteside's shooting, she had dismissed any idea of going public with what she suspected. Conquest had an informant in the police force and anything they did, any action they took, would be potentially known to him.

Look at what had happened to the Yilmaz family. Mehmet had said he had new information; a short while later he was dead.

Look at what had happened to Whiteside. Sent to investigate Conquest; now the victim of an attempted murder.

At home she showered, dressed and went into work where she checked on the disappeared boy. She felt sure that it was Conquest. She didn't believe in coincidences. The Somali girl, Baby Ali, both sexual victims, and now a twelve-year-old boy had disappeared.

She checked on the Whiteside investigation. He was still alive, barely, and they'd induced a coma, hoping that the swelling and bruising to his brain would gradually resolve itself. The bullet lodged in the front of his head had been successfully removed but it had caused a great deal of damage. The effect of that damage remained unclear. The forensics people were checking the bullets recovered from his body to see if they had any matches; the shell casings had been removed by the shooter. Hanlon sat alone in her office and thought of what she was about to do. She had no proof that would satisfy anyone. Her actions to date were guaranteed to get her suspended from any

investigation, if not the police force.

She scratched her head and opened a can of Diet Coke while she thought about the situation again. First, what she knew.

The number eighteen, written on a bunker, on a lock gate, then on a scrap of newspaper, was present at three separate crime scenes. This irrevocably linked the three crimes; it was beyond coincidence.

Whiteside in his phone message to her had said that eighteen stood for Adolf Hitler. Conquest's dogs were named after Hitler's animals. It was tenuous, but it was a link between Conquest and the crimes. There was another link too. Conquest was involved with Bingham. That spelled child sex. Two of the crimes were sexual in nature and involved children; the third, Peter Reynolds, was probably sexual in nature.

Whiteside had found information on Conquest that they didn't have on their own police records. That was almost certain proof of some criminal connection.

The Yilmaz family had been silenced after Mehmet had phoned the police and said he had new information about the woman who had taken Ali.

From these facts Hanlon decided that Conquest lay behind this. He had the temperament, the brains, the organizational ability and the money to carry it out. Hanlon also thought it a safe bet Conquest had someone on the inside. Conquest and Bingham were linked in this somehow. Conquest had at least three other people working for him. There was the woman behind the Baby Ali kidnap and the two men who had taken the Yilmaz family. Then there would be a fourth person, his Metropolitan Police informer. She suspected that Whiteside had obviously trusted whoever had shot him enough to let them into his flat. That's why she was assuming it was the woman, possibly even Conquest's contact in the Met. His mobile phone was missing. Hanlon guessed he had recorded the interview on that.

Hanlon drank more Coke and looked out of her window at the uninspiring view of the brick wall. If only she could find out what Whiteside had discovered. The Shapiro Institute would not allow her access; she would have to tell them she had lied to get Whiteside through their door. They were not an official Israeli government agency and would not be pleased that Saul had provided fraudulent documentation to a Met policeman. They would be very angry indeed at this breach in protocol. She had already, in their eyes, compromised their security and they were frantically, justifiably in their view, paranoid. That avenue was closed to her.

She wondered how Conquest could have known that Whiteside had been at the institute. Maybe he'd been followed. Maybe he'd mentioned it to Childs who had told someone else. She didn't suppose it really mattered how he'd found out. Maybe one day she'd have the opportunity to ask him.

Either way, Conquest had obviously decided that Whiteside, who was, as far as he knew, a bona fide journalist, needed dealing with and he had done just that. He must have got a nasty shock when he discovered he'd been responsible for shooting a Met policeman.

She couldn't make public her suspicions. Ludgate was leading the Ali murder enquiry and was in overall charge of the SIOs for the Yilmaz and Reynolds disappearances. He was viewed as a safe pair of hands and particularly good at handling the media. Much as she disliked him, she agreed. If she approached him with what she knew, it would be giving him her head on a plate. She doubted she could begin to calculate all the rules she'd broken, bent or infringed. Corrigan would go crazy. She might as well resign.

On the plus side, if she kept quiet, she was free to act as she saw fit. Hanlon's spirits rose slightly. She'd do it her way. She also had a team, if you counted Enver Demirel. She would be unconstrained by police procedural rules. She wasn't even all that concerned if what she did prejudiced the outcome of

a potential trial. She didn't want a trial; she wanted justice. Hanlon didn't really want to leave justice in the hands of a system she didn't trust, that she thought favoured the guilty over the inno-cent. At least she could rely on herself. She couldn't trust anyone apart from Demirel and she wouldn't even trust him fully. Well, luckily, she didn't need to tell anyone what she was going to do next. She picked up the phone and made a call. A while later she replaced the phone on its handset. Rabbit

Bingham, she thought. We'll meet again.

## 28

Alastair Fordham, the governor of Wendover Prison, studied himself in the mirror in his office. As usual, not a hair out of place. Fordham was an ex-Marine and it showed. He was also Cambridge educated and no stranger to the media. If there was a news item on prisons on *Newsnight* or a documentary, the chances were that Fordham would be there, giving the professionals' point of view. Fordham was held in high regard at the Home Office and strangely in the prison service, or the National Offender Management Service as it's officially known, as well. The two bodies rarely agreed on anything else.

Fordham had ordered his staff to extend all possible help to DI Hanlon. They'd never met but he knew of her and he admired her. He felt they were kindred spirits. Both had records of leading by example. Both had received medals for bravery. Both had been in trouble for disobeying orders.

At the beginning of the Afghanistan conflict, Fordham's men had come under withering fire as their patrol had crossed a river. Fordham had risked his life to rescue two young soldiers from certain death. For this action he was subsequently awarded the

Military Medal. So he felt a sympathy, a resonance, with Hanlon, as he would with anyone prepared to do what they had both done. They were both prepared to lay down their lives for others. Both had been decorated for it. He had a

great respect for bravery. His staff had been ordered to treat her with all possible consideration. He was looking forward greatly to meeting her.

He was satisfied with his reflection. As he brushed some imagined dust from his sleeve, he thought, I wonder what she wants with Anderson?

* * *

Hanlon waited in the interview room for Anderson to arrive. Prisons made her think of a strange mix of fortress and school. Even the way prisoners addressed the officers and visitors was archaically polite. It was like going back in time to a more mannered age.

HMP Wendover, one of England and Wales' hundred and thirty-one prisons, was Victorian. Like most Victorian buildings, it was designed to impress. It had massive brick walls, twenty feet high, the top few feet covered in a decorative, plain stone cladding, so it looked as if it had been capped by a stonemason dentist. The front gate was huge, panelled and studded like something from a medieval fortress. For someone arriving on foot it was a peculiar sensation to walk through the small door within the huge wooden portal. It felt like visiting a giant's castle.

Inside the enormous gate, in a side office off the vast, vaulted arch of the entrance, she was searched by an attractive blonde woman officer, signed a visitor's form and was issued with a pass. The fairytale world of the prison, a fairytale from the Brothers Grimm, not Disney, was emphasized by the discrepancy between the noisy rush outside and the disturbing tranquility within. The silence was almost oppressive.

A tough-looking, wiry, silver-haired prison guard, with the twin stars on his uniform denoting he was a principal prison officer, led her into the grounds of the prison.

From inside you could appreciate how big the place was.

The black, tarmacked driveway through the prison that they walked down was very wide and everywhere was immaculately clean. The only signs of life were three prisoners silently tending a flower bed. It was as peaceful and relaxing as a sanatorium out here. She knew that inside the cell blocks there would be a great deal of noise, but it was contained within their walls. Hanlon reflected that prisons were such places of extremes: it was either tranquil or a riot. There was very little in between. John, the guard who accompanied her, was a pleasant, laconic individual. Like most prison guards he seemed to have a good sense of humour. Hanlon guessed it was almost a prerequisite of the job; you had to be able to laugh or you'd

never last.

Any prisoner that they encountered greeted them politely. Hanlon was reminded again that prison was a strange place. There was always an atmosphere of strained civility mixed with the constant threat of violence. The last time she'd interviewed someone in a prison, the alarms had suddenly sounded and they'd found themselves in the middle of a lockdown. She found out later one of the inmates had had his throat slashed, the news of which had sparked a riot. She'd sat in a secure room while a flash flood of enraged humanity had seethed down the narrow corridor. Even for Hanlon it had been an unsettling experience. In one of the corridors today, she'd walked past a large, glass trophy cabinet mounted on the wall. In a school such a cabinet would contain trophies and cups. Here it contained a selection of home-made weapons, mainly shanks or knives, recently recovered. Razor blades set in handles, toothbrushes filed to needle-sharp points, ingenious arrangements of broken glass. There was even a wooden pistol fashioned by one of the inmates. It really didn't do to underestimate anyone in a

Category A prison.

They were walking past a low prison outbuilding. 'A wing,' said John with a jerk of his head. 'Sexual offenders.'

Hanlon nodded. Hello, Rabbit, she thought. Enjoying life in your hutch? The sex offenders had to be rigidly separated from the other prisoners, even to a certain extent from each other. The other inmates would have attacked them on sight. They were despised and they acted like a conduit, a lightning rod for the other prisoners' suppressed rage. There was a rigid social order in prison and the inmates took a kind of pride in their hatred of the sex offenders. It was their way of showing the world they too had morality, they too had standards. The sex offenders were good for the other prisoners' self-esteem. Whatever they were, they weren't nonces.

She thought of Rabbit Bingham, intelligent, witty, entrepreneurial, charming, self-deprecating, in many ways a catalogue of virtues, and a huge risk to any child he came within reach of. He, like virtually all child abusers, was totally without remorse. She doubted if Bingham even realized he was a monster. He'd told her in all seriousness that children often quite liked sex, it was a matter of how it was done. He'd dropped famous names of other well-known sex offenders into the conversation: Oscar Wilde, André Gide, Jimmy Savile, Roman Polanski, Gary Glitter, Stuart Hall. One day, he said, it'll be legal, like homosexuality. He also pointed out that marriage in many countries was permitted at the age of puberty, or below, and not fixed at some arbitrary figure. He told Hanlon that in some cases he knew of men who'd been led on by eight-year-olds. He himself had been broken in – his term – by a neighbour when he was ten and he'd come to love it.

'I'm talking from experience, Detective Inspector,' he'd said seriously. 'Children love sex.' Bingham, she had been reliably informed, had raped a three-year-old.

They all knew that the moment Bingham was released, he'd re-offend. She remembered how when interviewing him, Bingham gave nothing away, betrayed no one. Well, at that time she'd been constrained by PACE regulations. I wonder how you'll stand up to a more robust interrogation, Bingham, she thought. I know you're a monster. You fooled the judge who gave you the lightest sentence he could, you may even have fooled yourself, but I know you're evil and I will not regret what I'm about to do.

\* \* \*

Anderson was waiting for her in the interview room. It was furnished with two chairs and a table. The table was secured to the floor. Anderson was as she remembered him, tall, thin, and hollow-cheeked. He had grown his hair and it hung in rat-tails over his face. He looked ascetic and slightly crazy, like a killer monk, a clean-shaved Rasputin. John, the prison officer, looked enquiringly at Hanlon. His eyes said, are you sure about this?

Hanlon curtly ordered, 'You can leave us now.'

'Just press the button when you want me to come and get you,' John said.

The metal door closed behind him and there was an emphatic noise as the key turned with finality in the lock. They were alone together. Anderson sat down without being asked, on the opposite side of the table to Hanlon, and raised his eyebrows enquiringly.

'And what do you want?' he asked. He remembered Hanlon from the time before he'd been arrested. She hadn't been able to make that charge stick. He'd found out who was testifying against him. The witness had children. Anderson made sure he knew where they were, where they went to school. The witness withdrew his testimony and Anderson walked. No chance of

that happening in this case – five kilos of coke weren't going to disappear.

'I'd like your assistance, please,' Hanlon said.

Anderson smiled, a smile that didn't reach his eyes. Hanlon's own eyes were cold but Anderson's were dead. When he looked you up and down, it was as if he were measuring you for a coffin. There was no humanity in his bleak gaze. Both inmates and guards alike preferred the company of Andy Howe, the multiple murderer, to Anderson. At least Howe was human, even if badly flawed. Anderson would kill you or hurt you with as little compunction as a man might swat a fly, and with less compassion.

'I'm sure you would,' he replied. His accent and inflection were typically London. He spoke quietly. He didn't need to raise his voice.

Looking at him reminded Hanlon of how right she'd been to get him put behind bars. Anderson was a man untroubled by conscience or conventional morality. She reflected momentarily on the irony of the fact that she'd broken the law to get him in prison. Now, if he did what she wanted, and she was sure he would, she'd have to break it again to get him out.

Hanlon looked steadily in his direction. She didn't bother trying to maintain eye contact. She wasn't in a staring contest; she just needed Anderson to do what she wanted. Anderson had no intention of speaking first. He was in no hurry. By his own reckoning he had about ten years to go of sitting around behind prison walls. What was the rush?

'This prison is Victorian, you know,' said Hanlon conversationally. 'It's been here for 150 years. You'll be here a while as well. You'll be part of its history too. You could look into it, give yourself something to do while you're here. Architecture is very interesting; I think so anyway.' Anderson

studied his fingernails with feigned indifference.

'Perhaps you'll come to like it too. Inigo Jones, Sir Christopher Wren, Norman Foster, Vanbrugh, all the greats,' she added. Hanlon knew he must be wondering why she'd wanted to see him, but, of course, he wouldn't ask. She carried on.

'Or maybe, Mr Anderson, if architecture's not your thing, there's always history. Maybe you could study penal history while you're in here, since you're surrounded by it, so to speak.' She tugged gently at a strand of her hair. It was thick and coarse. It was hard to do anything with it.

'You'd have to do it the old-fashioned way. You'll have to use books, not being allowed Internet.'

'I know who you are, Hanlon,' said Anderson with studied menace. He raised his eyes. It was a look that would make most people flinch.

Hanlon leant across the table so her face was close to his. 'Good,' she said, very softly. He could feel her breath on his face. 'I'm glad.'

They held that position, staring now into each other's eyes for a few heartbeats. Anderson broke the spell first. He moved back in his chair. He was impressed by what he'd seen in the policewoman's eyes. It was almost like looking into a mirror. 'The copper that nicked me. I heard he got shot.' He smiled,

a parody of sweetness.

'That's correct. He got shot. He got shot three times to be precise. Two to the body. One to the head. That's why I'm here,' said Hanlon. 'He is a friend of mine, as well as a colleague.'

Anderson laughed. 'Do you think I was responsible, is that what you think? I thought you were supposed to be smart.'

'If I thought that,' said Hanlon, 'I wouldn't be talking to you. I'd be talking about you, to one of the many new friends you've got on your wing.' While Anderson digested this not so

veiled threat, she said, rather thoughtfully, 'There's a man in here, on A wing. Rabbit Bingham, do you know him?'

Anderson looked surprised. 'A wing. He's a nonce?' Hanlon nodded. 'He's a nonce.'

'I don't mix with nonces,' said Anderson. Hanlon sighed. 'That wasn't my question.'

Anderson asked, 'So what's he got to do with your sergeant?' Hanlon had had enough of beating around the bush. 'He used to be partners with the man behind the shooting, Harry Conquest. Conquest is also involved in the sex trafficking of children. I want to know where he keeps them captive. I also

want to know anything relevant to Whiteside's shooting.'

Anderson stretched luxuriously and flexed his powerful fingers. So that's why she's here. He was surprised by the request. The implication was clear. The DI was hardly likely to expect him to befriend this Bingham and gain his confidence, even if he'd been able to do so. The unstated message was, get him to talk. Beating people up for a confession or for information by the police had gone out with the ark and Bingham was safe in prison anyway, so she wouldn't be able to do it herself. He didn't doubt her capacity to do it, not now he had seen her eyes; he was just amazed she'd contemplate it. It would wreck any trial. He'd certainly never come across police violence in his dealings with them. Things had changed since his dad's day, as the old man frequently reminded him. Blah, blah, Kray twins, blah, blah, Charlie Richardson, blah, blah, George Davis. Not like the old days. He suddenly wondered if this was some kind of trap to make him attack another prisoner and get his sentence increased. He looked at her and decided it probably wasn't.

'He's a nonce, he'll be hard to get to,' he said. 'Even if I wanted to. Why should I?'

Hanlon ignored his question. 'I didn't say it would be easy,' she said. 'How you do it is up to you. And you will do it. There is another problem. One of time. Conquest has taken a twelve-year-old boy. He's diabetic with a limited supply of insulin. I don't think he'll last much beyond the weekend. You've only got four days.'

Anderson stood up slowly and leant on the table over Hanlon. 'And what do I get out of it? Unlimited access to Sky TV?' He spoke quietly, his voice low with sarcastic overtones. 'What could the Metropolitan Police possibly offer me in return for my help?'

'Nothing,' said Hanlon. He sat down again, surprised at the answer. He started to speak and Hanlon held her hand up to interrupt him. 'The police don't do deals like that. I, however, can get you out of here.'

Anderson looked around him theatrically and made an actor's sweeping gesture with his hand, taking in the barred windows, the iron door, the brickwork.

'How would you do that?' he asked her sceptically. 'Magic?' 'I'd tamper with the evidence that put you away,' said Hanlon simply. She looked at her fingernails, cut short and covered with clear varnish. She studied them, then put her head back and looked

at Anderson. She could see she had his undivided attention.

'I would break the seals on two of the evidence bags. We've got five kilograms of what we claim is your coke in our evidence room, on a shelf, in a box. All neatly secured and labelled. Possession of that coke is the evidence against you. QED. It's what you've been charged with, possession with intent to supply. You know that.'

Anderson was paying attention now, that was for sure.

'If there is any suggestion that this evidence is not what it seems, then the case against you has a massive flaw. Your brief

will demand a further examination of the evidence, claiming

that you were fitted up. We've got nothing to hide, we'll say yes. An independent examiner will determine that the evidence

– the drugs seized – has been tampered with, and this will come out in court. Some of the alleged cocaine will turn out to be, oh, I don't know, icing sugar, say. Dextrose. It hardly matters. It'll look as if you've been framed by an over-eager drug squad. I think that should be more than enough to have the case thrown out.' She paused to let this sink in. 'It could be argued that what you were nicked with never was cocaine, that our analysis was fraudulent from the start. Any lawyer, no matter how incompetent, would get you off on that. At the very least, reasonable doubt would exist. We'll be completely wrong-footed; no one will know what's happened. It'll be a shambles.'

Anderson was silent. She was certainly right. Evidence tam

pering would raise all kinds of issues: planting of evidence by the police, perjury, conspiracy to pervert the course of justice, and certainly reasonable doubt would be established. He'd walk. But could he trust her? He looked at the woman opposite. He knew he could. Hanlon was the real deal.

'You might even get some form of compensation,' she said helpfully.

But could he get to this Bingham? His mind was working furiously fast. Could he do it? He wondered. It was, as the DI had said, a problem of time. Yes, he could get to Bingham, but in such a short time? Usually time was in huge supply in prison; not in this case. Then that created the problem of bribing at least one of the screws, almost certainly more than one, to create a situation where he could get hold of Bingham for an hour. Half an hour would do, but Anderson hated being rushed and there'd be cleaning up to be done. It'd be ridiculous

to have Hanlon make good on her part of the bargain only to be charged with, and end up doing time for, assaulting Rabbit Bingham. But this was running ahead of things; let's deal now with the present, and with the most obvious question: 'This isn't official, is it? If any of this goes wrong, all bets are off, aren't they?' he said.

Hanlon was conducting a vendetta, that much was obvious. Whatever she was planning to do with the information it wouldn't stand up in court. Tampering with evidence would get her jailed. She must really have a thing about her colleague Whiteside, or really hate this character Conquest. Hate is a powerful emotion; he could sympathize with that.

Hanlon's mouth performed a smile of genuine sweetness and warmth for Anderson. Her eyes remained cold and hard. 'Yes, of course it's unofficial. If either of us gets caught, well, it's goodnight Vienna. But, Mr Anderson, let's not dwell on that unpleasant possibility, shall we? I'm sure we're both optimists at heart. You do your job and I'll do mine. If all goes to plan, and why shouldn't it, you'll be out in a few weeks, and

Conquest will...'

Anderson finished the sentence for her in his head. He'll be dead. It's what he would do. He wondered if she would be capable of it. She stopped speaking and extended her open hands with a kind of gentle shrugging motion. She looked at Anderson. It was a look he recognized. He had seen it in his own eyes in the mirror a few times. It confirmed his suspicions. It was reassuring to know the kind of person he was about to deal with. Amateurs and weaklings were untrustworthy. He could do business with Hanlon. He had a feeling Conquest wouldn't be coming to trial – at least, not in a legal sense. Hanlon had already passed judgement.

'Deal,' he said and they shook hands.

'Before the end of the week,' she said. He nodded. She pushed the button that would tell the guard to let her out and return Anderson to his cell. John, the principal prison officer, appeared in the doorway to escort her. 'The governor would like a word, ma'am,' he said quietly as the two of them left.

Mountfield, another screw, was standing behind him, ready to escort Anderson back to his wing. Anderson watched Hanlon go.

He didn't know who Conquest was but he was glad he wasn't in his shoes. Conquest, if Hanlon had her way, was a dead man walking.

## 29

It was night, and in her flat overlooking the Thames, flowing black, turbulent and powerful far below – a suitable metaphor for her feelings towards Conquest – Hanlon stood looking out at the water and the lights on the South Bank of the great river, thinking of Whiteside, thinking of Conquest, planning her revenge.

Enver had been wrong about which part of London Hanlon lived in, but not by much. She lived just off Upper Thames Street, close to Southwark Bridge, in the heart of the City of London. She could see it all now, understand it all, the chess game that Conquest had started and she had become involved in as his default opponent. Conquest's pieces were currently faceless, the two men who had abducted the Yilmaz family and the woman who had taken the Yilmaz child. They were also responsible for the death of the Somali girl and the attempted murder of Whiteside. Another major unidentified piece on Conquest's side

of the chessboard was his informant in the police.

He had more pieces but she was the White Queen. She could move anywhere; she wasn't restricted like the others.

She stood up and moved restlessly around the enormous room

that formed the main body of the flat. A spiral staircase in the corner of the room led up to the roof upon which she could sunbathe in the spring and summer. She had a small

bedroom, just big enough for a double bed, and a kitchen and bathroom. Hanlon rarely had visitors; she didn't like her personal space invaded by people. Even Whiteside had never been here. Officially, Hanlon's address was not this one; the flat itself was not in her own name. It's easy to be anonymous when you don't have friends.

She couldn't relax. The shooting of Whiteside was continually at the back of her mind like a piece of mental wallpaper. She had turned all the lights off in the flat and she paced up and down like a tiger in its cage, staring out across the dark expanse of the water to the lights on the south side. The wall overlooking the Thames was virtually one huge sheet of glass upon which she was projecting her thoughts like on a screen. She conjured up the image of Conquest's confident, smiling face. Conquest and Bingham. She thought about Rabbit Bingham. She might have guessed their paths were fated to cross again.

Bingham had earned his nickname from his teeth. The front ones were prominent and stuck out; the resulting name was almost inevitable. He had told her during an interview that obviously, as a child, he hadn't liked it, but things could have been worse. They could have been a lot worse. His face rose up before her like a hologram. Bingham was odd-looking. Tall and flabby with a skull-like face, he had lank, receding blond hair which had started to fall out when he was young. He told her he was already going bald when he was at school. As a kid he had been a strange mixture of effeminate and old.

He had informed her of all of this in some interview room with real urgency, as if it were important she understood him. He kind of latched on to her almost as if she were his friend. Whiteside he hadn't liked. He'd refuse to talk if Whiteside was in the room. Hanlon felt another spasm of rage shake her when

she thought that Bingham would be delighted to hear about what had happened to him.

Her memory took her back to Bingham. So, all in all, he felt he'd got off reasonably lightly with being called Rabbit. It sounded almost affectionate. It was the kind of name someone with friends had, and he had never been that sort of person. He had grown up, but the nickname stuck. Paul was his real name, yet he found himself telling people, 'My friends call me Rabbit.'

After leaving school he'd drifted into IT and discovered a talent for it. His paedophile tendencies, which grew stronger and stronger the older he got, had spurred him on in his studies. It's not my fault, he told Hanlon, I was born this way, I didn't choose it. The closed world of child Internet porn opened like a rare flower before the expert stroking of Bingham's nimble, caressing fingers on the computer keyboard.

He had served three years for the paedophile image collection on his PC's hard drive. Now he had only four months to go.

Conquest must have been combining his money and abilities with Bingham's paedophile connections and IT expertise, thought Hanlon. It was a kind of hideous, hellishly perfect marriage. Most paedo porn was Internet-based, but you needed a source and she could bet that the dead children had been part of it. Unless she found Peter Reynolds soon, he would be part of it too. Having no knowledge of the Nazi-obsessed Robbo, she was at a loss to understand why Conquest had been flagging up the bodies with the number 18, the Adolf Hitler code. Perhaps he was just crazy.

She sat down cross-legged on the floor in front of the window. The room was virtually furniture free. Hanlon didn't like furniture much. The only decoration was a signed, framed photograph of the artist Joseph Beuys, who stared impassively down from beneath his trademark hat at Hanlon's muscular back. She looked out at the night. Southwark Bridge was brilliantly lit above the darkness of the Thames. She was in a perfect lotus pose, but her thoughts were hardly meditative.

Anderson would get her the answer she needed. The boy would be in one of Conquest's properties and Bingham would know where. He would tell Anderson. Anderson would do whatever was necessary to make Bingham talk. Then Anderson would tell her.

Conquest was not going to stand trial. She would see to that.

## 30

Like all the sexual offenders at HMP Wendover, Bingham had to be strictly segregated from the other prisoners. He was a Category C prisoner, which meant staff thought he wasn't an escape risk (unlike Howe in B wing, who had nothing to lose) but was unsuitable for an open prison. As if by way of compensation, although nobody really felt sorry for him, Bingham had been given a coveted job. He got to clean the library for several hours a week when it was closed to other inmates. Bingham was one of Wendover's most trusted prisoners. He had no choice but to adhere strictly to security measures; it was what kept him alive. The library job was suitable for Bingham because it didn't need a team to do it, he was highly literate and, above all, a fanatic about cleanliness and order.

In fairness to Bingham, he did do a wonderful job. The small

library had never been so polished, dusted or well organized. Bingham enjoyed this task immensely. It was a change of scenery from A wing, extremely welcome in itself, and for a brief period of time he felt normal, as if he were doing a normal job in a normal place, like a regular person does in the outside world. He could almost forget he was in prison. He also liked the company of books. In another life he'd have enjoyed being a librarian.

Books were non-judgemental, unlike people. Here he had the company of other paedophiles: William Burroughs, André

Gide, Oscar Wilde, Lewis Carroll, Jean Genet. It was quite a distinguished list. He felt he belonged in that august company, not with these rough, unhygienic, uncultured criminals.

Today, however, he was surprised to find that Jardine, a prison officer who he didn't know well, was taking him, not down the usual series of internal corridors and gates that led to the library but on an unfamiliar route. This ended in the two of them standing outside A wing in the open courtyard that stretched over to a rectangular building. Bingham knew this to be the education block. Jardine looked at him imperiously. The screw was huge, six foot six and extremely powerfully built. He was a committed bodybuilder. Age was taking its toll on his sharply defined physique, and steroid abuse had also taken its toll on his temper and his skin condition, both poor. Unbeknownst to the prisoners but not to himself or Mrs Jardine, the steroids had also affected his virility, which added to Jardine's ill humour. Faded blue-green tattoos of a nautical style, anchors, mermaids, King Neptune, were inked into his skin. He was ex-Royal Navy. Rumour had it that Jardine was on the take but Bingham wouldn't know. He had never tried to bribe a prison officer; he wouldn't dare. Bingham was not a risk-taker; he knew himself deep down to be a coward, frightened of pain, frightened by threats. It was partly what had drawn him to Conquest. Bingham hero-worshipped Conquest's easy competence with violence. He wished he was brave, but he knew he wasn't. Jardine frightened him. He hadn't dared ask where they were going.

Prison was quite the worse thing that Bingham could have imagined happening to him. It was a terrifying place and he lived in mortal fear of the other prisoners. He had never visualized jail, not in his most vivid nightmares. He had always been so very careful. The only reason he was here was because an

ex-sexual partner (Bingham, who was a precise man verbally, would not have used the word 'boyfriend', and friendship had never been part of the equation) had shopped him to the police in a plea bargain attempt. What, after all, had he done? Looked at photos that he hadn't even taken. The regular sex trips he'd made to Thailand and Vietnam hadn't even come up in the trial. Besides, that was abroad anyway. The work he had done for Conquest had also remained secret. The organized sexual assaults, the recruitment of child prostitutes, the sex parties – none of this had come out.

Even if it had, he wouldn't have implicated Conquest. He had kept quiet during his interrogation out of a fear of Conquest as well as his love for the man. The police were sure Bingham knew quite a lot about the provenance of the imagery. This was correct, more than correct, but Bingham knew that if he implicated him, Conquest would have him killed. But it wasn't just that. He loved Conquest in his way. Love would have closed his lips as effectively as fear. So despite all the offers of reduced sentencing and lesser charges, his lips remained sealed.

'We've done some roster changes,' said Jardine to Bingham as they contemplated the empty yard in front of them. 'We heard that one of the prisoners was planning an attack on you in the library, so we're moving you to clean the education block instead.' He pointed at it. 'As you can see, it's isolated so you'll be safe there. Nobody will be able to get to you.' He smiled unpleasantly at Bingham. 'We wouldn't want anything untoward happening to you now, would we?'

Bingham caught a smell of halitosis from the officer's mouth and wrinkled his nose in distaste. Bingham, morbidly conscious of his own teeth, spent a great deal of time, which of course he had in abundance, flossing and cleaning and brushing. Plaque was his sworn enemy. His own teeth gleamed with almost

surgical cleanliness. Jardine's teeth were yellow with dark streaks of build-up between each tooth. Bingham shuddered inwardly. He found the smell of the decay disgusting.

'Thank you,' he said politely. A prison attack was what he feared most in life, with good reason. He sometimes had vivid nightmares about it. He could imagine with horrible three-dimensional clarity the shank, the home-made knife, ripping into his flesh, his blood spurting out. In his fevered imagination he had suffered this attack maybe hundreds of times. Shakespeare was right about cowards and their multiple deaths. There were three hundred and fifty men within the walls who would all be happy to do it.

The two of them walked across the tarmac to the building and Jardine let him in. His keys rattled in the metal door.

'In you go,' he said. 'Cleaning stuff is in a cupboard by the toilet. It's ten now, I'll be back at twelve. I want a good job doing, understood, Paul?'

'Yes, sir,' said Bingham.

He watched as the door closed. He frowned to himself. Jardine had departed with suspicious haste. The instructions were unusually vague. Normally everything in a prison was laboriously spelt out as if the assumption was that you were retarded. Things were ticked off on lists. Everything had to be accounted for. In the library the cleaning materials were checked off against columns detailing product type and quantity. They could, after all, be used to poison or blind someone. Due diligence was exercised to a tedious degree. Something did not feel right. The key turned again in the lock. He was alone in the building. Then he sensed movement behind him. He froze in fear. Not good. Not good at all. Bingham turned.

There, standing looking at him, was a tall, thin man he'd never seen before, dressed in prison denim. Long, unkempt hair obscured his face. The man's eyes gleamed dangerously. 'Hello, Rabbit,' he said softly.

Bingham's heart raced uncontrollably and he thought for a second he was going to faint. To be a nonce and alone with another prisoner could realistically only mean one thing. The attack wasn't planned for the library; it was planned for here and Jardine had delivered him to it. He felt the wet warmth in his jeans as he stared at the other man and lost control of his bladder in his terror. The other prisoner noticed the telltale change of colour in the material from light to dark blue. He shook his head but didn't seem surprised.

'Oh dear me,' he said softly and advanced swiftly on Rabbit, who was too frightened to move or speak. Bingham's nightmare had begun.

\* \* \*

Clarissa and Conquest stood on the quayside and watched as the small lorry carefully reversed off the boat that had come from the lodge on the mainland to Strood Island. The island was comma-shaped, nearly a mile long, and lay about a quarter of a mile off the Essex coast in the North Sea near Walton-on-the-Naze, the nearest town.

The island had a large nineteenth-century Gothic-style manor house on it that had been built by a Victorian businessman who had taken up the then relatively new hobby of sailing for pleasure. There was a small natural harbour on the coastal side of the island, protected from the sea by a low hill that rose up behind the house, and the harbour had been enhanced by a mole that ran out from the shore, leaving a gap suitable for a sizeable boat.

Conquest had bought the island about twenty years ago. It had been dirt cheap. No one wanted it. The house was dilapidated, falling down in parts. It had no electricity or gas,

the quay in front of the house on the island was in poor condition and the lodge that went with it on the mainland was in an equally rundown state.

At the time Conquest was still selling drugs. Ecstasy was the new kid on the block and new strains of grass like skunk were beginning to supplant black as the thing to smoke. The Dutch had control over the E so Conquest was spending a good deal of time going backwards and forwards to the continent. Twice now he'd been stopped, searched and questioned by French border control, alerted by his unusual travel history. With a motorboat, he could just sail over and bypass officialdom. Brittania rules the waves, thought Conquest. He had been using lorry containers from Rotterdam to Harwich to move the ecstasy. He felt he was having to pay too much to bribe HMRC officials and wanted to cut them out.

The idea of sailing the drugs over had never come to any

thing. But later, when he started going big with Bingham, the house on the island proved ideal.

The land surrounding the house had been landscaped to a certain extent and was mostly enclosed by a two metre-high wall built to protect the plants in the garden from the cold winds of the North Sea. There was a gap, however, that led to a field, originally put there for agricultural purposes to provide grazing for dairy cows. It was here that Conquest had decided to put the pigs. The fences surrounding the field had been strengthened and a dozen shelters for the pigs installed, with a wallow created for their comfort, and today the animals themselves arrived. There were six of them, five females and a tusked boar, all sizeable and pink. Conquest knew from Glasgow Brian, who was guiding them off the truck with a board and shouts of encouragement, that they were

Large Whites, and they would eventually weigh in at a couple of hundred kilos each.

When she was a young girl, Clarissa used to have an illustrated copy of the fairy story 'The Three Billy Goats Gruff', and the Troll who lived under the bridge was the very image of Brian. Like the Troll he was enormous, obese, very strong and covered in black hair. His teeth were yellowed and irregularly shaped, with occasional gaps where they'd been knocked or kicked out in fights.

A few years ago, he'd had a body to dispose of. A turf war had got out of hand and a rival biker had died in a fight at a meeting held to establish peace talks. Maybe unsurprisingly, the meeting had turned violent. The peace negotiators had agreed to come unarmed. All had brought knives or guns. Pete had a cottage with land attached and he farmed on a low-key scale. He'd volunteered to get rid of the dead Hell's Angel. He had experimented by quartering the dead biker and feeding him to the pigs that he kept on his smallholding. It was very successful. Pigs are omnivorous with big appetites and their forty-four teeth are capable of chewing through most organic things. The only drawback really was that small bones, like those of fingers or toes, passed through the pigs' digestive system fairly intact. They would be readily identifiable as human to the trained eye. They were too small and it was too time-consuming to search for them in the mud churned up by the animals or to go through their excrement.

It wasn't a foolproof system but it functioned well enough.

It would be possible to work out what had happened, but you'd need to know what you were looking for. It would have to be a pretty painstaking search by the police to find anything incriminating. They'd have to sift through a couple of acres of mud. It wasn't something you might stumble across. It was certainly better than burial or cremation.

With these pigs on the island, Conquest would now have a

ready-made waste-disposal system and, as he joked with Pete, it was very eco-friendly.

Clarissa watched the pigs as they nervously explored their new, unfamiliar surroundings. They snuffled the strange salt air with their snouts. Pigs have a keen sense of smell. They hadn't enjoyed the lorry journey and they were still unsettled. They were not in the best of moods. To Clarissa's eyes they looked monstrous. She wasn't a country girl and it was the first time she had ever seen a pig. They were the size of Chesterfield sofas and their eyes were disconcertingly intelligent. They gleamed. I'm not going in there, she thought, staring at their paddock from behind the barred gate where she stood watching them. Not if you paid me. They creep me out.

She turned and looked at the house behind her. The two downstairs front rooms of the house overlooked the island's jetty and, beyond that, the flat, green line of the Essex coast. One of the rooms was a lounge; the other, which had been a former snooker room, Conquest used as his office. In the course of his life, he had never bothered to collect art or mementos but occasionally he'd ended up with things salvaged from properties. He'd used these to decorate these rooms. It gave them a homely feel. The London address in the Bishops Avenue was kept on purely as an investment and for impressing clients; he didn't like living in it. It was the island that felt like home.

Among these random objects – a mounted tiger's head, stuffed fish, a framed poster for some music hall acts – was a pair of hunting spears, as tall as a man, with long, barbed iron heads, said to have been used by Hermann Goering at his enormous countryside retreat of Carinhall. Robbo, who worked for Conquest and lived in the house's basement, venerated these. He coveted them. Robbo worshipped the Nazis. The money that Conquest paid him, and he paid him very well, went chiefly on

Nazi memorabilia. The spears would have crowned his collection. Frequently he pestered Conquest to let him have them. 'Over my dead body,' Conquest said. They were vicious things, designed for boar hunting. Clarissa hadn't thought anything of them until she'd seen the size of an actual pig. One of the pigs in the field was indeed a boar, with protruding tusks that Glasgow Brian had explained were simply overgrown front teeth. Clarissa wouldn't dream of approaching it, certainly not armed with only a primitive spear, no matter how sharp or effective it might be.

Conquest had made a joke about someone called Rabbit and his dental similarities. How old's the boar? he'd asked Glasgow Brian. About five, said Glasgow Brian. Conquest had laughed and said, 'That's the age Rabbit likes them. Maybe a bit too old for him in fact. He'll be here in a few weeks, I'll introduce them. They'll get on.'

Rabbit Bingham was currently in no position to appreciate jokes. He was fastened to a wooden chair in a capacious store cupboard in the education block. The cupboard was built into the building itself, part of its actual fabric. Its walls were brick, its door metal-panelled wood. His arms had been duct-taped to the chair, his legs to those of the chair with tape round his ankles. More duct tape secured his mouth.

Bingham's trousers and underpants were currently around his ankles too and Anderson was looking at him expressionlessly. Anderson had closed the door of the cupboard, which was more like a small room. He sat down on an upturned bucket directly in front of Bingham. Light came from a candle that Anderson had lit, which made the scene look like something from medieval times. A scene from the Spanish Inquisition painted by Goya. Sweat trickled down Bingham's forehead, occasionally stinging his eyes.

Anderson said in a conversational tone, 'These walls are surprisingly thick and so is the door. I don't think anyone will hear you scream but I don't like noise, so I'll leave the tape on for now.' He paused for effect. 'Now, doubtless, you'll be wondering why you're here.'

Bingham shook his head helplessly, a wordless pleading for mercy.

Anderson took a pair of latex gloves from his pocket and pulled them on slowly and thoughtfully. He had heard that the anticipation of pain is almost as effective as pain itself. He wasn't sure. One day he would ask but usually when he'd finished with someone, they were in no fit state for measured reflection. They were pathetically grateful to be alive even if the gratitude was mixed with extreme pain.

He leant forward and said, 'This isn't about you, Rabbit.' He studied his gloved hands carefully. 'Your friend Conquest has taken a boy and I want to know where he's put him. That's fairly simple, isn't it. You are going to tell me where, aren't you? I'll just repeat that for you, you don't look all there, Rabbit. Do try and concentrate. I want to know where Conquest would be keeping a boy. You're going to tell me, so you might as well get it off your chest now.'

It wasn't a question. Anderson's freedom, ten years of his life, rested on Bingham telling him what he wanted to know. He would talk. Unable to speak, Bingham's responses were limited to a yes or a no. A nod or a shake of the head. Had he been able to talk he would have tried to plead ignorance or buy time.

He knew exactly where the boy would be held. It was where he intended to stay after he left prison. He shook his head. Anderson sighed as if he'd been expecting this. He put his hand in his pocket and took out a Zippo lighter.

He flicked the lighter and a ragged yellow flame appeared. Anderson and Bingham both looked at the flame, then Anderson shook his head sadly and leant forward with the lighter. His other hand took Rabbit's penis. Bingham's agony began.

A little while later for Anderson, a lifetime later for Rabbit, he extinguished the flame, 'Well?' Bingham shook his head. His face was wet with tears. Unable to scream, unable to move, he had just endured pain like nothing he could have ever imagined. Anderson put his head close to Bingham's.

'It won't get any better. I've only just started. Tell me what I need to know.' Anderson re-applied the flame. A thin plume of dark smoke rose and the smell of burning flesh started to fill the room.

Bingham's head started nodding frantically. Anderson put away the lighter and took out a pen and paper. He removed the tape from Bingham's mouth and listened carefully as he told Anderson the location of the island and where the boy would be held.

'Now that wasn't so hard, was it?' said Anderson. He looked with distaste at Bingham.

Anderson had grown to dislike Bingham greatly in their short meeting. He opened the cupboard door and glanced out to check the time against the clock on the wall. An hour before Jardine would reappear to take Bingham away. He had paid Jardine a great deal of money for this. It was hugely expensive but money was not a problem for Anderson. Included in the deal was another bribe for the warder in charge of the relevant security cameras, another five-figure sum. He'd promised Jardine he wouldn't kill Bingham. Neither of them wanted Bingham dead. He smiled to himself. Bingham noticed the smile and, like a dog eager to ingratiate itself to his master, smiled back, despite

the pain. It was all over now. He had done as Anderson had asked; he had betrayed Conquest.

Anderson leant forward and replaced the tape, which had been hanging by one corner from Bingham's cheek. He patted it gently. 'I guess they call you Rabbit because of your teeth,' he said conversationally.

Bingham nodded. He was wary but he'd done everything asked of him. A bargain was a bargain; it was only fair. Surely to God this was the end of it.

Anderson reached behind him. He had a brick in his hand, a conventional house brick. Nothing special. Without warning he slammed the end into Bingham's mouth. Bingham's head snapped back with the force of the blow. Anderson had to restrain his immediate instinct, born of a number of vicious fights in pubs, car parks and streets, to slam the brick, or his hand, into Bingham's exposed throat. He pushed his fingers against the rapidly swelling skin of Bingham's upper lip to check the damage he'd done. He felt the ridge of Bingham's front teeth with the tips of his fingers. They were still surprisingly intact. Blood seeped from around the black strip of duct tape that dramatically punctuated the very pale parchment of the skin on Bingham's face.

It took two more blows before Anderson was satisfied.

Rabbit Bingham would need a new nickname.

# 31

In Brussels, Lord Justice Reece showered carefully and washed his thick, silver-grey hair. He looked at his face critically in the bathroom mirror. He had never been good-looking, his lips were wide and blubbery, his eyes slightly bulging, his face fleshy, but his ugliness had worked to his advantage. People don't want their lawyers to look like male models. They want ability, they want reassurance, and Reece's messianic self-confidence, boosted by carefully chosen, high-profile pro-bono work and remorseless media networking, had made him very reassuring indeed.

Before he had become a judge there were few TV or radio programmes about civil rights that didn't feature Reece. He'd made his name in the law by championing unpopular causes and the downtrodden, but only if they were also popular media topics. He was also a fixture on the lecture circuit, a regular at places like the Oxford Union and the Cambridge Union Society. He had many friends in the BBC. He had adopted a strategy of professing modesty, but reluctantly appearing in the full blaze of publicity for 'moral' reasons. Media fame had brought high-profile cases, which in turn brought the ability to charge astronomical fees. Representing the underdog and fighting injustice was lucrative work for Reece, but of course he'd only do it if there was interest from the intelligentsia. Before

becoming a judge, Reece was a multimillionaire from his legal practice but he kept this quiet from the public, who viewed him as an ascetic seeker of truth. Now he had set his sights on bigger things than fame or money. Now he was after power.

The interviews he had attended in Strasbourg for the presidency of the European Court of Human Rights had gone extremely well the day before, he knew that. He had expected nothing less. The questions he had been asked, the outline of the future for the law he'd been invited to express, could have been expressly designed to play to his strengths. The legal profession usually draws its top tier of lawyers from a particular class, connected, arrogant, ambitious, wealthy; it's an exclusive club. The role of a senior legal position is not concerned with justice or ethics; it is primarily to safeguard salaries, reputation, power and status for the legal profession. Lord Justice Reece was a highly safe pair of hands and well used to dealing with civil servants, government and the European Union. He spoke their language, bureaucracy, and he spoke it fluently, mellifluously and persuasively – it's a universal language, the Esperanto of power.

That morning he would meet the advisers to the French

and German Justice ministers – agreeable, civilized, likeminded, legal minds. Then there would be a long lunch and another meeting. In the evening, dinner with the EU Justice Commissioner at Bruneau, one of Brussels' best Michelin-starred restaurants, centrally located in Avenue Rousting in the shadow of the Koekelberg.

Reece liked to think of himself as a gourmet. As a child he'd had to endure the horrors of English boarding-school cooking, the lumpy mash, the lukewarm, gristly, grey mince with its congealing gravy, and tapioca pudding. Now he was a Michelin Guide addict. Any trip to any city for whatever reason

would find Reece booked into one of the red guide's entries, and nine times out of ten someone else would be paying. He was particularly looking forward to Bruneau as he'd never been before; he only knew about it by repute. Its chocolate soufflé was said to be superb, as was the cheese board. The rack of lamb was legendary, the turbot alone worth the enormous EU fisheries subsidy.

The 200 euro set menu came with a selection of recommended wines. Reece was particularly pleased by this. He was knowledgeable about food but choosing the correct wine was such a terrible problem. Choice itself was the first hurdle. You were normally faced with a massive leather-bound menu containing the names of hundreds of wines, making selection haphazard at best. Then there was the question of which vintage to go for. He had an app on his phone which had more or less sorted this problem out. The year 2005, for example, was a superb year for Bordeaux, but which one? You could take a risk and go with the sommelier's recommendation, which could be, and often was, based on what would give the restaurant the best profit margin, or, scandalously in his opinion, what needed using up. Having the choice made for him lifted a huge burden off his shoulders.

Then he would fly home on the Wednesday, back to his

office in the Inns of Court, and Thursday would see him alone with the boy, for forty-eight hours of pure, sensual pleasure. It would be the culmination of a dream.

Reece had experimented with rent boys, courtesy of Bingham, over on the island, but lived in fear that one of them would recognize him from his many TV appearances. Bingham thought the chances of this happening were practically zero. How many rent boys, he'd asked Reece scornfully, watched *Newsnight* or *Hard Talk* on BBC News 24? Almost certainly zero. But to

reassure Reece, he had come up with the idea that the judge should wear a mask, an idea he'd adopted with great enthusiasm. But sex with prostitutes wasn't what he wanted and he also didn't like having to take precautions. He wanted a pure, untainted body; he wanted sex free of condoms. He wanted a boy that he could use without fear of contracting AIDS or a pernicious STD. Reece felt he had done more than enough to deserve it. It was really what he was due, what he was owed by society for his rare legal expertise. Bingham had reassured him on this. It was only right he should receive his due reward. You are a guardian of civilization; without you we'd be at the mercy of racists and fascists. It's people like you who preserve decent society, said Bingham, and it's only right that an exceptional man gets an exceptional reward. He strongly believed that the labourer was worthy of his hire. The law was there to protect children from predatory perverts, but he was the embodiment of the law. He decided what was just and what was unjust, and only a keen mind like his was able to make these distinctions.

He decided what was legal.

Society is run, Bingham had assured him, on utilitarian principles: good was what was good for the greatest number of people. Since Reece, with his masterly legal mind, a man in a hundred million, had seen fit to devote his stupendous intellect to the good of society, it was only fair that society pay the reward. Reece, in taking Peter Reynolds, would only be taking a tiny part of what society owed him.

The judge had nodded.

Render unto Caesar that which is Caesar's. Come Unto Me.

\* \* \*

Hanlon sat in her dusty office, wearing her usual impassive face but inside screaming at her mobile to ring. She hated having

to rely on other people, but there was nothing she could do to hurry Anderson. The rolling TV news still carried reports on the missing Peter Reynolds, mainly live from outside New Scotland Yard. It was infuriating that she felt she knew the truth but was powerless to act. She had everything and nothing. There was a figure out of Greek mythology called Cassandra, who had the gift of seeing the future, but her curse was that no one would believe her. That's what I am, she thought bitterly, a modern-day Cassandra. Come on, Anderson, call me!

\* \* \*

Back in London, Kathy was eating a Ryvita and drinking water. The coarse crispbread scoured her tongue and palate and she found its abrasive texture somehow comforting. She would have liked to be able to hurt herself, to gash herself with a razor blade, for example. The pain would have distracted her, and it would have been a sympathetic magic, as if by drawing bad things down to her own body she could take them away from Peter. She had another piece of crispbread. Normal food would have made her vomit. Until Peter was found, the thought of eating revolted her. She knew she had to have enough to function, so she didn't collapse, but crackers were all she could really face. Her sleep at night was fitful at best, more like drawing a thin grey veil around her than the oblivion she craved. She lay on her bed, drifting in and out of consciousness. She refused sleeping pills. Peter might be found at any time and she had to stay sharp.

Peter may not have been able to guess why he had been kidnapped but Kathy could imagine all kinds of terrible reasons. She didn't dare think about them. Her head felt as if it was going to explode, like it had been pressurized. When she was awake, her thoughts virtually shut down. She didn't want to think. She was like a TV on standby. It wasn't a comforting,

meditative state of non-ego, of awareness; it was a pointless, numb nothingness. She couldn't bear to think. Life for Kathy was a prolonged, silent, howl of pain, separation and dread.

Rabbit Bingham was in the prison infirmary. The second degree burns to his penis would require a skin graft; the smashing of his mouth would result in the extraction of what was left of his upper and lower front teeth. The damage to the soft tissue of his lips was also extensive and had required a lot of stitching. Bingham had refused to name his attacker.

Drifting in and out of consciousness from the morphine they'd given him for the pain, he told the guards he'd fallen down stairs and hurt his mouth. The burns he claimed were self-inflicted. They were a sex game gone wrong.

Alastair Fordham, the governor, was in a state of understand-able rage. He didn't care about Bingham as a person, nobody did. If the story leaked out to the press no one would care that a paedophile had been seriously injured in prison. But although non-newsworthy, what Bingham most certainly had become was both an administrative headache and the subject of an embarrassing investigation.

To a certain extent, Fordham didn't care about the cost and the administrative hassle of Bingham being sent to a mainstream hospital. He was hardly a flight risk. Certainly, with the condition his genitals were in, he posed no threat to children. Added to that, it would be a while before he could even move a muscle in his lower limbs, much less run away.

What Fordham did object to was being made to look as if he couldn't control his own prison and the implication, the clear conclusion, that whoever did this had inside help. The assault on Bingham must have had the tacit support of at least one of the prison officers. Almost certainly more than one. Fordham

was a pragmatist, he knew that with more than three hundred dangerous prisoners on site, not to mention the ever-present problem of bribery, a certain amount of trouble was inevitable. Prison officers are not well paid, they have difficult working conditions and some of the prisoners in their care have access to huge amounts of money. Blind eyes were often turned inside. The presence of illegal substances, a given. Arguably, anything that calmed a volatile prison population down was not necessarily a bad thing. You'd be a fool to think otherwise. Fordham was not the kind of man to launch a moral crusade over anything. But this was provocatively bold. It was an in-your-face challenge to his authority. Bingham had been discovered in the library he was supposed to have been cleaning. There was no trace of the violence that had been inflicted on him to be found, so the assault had obviously taken place elsewhere. A quick enquiry revealed that several key CCTV monitors had 'malfunctioned'. Certain key officers had become very forgetful, either because they were involved or were unwilling to voice suspicions. The general amnesia seemed contagious. Nobody knew anything. It would be useless asking the prisoners. Nobody would dare implicate Anderson. No one was

going to grass.

The assault also had the effect, like any violent incident in a prison, of creating a hysterically ugly mood. Prisons are very finely balanced places; they rely as much on the prisoners making it work as the staff. They were all in it together. But they are febrile, hothouse environments and the effect of Bingham's attack was like poking an anthill. The natives were restless. He'd had to cancel leave and put on extra shifts. The last thing he needed was a riot. That really would be the icing on the cake. Fordham was furious about this damage to his reputation. Other governors would be rubbing their hands.

Fordham personally suspected Anderson. He had the show-man's flamboyant touch, the imagination, that most of the other prisoners lacked. Everyone knew the reason for his 'Jesus' nick-name. Fordham also harboured a feeling that it might be connected with Hanlon's visit. He didn't believe in coincidence. Not in prison.

When he'd been in the army, in Iraq and in Afghanistan, Fordham had seen torture of suspects first hand, or 'enhanced interrogation' as the army put it. He wasn't squeamish – you can't fight a war with clean hands – and having met Hanlon, he knew that neither was she. Well, he wasn't going to launch a complaint to the Met, to Hanlon's boss, or to air his suspicions; by nature he believed in closing ranks, but he certainly wasn't going to make life easy for anyone.

He ordered an immediate cell lockdown on Anderson's wing and a thorough search. He put his most trusted men on this. Rip the place apart, he'd told them. Prisoners are only allowed a certain amount of personal effects, more or less enough to fill two shoe boxes, but stuff still accumulates. Anderson's phone, minus its SIM card, was discovered. An incandescently angry Fordham – what else was Anderson up to? – ordered Anderson strip-searched, with replacement clothing issued, and that he be put in a holding cell indefinitely until Fordham had decided exactly what to do with him.

* * *

Anderson paced his solitary confinement cell angrily. He hadn't had his phone with him when Bingham had grassed Conquest up. It had been in its secure hiding place that had turned out to be not secure at all. He guessed that Hanlon wouldn't be allowed to see him, no one would be. He'd demanded to see his lawyer and was told his request would be considered. That could be days, maybe weeks. Today was Wednesday; if he

couldn't tell her where Bingham thought the boy was being held by Friday, the deal was off. All of this would have been in vain. Not only would he lose the money, which he didn't particularly care about, but he would lose his chance to get out of jail. If he'd been in the main part of the prison he could have found someone who was due a visit that week to pass a message on; that wasn't going to happen now.

He'd requested via one of the prison officers that he be allowed to see Hanlon. He was given a frosty reply that the matter would be looked into. He had to get a message to her, but he couldn't see how.

As Fordham expected, he received a formal request from DI Hanlon for a further meeting with Anderson. This chimed with the Anderson request to see her. It confirmed the governor's suspicions. No way, thought Fordham. You've got a bloody nerve, DI Hanlon. This was turned down until a thorough review of Anderson's conduct had been made.

Hanlon sat in her office, frustrated and worried. She had known that calling the prison would be a bad idea, but she hadn't been able to resist. Every moment she didn't find Peter increased the danger he was in and increased the pressure on her. The same thoughts ran over and over in her head like a washing-machine cycle. She knew Conquest had the boy, but she had no real proof.

She had nothing she could take to even the tamest of magistrates. Even if Corrigan were to go crazy, throw caution to the wind, and agree with her, she still had no idea where Peter was being held. A man like Conquest, with a property network, could have him almost anywhere. Conquest would never tell her where the boy was. She knew that even if she had incontrovertible evidence – a busload of witnesses, forensic evidence, the whole thing on film even – Conquest wouldn't

talk. It would be beneath his dignity. There was nothing she could threaten him with.

The thing that really got to her was that she was certain Anderson had fulfilled his part of the bargain. The answer as to where Peter was lay maddeningly close, but just out of reach. Suddenly she thought of Cunningham. Her heart leapt at the thought. Momentarily a golden scenario unfolded in her imagination: Cunningham in an interview room alone with Anderson, the information passed on, the lawyer phoning her from the prison car park. Surely Anderson was entitled to see a lawyer? Cunningham could get the access that Fordham had denied her. After her calls to the governor went unanswered, his secretary stone-walling her, she'd called a couple of people she knew in the prison service and they'd made discreet enquiries. They quickly found out what had happened at HMP Wendover and filled her in on Anderson and the sorry state of Bingham. That's how she knew Anderson had succeeded. If Bingham hadn't talked, Anderson would have killed him out of annoyance. They also let her know about the governor's frame of mind. She was persona non grata. Everyone was.

Hanlon didn't have many friends; in some respects she didn't have any, not in the conventional sense. She strongly disliked socializing. She didn't really understand it. Hanlon had little time for Jean-Paul Sartre but she did agree that hell was other people. She would never meet or talk to anyone purely for the pleasure of their company; she hated small talk. Fortunately, friendship doesn't have to be a two-way street. If you admired Hanlon you had to accept that there would be a great deal of giving with very little reward. There were, however, more than a few people, a significant number, who liked Hanlon very much and were prepared to go to great lengths to help her. People like Corrigan and James Forrest. People like Laidlaw

and Brudenell, the evidence storage manager, who had given Whiteside the clothes when they'd trapped Cunningham. The prison service people she knew were in that category. But even they couldn't reach Anderson.

She sipped a cup of coffee, black as her mood, and tried to think how she could get access to Anderson. Whatever she did, Fordham, already suspicious of Anderson, would smell a kingsize rat. No way would she be allowed to see him. Eventually yes, but not in the limited time frame that she was operating within. Nobody would be allowed to see him. No visitors for the foreseeable future. Peter would be dead by then.

There was a knock on the frosted glass of her door. She looked around her storeroom-cum-office gloomily. This is where they put the furniture that's too old-fashioned, that they don't want but don't know what to do with, the stuff that's useless, she thought to herself, a suitable metaphor – in Ludgate's eyes – for me. At this moment, I tend to agree, she thought.

'Come,' she called out and Enver's paunchy frame entered the cluttered room. His jacket was folded across his left arm and his stomach strained against the fabric of his shirt. Hanlon was pleased to see him despite her unaccustomed gloom. There was something very reassuring about Enver. She motioned to the chair opposite and Enver sat down, gingerly, as if he didn't quite trust it to carry his weight. Hanlon filled him in on the Anderson story. 'Which prison is he in again, ma'am?' he asked her as she told him about her inter-

view with the crime boss. As she did so, Enver felt a growing sense
of pleasure, no, make that delight, at being able to provide some
possibly good news. It was about time something went their way.
Hanlon finished her narrative. Enver stopped playing with his
moustache and looked at her. 'When all this began, ma'am, when
my uncle got me to agree to help Mehmet Yilmaz, I was kind of
annoyed because

my community, Turks, had pressurized me with the "you're one
of us" argument. You know, blood is thicker than water, don't forget
where you're from, that sort of thing.'

Hanlon nodded.

'Well,' he said, 'if that's the case, it cuts both ways.'

Hanlon looked at him with interest. Enver continued, 'My
cousin's wife is a prison officer at Wendover. I've put myself out for
Uncle Osman, it's about time he returns the favour. Time for him to
put a bit of pressure on his son.'

'Will she do it, though?' queried Hanlon. It was like a gift from
God but she didn't want to get too excited. It was a lot to ask. If
Fordham found out one of his officers had made unauthorized
contact with Anderson, he'd be furious. It would be a sackable
offence.

Enver stroked his moustache. He looked at Hanlon. 'There's a
Turkish saying, "*Bilemmek ayyup degil, sormamak ayyup*". Do you
know what that means?'

'No,' said Hanlon. It sounded strange to hear Enver, with his
London accent, speaking a foreign language. The sonorous Turkish
words rolled off his tongue fluently.

Enver stood up. 'I do,' he said, somewhat smugly. 'I'll go and
arrange it. I'll see you later, ma'am.'

Gently, but triumphantly, he squeezed his way back through the
furniture towards the door. Hanlon watched him leave with what

she realized was growing affection. She hoped to God that Enver's cousin's wife would help.

I wonder what the saying meant, she thought. If that gloomy sod can look cheerful, it has to be a good sign. Hanlon's mood brightened for the first time in days. She began to make plans for action when, not if, she got the information she needed.

## 32

---

'Not knowing is not shameful, not asking is.' That was the meaning of the proverb. It was time to ask for a favour. If Hassan demurred, Enver would call his father, the imam. Enver texted Hassan, who he'd always got on well with, and checked the shift patterns of Julie Demirel, Hassan's wife. She was working that day and would be home about five. The other question was, yes, she'd be working Thursday. Enver arranged to meet her that evening. He could imagine the puzzlement his request to see them would have caused. Enver rarely left London. He'd never been to their house before, although they probably saw him at least a dozen times a year when they came up to London, to Southgate, home of the extended Demirel family, for family do's. He thought there was a reasonable chance they'd cooperate. With luck, they would know where the boy was being held within twenty-four hours. He texted Hanlon to that effect and

got a laconic 'good' by way of reply.

Enver put his phone away. His police station was frenziedly busy. The Reynolds disappearance may have elbowed the Whiteside shooting off the front pages but Whiteside was one of their own. The thoughts of most officers were centred on the Whiteside shooting. He was still in a coma, stable but with an uncertain prognosis. In everyone's mind was the thought that whoever had done this was quite likely to kill again, or had

killed before. Although Whiteside wasn't dead, the attempt on his life had been unambiguous and so it was being investigated by a murder investigation team. This MIT was being led by DCI Simon Harding, an affable, well-respected officer with a reputation for pedantic thoroughness. The MIT team in charge of the Yilmaz family was still in the charge of DCI Murray. They'd been elbowed to one side in terms of importance by the Whiteside shooting. Both teams were working out of the same station, the two incident rooms separated by a corridor. Supervising the two MIT teams was the Specialist Crime Directorate's Homicide Command, represented here by DCS Ludgate. Despite his dislike of Ludgate on a personal level, Enver was impressed by the stamina and energy that Ludgate was putting into everything. He was inspirational. He guessed maybe these cases would be Ludgate's last hurrah before he retired, and he wanted to leave with a reputation enhanced by the investigations. There were about thirty police working on the Whiteside shooting alone; the station was full to bursting. The only quiet room in the place was Hanlon's office-cum-

storage facility.

Baby Ali's death and the Yilmaz disappearance had slipped far down the agenda. His investigative team numbered four: DCI Murray, heading it, Enver, and two constables. There was no media interest in the child's death and none of the crusading zeal that a cop killer creates among his fellow officers. There was no 'it could have been me' or 'there but for the Grace of God' feeling about the Yilmaz family. They were a footnote now in Haringey's crime stats. There was even, as Corrigan had predicted, a growing feeling that maybe they hadn't been killed. The theory was that faced with the possibility of deportation, the Yilmaz family had staged their disappearance. And there was no proof they were dead. After all, where were the bodies?

Murray, as far as Enver could see, was doing everything reasonably well. He was a conscientious officer despite the rumours that the Yilmaz family was alive. Until the axe fell on the investigation, and he was secretly convinced the time was not very far away, he'd do his best. With Enver he was very hands off. He was inclined to leave Enver very much to his own devices after Corrigan's descent on the investigation. He issued Enver with basic investigative duties, particularly liaising with the local community and the sexual assault unit together with the child abuse unit.

Murray was investigating racial attacks on Turks as well as the obvious paedophile angle. Enver felt increasingly uncomfortable watching the vast display of resources that the two investigations were consuming. The media briefings, the endless interviews, the progress meetings, the liaison committees that were needed to make sure that nobody else was holding a vital piece of the jigsaw, the logjam of logistical problems as detectives were taken away from different cases – when two people, he and Hanlon, knew who was responsible. Or, more accurately, he felt, thought they knew who was responsible.

Then there was the ongoing fact of Peter Reynolds' disappearance. That was the real focus of most of the Met's resources. It was Whiteside's misfortune to have been shot when something as newsworthy as Peter's disappearance had happened. It was a huge news story. BBC, ITV, Sky, and all the newspapers were covering it. Hanlon's point, that there was no way of knowing where he was being held except via Anderson, was horribly true. Enver didn't know what she'd said to Anderson to get him to cooperate, but obviously it wasn't police approved. Given that, would they even be able to legally act on the information as to where the boy was? It had after all been acquired through

torture. A human rights lawyer would say they had no right to act on it, even if it meant the rape and murder of Peter. Bingham's rights had been well and truly violated. It was all so difficult. Many times Enver had wondered if he was doing the right thing. Should he go directly to an increasingly harassed Ludgate? The DCS was doing a difficult job with tremendous skill and energy. He was at almost every key meeting for the investigations, he put in a staggering amount of hours and, since he was coming to the end of his career, none of this would result in promotion or financial reward. Maybe, Enver felt, he should go to the assistant commissioner? As far as he could tell, Hanlon's decision to play this alone was based mainly on a feeling that somewhere in the police force, Conquest had a source of information. That to involve the Met would be to tip off Conquest. But there were many informants in the Met. It went with the turf. If you adopted that attitude, nothing would get done. You might as well give up and go home. Or, if you were concerned about the Met, you could use a neighbouring constabulary. Surrey, Herts or Kent and Essex, for example. What if Hanlon's go-it-alone policy was directed purely by personal revenge and she had suckered him in to help. Yes, she was charismatic, but so, by all accounts, were the Kray twins.

That didn't make them wise leaders.

One of Enver's worst fears as well was that Corrigan was right. That she was going to take the law into her own hands and he would end up arrested as an accomplice to a police execution. That Hanlon would blow Conquest's head off in revenge for Whiteside. He certainly believed her capable of it. His own defence would look pathetic. I helped her because I believed in her. That was no defence at all.

Enver's own emails to Corrigan had been masterpieces of selective information and factual avoidance. He had been greatly

helped by Fordham not making official his feelings that Hanlon was behind the Bingham attack. His own concerns about the DI's behaviour he kept to himself.

Looked at dispassionately, Hanlon created chaos. She was anarchic. Arguably, it was her fault Whiteside had been shot. She had undeniably already got one prisoner severely injured, with another locked down, and induced a state of simmering tension into a maximum-security prison. He suddenly wondered how Julie would react to being asked to help the person indirectly responsible for all of this. The person who had created havoc at HMP Wendover, her place of work.

Enver shrugged to himself. He was innately fatalistic and he knew, deep down, he believed in Hanlon. He'd keep helping until some kind of conclusion was reached. To that end, he picked up the phone and called his cousin.

\* \* \*

Conquest stepped into his car and drove out of the underground garage he'd had built under the mansion in the Bishops Avenue, then headed for the North Circular. Underground was the new black for property developers. Whole streets in Knightsbridge, in Camden and Chelsea were being underpinned as builders – despite the anguished objections from neighbours, lives blighted by dust, noise and vibration – dug deep down to add extra floors to already large houses. Conquest's own property company didn't handle very much high-end housing but he often thought to himself, who would really want an underground swimming pool and an underground cinema? How often were things like that ever used? They were the multimillionaire's equivalent of a pasta-maker. Nobody ever used them. In years to come, he thought, a new generation of property developers will be ripping all this out, wondering what had got into people at the time. He smiled at the thought. He was hugely happy.

He slid a CD of Furtwängler conducting Wagner's *Die Meistersinger* into the slot on his Bose in-car music system, and pointed the Maserati in the direction of Essex. Now there was something that had stood the test of time. Music and sex, they'd go on forever. He pressed the accelerator and felt the surge of power and the roar of the engine complementing the beauty of Wagner's opera. The Yilmaz family was gone; in a fortnight the investigation, although officially open, would cease. Whiteside was no longer a threat; soon his police insider would start rumours it was a gay ex-lover who might be behind it, and according to his police source, the Reynolds investigation was going nowhere. The music was golden, the car was golden, everything was golden, especially his future.

The judge relaxed with a glass of champagne at Brussels Airport, waiting for his flight to City Airport London. It had been a productive couple of days. For the judge, productive was synonymous with fun. He had a huge capacity for hard work, and the meal last night at Bruneau had been memorably wonderful – even better than he had expected. It was over the chocolate dessert, as miraculously light as he'd hoped, that he'd learnt unofficially the job was now his for the taking. That meant many more agreeable Michelin-starred lunches, as well as a wonderfully generous pension when he retired and first-class travel complete with chauffeured limousines. But these were fripperies. These were his already.

The best thing about his new job, of course, was the power aspect. To be President of the European Court, that had a ring to it that the judge found exceptionally pleasurable. He would be more powerful than a Prime Minister or Chancellor or Home Secretary. They would come and go on the whim of an electorate, while he carried on, above all of that. His

judgements could determine the fate of states. What enhanced the feeling was the knowledge that two of his UK colleagues, who he knew coveted the post, would not get it. When you reach the judge's eminence, when you've climbed to the top of the mountain, it's not just enough that you succeed; others must fail. He lifted the champagne flute aloft in a silent toast to his own glittering future.

But later, as he took his seat on the small BAE 146 Whisper Jet that would fly him back to his luxury penthouse in the City, it wasn't the career triumph that was foremost in his mind. It was the delights that were waiting for him on Strood Island.

Come Unto Me.

The judge didn't know the name of the boy, or his background. These were unimportant and, anyway, he didn't know or care what would happen to the child after he had finished with him. He would cease to exist, Conquest would see to that. But before he met his maker, the boy would fulfil a destiny of sorts as the boy bitch for Europe's most brilliant legal mind. He would be wearing his mask, as suggested by Bingham.

He owed Bingham a lot for that suggestion. It had been so liberating. Before the mask he had been consumed with fear that he might somehow be recognized by one of his infrequent boy-prostitute lovers. Bingham had mocked this idea. Rent boys do not know the faces of prominent judges. But he could envisage a chance glimpse of his face on TV or a newspaper, the rent boy phoning a red-top, the reporters digging deep. If only we had a sensible anti-privacy law, thought the judge, like they do in France, then I wouldn't even need to worry about things like this. The Leveson Inquiry would put the brakes on journalists, who the judge feared more than anyone, but it wouldn't stop them. He turned his mind away from thoughts about how best to muzzle the press. In Europe he'd have more

power to try to curb their excesses. It would be a tragedy for the law if unwelcome journalistic investigations were turned on the judiciary. Ordinary people did not understand how judges' minds worked and they should not be accountable to the electorate. They were the ones in charge; they served Justice itself.

The judge found himself salivating at the thought of enjoying the child, of running his learned tongue over the boy's flesh that evening. Every night he'd thought about the boy and what he would do to him in great detail. He had dreamed about removing his clothes, running his wrinkled hands over the boy's smooth body. The judge had a well-deserved reputation for thoroughness, he was proud of it, and Peter Reynolds would get to appreciate this gift in the flesh. Not many people have the chance to make their dreams come true. The judge was one of the select few.

You were allowed to use your phone on the plane. The judge emailed Conquest to see if he could come down that night. The answer came back immediately: yes. The judge smiled in delight and sent some instructions as to how he wanted the child preparing for that evening's entertainment. He would have three days with him. He breathed deeply in excited anticipation. Three days, seventy-two hours. He would make the most of every minute. *Carpe diem.* It's what he deserved. It was, after all, only just. God, he was excited.

\* \* \*

Peter counted the scratches on his cell wall. One scratch per injection, that meant four scratches per day. He now had eighteen, so he figured that today was still Wednesday. When there was no clock, no natural light, it was hard to keep count. The hatch on his door rattled and opened and his evening meal, tonight a pasta salad with tuna, was delivered. Today he'd given

in to unhappiness and, hiding his head in Tito's fur so no one could see, cried a little. He was so alone and he didn't know why he was here or, worse, how long this would last. The dog sensed his misery and gently licked his face and hands, which comforted him a little. He so wanted his mother.

He drank the lemon-flavoured water that had come with his meal and gave himself an insulin injection based on the carb count on the tuna salad packaging. Shortly after he'd eaten, he started yawning deeply. He was feeling very tired all of a sudden. It crossed his mind that he might have been drugged but he was too sleepy to care, and before he did actually fall asleep, he thought, *I don't mind anyway, perhaps when I wake up it'll be in my own bed, perhaps I'm going home.*


And forty miles away in London at the City Airport, Lord Justice Reece walked down the metal staircase from the plane, down to the black tarmac. There was a smile of happy anticipation on his lips. Tonight's the night, he thought, tonight's the night.

## 33

Julie Demirel had known Enver more or less as long as she'd known his cousin Hassan, now her husband. Julie was an attractive blonde in her early thirties, her good looks, in her opinion, let down by her legs. *I've got fat thighs*, she would think to herself gloomily. Thunder thighs. Hassan didn't seem to mind. It was all right for him, she thought, he had lovely legs. Now she was the mother of two small children, aged four and six, and she was too preoccupied with them and her job to worry about the lower half of her body. She was pleased to be seeing Enver, she liked him a lot.

Most people found it strange that she worked in a male prison but Julie didn't mind it. It was unsurprising, people's surprise. Prison is a place universally dreaded. In her experience, people assumed you were locked in a life-or-death struggle with insanely violent depraved criminals. Well, in twelve years as a prison officer there had undoubtedly been moments, but what her friends failed to realize was that you had to be firm, not brutal, and most of the inmates were reassuringly normal. Anyway, prison for Julie had run in the family. It was normal for her. Her dad had been a prison offi-cer, most of his mates had been in the service, one of her brothers was in the probation service and she'd grown up with it. Now, many of her friends struggling financially or with job insecurity were looking at

her job in the prison service with a certain amount of envy, although in Julie's opinion few of them would last five minutes. You had to be tough to survive in there and most civilians, she felt, with a certain amount of good-natured contempt, simply couldn't hack it.

The attack on Bingham had undeniably hit the prison hard. Every officer fears a riot and a good deal of prison rules are there to create an atmosphere of normality, of acceptance, so that everyone could get along with as little friction as possible. She guessed it was like being stuck on a submarine. There had to be a certain amount of consensus, give and take on both sides. No matter what happened, you couldn't just storm out or slip away. You were trapped in it. The Bingham episode was similar to throwing a large piece of concrete into a small pond. It had landed with one hell of a crash. It had created a very ugly atmosphere.

Like everyone in the prison, from governor to cleaner, from the lowest- to the highest-profile prisoner, she had speculated on who, why and how it had happened. More or less everybody suspected Anderson. Why he had done it was a question more for the guards than the prisoners. Why not, the prisoners would have answered. Who cares? Shit happens. Some of the murderers had committed their crimes in an alcoholic- or drug-induced blackout and couldn't remember why they'd killed, indeed sometimes who they'd killed. One or two of them had very tenuous grounds for murder. 'He looked at me in a funny way' was one reason frequently given. The last question, how it had happened, was particularly pertinent for the authorities.

In Julie's opinion, at least three staff would have to be involved. She could think of half a dozen likely candidates. It would be such an easy thing to rationalize. Bingham was a child sex offender, no one really cared what happened to him,

no tears would be shed. It would be hard to find the culprits. They would all, herself included, close ranks. The prison officers had a siege mentality stronger than the prisoners. More or less everyone who was not a prison officer was an enemy. Anyway, those responsible would say, if ever they were found, well, no one escaped. No one innocent had been hurt. So what. Easy for others to talk, they didn't have to live on a prison officer's salary.

The main issue raised was, of course, one of corruption. A great deal of money must have changed hands. And now Enver, who she liked a lot, was explaining that a police officer had sanctioned the assault. Well, thanks a bunch, DI Hanlon, for shitting on our living-room carpet. You don't have to deal with an enraged prison governor, three hundred plus over-excited prisoners, an enquiry, and an internal affairs audit of your finances and spending to check you haven't suddenly become unaccountably rich.

Well, she thought, that answers the why to a certain extent. Because of the bloody Metropolitan Police. Hassan, her husband, didn't seem to understand. So what? A prisoner assaults a prisoner. Who cares? Julie knew there was little point explaining to him there had to be rules of justice. She found the whole thing scandalous above and beyond the temporary annoyances. She was a deeply moral person. How would the Metropolitan Police like it if the Prison Service started meddling in their work? Outrage was tempered, though, by the victim's status. She would cheerfully kill anyone who harmed Aydin and Rifat, her boys, something Enver was exploiting none too subtly. 'There is a missing boy, a twelve-year-old, and if we don't find him soon he'll die,' said Enver. He'd used this argument

several times already.

'That's not the point,' replied Julie.

Enver shook his head. He looked at Julie, who he could see was getting angry. Her cheeks were dangerously red. 'It's exactly the point, Julie. We' – by 'we' he means 'me', thought Julie – 'we have the choice. We can either save him or we can choose to do nothing. And then he'll die horribly after being sexually assaulted. Repeatedly sexually assaulted. I was there when a toddler, a baby almost, was pulled from a canal after being raped at least a dozen times. We're not talking about abstract justice. That could be your child, Julie.'

'That's enough, Enver,' said Hassan. He was getting cross himself now. He repeated himself in Turkish. 'Yeter, Enver.'

And in one sense it was enough. Julie agreed to do what he was asking. It was enough to make Julie agree to speak to Anderson the following day. Enver felt no sense of triumph or victory. He felt ashamed of himself for the moral blackmail. 'We just need to know where,' said Enver urgently. 'Just an address.'

'Just an address,' said Julie, 'and no one will ever know where it came from? I won't be implicated? Fordham won't find out? He'd go spare.'

'No,' replied Enver. 'This is all very much unofficial. That much is certain.'

* * *

On Strood Island, Conquest, Clarissa and Robbo, who was the permanent caretaker there, looked at the TV monitor that showed Peter's cell. The cell had been a former wine store in the cellar underneath the house and modified for its current purpose a couple of years ago. The boy was now sound asleep from the Rohypnol that had been added to his juice. The judge, in his rather detailed instructions, had wanted the boy unconscious when he arrived. He wanted about five hours, while he explored his unresisting body, before he woke the sleeping beauty up.

Robbo was an expert at drugging victims. He'd had quite a bit of experience now, working for Conquest.

'Shall I take him upstairs now?' asked Robbo with a grin. When Conquest had first met him, back in the Eighties, a fellow Hell's Angel, Robbo had quite long hair. Now he was a neo-Nazi skinhead, a devotee of tattoos, or body art as he preferred to call it. Most of Robbo's tattoos had a similar theme: eagles, iron crosses, provocative slogans. 'Arbeit Macht Frei' – 'Work makes you free' – the words above the gates at Auschwitz, were tattooed across his shoulders. He was a dedicated bodybuilder and the steroids that he took to enhance his muscle mass had left him with a perpetual acne-covered

back and an eternally angry mood.

The 'upstairs' to which he was referring was a large double bedroom, fitted with a bank of cameras that were motion sensitive and would record the action automatically so the judge would have a permanent record of his activities for future, pleasurable viewing. Robbo would edit them to form a coherent, sexually exciting, whole. The judge liked to dress up. Robbo, like some repellent butler, had already laid out upstairs the costume the judge liked to dress up in. He would be wearing a black, latex mask whose eyeholes were covered in a fine silver mesh, preventing any form of recognition. There was a wide selection of sex toys in the room, mainly relating to pain: whips, handcuffs, nipple clamps, tongue screws, the full range of S&M panoply. Conquest liked to call the room the Bridal Suite. It seemed appropriate.

Conquest hoped the judge wouldn't be too enthusiastic, wouldn't get too carried away. He didn't want the boy dead too soon from internal or external injuries. He needed to film him with

Robbo and Glasgow Brian for Internet distribution after the judge had finished and before disposing of him. Peter

would fetch a very high price. Conquest always needed funds. There was a potentially very large market for what would be Peter's one and only sex film.

Outside the house, in the field, the pigs had been put on strict rations. Conquest wanted them starving by the time everyone in the house had finished with the boy. Pigs can be very aggressive. He was toying with the idea of putting Peter in with them while still alive and seeing what would happen, how long they would take to finish him off. The pigs had been brought up to eat dead and occasionally dying animals. It would be interesting to see what they would make of the boy. He would get Robbo to film it anyway. He was sure there would be a specialist market out there for that kind of thing. Bingham would know. He missed Bingham and his technical expertise as well as his infallible commercial sense.

Conquest looked at the boy, still wearing his school trousers

and shirt. His arm was curled round the dog. He smiled, pleased with his foresight. He had put the dog in with the boy and given him the books because he hadn't wanted the child to go to pieces. He wanted Peter to look his best for the judge and not be some gaunt, sobbing, hysterical mess. He'd learnt from experience. A previous guest in the cell had committed suicide in a state of despair. It was rare for children to do this – unlike adults they could have no conception of the horrors that awaited them and they were valuable commodities, things in which he'd invested a great deal of time and effort. It paid to look after them. He'd keep the dog once Peter was gone. Conquest quite liked dogs. He looked at his watch; the judge would be here in an hour or so. Then his fun could begin.

'No,' he said. 'Leave him here for now. We'll move him

when Reece arrives.'

Lord Justice Reece relaxed back into the luxuriously soft, leather upholstery of Conquest's Mercedes as he was driven through the outskirts of East London towards the highway that led to Essex and the island. He was humming an old pop song to himself, he couldn't remember the name of the artist – 'Tonight, I celebrate my love, for you' – when his phone went. He pulled on his reading glasses in irritation and looked at the small screen. It was his office, his secretary.

'Yes?' he said angrily. He had left strict instructions not to be disturbed, unless it was absolutely necessary. His secretary was a highly competent woman called Caroline who had been with him for over thirty years now. Reece prized loyalty. Caroline would have crawled across broken glass for the judge if she'd had to, she thought he was wonderful. She said briskly, 'I know you left orders not to be disturbed, my lord, but the Cabinet Office want to see you tomorrow morning. I told them you were officially on holiday, but they insisted.' She lowered her voice confidentially. 'It could be the one. The big one,' she said. She was far more excited than he was; she felt his talents had been criminally overlooked.

Reece smiled appreciatively. As a Lord Justice he was auto matically a KBE, a knight, and could call himself Sir Crispin Reece, but he was not a full lord, entitled to a seat in the Upper House, and he wanted that honour. He had plenty of money now. More money was always nice, but it had ceased to delight him. Power, though, and titles, well, that was beyond mere money. He had campaigned assiduously for elevation to the peerage, flattering the egos of politicians he despised, sitting on committees he had no interest in, so his name would be more noticeable. Lord Reece of...? Well, that was a question to ponder. A very nice question to ponder. A shame his old sadist of a house master wasn't around to see it; he'd always

predicted abject failure for Reece, a view shared by his parents who had taken any side but his. He hummed the first bars of 'Come Unto Me', the old school song.

'What time?' he said.

'The Permanent Secretary wants you at 2 p.m.' she replied. 'Get back to him. I'll be there,' he said curtly and pressed the button to end the call. The present government was sucking up to him now he looked like getting the top job in Brussels.

He stretched luxuriously in the back seat of the car. Life could hardly get better.

The boy would have to wait until Thursday night. He couldn't give the child the time that he felt he deserved. He wasn't going to be rushed. He could spend the night on Strood Island, travel back up to town in the morning and then back again in the evening, but this, he felt was out of the question. He wanted to give his full and undivided attention to what was going to be the sexual highlight of his life. He ordered the driver to turn round and take him home to Mayfair. He texted Conquest the change of plan.

A pleasure deferred. It was one of the signs of a higher being.

## 34

Julie stood outside Anderson's cell. It was Thursday afternoon; she was working the two until ten shift. She had often been responsible for the solitary punishment cells in the past – it was felt that a woman might have a calming effect on the more disturbed inmates – and getting to Anderson was simple. It had been a while since the cells had been used. Solitary confinement was out of fashion at the moment, but not illegal. It was regarded as counterproductive and of questionable human rights ethics, but Fordham's towering rage had put one of them back into use for Anderson's benefit.

She had been forced to wait until four o'clock, when she'd visited the guard on duty, started a conversation – not hard, she knew he found her attractive – and volunteered to check on Anderson. He smiled as he gave her permission. Quite a few staff had been along to have a closer look at their new celebrity prisoner. As she turned her back on him she could feel his gaze lingering longingly on her backside.

The walk to the cells was short; the other cells were untenanted. She opened the flap below the eye-level viewing window to speak to Anderson. He was standing up, his back turned to her.

'What do you want?' he asked, his voice flat and uninflected.

The accent was unassertive London.

'Hanlon sent me,' she said. 'I need an address.'

Now he did turn round. It was the first time she had ever seen him in the flesh. He had shoulder-length rat-tailed hair, a thin, almost malnourished face and very deep-set, intelligent, dark eyes. His shoulders were narrow and his hands, which hung by his side, seemed disproportionately large. Julie felt the presence of an overwhelming malevolence coming from Anderson and a feeling of great strength. The hands, with their bitten-down fingernails and long, strong fingers, looked very powerful. They belonged on an animal; they were the kind of hands capable of tearing someone to shreds.

It wasn't just his reputation that made him so menacing. She had long lost count of the number of convicted killers she had met, there were plenty in the prison itself right now, but none had come close to Anderson when it came to intimidating power. Julie didn't scare easily, she couldn't do the job if that were the case, but he scared her more than any prisoner she had ever met.

Anderson walked up to the door and looked at her through the small, open flap. She was very grateful to have the heavy steel door between them.

'Tell her, Strood Island, near Walton-on-Naze, Essex. Repeat that.' He spoke softly. He didn't need to raise his voice. People paid close attention to what he said. His face was framed in the metal hatch like a compelling portrait of evil. She could sense the power emanating, radiating, from him. His gaze was hypnotic, compelling. Julie felt a sensation akin to vertigo, that overwhelming desire to jump, except in this case it was the need almost to beg him not to hurt her. Like a bird hypnotized by a cat, she thought. She repeated the words he'd spoken.

Anderson nodded satisfied, then he said, almost as an afterthought, 'Tell Hanlon, Conquest is a supplier, not a user.' Then he turned away from her. His back was a sign the conversation was over.

Julie closed the flap and walked away. As she did so, she felt Bingham had probably got off relatively lightly. That man was capable of far worse.

At half four, the first opportunity she got, she texted Enver with the information.

An hour later, he and Hanlon drove out of London, east, heading for the Essex coast. Hanlon had used that hour for some frantic, last-minute research. She had an excellent series of contacts in Essex and, because it was her, they dropped whatever they were doing to help. Shortly after they left, so did the judge, at the wheel of his own Porsche. His meeting, too, had gone well. His suspicion had been more than confirmed that the Home Office, knowing of the Brussels appointment, wanted to get into the judge's good favour by the offer of a peerage. The stronger the ties that bound him to the UK government, the more chance of his reaching judgements favourable to his country of birth, that was their hope. The civil servants he had just met, always deferential, were now treating him like uncrowned royalty.

Hanlon drove in silence. They had first of all gone in her Audi to a car park in Bow where Hanlon had swapped her car for an old Volvo estate that smelt of dog and had bits of straw in the boot. Its bodywork was covered with mud and dust. Stickers saying 'Support the Countryside Alliance' and 'I Slow Down for Horses' were stuck on to the hatch window. He guessed she'd borrowed the car. He assumed it was because her own Audi was too well known to the officers she worked with. Hanlon, unsurprisingly, drove fast and well. Enver was glad she was at the wheel. He rarely drove, he didn't need a car in London, and knew he was at best an indifferent driver. He had

a feeling that if he were driving, it would be nerve-racking, like doing a test again.

'What will we do when we get there?' he asked. They were leaving London now and heading deep into Essex. The traffic was light and they were making good speed.

Hanlon turned her head momentarily to look at him. 'Rescue the boy. We'll worry about the legalities later.'

Enver sighed and stroked his moustache pensively. In other words, there was no plan, or if there was, he wasn't privy to it. He was used to meticulous planning, diagrams of the premises to be raided, photographs, ball-park figures as to the number of suspects likely to be present, risk assessments. Not 'Rescue the boy'. That wasn't a plan. That was a statement of intent. He made a mental note that he would never complain again about excess tactical planning as he had in the past.

They drove past the small seaside town of Walton-on-the-Naze and along the road that bordered the sea. Enver had never been to this part of the world and he was surprised by how attractive it was. He wasn't used to the countryside. The last time he'd seen so much green was on Hampstead Heath a few years ago in an operation targeting muggers. To their left, inland, rose slight hills with bushes and small trees; to their right, where the land gradually fell away to the sea, were flat fields dotted with sheep and cows. A couple of miles from town, just off the main road, they came in sight of the sea itself and Enver was moved despite himself, by its immensity.

Hanlon slowed and pointed. 'Down there,' she said.

There was a narrow, tarmacked track that ran from the road they were on and led down towards the water, glinting blue and silver in the late afternoon sun. At the bottom of the private road lay a small, detached house. There was a sign on the road, its paint peeling, barely legible as they drove past:

'Strood Island Lodge'. Half a mile or so out to sea lay a long, narrow island with a single hill in the middle. Below the hill, facing the coast, they could see a sizeable white-painted building. Enver felt the adrenaline levels in his body begin to rise now their destination was in sight. That was Conquest's island and that was where, if Anderson's information was correct, they would find the boy.

Hanlon slowed the car but kept driving for another mile before she pulled into a lay-by at the side of the road and switched the engine off.

'Wasn't that the road down to the island?' asked Enver. He had a feeling he was in for a cross-country walk he certainly didn't want and was definitely not dressed for.

'Yes,' said Hanlon, 'but we're not in London now, Sergeant. We can hardly drive down there and mingle with the traffic and the crowds. We're in the countryside. We need to be inconspicuous, that's why we're in this car not mine.'

She didn't add that her car was known to quite a few police officers, which is what Enver had suspected was the case and, even if it wasn't recognized, a trace on the number plate would reveal her as the car's owner. Conquest would surely not fail to have a check on any unknown vehicles parked suspiciously nearby. Her Audi was a city car, the battered four-wheel drive Volvo estate, its paintwork scratched and dented, looked as if it belonged here in the country.

Strood Island was a good choice for a place that Conquest wanted to keep a prisoner. Even if you got out of the house, surrounded by sea, you'd need a boat to escape. You couldn't shout for help or attract anyone's attention. Once you were out there, you were trapped. Hanlon knew from a land registry search she'd done earlier that he owned most of the farmland around, land was cheap round here, and she'd noticed as they drove along that he'd had it rigorously fenced off. There was no danger of any ramblers straying on to it or, more to the point, anyone posing as a rambler. She guessed that if worst came to the worst and the police wanted to place surveillance on the place, it would be practically impossible. Wherever they hid, they'd stand out like sore thumbs. Her respect for Conquest's organizational skills, already high, rose another notch.

She had learnt from a trusted source in the Essex police constabulary that the track they had driven past led down to a lodge that served the island house. There was a small slipway, a jetty, and moorings for two boats. One was a six metre delivery boat with a shallow draft, used for delivering bulky supplies, the other an eight-seater motor cruiser for passenger use. There was also a small rowing boat with an outboard that was used for single passengers or more informal journeys.

Hanlon got out of the car and Enver did the same. He hadn't come prepared for the outdoors and Hanlon hadn't thought to warn him. She'd forgotten that city-dwellers are peculiarly ignorant about the countryside. He shivered in the chill sea breeze. It must have been about ten degrees colder than London, if you factored in the offshore wind. He was wearing another of his cheap, dark suits. Hanlon thought, he obviously thinks it's a bad idea to spend good money on work clothes. Someone might throw up over you if you nick them when they're pissed, or they might get ripped in a fight. It never occurred to Hanlon that Enver thought his suit perfectly acceptable. He would have been mortified to know her opinion of it. Whiteside, Hanlon thought, always wore great clothes. He used to joke sometimes, especially on undercover work, that you never know when your time will come, so you'd better look smart for the big occasion. She wondered what he'd been wearing when he'd been shot. She hoped it was something nice. God, how she missed him.

Enver's lightweight, polyester tie flapped in the wind that blew his hair over his face as he stood looking at Hanlon. She was wearing a dark blue tracksuit and dark training shoes. She had a small, expensive-looking rucksack with her. She looked ready for anything, thought Enver. Not like me.

They closed the car doors behind them and she locked the vehicle and gave Enver the key. She took a similar one with the Volvo logo on it, put it in a small plastic bag, and hid it under a stone in the grass by the lay-by.

'That's the spare,' she said. 'Just in case. Remember where I put it.'

That little gesture brought home to Enver, as nothing else had, the danger they were in. Nobody knew where they were. Come to think of it, he only had a vague idea himself. Conquest had killed or had ordered the killings of at least several people that he knew of; the man wouldn't care if he added to it. He certainly had very little to lose. Once again, Enver questioned his sanity in following Hanlon. Yet he could appreciate her worry that the mole might tip Conquest off, giving him time to dispose of the evidence by killing the boy. Enver thought, if we die, he dies anyway.

He looked around at the unfamiliar countryside, the flat, featureless fields, the enormous expanse of sea, and suddenly craved the certainty of buildings and the proximity of people. He wanted the safety blanket of London. If anything happens out here, Enver thought, no one would ever know. In London you can always shout for help. Not out here. Only the gulls would hear.

'Have you had enough of the view, Sergeant?' said Hanlon acidly. 'Come on.'

A stream in a culvert disappeared under the road where the lay-by was, and flowed down across the fields towards the sea.

From the road you could see its route, lined with bushes and scrubby trees stunted by the cold, salty winds that blew in off the sea. Hanlon intended to follow it downstream. Walking across the fields would make them visible from the lodge; the undergrowth flanking the stream would screen them from sight. She climbed gracefully and lightly over the waist-high barbed-wire fence that ran next to the lay-by, putting her feet on the wire close to where it was attached to one of the upright posts, so it didn't sag under her weight. She jumped over and Enver tried. The wire bent alarmingly as he trod on it and his foot slipped.

'Be careful, Demirel, you cretin,' hissed Hanlon angrily. 'If you cut yourself open on that wire you'll be no good to man or beast. I'm not driving you to fucking Colchester A&E! Put your jacket over it!'

It was the first time he had ever heard her swear and it gave him some idea of the stress she must be under. He had almost forgotten that Hanlon was human and might well have feelings. He was coming to think of her as robotic, devoid of emotion. Enver did as he was told, now straddling the wire, his suit jacket protecting his groin from the barbs. He got over and the fabric caught on the wire and ripped as he removed it. He sighed to himself as he put it back on. There was a big tear in the material. It was going to be a long night, he thought. A long, cold night.

The stream had cut its way into the earth over time, creating a kind of trench, and it zigzagged down to the sea a few hundred metres distant from the lodge. The two of them followed it down until they were parallel to the house. Hidden from view of the windows by tough, thorny gorse bushes and buffeted by the endless salt wind from the sea, Hanlon and Enver lay on the ground, looking towards the lodge-house. Hanlon had

taken a pair of binoculars from her rucksack and they were pressed to her eyes as she studied the terrain.

Enver's shoes were covered in mud and waterlogged. His trousers were filthy and the fabric was soaked with water. He was very cold. Hanlon, by contrast, looked in her element. Enver's father used to take him hunting when they went back to Turkey, to Rize, where the Demirel family had come from. They used to go there on holiday; it was up by the then Russian border. Now it would be some other independent former Soviet Republic. It had been equally uncomfortable. Enver remembered his father's suppressed excitement as they drew near their prey, his old rifle in his hands. He sensed the same emotion in Hanlon but didn't share it. This is what they were doing now, he thought, stalking Conquest before striking.

He hadn't liked hunting then either, come to that. He'd

wanted to go to Fethiye or Kas, sunbathe, go swimming, look at girls. They never did, of course. They went to sodding Rize. There was a lot of rain, he seemed to remember, and a disproportionate number of mosques. They were very religious in Rize. No bikinis there. The noise of an engine broke his train of thought. A Porsche drove down the narrow strip of road and stopped outside the house. Enver saw the driver's door open and simultaneously a man appeared from the lodge. He'd either heard the car or been expecting it. Then someone got out of the car. He heard an exclamation from Hanlon. She obviously recognized the driver.

'Who is it?' said Enver. She handed him the glasses. He put them to his eyes and adjusted the focus. The magnification was excellent and the resolution high. There, talking to the lodgekeeper was a man who he recognized from his TV appearances as a prominent, crusading QC. Not that long ago he'd heard the man had been made a judge; the papers had talked about a poacher

turned gamekeeper. The man in the car was Lord Justice Reece. The last time Hanlon had seen Reece was when Bingham was sent down. Reece was the presiding judge at the trial. She was beginning to feel a strange sense of fate about this investigation. The protagonists had all met before. Reece, Bingham, Conquest. Bingham was connected to her by his past trial and his current role as unwilling informant. Anderson was linked by virtue of proximity to Bingham and as a direct result of

Hanlon's vendetta.

Reece was a surprise. She guessed it shouldn't be. Sex crimes were democratic, they cut across all bounds of class and money and societal divide. Why should a paedophile judge be worse or more unusual than, say, a famous paedophile film director or child rapist pop star, DJ, TV presenter or actor? Or carpet fitter, labourer, postman or bank clerk, come to that? She supposed because it was a double betrayal, a betrayal of the innocent and a betrayal of justice. Hanlon was ambivalent about the law, but she was passionate about justice. Corruption and hypocrisy turned Hanlon's stomach. She preferred the company of criminals like Anderson. They didn't pretend to be anything other than what they were. Anderson was at least honest. He might nail people to doors but he didn't bleat about upholding their human rights while he did so, or righting wrongs. Reece was far worse. Anderson's words to Julie Demirel came back to her as if borne on the sea breeze, 'He's a supplier, not a user.' Reece would be the customer. Hanlon clamped her jaw tight in impotent rage. She wouldn't be able to do anything until evening, until darkness could cover her movements.

She watched through her binoculars as Reece parked the

car and the man from the lodge pulled a small rowing boat in from a mooring buoy with a rope on to the shore, a running mooring as it was called. The judge climbed in awkwardly and sat

uncomfortably in the bows. He was obviously unused to boats. The boatman handed him his suitcase, tied the mooring up with a sheet-shank, then pushed the old clinker-built boat out into the sea and jumped gracefully into the stern as it moved away from the shore. He started the outboard motor and they headed off towards the island. The boat's keel bounced a little on the choppy surface of the sea. The judge sat stiffly on the thwart, clutching his suitcase as it balanced awkwardly on his knees. Hanlon's eyes narrowed thoughtfully as she examined the water. She was thinking of currents, tides and wind strength. She looked at her watch: seven o'clock. Maybe an hour, an hour and a half, before it was dark enough for her.

* * *

Peter had spent the day feeling lethargic. He wondered why he felt so tired. Perhaps he was ill. He had finished *Animal Farm* and was rereading it. He had cried when Boxer, the horse, was taken away to the slaughterhouse. He felt a certain kinship with the animal, bewildered by events he couldn't understand and beyond his control. Deep down, though, he didn't really think anything bad was going to happen to him. He had a child's faith in his own immortality.

This lunchtime there had been a welcome variation in his routine. He had been given soap, shampoo, a towel and clean clothes, jeans, underwear, a T-shirt and a fleece, all in his size. He took a shower for the first time in a week, revelling in the sensation. He was a bit concerned about the TV camera in case it saw him naked, he was a shy boy, but he'd lived with the camera so long now he hardly noticed it. He put his new clothes on and played with Tito for a while. He was feeling a lot better. He suspected that the clothes might be a sign he was going home. His heart thudded with wild excitement at the thought.

On the other side of the heavy steel door the judge, recently arrived on the island, watched him play with the dog through the one-way spy hole at eye-level. His eyes drank in the boy's physical grace, his long-limbed beauty, his straw-blond hair. The thought that soon the boy would be his to do his bidding was incredibly arousing. Saliva flooded his mouth as he watched unseen. He played various sexual scenarios in his head and decided that, as before, for a while he would want the child unconscious while he explored his body for a couple of quiet hours at least. He found the thought incredibly arousing.

The judge believed himself to be a connoisseur of pleasure. He wouldn't tip a fifty-year-old brandy thoughtlessly down his throat out of the bottle, or guzzle a Roux brothers' meal as though it was motorway service-station food. No, beautiful things should be savoured, and he fully intended to savour Peter. He would take his time. This treat had cost him a great deal of money but it would be worth every penny.

The child was due to eat soon. The judge had already issued his instructions to Conquest and the Rohypnol would be given in his drink, as it had been the day before. He'd allow time for the drug to take effect, and the child would be delivered to the Bridal Suite in the upstairs part of the house at about nine o'clock. He turned and went up the stairs that led to a door beside the kitchen in the entrance hall, and walked up the broad, heavy, carved wooden stair-case to his bedroom. Conquest had offered him food but the judge had tasted Robbo's cooking. He shuddered at the memory. It was as crude as Robbo. It was as criminal as Robbo. Such things really shouldn't be allowed; they certainly shouldn't be encouraged. The only people in the house tonight would be Robbo, Conquest, Clarissa and the judge.

Upstairs in his room the judge stripped slowly, and wrapped his aged, thin, naked body in a silk, Chinese robe and laid out what he would need for later. Viagra to sustain himself, he needed to last. Cocaine, to heighten his pleasure, and a bottle of 1986 Premier Cru Margaux, his favourite Bordeaux. He also had a pack of three Cohiba Esplendido Cuban cigars. He looked up in irritation at the smoke alarm on the ceiling; he would have to lean out of the window because of Conquest's ludicrous smoking ban. He turned on the TV and selected the channel that would bring him the feed from Peter's cell. He rewound the image and watched the boy undressing for his shower, making judicial use of the freeze-frame. He looked at his watch. Not that long to go really. He stared hungrily at the boy's buttocks. Very soon, oh yes, it would be very soon now.

\* \* \*

Enver looked at his watch. It was eight o'clock. The sky was darkening and soon it would be night. There was a three-quarters full moon in the sky, but it was obscured by cloud. The boat, minus the judge, had returned from the island and lights showed in the lodge. They also showed around the lodge as well. The jetty and foreshore were floodlit. There was no possibility of taking one of the boats unobserved. He wondered how they would get over to the island. There seemed no chance now. For a delirious moment he hoped they would call in the police on some spurious excuse. Hanlon would think of something. The boy was over there, there was an Appeal Court judge over there, Conquest was over there presumably, what more did they need? Everybody could be scooped up in one fell swoop.

He had tried talking to Hanlon about what they would do, but had been rebuffed. Now she turned to him. 'Come on, Sergeant. Follow me.'

He knew then they wouldn't be calling for help. His hopes faded and reality set in. Hanlon would say, yes, they could call for help and with a high court judge barring the door which copper would dare enter the premises? They'd need a search warrant and what magistrate would issue one based on their evidence? Enver thought, maybe we could stretch the PACE section

18, which permitted an inspector to search premises if the suspect was in custody. They could claim Bingham qualified, albeit indirectly, and hopefully if they found the boy they'd be home and dry. Then he thought, and if Conquest has him elsewhere, we'll be found guilty of causing Bingham's torture. We have broken so many rules, so many laws, we'd make police history and not in a good way. No, there was no question of outside help. They'd be doing this the hard way. Hanlon's way, as she'd doubtless intended all along.

Hanlon slithered backwards on her hands and knees, Enver following, and they dropped into the gully where the stream was. They followed its path down to the beginning of the beach where it trickled across the pebbly sand, into the sea. On the island they could see lights in the window of Conquest's house. The lodge to their right was about five hundred metres away from where they stood, ablaze with light. Enver guessed they would be practically invisible in the gloom.

A sand dune screened them from view of the house. Hanlon turned to Enver. She looked at her watch. 'What time do you make it?' she asked.

'Ten past eight,' he said.

'Fine. I'm going over there.' She pointed to the island. In an Iron Man triathlon, Hanlon could swim 2.4 miles at sea in an hour and a half. This was only half a mile, but there would be currents and the sea was choppy. Still, she reckoned she could do it in half an hour. On the plus side, the salt water would be buoyant and she certainly had all the motivation she needed. 'If I'm not back with the boy by ten, call for backup. You can

get a signal from the car, but my phone's dead down here, have you got a signal?'

He took his phone out of his pocket and checked. No signal. 'No,' he said bitterly, thinking, we wouldn't have this problem in London.

'How are you getting over there, ma'am?' he asked, feeling stupid.

Hanlon stood up and unzipped her tracksuit jacket. She took her training shoes and socks off, then her T-shirt and tracksuit bottoms. She was wearing nothing now but black Lycra shorts and sports bra. Her supple, muscular body gleamed palely in the fitful moonlight. Enver suddenly thought with a shock, she's unbelievably attractive, and then smiled at how ridiculously inappropriate the thought was. Then he smiled again at the cliché of the ugly duckling's transformation into a swan, like in a film when the unattractive girl turns out to have been a stunning beauty all the time. He should, by rights, now gasp in amazement and say, 'My God, Detective Inspector, you're beautiful.' Of course, he thought, Hanlon was perfectly aware of how attractive she was. She just didn't choose to show it. He thought too, thank God it's not me having to take my clothes off, I can't imagine DI Hanlon swooning in delight at the sight. 'Why are you grinning like that, Sergeant?' she said in an

irritated voice.

'I was just thinking you're a very beautiful woman, ma'am,' he said, with mock solemnity.

She nodded her head in her Hanlon equivalent of laughter. It was an almost Whiteside comment and it cheered her up more than she could say. 'I know that,' she said, matter-of-factly. She stuffed her clothes into the small bag. It was obviously waterproof. She turned and said in a warning tone, 'Ten o'clock.' He nodded and watched Hanlon as she walked

down to the beach and slipped into the water, as sleek as a seal or a porpoise.

\* \* \*

A mile or so away from them, the unknown man whom Hanlon had named the Joker was examining the Volvo with a flashlight. His brow was furrowed thoughtfully. He was 90 per cent sure it was hers, but he was a man who liked to know. If it was Hanlon's, then he was sure he could guess her next move. He walked over to the barbed-wire fence and by the light of his torch looked carefully. Hanlon's light feet had made no trace on the ground, but he could see in the bent grass the marks of shoes and some deeper prints from a heavier weight than the detective inspector's. There on the fence was a torn piece of cloth caught on a barb of the wire. He smiled grimly and nodded to himself.

He climbed over himself, first breaking open the shotgun

he was carrying for safety purposes. The two copper shells gleamed in the moonlight. He himself was no longer young and he was cautious with firearms. He didn't want any accidents. He walked down to the stream and in the mud by the side of the water he saw the confirmation he was looking for. There they were, the two sets of footprints he was expecting. He smiled to himself. The Volvo had been a neat touch and he congratulated her forward thinking. She'd guessed he would investigate any stray vehicle, and she had nearly had him fooled. The Volvo was perfect. He'd been checking for either her Audi or a car he would associate with that fat idiot sergeant. He snapped the shotgun closed and slid the safety off. He was not the kind of

man who underestimated Hanlon.

## 35

Half an hour later Hanlon emerged from the sea, downwind of the jetty, just in case Conquest had brought his dogs. She was bitterly cold and her body ached with effort. Natural swimming, as opposed to a pool, is by its very nature unpredictable. She had guessed before she entered the water that it would be tough, but the current had been stronger than she'd imagined and the sea viciously choppy. It was only as she reached a few hundred metres from shore and entered the protection from the offshore breeze of the lee of the island that the water became calmer and she could relax. It had been more of a battle than she'd anticipated. She was now about a hundred metres from the simple, block-stone jetty. The rocks around her were large and black, their surface a mixture of slick, slippery stone and cheesegrater-rough barnacles, fringed with iodine-smelling bladderwrack seaweed. She felt her way to the dryness of the tideline, careful not to cut her feet on the sharp edges of the mussels that were attached to the boulders, unzipped her bag and quickly put on her clothes and shoes. Now she pulled a ski mask over her head, so that only her eyes were visible. On her hands were dark, fingerless gloves. There would be no white flash of skin colour to give her away. She was completely invisible in the shadows. She studied the house in greater detail while her heart rate slowed

after the exertion of the swim.

Like the lodge on the mainland, it was brightly lit by spotlights. She couldn't see or hear any dogs, which she was grateful for. The building was Victorian, fairly unremarkable. She guessed it would have half a dozen bedrooms upstairs. She had no way of knowing how many people it contained. The two front rooms had lights on behind drawn curtains. The front of the house gave on to a lawn and a grey stone balustrade with a stone staircase, both mottled with patches of lichen, which led down to the illuminated jetty. The side and rear of the house were in darkness.

Hanlon made her way to the back of the house. The fact that there were lights on in the front rooms led her to think that was probably where Conquest was. She guessed that one would be a living room with a sea view, it was the obvious place for a lounge; the other, she had no way of knowing. She crept round the side of the house. The hill she had seen from the shore of the mainland was directly behind it. The house was practically built in to the rock, snuggled up to it as if for comfort. She guessed that the winds coming from the sea would be so strong that it made sense to position the house in the lee of the high ground. It was this shelter too that protected the small harbour and made it viable.

She climbed up the hill through pungent low bracken and

tall grass – the gradient was practically sheer – on hands and knees until she was parallel with the eaves and guttering, and looked again at the back of the house.

From her current position, she could see into the windows of three rooms at the rear. One, on the right, was in darkness; the one in the middle was brightly lit. It had no curtains and its windows were frosted glass. Obviously a bathroom, she thought. The third set of windows on the left were curtained. They'd been drawn but not fully and, from where she was

crouching, some six or seven metres away, she could see the end of a bed and a pair of naked legs. As she watched, the legs swung off the bed and in a sudden movement the curtains were drawn back. There, framed in the window, the open robe exposing his stick-like limbs and naked chest with its sparse, grey hair and pendulous, aged, man-breasts, was the figure of Lord Justice Reece.

He lifted up the sash of the window about thirty centimetres and lit a cigar. It was sizeable, about the length and thickness of a candle, and she could see its tip glow red periodically as he puffed on it. Momentarily she wondered why he was leaning out of the window to smoke it, like a guilty schoolboy. Then she saw the plastic circle and flashing warning light of a smoke alarm on the ornate ceiling with its moulded decorative plaster friezework. She guessed that any smoking inside the room would trip the alarm.

Reece turned round as if summoned by someone, so she could see his back, and the door to the bedroom opened. As she watched, the muscular back of a freakishly tattooed shaven-headed man came in, carefully walking in reverse, pulling a trolley. It was like room service in a hotel, except lying on the trolley, without moving, was the body of a fair-haired boy. Her heart beat faster; this had to be Peter. She saw the man speak to the judge and the latter point to the bed. The tattooed skinhead lifted the boy carefully as if he weighed nothing, the huge muscles standing out on his body like an anatomically correct drawing, and laid him gently down. Then he withdrew from the room, taking the trolley with him and closing the door. There was a bolt on the door and she watched the judge as he pushed it home to make sure he wouldn't be disturbed. He stood looking at the boy, one hand playing gently with himself, the other holding a glass of red wine that he sipped

carefully. He shrugged off his robe and Hanlon saw his flabby, elderly buttocks, their loose skin swaying as he walked round the bed like a predator eyeing its prey, on his spindly legs. Then he turned and went to the curtains and pulled them across. As he did so, Hanlon saw he was fully aroused, the shaft of his tumescent penis swollen with heavy, dark blue veins.

She unrolled herself from the crouch she was in and slipped gracefully down the hill to the back of the house. Below the lighted window of the bathroom was a thick drainpipe. As she had hoped, it was the same age as the house, made of cast iron. It wasn't a modern, thin plastic one. It would easily take her weight. She pulled her shoes and socks off, tied the laces together and hung the shoes over her neck. She started climbing the drainpipe. Its surface was pitted and corroded and it provided a wonderful non-slip surface for her powerful grip, while the rough stone of the walls of the house gave her purchase with her toes and the soles of her feet. Like all climbers, she leant hard into the surface she was climbing up. She excelled at climbing. She had that wonderful mix of a head for heights, balance, mental and physical, and huge strength. Hanlon could do one-armed push-ups and she could also pull her own body weight up by her fingertips on one hand. The ascent for her was ridiculously easy.

She hung from the window ledge of the bathroom by the fingertips of her right hand and reached over with her left hand to the ledge of the bedroom. Then she tightened the muscles in her arms and pulled herself up so she could see through the crack in the curtain. The judge had lifted the boy's T-shirt up to his chin and was staring lustfully at his naked chest. He leant forward and gently stroked the boy's nipples. He sat down on the bed next to the boy and licked his thin lips. Hanlon placed her shoes on the window sill and slid silently

into the room, lithe as a snake. As she did so, she pulled a length of cord from the right-hand pocket of her zipped top. At each end was a loop. She slipped her hands through these loops. The judge's back was to her. His tongue extended as he bent his head forward to lick the boy's body. As he did so, in one swift motion, Hanlon threw the cord over his head, around his neck, planted her knee in the judge's back and pulled. While she did this, her hands crossed over each other and the cord bit savagely into the scrawny neck. She stood up, pulling the judge with her, the man making almost inaudible choking sounds, his eyes bulging, his erect penis, a bulging, blue-veined pole, maintained by two Viagra, incongruously dancing and jerking in front of him as they moved, in an obscene shuffling dance. His hands clawed ineffectually at the cord which closed his windpipe, cutting off his air supply. Then his knees gave way as he lost consciousness and he slid to the floor.

Hanlon checked her watch, five past nine. She went over to the boy and examined him. He seemed unhurt, there were no visible injuries and there were no marks on his wrists to suggest he'd been restrained. He was breathing comfortably and deeply; he'd obviously been drugged. On the bedside table was an unfamiliar type of syringe with a very small needle and next to it was a small, black, plastic machine about the size of a pack of cards. She remembered that the boy was diabetic; this then must be his insulin and the machine for checking his blood-sugar levels. Well, if all went to plan, she'd be able to get him into the hands of a doctor soon enough and if things didn't work out, then maybe he'd be better off not waking up. She knew that Conquest would never release him alive. His body would either never be found, or be dumped somewhere prominent with the number eighteen written nearby.

She slid her arms under the boy and lifted him up, then laid him gently down on a rug on the floor. She looked at the now empty bed. It had a sturdy wooden headboard and the posts which formed the legs at the bottom rose in twin carved wooden columns above the mattress. There were buckled restraints attached to both headboard and posts so a body could be tied down on the bed, legs and arms splayed out. She picked the judge up and secured him tightly, face upwards, like a skinny, wrinkled starfish. He stirred and moaned.

There was a jug of water on the table next to a bottle of red wine with a faded label, and a mirror, a razor blade, a silver straw and a folded bag of what she guessed was coke. Next to the table was a shoulder-high, Victorian, ladies' screen with three hinged panels so you could conceal yourself while undressing or dressing. She looked behind it and there on a dainty ormulu table with ornately gilded legs was a mask and a studded codpiece. Her lips curled in contempt. She picked the mask up and looked at it. The mask's eyes were covered in a kind of gauze so you could see out but not in. She guessed that the judge was too cowardly to meet the gaze of his victim. He had to hide behind a disguise. Above this table was another set of drawn curtains. Hanlon opened them a crack and looked out. These windows overlooked more lawn surrounded by a wall which had a section of fence and through there, in a field partially lit by the house's floodlights, she could see a large animal. A pig was standing looking in her direction. She was aware of movement behind it and guessed that maybe there were more pigs in the field. Narrowing her eyes, she could just make out in the moonlight a couple of rudimentary shelters for

the animals to provide shade from the sun.

Satisfied, she closed the curtains and picked up the jug of water. She also selected a couple of items from a coffee table

that contained sex toys. One of these was a ball gag. She leant over the judge and pinched his nostrils closed. He automatically opened his mouth to breathe and she inserted the black rubber ball into the opening, releasing his nose, then slid the straps round his head and secured them tightly. She slowly tipped the water over the judge's face and his eyes flickered and opened as he regained consciousness.

Then, as his oxygen-starved brain readjusted itself, he focused on Hanlon. His head jerked wildly as he struggled in his restraints and he made muffled noises behind his gag. She held one of the nipple-clamps she'd taken from the table in front of his eyes and watched as they widened slightly. She leant forward and positioned it over the judge's left nipple and then started screwing it tight. She watched as his eyes filled with tears and his body tautened with pain.

'Good. I can see I've got your attention,' said Hanlon. 'When I take this gag off you're going to tell me how many people there are in this house, do you understand?' She screwed the nipple clamp tighter and the trickle of blood running down his chest intensified. 'Another turn on this and you'll be able to wear a nipple ring.'

The judge nodded frantically. Hanlon showed the judge the razor blade she had taken from the table. The judge now looked absolutely terrified. 'Don't try and scream for help,' said Hanlon. 'If you do, I'll cut your throat.' She pulled the ball of the gag down. Reece swallowed nervously.

'Three,' said the judge. 'Me, Conquest and the girl, Clarissa.' Hanlon replaced the gag and took hold of the clamp. She screwed it as tight as it would go, completely through the soft flesh of his nipple. The judge's body bucked against his restraints. Blood trickled down his chest through the pierced nipple. 'Don't lie to me,' said Hanlon. She stood up and walked

to the table. She picked up a paddle and returned to the judge. His erection had subsided now and she could plainly see the wrinkled sac of his scrotum. Three times she slammed the paddle into his testicles. The judge writhed and whimpered through his rubber gag.

'I'd tell the truth, the whole truth and nothing but the truth so help me God, if I were you,' said Hanlon.

The judge nodded frantically. She removed the gag. Lord Justice Reece was crying with pain, tears pouring from his eyes, and mucus dribbled thickly from his nose. His chest heaved as he sucked in air to vainly try and dampen the fires of agony that burnt in his groin and chest. It was hard to know which hurt more.

'Four,' he gasped. 'Me, Conquest, the girl and Robbo. I swear. I swear it's only the four of us. Please don't hurt me any more.'

'Robbo will be the skinhead?'

The judge nodded. Hanlon was pleased. It was better than she could have hoped for. Only four. And one of them was tied to a bed. Not that the judge, bereft of a supportive legal apparatus, was much of a threat to anyone. She guessed it was maybe the first time in his life anyone had deliberately hurt him. He would have no point of reference. He could hand it out, but he couldn't take it.

'Can you get him up here?'

The judge nodded. He moved his head so he was looking at an old-fashioned bell pull. 'With that,' he said. He was eager to be cooperative now.

Hanlon looked around the room. The only weapon she had with her was her knife and she did not want to be in a fight in close proximity to the massively muscled Robbo. She guessed, well, she knew, he would be no stranger to violence. She would

bet it was Robbo who had slammed Mehmet's head into the kitchen counter, shattering his skull. If he managed to pin her down with his weight, she would in all probability lose. To lose meant to lose everything. She had no intention of doing that. The bedroom was dominated by a huge Victorian fireplace,

its hearth decorated with glazed tileware. There was a set of fire irons of a scale in keeping with the large fireplace, including a poker the length and thickness of a crowbar. Hanlon replaced the gag in the judge's mouth and went over and picked it up. She hefted it thoughtfully in her hand, feeling its solid weight. It was perfect.

She covered the judge with a blanket so only his bound wrists and ankles were visible; the rest of him, including his head, was an amorphous mass under the cloth. Then she unbolted the bedroom door, tugged the bell-pull and stood behind the old-fashioned screen. The judge's mask stared at her balefully with its faceted eyes.

A couple of minutes later, she heard the stairs creak under a man's heavy weight and the handle of the bedroom started to turn. Her grip tightened on the iron bar as she waited.

## 36

DCS Ludgate slowly followed the twin sets of footprints down the stream. For a solidly built man, he moved silently and gracefully. The gun with its double barrels was comfortingly heavy in his hands. One for you, Hanlon, he thought, and one for you, Sergeant. He had no doubt that the other set of prints belonged to Demirel. Hanlon attracted these hangers-on, he thought dismissively. Other women have dogs, she has Metropolitan Police sergeants. She should get them chipped for when she loses them. Not that Whiteside was exactly lost. Not geographically anyway. How that stupid bitch Clarissa had managed to cock up shooting him in the head, God only knew. It wasn't the kind of mistake he'd make.

He came to where Hanlon and Demirel had climbed up the steep muddy bank to look at the lodge. He stood and looked at the prints and divined what had happened. Two sets up, two sets down. He moved slightly downstream and sure enough he picked up their tracks again. He was puzzled now as to what they would find or do on the beach. Had Hanlon arranged a boat? She was certainly far-sighted enough to do that. He was creeping forward now, every nerve strained. They had to be very close.

The banks of the stream widened and flattened as it spread out to the sea, and then suddenly visible in front of him, he saw

Demirel. He was crouched by a sand dune, his back to Ludgate, staring at the house on the island through binoculars. Ludgate noticed prints in the wet sand among the shingle and they led to the sea. They were footprints now as opposed to shoe prints. He shook his head in wonder. The crazy bitch must have swum over there. He hated Hanlon's guts, but he had to admire her bravery and astonishing physical fitness. It would have been understandable for Ludgate to speculate wishfully that she might have been swept away by the powerful current, but he had absolutely no doubt Hanlon would be equal to the challenge. Keeping an eye on Demirel, he fished his iPhone out of his pocket. Still no signal. He'd have to call Conquest from the lodge. He put the phone back in his pocket and slowly and quietly walked up behind Demirel. The noise of the wind from the sea masked any sound he made.

He walked to within two metres of Demirel. 'Stand up,

Sergeant, and don't turn round,' he said quietly. He watched, satisfied, as Demirel froze. 'I'm armed. If you turn, I'll fire.' He watched as Demirel painfully, slowly got to his feet, keeping his back to him as instructed. Ludgate shook his head. And I thought I was unfit, he thought. 'Turn round slowly now, hands outstretched where I can see them. I'm sure you know the drill.' Enver did so. He recognized the voice immediately and was surprised by how unsurprised he was. It was as if he had known all along that if Conquest did have a man in the Met, it would be him. He looked now at Ludgate, saw his sparse, reddish-brown hair blown over his balding head, his fleshy face with the small, piggy eyes unwavering as they held Enver in their stare, the shotgun rock steady in his freckled hands. Enver knew that Ludgate wouldn't hesitate to shoot him. Now Enver knew Ludgate was implicated, he wouldn't be allowed to live. That much was certain. The only reason Ludgate hadn't

pulled the trigger was almost certainly because he didn't want
the messy business of clearing up afterwards. At this range, bits of
him, chunks, would be spread all over the place. Enver was sure
Ludgate had a cleaner death lined up for him than blowing him
into shreds with a shotgun.

He was surprised by how unafraid he felt, surprised and grateful.
Although he'd climbed into a boxing ring many times, a thing most
people would be terrified to do, he'd never thought of himself as
brave. He was pleased to find he was. He'd have hated to go to pieces
in front of Ludgate. If anything, he was strangely calm. Barring a miracle, he was a dead man. He breathed deeply and looked around him
at the enormous expanse of sea and sky. They were beautiful. There
were worse places to die. What did upset him was the feeling he had
let Hanlon down. She would be relying on him and he was useless.

'Take your jacket off, Sergeant. Good. Now your shirt and tie.'
Ludgate was concerned about two things; concealed weapons was
one of these. The other was a key. Police handcuffs have a universal
key and Ludgate did not want to have to body search Demirel to
check he didn't have one concealed about his person. He made the
sergeant strip down to his boxer shorts. His clothes lay in an untidy
pile on the beach as if he'd gone for a midnight dip. He shivered in
the cold wind, his skin covered with goosebumps.

'Good, Sergeant. Now turn round facing the sea. Good. Arms
behind your back.' Holding the shotgun with one hand, Ludgate
advanced towards him and, both barrels pressed upwards into the
rear of Enver's skull, handcuffed his hands one by one behind his
back.

'Now sit down on the ground, back to me. Slowly now.' Enver
did so and Ludgate gathered up the sergeant's clothes and shoes,
and hung the binoculars around his neck.

'OK, Sergeant. Stand up now. That's good. Now head for the

house.' Enver winced as his naked feet scrunched painfully on the stony beach. Ludgate followed behind him, the shotgun cradled in one hand.

* * *

Back on the island there was a discreet knock on the oak-panelled door of the bedroom. Robbo had arrived. Hanlon waited, the door opened and Robbo came in. He stopped uncertainly, looking at the bed in puzzlement. Seeing the hands and feet, the body covered with the blanket, he assumed it was the boy, but where was the judge?

Hanlon sprang from behind the screen and brought the poker down in an overhead arc aimed at Robbo's head. Robbo sensed, rather than saw, the movement. His response was instinctive, born of years, decades, of violence. His left arm, coated in heavy, protective muscle, swung upwards to block the blow. He grunted in pain as the heavy, iron poker smashed into his arm, fracturing the bone, and his right fist swung at Hanlon. She ducked and felt it graze the top of her head, and then she straightened up and drop-kicked Robbo in the groin.

It was exactly the same kick that Enver had seen in the gym in South London. The same kick that had lifted the heavy bag, all forty kilos of it, up high on its chains. Robbo gasped in agony and doubled over, his face contorted with pain. Hanlon stepped forward, her left knee scythed upwards into his face, and as she did so she dropped the iron poker, clasped her hands together, fingers interlaced, and slammed his head downwards to meet her knee coming up. There was a dull thud, a muted breaking sound, as the bones in his nose, his gum, upper teeth and cheekbones smashed, and Robbo went down. Even then he wasn't finished. He tried to pick himself up off the floor, his face a bloody mask, and as he did so Hanlon snatched the

poker from the floor and struck him as hard as she could in the right temple, driving the shattered bone of his skull into his brain. He collapsed on to the carpet face down. A thick, dark red pool of blood slowly formed around his head. His breathing sounded ragged and wet and then slowly ebbed away into silence.

She looked around her. The blanket had come off the judge's head as he had struggled to free himself and he looked at her, wide-eyed with terror. Hanlon pulled the ski mask off her face and shook her hair free. Yes, Lord Justice Reece, this is what I look like, look at me, look at my face. Her eyes blazed with bloodlust. I don't need to hide behind a mask, she thought. She strode to the door and closed it, stepping over Robbo's body as she did so with as little thought as if he had been a rug. She walked back to the bed and checked on the boy who still lay there on the floor, unconscious.

She went to the table where the boy's insulin was. She was well aware how dangerous it could be. Hanlon knew that insulin in a healthy person would lead to coma and death. Years ago, she had been a constable on a murder investigation where this had happened, a husband and wife thing, not too dissimilar to the death of Sunny Von Bülow, very possibly inspired by it. Insulin had recently led to several hospital deaths in the north of England when saline drips had been deliberately contaminated with it. She picked up the boy's syringe and looked closely at it to see how it worked. It was simple enough. She twisted it experimentally and it clicked as a number of units were dialled. She decided that twenty would prob-ably do. She'd make it fifty to be on the safe side. She turned the injection pen and saw it would allow her to go up to thirty-three. Well, if that was the maximum dose for a type-one diabetic, it would surely be more than enough for a healthy adult.

She thought of the boy's mother, she thought of Whiteside, she looked at the tranquil face of the boy himself. She thought of the charred body of the Somali girl and the drowned corpse of Baby Ali and his dead family. She looked at the judge, then at the syringe. An expression of terrible fear spread over his face as he guessed what she was intending to do. He caught her eyes and silently shook his head, pleading with her not to do it. Hanlon's face was expressionless, her eyes cold, hard and distant.

She saw Whiteside clearly in her mind's eye. It was an image, a memory from the past, a couple of years ago. It was before he'd grown his beard. They'd arrested a pompous financier for conspiracy to pervert the course of justice and Hanlon had roughhoused him a little, slammed him against a wall, if she remembered correctly. He'd said, who do you think you are? He had been more outraged than hurt. Whiteside had answered for her, she's the face of postmodern feminist policing, sir, get used to it. She smiled at the memory. Now Mark was lying in a hospital bed, his head shattered, his body damaged beyond repair, all to protect Conquest and his wealthy customers. Whiteside would never make her smile again. The judge saw her face soften and for a second hope blazed in his heart. Then he looked at her expression as she turned her head back to him. It was the face of a beautiful Medusa. It was then that all hope died for Lord Justice Reece.

Hanlon sat on the bed next to him. Tears were streaming from his eyes now; he could see no mercy in her face. No humanity at all. Hanlon moved the blanket aside. She looked with dispassionate distaste at his body, his thin limbs, his pot belly, deciding where to put the syringe. He felt the prick of the needle as Hanlon injected him in his groin, near the base of his penis. It seemed to her appropriate. She was sick of the powerful and the connected evading justice. She could even envisage a scenario where the judge would be allowed to walk because it was deemed politically expedient, his arrest considered detrimental to the public good. His trial might undermine faith in the incorruptibility of justice. She covered him up with the blanket, ignoring the mute appeal in his eyes, and wiped the syringe clean where her fingers had touched it, removing her prints with a medicated tissue from a box on the table. Then she crouched over the corpse of Robbo, putting the syringe in his right hand and closing his fingers around it tightly, before holding it with another tissue as she placed it back on the table where she had found it. She glanced at it dispassionately. When SOCO arrived to investigate what had happened, let Robbo take the blame for the judge's death.

She went back to where Peter lay on the floor and manoeuvred him underneath the bed. Hiding him was the only thing she could think of doing with him. She looked around the room one last time and took her phone out of her bag to check it. No signal. There was no landline in the room either. She guessed that Conquest had never bothered to have one installed. Somewhere in the house would be a satellite phone like those used on boats and ships, but she had more pressing problems. Two down, two to go.

Time for Conquest.

## 37

It was as Hanlon had guessed. There was a satellite phone in Conquest's study. It was a new Inmarsat and it rested on a docking station behind his desk. He had toyed with the idea of getting a landline installed, the expense was no deterrent, but what he didn't want was outside intrusion on his privacy. Conquest believed you could not be too careful. The satphone was fine. It rang now. He picked it up and listened carefully. Clarissa watched as, still holding the phone, he went to the gun cupboard in his study, opened it, and took out a .22 rifle and a box of shells. The Makarov pistol was at the bottom of the North Sea about two miles from the island. He had two shotguns in the cabinet as well as the rifle, but he had no intention of blowing holes in his house or painting walls and ceiling with Hanlon's blood and tissue. If he did have to shoot her, he'd keep it neat. Conquest doubted it would come to that. He had every faith in his abilities.

'Sure, Jim. Understood. No, we don't need help. I'll handle this myself,' he said with finality and put the phone down. He slid the bolt of the rifle back and put a bullet in the chamber of the gun. He gently pushed the bolt back into position.

'Hanlon's on the island,' he said to Clarissa. He threw over the remote to her and she nodded, using it to switch on the TV and access the channels that were connected to the CCTV cameras

in the house and garden. There was a full bank of monitors down in the basement where Robbo had an office adjacent to his bedroom, next to the cell that Peter had occupied. On Conquest's TV, in his study, you had to view the camera shots individually. Clarissa quickly ran through the options in the house with rapid clicks on the remote. A series of images filled the high-resolution TV screen, one after the other.

The cell. Empty apart from the dog. Robbo's office, empty.

The hall downstairs, then the landing upstairs, empty. The Bridal Suite. Here was Robbo, face down on the floor,

his head haloed in a rusty red stain. The judge, spread-eagled naked on the bed, gagged and bound, his eyes closed. His chest moved, he was obviously still alive, and sitting on the bed, tying her training shoes, Hanlon.

Conquest studied the picture and frowned, deciding on his options. 'Wait here,' he said.

Clarissa nodded. She watched him through the half-open door of his study as he gracefully, silently, ran up the stairs, rifle in hand. She moved closer to the door and now she could see two images, one on TV of a two-dimensional Hanlon tying a final double knot in her shoe and standing up from the bed, and one in real life of a three-dimensional Conquest taking a position by the door. He clicked the safety on the rifle and held it above his shoulder by the barrel, like a club, or like a baseball player waiting for the ball.

Clarissa watched as Hanlon clicked the blade of her gravity-knife out and gently took hold of the door handle. She signalled to Conquest above her. He glanced down and she mouthed the word 'knife' exaggeratedly, miming a stabbing action. He grinned and gave her the thumbs-up sign. A gun would have complicated matters, but not a knife. He would bet good money

that the policewoman had never used a knife in a fight in her life. He had.

Crouched outside the door, waiting for Hanlon, Harry Conquest was now enjoying himself hugely. This was like old times. This was what he'd been so good at as a teenager, the reason he'd been accepted into the Motorcycle Club. A stunning ability for violence. It had been twenty-five years, he guessed, since he'd been in a serious fight. One that meant life or death. Once, they'd been commonplace. To join the Angels, to be accepted even as a Probationer, he'd had to go Angel bashing, driving out to pubs frequented by rival motorcycle gangs and picking fights. Vicious, bloody brawls in bars and car parks. Your life hung in the balance as the fists and the steel-toed boots swung or glasses were smashed and used as weapons. He still bore the scars. And Harry had been exceptionally talented at violence. He was proud of his reputation. Then, once he was in the Angels, a more professional level of hurt, debt-collecting, often drug debts from dealers. Conquest had a bloody past and he'd been very good. As he stood there, feeling the adrenaline course through his body, he felt the years drop away. Life had been so much more fun then.

Today, he was richer and more successful than he could have

believed possible, a multimillionaire he guessed, but part of him suddenly hankered for the old days, the excitement. The drugs, the booze, the partying, the women, maybe even the camaraderie. He'd got to the top, but a pinnacle is a lonely place to be. Life had become too corporate, too planned, too controlled. He'd never be young again, but tonight he'd stop time for once, he'd be the man he once was. Tonight he'd really live again.

He was looking forward to taking down Hanlon. She was a

worthy opponent. She'd managed to deal with Robbo, that in itself
was an achievement. Very few men could have done

that. And she'd swum all the way here as well. He had to admit
she was good.

Clarissa gestured frantically and he smiled. She was coming. He
saw the doorknob turn, then the door opened and Hanlon strode
out. Conquest admired that. She didn't creep out, she boldly
stepped out. As she did so, he moved his right foot out and swung
the rifle in a powerful arc. The wooden stock hit Hanlon on the left
upper arm. The bone broke on the impact. The power of the blow
knocked her off balance and as she started to right herself, to
launch the hand containing the knife at Conquest, he slammed the
rifle butt into the side of her head. She collapsed on the floor, not
quite unconscious but dazed, and Conquest kicked her in the stomach. He heard her gasp as the wind was driven out of her, and she
doubled up and let go of the knife. He booted it away with his foot.
It fell through a gap in the bannisters on to the polished, parquet
floor below, where Clarissa picked it up. He kicked Hanlon again,
viciously in the guts, and she retched.

Conquest moved forward, the rifle tucked under his right

arm, and grabbed a handful of Hanlon's thick hair, still damp
with seawater, and half pulled, half dragged her downstairs. He
guessed that she was barely conscious but she made no sound of
pain, although she had to be in agony from the left arm that hung
down uselessly by her side. Her chest twitched spasmodically as
she tried to breathe through a crimson haze of pain. He moved
quickly down the stairs, his fingers laced tightly through her wiry
hair, the base of her spine and her heels thumping rhythmically on
the carpeted stairs as they descended together.

He pulled her into the study, her backside sliding across the
polished hall floor, hauled her to her feet, and pushed her down

into an armchair that faced his desk about three metres away. She collapsed into it and sat awkwardly. Her head was bent

forward and her right hand held her left arm, trying somehow to deal with the break she could feel in the bone. Her breathing was rasping and irregular. Her body was a mass of pain from her broken arm, to her agonized stomach, to the pain in her lower back.

Conquest pushed his chair out from behind the desk and dragged it round so he was sitting directly in front of her. He slid the safety catch off the rifle while he waited for Hanlon to recover. He called Clarissa over to him and told her to go upstairs and check on the judge, also to try to find the boy. As she left the room, Hanlon raised her head and looked directly at him.

'What have you done to the judge?' demanded Conquest.

Hanlon had no intention of replying. She doubted Conquest would be able to do much about it even if she told him; was there anything you could do to remove insulin? But she didn't want to take the chance. She couldn't see how he would get the judge into a hospital without seriously awkward questions being asked: how and where did this happen? You could hardly pass it off as an accident. The judge was doomed. And so too, she felt, was she, but right now she couldn't think about that. Her entire body was on fire with pain. Her head, her stomach, but everything was dwarfed by the agony of her broken left arm.

Conquest looked relaxed and content in his office chair. He had won. Another day, another challenge, another fight, another victory. The barrel of the rifle pointed unerringly at Hanlon. She looked at him through her pain with a new respect. Conquest certainly knew how to fight, she thought. Once again she thought of Whiteside. He would have made some remark about Conquest knowing the way to a woman's heart. 'He sure knows how to impress a lady,' or something similar. She smiled grimly to herself.

Conquest's eyebrows raised slightly as he saw Hanlon's lips

move in amusement. He suddenly wondered if maybe she really wasn't all there mentally. She must surely know she was going to die. He could hardly let her live.

Clarissa came back into the room. Hanlon looked at her, no trace of a smile now. So this was the girl who had shot Mark. She was medium height, Mediterranean colour, olive skin and dark eyes, a distinctive crescent scar between her eyebrows. She leant forward and whispered into Conquest's ear. He nodded.

'Where's the boy?' he asked.

Clarissa had told him he was nowhere to be seen and that the window was wide open. He must be somewhere in the grounds, he couldn't get off the island, thought Conquest. Hanlon must have lowered him out of the window. Well, he's no threat. We can always find him later and dispose of him. It didn't look as if the judge would be needing him any more. According to Clarissa he was in some kind of coma. Whatever it was, she couldn't wake him up. It was going to be an annoying and time-consuming clean-up operation. Hanlon, her sergeant, the boy and the judge. Not to mention Robbo. All would have to be disposed of. Hanlon was staring at Clarissa. Idiot, she was thinking. You didn't even look under the bed.

Hanlon met Clarissa's eye. 'Did you shoot him?' she said.

Hanlon didn't say his name. She didn't want her to hear it, to know it. She wasn't fit for that. Clarissa smiled sweetly and put her hand on Conquest's shoulder. It was a possessive gesture, almost as if she thought Hanlon was some kind of threat.

'Yes,' she said proudly, 'I shot your Sergeant Whiteside. Did it upset you, was he your lover?' She studied Hanlon's face.

It was impassive but it was obvious what she was thinking. Hate is always transparently obvious. Conquest felt Clarissa's hand tighten on his shoulder. 'When I shot him in the face, I laughed,' she said. Her voice was ugly now, harsh. She had the actor's way with delivering words; they carried clearly across the room like whip cracks. 'I hear he's still alive. Maybe not the same man he was, though. When he kissed you, did he drool? I hear he will now.' She laughed out loud. She had a pretty, tinkling laugh.

Hanlon felt the rage flare up inside her like phosphorous burning, a white-hot flame. She welcomed it. It burnt away her pain and transmuted it into fuel for her anger. She looked at the clock on the wall above Conquest. It was nearly ten o'clock. Soon Enver would phone for backup and the police would arrive. All she had to do was stay alive for another maybe quarter of an hour. The police helicopter would be first on the scene from the Air Support Unit; they'd be happy. It cost about seven hundred pounds an hour to use the thing; the rescue of Peter Reynolds would go a long way to justifying its budget. There was a Marine Unit with a fast RIB vessel that could be here within half an hour based somewhere along the Essex coast, which would bring more police. She closed her eyes and felt relief wash over her. No matter what irregularities she had committed, Conquest wasn't going to wriggle out of this.

There was a peal on an old-fashioned doorbell, which rang through the house. It was literally a bell on a chain, it wasn't electric. It jangled almost cheerily. Hanlon thought for a moment that Enver must have pre-empted the agreed time and called in earlier than he should have done. Well, she wouldn't complain. Conquest jerked his head and Clarissa disappeared. She heard a bolt being drawn on the front door. It echoed loudly in the hall, followed by voices, and Clarissa re-entered the room. It was then that all hope ended for Hanlon.

Clarissa was followed by Enver with Ludgate bringing up the rear, a shotgun pressed into the sergeant's back. There would be no rescue. The cavalry would not be coming.

## 38

Enver was now sitting on a chair as well as Hanlon. It was a very sturdy, wooden chair with a high back. It was like a simplistic version of a throne. Its broad arms had leather straps and these secured Enver's wrists, so he was tied to it. He was naked apart from his baggy blue boxer shorts and, free of restrictive clothing, you could make out the body of the athlete he once was. There was a lot of flesh there but you could see the solid frame beneath. Hanlon had watched him testing his restraints, his biceps swollen with muscle, writhing like snakes with the effort. His chest was carpeted with black hair and his jowly face dark with stubble. He was bear-like. Ursine, thought Hanlon, that was the word. If I get out of this alive, by some miracle, I'll teach it to Corrigan. He can add it to his list.

Conquest sat near him, the rifle still unrelentingly trained on Hanlon. Ludgate and Clarissa sat on a sofa. Ludgate's shotgun was broken open and lying on Conquest's desk.

Ludgate said sourly, 'Well, isn't this cosy.' He was beginning to feel highly vulnerable, more than slightly edgy. Although he knew that Hanlon had not so far confided in anyone other than Sergeant

Demirel, he felt there could well be fallbacks that she'd set up. He would have done that. He could imagine her arranging with one of her small but devoted fan base something

along the lines of 'In the event of my not contacting you before, whenever, please inform Assistant Commissioner Corrigan, etc., etc.' Like Hanlon earlier, he had an ear cocked for the telltale sound of a helicopter or the roaring of powerful outboards.

He would have liked to see a lot more action on Conquest's part, certainly more of a sense of urgency. At least to get rid of Hanlon and Demirel, for a start. Then there was Robbo's body upstairs and the judge lying up there unconscious. God knows what Hanlon had done to him. And somewhere, out on the island, was the boy. It was a mess. He glared at Conquest and Clarissa. They'd make a lovely couple splashed all over the papers. He could see the headline now, 'Monsters', something along those lines. He'd be a footnote, but he'd end up doing a full-life tariff all the same.

His thoughts were broken by a harsh laugh from Enver. Such was Hanlon's magnetism, that the three of them hadn't been able to take their eyes off her, and they'd almost forgotten the sergeant was there.

Enver had been looking around Conquest's study, at the five of them together. Ludgate looked at him angrily.

'Something funny, Sergeant?' he said.

Enver replied, 'I was looking for the sign.' Frowns appeared on puzzled faces. 'The one that says, "You don't have to be crazy to work here, but it helps". That one,' he explained. 'You've got two bodies upstairs, a kid on this island that just about everyone in Britain is looking for, two police missing, one a senior officer, do you really think you're going to get away with this?'

Hanlon nodded her head in agreeement. She could visualize Forrest and his SOCO team carefully going over Conquest's house searching for traces of her presence. Then she thought, the only person who knows of its existence is Anderson. Would

he tell anyone? Probably not. Conquest could well get away with it. Ludgate might even end up heading the investigation for her and Enver's disappearance. Conquest smiled bleakly as if reading her thoughts and he allowed the barrel of the .22 rifle to point towards the floor. There was a sharp crack as he pulled the trigger. The bullet drilled a neat half-centimetre hole through Enver's naked right foot. Enver gasped, then grimaced in pain and clamped his jaw shut. Blood trickled from the hole in his foot. Conquest slid the bolt back and ejected the spent cartridge case. The polished copper casing tumbled to the floor. 'When I want your opinion, I'll ask for it. But in answer

to your question, yes,' he said simply. 'Yes, I think I will get away with it. Why not?' A thin wisp of smoke drifted upwards from the chamber and Conquest inhaled it appreciatively, like a man sniffing perfume. He took another full cartridge from a box by his side and reloaded the rifle. He slid the bolt back and pointed it at Hanlon.

'Of course,' he added thoughtfully, carrying on his train of thought and looking at Enver whose eyes were moist with tears of pain, 'even if I don't, I'm afraid neither of you two will be around to see it.' He turned his eyes to the figure of Hanlon. The rifle barrel followed his gaze. So it ends here, she thought to herself. Her only regret was that she had brought Enver into it. He was paying for her arrogance, her hubris. Another word she'd never get to teach Corrigan.

'Stand up, DI Hanlon,' said Conquest. Slowly she complied, and drew her aching body straight, with pride, as if she were on parade. She braced herself for the impact of the shot.

'Jim, could you hold her wrists behind her back.'

Ludgate stood up and warily did as he was told. Hanlon with a broken arm was still Hanlon. He heard her hiss with pain as he took a very firm hold of her. Her wrists were slim

and hard with muscle. He could smell her damp hair. He was careful not to put his face too close to her head in case she drove it backwards in a reverse headbutt. Similarly, he was very conscious of her feet. He didn't want her stamping on his instep. He was nervously wondering too about the penetrative powers of Conquest's rifle. He guessed the bullet that had gone through Demirel's foot was embedded in a floorboard. He wondered if Hanlon's body would stop a shell or if it would keep on going through her into him. Can't we just kill them now, he thought, without all this faffing around?

'Where's the boy, Hanlon?' Conquest asked. She shook her head. He turned his head to the woman. 'You ask her, Clarissa,' he said.

Clarissa nodded and stood up. She walked over to Hanlon and pulled on a pair of black, leather gloves that Conquest handed her. She smiled at Hanlon and then slapped her across the face with the palm of her hand and then again with her back hand. Her leather gloved hands made dull thuds on Hanlon's skin. 'Where is he, bitch?' she hissed. Hanlon said nothing. Her face was marked crimson from the blows. Clarissa started again, grunting with effort.

Enver watched in misery as Clarissa slowly, viciously, venomously, beat Hanlon senseless. She made more noise, grunting with effort, than Hanlon, who endured the assault silently. Hanlon didn't say a word. Clarissa varied the attack on her face with blows to the body. It seemed to go on for a very long time. Clarissa was badly out of breath when eventually Hanlon's legs gave way as she collapsed from either unconsciousness or pain. Enver saw her knees go and her body slump. Ludgate's face tightened as he took the strain of her dead weight. He let her fall to the floor and she lay there, face down, on her left side on top of the broken arm. Her eyes were closed.

Hanlon's features were a mask of blood. Enver guessed the skin around her eyes and mouth had been cut by the beating she'd taken from Clarissa, who stood there over her, panting. Her face and hair were spattered with Hanlon's blood and there was a big smear of it down her dress where she'd wiped one of her hands without thinking.

'Go and wash and get changed,' said Conquest. 'And I want those clothes you're wearing binned. We'll have to start removing evidence. Jim,' he said to Ludgate, 'go with her and bring back a roll of bin bags and duct tape. She'll show you where they're kept. About time we did some cleaning up around here.'

Hallelujah, thought Ludgate. Sanity prevails at last. And I, for one, could do with a drink, a Scotch, a bloody large one. Conquest was notoriously abstemious and he rarely offered people a drink. Guests, maybe; those on the payroll, never. Robbo liked a drink, though, had liked a drink, there'd be whisky in the man's room. He'd have one down there. Robbo was hardly in a position to say no. The two of them left the study, closing the door behind them.

Conquest glanced at the unconscious Hanlon. He shook his head irritably. Four bodies to get rid of. Two upstairs, one down here. And the boy would make five. He looked at Enver upright in his chair, eyes virtually closed as he fought the pain in his shattered foot. He'd have to take them to Glasgow Brian in Essex to dispose of. The pigs could only eat so much and he didn't want to risk burial at sea. The bottom round here was shallow and sandy. Even weighted down someone could end up entangled in a fisherman's net and be brought to the surface. He stood up and stretched, and swivelled his chair round to use the laptop on his desk. He switched it on and bent his head. He thought to himself that he'd better email Brian and warn him they were coming. There was a Mitsubishi pickup truck at the lodge, they'd be able to get the bodies in there while it was still dark and head off to the farm about six in the morning.

Behind Conquest's back, Enver saw Hanlon's eyelids flicker. He stared intently at her, hardly daring to breathe. Then, suddenly, her eyes opened. Hanlon was back.

## 39

Hanlon's right eye opened suddenly. It was startlingly clear against the dark, red blood that covered her face. Hardly daring to breathe, Enver watched as she blinked twice. Then Hanlon rolled her weight off her left side and lay, face down on the floor. To the right of him, Enver was conscious of Conquest tapping one-handedly at the keyboard of his laptop. He was still sitting with his back to Hanlon. Enver was terrified that he might turn round.

Hanlon didn't move for a couple of heartbeats that seemed to extend into eternity and then, pressing up with her right hand, her broken left arm useless, as though doing a yoga exercise, or attempting a one-handed press-up, she pushed her chest and shoulders upwards like a cobra. Still Conquest frowned at the screen. Next to him on the desk was Ludgate's shotgun. Propped and leaning against the sofa was his rifle. Enver hardly dared to breathe.

Now Hanlon, in a fluid, graceful motion slid her knees forward and straightened up. She stood looking at Conquest's back. Her dark hair was matted with her blood that obscured her features like a mask. Her other eye was swollen shut and her left arm hung uselessly by her side.

Her head turned left and right in an almost machine-like, robotic way as she scanned the room with her good eye.

Hurry up, hurry up, willed Enver. Mounted on the wall, above where Hanlon had been lying, in parallel at a forty-five degree angle, were the two boar spears that had reputedly belonged to Goering. The spears that the dead Robbo had coveted. Very gently, Hanlon lifted one off its brackets where it was resting. She narrowed her eyes with the effort. It was nearly two metres long with a sixty centimetre barbed steel tip, ending in a needle-sharp point. It was very heavy, but beautifully balanced. She manoeuvred the spear under her right arm like a knight with a lance, then she ran at Conquest.

He must have heard or sensed something for, as she started her charge, he stood up and wheeled round, but he was far too late to react. The tip of the spear caught him in the sternum, just below the V of his ribcage, and kept going. Enver saw the fabric of his white, heavy cotton shirt pushed out, tentlike from his back, before bursting open as the tip of the spear emerged through the material, red with blood from his body. Conquest's mouth was open in shock and pain in a soundless scream as the spear drove through him, and Hanlon stared triumphantly into his face, her right hand grasping the shaft of the weapon slick with the blood which was pouring out of his chest, trickling heavily from his mouth and flowing down his back from the exit wound. The white fabric of his shirt was now dyed a deep, deep red. Enver had never seen so much blood, it seemed endless.

Conquest still made no real sound apart from hoarse gasps.

He and Hanlon were about a metre away as they faced each other, separated by the shaft of the spear. Hanlon advanced on the dying Conquest, the forward pressure of the weapon as it sank further into his body pushing his legs and lower back against the edge of his desk, trapping him. As she moved forward, gripping its shaft, yet more of the spear emerged from

Conquest's back. Centimetre by bloody centimetre she moved forward jerkily, Conquest's body twitching as more and more of the metal slid into him, until their bodies were touching, chest to chest, separated only by the width of Hanlon's hand on the spear. Her thumb was pressed against his chest, her little finger against her own. Her face was so close to Conquest's, their noses were only a couple of millimetres apart. It was almost as if they were lovers.

More blood trickled out of Conquest's mouth, his white teeth were stained vampirically with the stuff, and Enver could see his lips move as he tried to say something. Hanlon stared into his dying eyes, and Enver heard her hiss, 'Mark sends his love.' And she gave the spear a final jerk upwards, lifting Conquest off his feet. The light in his eyes was finally extinguished and his head slumped forward.

Hanlon put the spear down. The end of the shaft was so long it rested against the raised hearth of the fireplace, propping Conquest upright against his desk so it looked like he was standing. Hanlon stood, seemingly lost in thought.

'Ma'am!' said Enver, urgently. She shook her head as if to clear it and went over to him. Quickly, she one-handedly undid the straps that secured his arms. Enver stood up. As he did so, he immediately sat down again, wincing at the agonizing pain in his foot. It was then the door of the study opened and Ludgate and Clarissa stood, framed in the doorway.

Clarissa took in the sight of Conquest's bloodsoaked corpse, skewered by the spear, and the dreadful sight of Hanlon, covered in blood, both her own and Conquest's, as if she had been dipped in it by a giant hand. Clarissa couldn't believe that this had happened. It was like some kind of dreadful reverse miracle. Like Lazarus, back from the dead. She clapped a hand to her mouth to stifle a scream and stood, paralysed by the scene. Ludgate reacted more robustly. It was obvious what had happened, God knows how it had, but that wasn't the problem. Hanlon was. The bloody woman had got free. Demirel was still sitting where he should be; he concentrated on the DI. He could see the shotgun out of Hanlon's sight on the desk, concealed by Conquest's body and the upright screen of the laptop. She was closer but didn't know it was there, and Enver was still restrained in the chair.

He jumped forward to seize the gun. Even if Hanlon managed to pick it up, she only had one hand and the broken-open shotgun needed two to close it shut and work it. Then, without warning, Enver was upon him.

He had seen Ludgate move and he sprang out of his chair, ignoring the agony in his foot. As Ludgate's fingers reached for the stock of the gun, Enver's fist crashed into the side of his head. As a fighter, Enver's strengths had always been as a puncher rather than his ability to move well. He would never have reached the top because of this, but in a brawl he was unparalleled. Style hardly mattered. The extra ten kilos he was carrying as surplus weight only added to the power of the mass behind the punch. Ludgate literally saw stars from the force of the blow. It was like being hit with a sledgehammer. He sprawled across the desk, coating himself with Conquest's blood which had pooled in a sticky puddle on the wooden surface from the exit wound in his back. His outstretched arm sent the shotgun sliding across its surface and it fell to the floor next to Hanlon. There were two loud thuds as a left and a right hook slammed into Ludgate's kidneys, one and two. His lower back exploded with the pain and he nearly blacked out, then he was dragged off the desk on to the floor, face upwards with Enver on top of him.

Ignoring the shotgun, Hanlon picked up the rifle and called out as she exited the room, 'I'm going after the woman. The boy's upstairs. Go and find him. Get backup.' Enver nodded. He was sitting on Ludgate's chest now, his knees pinning the DCS's arms to the floor. He drew back his fist. Demirel's face was maddened with bloodlust. Even in the ring he had never felt anything like this level of visceral hatred. Ludgate had meant to kill him and Hanlon. Enver's dark brown eyes were sleepy no more. All Ludgate could do was lie there helplessly, trapped under Enver's weight, and await the blow. Enver's fist was huge.

Clarissa had run into the hall while Enver and Ludgate were struggling over the shotgun on the desk. Her tight dress made movement hard and her high heels were impossible to run in. She kicked her shoes off and looked around desperately. The house suddenly seemed like one huge cage. Upstairs were the two bodies and she didn't want to join them. The ground floor had Hanlon. Downstairs, she feared being caught like a rat in a trap. She had seen what Hanlon had done to Conquest, God knows what the woman would do to her if she got her hands on her. Then, suddenly, like some hideous vision of an avenging angel of death, as if reading her mind, Hanlon herself appeared in the doorway. She was coated in blood, both hers and Conquest's, and under her arm was his rifle. Clarissa moaned and backed away from Hanlon in terror, then ran for the front door and outside into the night.

Clarissa hurried down the steps and stood irresolutely look

ing around her. Her heart was thudding wildly. It was like a dreadful nightmare. What to do? What to do? She looked one way, then another. Her mind couldn't think, she was panicking so much. It was like some horrible dream, hyper-real yet insane. The house's bright security lights bathed everywhere within thirty metres in a harsh, white radiance. She could see the boat Ludgate had arrived in pulled up on the shingle next to

the jetty, but she could never get it into the water in time. She sobbed in panic. Hanlon was coming. On the other side of the house were the rocks and she knew they'd tear her bare feet to pieces. The door of the house crashed open, and there stood the terrible, blood-spattered figure of Hanlon. Behind the house was the sheer slope of the hill. She had a sudden vision of climbing it on her hands and knees, then a sudden jerk on her ankles in the darkness as Hanlon seized her and pulled her down into the terrible strength of her arms. She ran for the paddock, forgetting momentarily about the pigs.

* * *

Enver finished tying Ludgate's arms behind his back with duct tape. His ankles were tied with the same material. He sat him upright and ran more tape around him, securing him to the leg of a heavy, mahogany table in the room. He tugged experimentally at the tape and nodded in satisfaction. The DCS wasn't going anywhere. He picked up the shotgun and wondered as he did so, what the aftermath of all this would be. Enver's mind usually ran very much on procedural lines. Tonight was unparalleled as far as he knew in police history. He laughed, slightly hysterically. He'd have to write a report. He laughed again, so hard that tears welled from his eyes. Where would he begin?

The assistant commissioner had wanted Enver to make sure Hanlon caused nothing untoward to happen without him knowing about it. Look around you, sir, thought Enver. Welcome to normality, courtesy of DI Hanlon. Conquest pinned with the spear like a butterfly, the DCS bound and gagged, he himself naked apart from his boxer shorts, with a bullet hole in his foot. Perhaps he should give Corrigan a ring, he thought, put him in the picture. Better still, he could take a photo on someone's phone and send it to him. This idea precipitated another gale of laughter, he was sobbing now as he laughed,

tears rolling down his cheeks. His stomach muscles were starting to ache. He wiped his eyes and tried to relax.

Conquest's TV was still flickering through its selection of fixed camera images from the house. The Bridal Suite came on, with clear images of the two bodies: Robbo's and the judge's. Hanlon's handiwork, he assumed. Enver guessed there would be a control unit somewhere, probably in the cellar. Shotgun in hand, just in case, he limped across the study, wincing with pain, then crossed the hall and hobbled down the staircase through the door he'd noticed earlier.

At the bottom of the broad, stone stairs was a corridor running under the house with several doors, all open except one. The one that was closed had a prison cell style door. Enver looked through the viewing glass. The room was empty except for a small brown and white dog. He recognized it as a spaniel. His colleagues in the drug and bomb squad often used them. It was one of the few breeds he could identify; dogs used by the police were breeds he knew – Labradors, German shepherds, spaniels – and dogs he thought of as criminal were pit bulls and Rottweilers. He wasn't a dog person.

In the cell, he could also see a school blazer and a couple of books. This must have been where they'd kept the boy. He tried the handle experimentally. The door was unlocked and as it opened the dog ran out and stared up at Enver expectantly. It wagged its tail hopefully. It seemed happy to be out of the cell. The man and animal looked at each other and Enver shrugged. He guessed the dog might as well come too. One of his colleagues would look after it later. He limped on down the corridor, slowly and painfully, the dog at his heels.

He found a bedroom where he guessed the dead man upstairs

had slept. Its walls were decorated with violent, pornographic images and there was a table with drugs paraphernalia and

stacks of porn DVDs, bodybuilding manuals, bike magazines and some books on Nazi Germany. Some of the drugs were prescription and he looked at the bottle labels for painkillers. He found some diazepam that looked promising and swallowed three. The adjacent room was a bathroom, leading to a kind of utility room which contained computer equipment, a couple of professional-looking servers, filing cabinets, film equipment neatly labelled and stacked on racking, and a table with a bank of monitors and the CCTV camera system's controls.

Enver knew a lot about CCTV systems and this one was simplicity itself. It was old-fashioned, it still had actual tape, and it took him only a couple of minutes to rewind and wipe it clean. There was now no visual record of whatever Hanlon had done upstairs, or the death of Conquest come to that. That'll make the IPCC's job a bit harder, he thought. They can rely on Hanlon's version of events. He nodded in satisfaction and patted the dog on the head. He switched the system off and, accompanied by the spaniel, headed upstairs. Time to try and find the boy.

\* \* \*

Hanlon followed the retreating figure of Clarissa at a brisk walk. Her arm was still agonizingly painful but the adrenaline coursing through her more than compensated. The relief at still being alive was incredible. She had never felt so euphoric. Even the shrill pain from the break in her arm reminded her she was still alive, the boy was still alive, Enver was still alive. And her enemies were dead. Conquest, dead. Robbo, dead. The judge, dying. The sight of the moon and the clouds in the night sky, the occasional glimpses of stars, the scent of the earth underfoot and the smell of the sea, the noise of it breaking on the shore in a series of whooshing audible dips and troughs was amazing. Everything was hallucinatory real.

She put her head back and laughed with the pleasure of it all. Clarissa heard the laugh, carried by the wind. She was crying now and almost blinded by tears as she ran and ran, pursued by the grim figure behind her.

Hanlon saw Clarissa in the distance in front of her reach a barred fence and hesitate briefly, looking into the field and then back at Hanlon. Scylla and Charybdis, a rock and a hard place. The DI behind, the pigs in front. The moon was momentarily revealed from behind a cloud and light glinted off the rifle. Clarissa remembered the way Hanlon had looked at her. She thought of what Hanlon had done to Conquest. She saw again in her mind's eye the body of Robbo on the floor, and the judge, dying, tied to the bed. She knew Hanlon would have no mercy. She looked over into the field at the pigs and climbed over the fence, into their field. She was more frightened of Hanlon than of the Large Whites.

* * *

Enver looked around the Bridal Suite. The judge was still breathing, but Enver thought his face looked oddly shrunken. The insulin that Hanlon had given him meant his body was hypoglycaemic, the sugars in his blood now dangerously depleted. He had slipped into a diabetic-style coma induced by Hanlon's injection and already the irreversible process of brain damage had begun. If the judge had been fitter, if he hadn't had so much alcohol or cocaine and Viagra in his system, his body might have been able to fight back. Peter would have recommended an injection of glucagon, he had some in his schoolbag, but Peter was still in his drugged sleep.

Enver couldn't have cared less about the judge. To be honest, it was better for him and Hanlon if the judge was dead. It was Peter that concerned him. He looked for the boy behind the curtains, feeling as if he was playing hide-and-seek. The

boy was not there and then Enver bent down. There he was, under the bed, still unconscious. Enver tried to move the bed to one side but it seemed fixed to the floor, so he gently pulled Peter out. The boy stirred and Enver noticed his eyelids flicker. He didn't want the boy waking up and seeing the glassy-eyed corpse of Robbo, or the naked judge come to that, so he cradled him in his arms – the boy felt feather light – and, limping heavily, gasping with the pain, carried him outside the room to the landing. The dog followed. Enver gently carried Peter down the stairs to the hall. The pain from his foot was a lot less and he guessed the opiates in the pills must be starting to kick in. He sat on the bottom step and put the boy down on the floor. Through the doorway he could see the still erect body of Conquest, the spear end clearly visible. He went into the room, collected the handset from the satphone docking station and returned to the boy's side, closing the door behind him. He didn't want the boy to see that bloodstained corpse when he came to.

The dog was gently licking Peter's face. The child opened

his eyes suddenly and looked around startled. The first thing he saw was a very large, hairy man, naked except for a pair of pants. He froze in terror, wide-eyed. Then he saw Tito. He put his arms round the dog and Tito pushed his muzzle into his face and sneezed with pleasure. The man held up both hands placatingly. He had a pleasant, open face and an old-fashioned moustache. 'It's OK,' he said, 'I'm a police officer.'

Peter looked at him suspiciously. He certainly didn't look like one. 'Where's your badge?' he asked.

The man smiled and started to laugh. Peter held Tito close to him. 'It's a long story, Peter Reynolds,' he said. 'Let's phone your mum, shall we.' Peter nodded and the man handed him what looked like a large mobile phone.

'Go on,' he said. 'Use that. Phone her. She'll be worried about you.' Peter took the phone suspiciously and dialled his home number. It rang once and he heard his mother's voice, 'Hello?'

\* \* \*

By the time Hanlon reached the fence, Clarissa was halfway across the field. The pigs were following her. Pigs have very sensitive noses. Despite her orders from Conquest, Clarissa hadn't bothered to change. She'd assumed that they would kill the two police and bag the bodies, and her new clothes would get equally contaminated, so she'd left the dress on. It was a mistake.

The pigs were hungry. They scented the dress and snuffled and grunted deeply. They smelt food. Their eyes gleamed. Conquest had wanted them starving so they would make quick work of Peter's body. They were starving. Now, they could smell Hanlon's blood on Clarissa's clothes. It was what they'd been trained by Glasgow Brian to respond to.

Clarissa heard them grunt and turned and saw the pigs trotting after her, in a dreadful procession, led by the boar. The fitful moonlight shone on his sharp tusks. She increased her speed as her fear grew and the pigs, maybe smelling her terror as her eyes dilated, her heart pounded and sweat and tears streaked down her face, picked up their pace too. It was an uneven race, a race she couldn't win. She doubled her speed. The pigs followed suit. Then her bare feet, wet and muddy from the grass field, slipped, and Clarissa fell. Boars are very aggressive animals and when he saw her stumble and fall, he attacked. She was just getting to her feet when the boar was on her. It bucked, then scythed its head upwards, and its tusks and snout thudded into her bent-over stomach. The knife-sharp, strong tusks ripped through her blouse and skin into her gut.

She cried out and doubled over. Now there was a great deal of blood to attract the animals, blood and soft, warm food. They went into a kind of feeding fury, butting each other out of the way, their sharp hooves trampling and stamping as they fought for the meat beneath them.

Hanlon leant on the fence. She heard Clarissa screaming for maybe a minute and a half before she died. The pigs were on top of her in a bucking, tearing frenzy as their prey struggled helplessly beneath them. Then, as her movements stopped, the pigs grew quieter and calmed down as they started to feed, grunting with pleasure, their stomachs filling. Hanlon could hear them from where she stood. She laid the rifle down and started to walk back to the house.

As Hanlon reached the half-open front door, she stopped and listened quietly. She could hear a boy's voice talking. 'Hello, Mummy. It's me, Peter. Yes, I'm fine. I'm with a policeman now, his friends are coming. Yes. I love you too. Oh, Mum, I've got a dog now, please can I keep him. Thanks, see you soon. Mum, I love you.'

Then she heard Demirel's voice. 'This is Sergeant Enver Demirel, Mrs Reynolds. Metropolitan Police. Your son is fine. Please could you pass me on to my colleague who I'm sure is with you. Thank you.'

Hanlon sat down heavily on the doorstep, staring over the sea. She didn't want the child to see her coated in blood. Enver finished speaking and she heard him tell Peter to wait a moment with the dog and not to move, while he spoke to his colleague.

He padded out to join her and sat next to her as they looked out together at the mainland. He thought, from a distance we must look like some couple enjoying the romantic moonlight over the seascape, then, when you look more closely...

'Do you know what Rize province is famous for, ma'am?' he asked.

'Tea,' she said simply. Enver nodded. He felt hugely tired. He didn't ask what had happened to the woman. He looked at Hanlon, her hair a wild mane, her face streaked with blood.

'I thought you'd know that,' he said as he stood up. He could hear the sound of a helicopter on the night air. He'd better go and rejoin the child.

Hanlon looked up at him and smiled. It was the first time he had seen her do that. 'Thank you, Sergeant,' she said simply. 'Thank you.'

## MORE FROM ALEX COOMBS

We hope you enjoyed reading *The Stolen Child*. If you did, please leave a review.

If you'd like to gift a copy, this book is also available as an ebook.

Sign up to Alex Coombs' mailing list below for news, competitions and updates on future books.

http://bit.ly/AlexCoombsNewsletter

Explore the next book in the The DI Hanlon Series, *The Innocent Girl*.

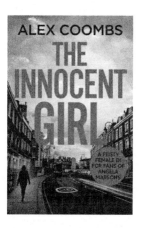

# ABOUT THE AUTHOR

**Alex Coombs** studied Arabic at Oxford and Edinburgh Universities and went on to work in adult education and then retrained to be a chef. He has written four well reviewed crime novels as Alex Howard.

Visit Alex's website: www.alexcoombs.co.uk

Follow Alex on social media:

facebook.com/AlexCoombsCrime

twitter.com/AlexHowardCrime

bookbub.com/authors/alex-coombs

# ALSO BY ALEX COOMBS

*The DI Hanlon Series*

The Stolen Child

The Innocent Girl

The Missing Husband

The Silent Victims

*The Hanlon Private Investigator Series*

Silenced For Good

Missing For Good

Buried For Good

## ABOUT BOLDWOOD BOOKS

Boldwood Books is a fiction publishing company seeking out the best stories from around the world.

Find out more at www.boldwoodbooks.com

Sign up to the Book and Tonic newsletter for news, offers and competitions from Boldwood Books!

http://www.bit.ly/bookandtonic

We'd love to hear from you, follow us on social media:

facebook.com/BookandTonic

twitter.com/BoldwoodBooks

instagram.com/BookandTonic

Printed in Great Britain
by Amazon